For my family

Acknowledgements

I'd like to sincerely thank a number of people who without their help this book would not have been possible.

My friends from the Shinnecock Nation, in particular Autumn Rose Williams and her mother Lauryn Randall, aquaculturist and keeper of the traditions Ruben Valdez, Andrina Wekontash Smith, and the forever-inspiring Dyani Brown @SingleRedFemale. Friends and members (or former members) of the local East End press corps Will James, Rohma Abbas, Carolyn Kormann, Marissa Maier, Beth Young, Stephen Kotz, Joanne Pilgrim, Virginia Garrison, Michael Wright, Larry The Birdman Penny, and Taylor Vecsey. And a special shout out to Bill Henderson of Pushcart Press.

To my earliest readers, thank you for your patience and unvarnished opinions: Lawrence LaRose, Josh Simons, Richard Pelletier, Gabrielle Brooks, and Clare Wolfe. The inestimable Dana Spiotta at Tin House Summer Workshop. All the good people at the Southampton Writer's Conference, with special props to Meg Wolitzer, Helen Simonson, and Nick Mangano. Lisa Gallagher at DeFiore & Company, who suffered through several drafts with me. Much love and special thanks to the following dear friends for their continued help and support: Kara Westerman, Mike Solomon, Rachel Pelz, Mike Perrotta, Kathie Russo, Elliot Groffman, Sean Moore, and Ken Sacks for helping point the way in my philosophy research. Tom Perrotta, who belongs in his own category. And to my family—Pablo who showed me how to rap, my expert teen and Spanish dialogue coach Miles, and Mary Ellen, who with her finely tuned BS meter shamed me into making something merely good better.

“The love of the beauty of the world... involves... the love of all the truly precious things that bad fortune can destroy.”

Simone Weil, *Waiting for God*

Summer

Chapter 1: Thursday, Beach Lane – The Surfer

Fredy Gomes tossed his surfboard in the back of his Dodge Ram, torqued up the stereo's volume, and eased into the bucket seat for the ride out to Beach Lane. As he drove along Pantigo, windows down, he checked out the flags across from the old Hook Mill at the entrance of East Hampton Village. Their expansive furl told him the wind was coming offshore and there'd at least be a chance for a few small tubes. He slowed through the traffic light at Newtown, watching for cops who might be looking to bump their early season ticket quota. Past the closed up boutiques. The movie theater. The worn, 18th century New England-style houses. Past the old cemetery, its rubbed-stone tablets casting crooked shadows over the bones of early settlers. Past the ducks and swans floating out on Town Pond; a lone egret, wading soldier-like at the far end.

Fredy flipped open his mobile and dialed his friend Dylan to ride out with him. Dylan was Fredy's bone reader, a freakin' surf Zen wizard. The dude could tell you what the conditions were without him even ruffling the bedcovers. Which sometimes made it difficult to convince him to get his ass out of bed.

"I don't know. What are you listening to anyway?" Dylan asked, his still-sleepy voice yelling over the music blaring from Fredy's car speakers. A barrage that sounded like Beach Boys on meth.

"Mood Kill."

"Again? You got to get off of that shit, dude."

"It's the *only* shit. *'Another year and nothin' to do,'*" Fredy screamed-sang into the little phone speaker.

"I'm not feelin' it today, Fredy."

"C'mon. Come out with me."

"Nah. Yesterday was dead. Today will be dead—just nuggets.

Lucky if you get two feet. Promise me four and I'll get my ass up. I'll chill with you later."

"Whatever, dude. Your loss."

Screw Dylan.

This was Fredy's time: the matchless present.

Fredy pulled up to the Beach Lane parking lot, dropped wheels onto the sand and rode a mile down the beach past another pond—the big one, Georgica. Out near the jetty where the sand formed a reliable break and the waves fanned out toward the shoreline. A layer of early morning fog hovered over the water's cool surface blocking his view, so he left his truck in the parallel tracks he had followed down the beach and walked to the shore to get a closer look at the conditions.

Dylan was right, as usual. There were maybe two or three-foot swells out there to work some tricks. Fredy tossed his T-shirt and cargo shorts in the front seat, pulled on his rash guard, picked up his board and headed into the water. He'd come back again later at high tide and see if things had picked up. And there'd probably be more guys from his crew there after seven o'clock to post up with. At least they could smoke a joint and build a fire and maybe get some kind of party going after the sun went down. The school year was almost over and he and his friends were hoping to hook up with some high schools girls before the official start of summer—and the onslaught of summer people.

He paddled out, spun toward shore, and legs dangling, waited for the right wave to take him.

Soon he was up, working a couple of quick turns and front side snaps. His movements were graceful, almost automatic. He watched the bursts of light dance off the water's surface under the fog line, like thousands of mini explosions feeding mad energy directly to his brain. And like that, the brain-fog pressing at the back of his skull began to lift. While dropping into the next breaking wave and hitting the lip he let himself forget the first hard rule of surfing: the ocean is your boss. Instead, he and the wave were a single indissoluble entity. There was no "Fredy," no "beach" or "break." No concern for earthly things beyond this, the sublime moment of slipping through an arc of watery bliss.

After a few more runs, he was getting bored and decided to try something different.

The best waves broke in front of the jetty and peeled off to the right all the way to the beach. He paddled into position, spun, dug the board into the bulging peak and popped up as the board sprang forward and down as the lip threw and the pocket opened. Within a millisecond he was flying in a small barrel and the universe was smiling. Paddling back out he visualized the no paddle takeoff he had done to get the tube. It reminded him of a grainy, amber-tinted Super-8, an old-school surf film he had seen somewhere online.

And there was something else.

During this last run he caught something in his peripheral vision, something on the last bit of rock jutting out from the jetty. It was tough to make out—the early morning fog was only beginning to lift. Probably a kite left by one of the rich kids who were always flying them out near Georgica Pond on the weekends. Fuck, he might even take the kite home and give it to Elijah if it wasn't too messed up. They'd take it out to Promised Land where all the wind surfers gathered and see if they could get it to fly. He decided then to ride in to shore and walk back out on the jetty to get a closer look.

Though the rocks were slippery-wet and pockmarked, he found it easy to keep his balance. He'd set his mark with one foot on the rock's highest point, pause, then make a perfect landing over water on the next. He continued on this way until climbing further out where the rocks grew larger and pushed against each other, up toward the sky, accumulating into a massive gray monument placed there by what had to have been some ancient tribe. Just before he reached the end, he somehow misjudged the next big rock. As he shifted his weight to one of the taller, sharper ones, he fell and cut his hand deep. Blood pooled from newly white, open skin. His hand throbbed with pain. Cursing himself, he got back up and continued on, droplets of blood trailing him as he went. When he reached the jetty's end, he leaned his long lanky body on his good foot and peered over the edge.

There, on the headland, lay a young woman, her arm raised over her head as if waving hello.

Hello.

It wasn't a rich kid's kite. It was a girl and she was dead.

Fredy scanned the beach for signs of people. Usually at this time on a Thursday morning there'd be at least a few middle aged beach ladies out with their black and white plastic poop bags walking their dogs. A few stray joggers or maybe a yoga group doing whatever it was they did. There was nobody.

He stood stock-still over the dead girl's body.

Why the hell didn't Dylan come? Dylan would totally know what to do.

Fredy's instincts were telling him to get the hell out of there as fast as he could. To go back to his truck and wrap his injured hand. But something, something he couldn't quite explain, demanded he keep his uninterrupted gaze on the girl.

God she is so beautiful.

He hustled over to the other side of the rock to get a better look.

The girl lay there on her back, her dress caught up on the jetty's eastern side. The twisted dress fabric acted as a kind of anchor that wrapped itself tightly around one of her arms, leaving her other arm dangling free. Her thin body, her long hair and short, gauzy dress undulated with the rising and falling of the water against the rocks. Like a dancer, he thought. And the dress, stretched and knotted away from her this way, left her almost completely exposed.

The girl's unending stare startled him at first—but he couldn't look away. The sun lit up her broad open face, her delicate nose, her sharp cheekbones. Her teeth were as shiny as pearls. And her plump lips, once luscious and kissable, were now cracked and drained of color.

Bending and leaning closer, Fredy noticed bluish bruises on her otherwise unblemished legs. The sheer fabric of her underwear had been torn and pulled down slightly, revealing a distinguishing mark. Right below where the top of her panties should have been, next to her shaved pubic mound was a tattoo. A blue five-pointed star.

The sky overhead was just starting to clear. And for the first time since he got out of the water, Fredy could feel the mix of sun and salt prickling his skin under his rash guard.

He moved back over the rocks toward the beach, making sure not to get caught up on the same rock that tripped him. Once reaching dry sand, he ran over to his truck, found a rag to wrap his hand and stop the bleeding, and retrieved his cell phone from the pocket of his shorts. Barely holding the phone steady, he hit the "Redial" button. Then something changed his mind. He pressed, "Stop," before the call could attempt a connection.

He made his way back along the jetty taking greater care. And, trying as best he could to steady himself on the slippery rocks, he took a picture of the dead girl's face. He then adjusted the mobile camera's zoom and took a close up of her tattoo. He hit the "Redial" on the phone and waited for the first ring.

C'mon, c'mon, c'mon. Fucken no cell service.

He sat down on one of the rocks. The blood was still streaming from his right palm, soaking the rag red. He checked out the beach again, both directions, still no one in sight. He took up his phone and pulled up Dylan's name from his contacts. Hands trembling, he attached the two pictures he'd taken and tried typing out a text:

Dude u my gong vlcll tths. U R not going 2 FCKNG belive ths_

Chapter 2: Thursday morning

"Paul, you there?"

"Jeanine? What the hell time is it?"

"I know it's early Paul but I wanted to catch you. You never answer your cell."

"Okay. What time is it?"

"I got the appointment. With the lawyers. They can do it tomorrow afternoon at four in my office," Jeanine said. "Can you try to make it, please? You don't know what a bitch it was getting everyone's schedule to line up."

"You called *my* lawyer?"

"Just make sure to show up, okay?"

"Sure. Four o'clock. Is that it?"

"How are you doing?" she asked.

"Oh, you know."

Paul forced his eyes open and scanned the mess of his bedroom. Lately he'd been forgetting which pile of clothes was clean or if any of them were. This may have been acceptable if he was still in his twenties, thirty even. At least he'd feel culturally relevant. But at forty? At a certain point he'd passed through bohemian and earned his way to pitiable. He should probably get a cleaning lady. But then he'd have to tell people he had a cleaning lady. Could you even say "cleaning lady" still?

"You saw your friend Goldberg's piece in *New York* magazine about the mayor's sexts with his mistress I suppose," Jeanine said.

"Yep."

"It was pretty good. I actually read it," Jeanine said.

"I can see why you might. And yes it was. Good I mean.

Goldberg's a good writer."

"I didn't mean—we did the right thing, Paul."

"What's that?"

"Moving out here. For Connor."

"Sure we did, Jeanine."

"Don't forget. Friday at four. Put it in your phone."

"I don't have that kind of phone."

"Then write it down. You're a writer, right?"

"Bye, Jeanine."

"Wait. Don't hang up. Your birthday is this weekend. What do you want? I can tell Connor to get you something."

"I can't think right now, Jeanine. Surprise me."

Okay, that was fair. He could take the dig about the sexts. But did she have to mention Goldberg? Goldberg, the punk Paul trained and edited for three years until he took over Paul's job at the magazine? The kid—sure, Goldberg was thirty-two now but Paul still thought of him as a kid—was *obliged* to think of him that way—who just got a book deal based on a story Paul researched and wrote years ago? A story the bosses originally refused to publish because they deemed it not sensational enough, even though it had everything: political corruption, sex, his beloved Brooklyn?

Paul got out of bed and moved to the kitchen to put on some coffee. He turned on his old police scanner, low volume, and turned up NPR news on the little kitchen clock radio. The doubling of static wasn't the most relaxing soundtrack to his mornings but you never knew. There was always a chance of a fire, a horrific accident or maybe an old local who died in his sleep. The last decent thing to come over was a report on the guy who shot his wife in a murder suicide in their marital bed. The couple was in their late 70s and had been happily married for over forty years so it wasn't a story most people wanted to hear—no jealousy or cheating or extreme passion—only sadness and loss for the family (she was dying of brain cancer; he chose not to go on without her in the most selfish way possible). Worthy of a couple of paragraphs at most.

Paul started up his microwave to heat some leftover oatmeal (more static) when he thought he heard a voice coming over the scanner, one he didn't recognize. He lurched toward the dial to turn up the volume and turned down the news. Two male voices were talking now; one of them clearly agitated, spitting words out between breath gulps.

—I think we got—a dead body.

—You *think*? Where is the deceased?

—On the jetty—out near Georgica Pond, copy?

—Did you touch the body?

—Um, no. It's not going anywhere—I mean she's caught up pretty good on the rocks.

—She? Did you get a positive ID that it's a woman?

—Yeah, she's young. I'd say about eighteen or nineteen. And, look I mean she's—

—who is watching the bod—

"Goddam it!"

Paul tried tuning in all the possible channels but the signal was gone. Georgica Pond. The closest beach entrance was Beach Lane. It'd take him ten, fifteen minutes tops.

* * *

"I know you," the woman said when he first approached.

The two of them were the only ones in the parking lot, aside from the police and emergency crews. He could see detectives in blue windbreakers and uniformed cops walking the beach west toward Sagaponack, searching. An EMT vehicle sat vacant, lights flashing, its doors spread wide as angel's wings. Yellow police tape fluttered in the breeze behind her. She looked as if she'd been crying.

"How do you know me?" Paul asked.

"You came to my house once. Years ago," she said.

"Huh."

"You don't remember? You were doing a story on us, the tribe I mean. You came to my mother's house, JoAnna Jones. I'm Merika." She reached out her hand for him to take.

He remembered. Ten years before, soon after he and Jeanine moved to the East End full time, Paul had interviewed her mother for the paper. A story on the Shinnecock Indian tribe's years' long struggle for Federal recognition. JoAnna was a senior member of the tribal council then and handled most of their local press relations. He recalled being impressed with her grace and intelligence.

Merika must have been only eighteen or nineteen back then, attractive but not pretty in a conventional sense. A skinny girl with long hair styled in traditional braids. He tried to square his memory of that serious teenager with this woman standing before him. Her long, black hair was no longer braided but twisted into tight cornrows in front, falling straight to the middle of her back. And her figure had filled out considerably in the intervening years. She had brown skin that freckled around a broad uneven nose and was wrinkled slightly around her brow, a sign of maturity that also lent her the appearance of approachability. But it was her eyes that showed the most striking change: they held an intensity undiminished by her apparent weariness.

“What happened here?” he asked.

“I don’t know. I just got here myself. I overhead them saying something about a girl washing up on the jetty, out near Georgica Pond,” she said.

“I heard the call on the police radio,” Paul told her. “The cop who found her said she was young, maybe eighteen. He sounded really shaken up—I mean more than someone who happened to find a dead body, if that’s possible.” He wasn’t sure why he was telling her this. “Did you see them bring her out?”

“No.”

He took in Merika’s sandals, her summer dress. She couldn’t have been here jogging or dog walking. “Can I ask you why you’re at the beach alone this early?”

“No.”

An awkward silence. The wind flapped ropes against a nearby flagpole.

“I’m sorry but I can’t tell you,” she said, biting her lip.

One of the detectives, a guy in a rumpled suit, shaved head and a serious expression under his goatee, strode from the beach over to his car, a black Crown Victoria with county plates. He was tall, well over six feet, and the reflection shining off the top of his head made him appear even taller, especially when he sat. The detective pulled out his mobile and made a call (reception sucked on the beach once you got past the end of the blacktop). He was close enough for Paul and Merika to overhear.

—“Yeah, we still haven’t found her. We’ve been searching the whole beach... I know, it’s crazy... Will Clifford, *Clif-ford*. Like the big red dog... my kids—forget it... Yeah, the guy’s a newbie... Sure, sure.

I'll tell 'em."

After the detective hung up, Paul walked over to his car. His driver's side door was cracked open, and he had one spider leg extended out, a polished black oxford resting on the blacktop. He looked beat.

"Did I hear you say the girl was missing?" Paul asked him.

"And who are you?" The guy straightened his shoulders and did that head bob thing cops do, let their chin do most of the talking. His police radio crackled with a woman's voice calling out numbers and addresses, nonsense.

"Paul Sandis. From the *East End Times."* He showed the detective his press card.

Another chin jut. "Reporter? Yeah, you heard and saw nothin' here. A simulation. We're doin' a drill, that's all. Why don't you and your girlfriend go on home?" the detective said, the chin pointing toward Merika.

"Sure," Paul said. He held up his notebook and pen. "And what's your name, detective?"

"Fuck you. That's my name." He eased out of the Crown Vic and stood up, placing his body close to Paul. Then he closed the door and passed under the yellow tape in the direction of the beach.

Paul wrote down the license plate number, put away his notepad and walked back over to Merika.

"Can you believe that guy?" he said.

She reached out and gently placed a hand on his shoulder in a way that felt tender and familiar yet seemed to have a more immediate purpose, as if she was trying to steady herself against a considerable burden. The gesture surprised him but he welcomed it.

"Love is so fragile," she told him.

Not "*life* is so fragile," an expected thing to say under the circumstances, but "*love* is so fragile," a qualification Paul found strange and deeply moving.

"I know," he said but couldn't think of anything else to add.

She drew back her hand from his shoulder, as if she'd touched something hot.

"I know he told us to leave but will you stay and talk with me? I don't want you to go just yet," she said.

"Sure. What should we talk about? "

"I don't know, tell me something about you. What about your job?"

He told her about his work at the paper. The crappy hours, the lousy pay. She was a good listener.

"Hey, you get to tell stories. That's something," she said after he'd finished his list of complaints.

"Ha, I guess." He wanted to tell her he didn't always do this. He'd been a journalist. For *real* magazines. In the city. Even won a National Press Club award (shared, but still). "So, is this your regular beach?"

"No."

"You staying close by?"

"Um, no."

"What brings you here then?"

"Nothing in particular."

"And so I shouldn't ask you any more about that?"

"Yes."

"At least I got you to say 'yes.'"

Down along the shore, one of the police dogs began barking, setting off a chorus of yapping dogs. He and Merika moved closer to the yellow tape to see if they could tell what was going on but it looked like the dogs had only uncovered a dead fish or horseshoe crab.

"My younger sister, do you remember meeting her that day?" she asked.

"I remember. Is she—"

"—and, my mother."

"Yes?"

"They liked your story."

"Thanks."

Of course he stayed. He would spend a good part of an hour talking with her, trying to get a fix on her. But she would end up sharing nothing else about what had happened that day or why she was even there.

Chapter 3: Friday morning

Pandora, that little bitch.

Wasn't it because a *guy* told her not to open it reason enough? Or was it her weakness for nostalgia that made her do it. Yet here Jeanine was, X-acto knife in hand, ready to slice through the top. The only thing separating past from present a sliver of clear tape.

"Whaddya want to call this one?" one of the packer-movers had asked her then, holding a marker in his fist over the brimming cardboard box.

"I don't know, how about 'My Old Life,'" Jeanine said. "Here, let me close it up."

Once through the tape labeled just that, she went straight to the photo albums looking for pictures of Paul (*Hey Babe, remember we used to make these?*). So many of the pictures were of her and Connor. Connor by himself. Her by herself. Smiling, laughing, pouting. Her hand trying to block the lens. *You guys look beautiful* he'd say. And she'd let him shoot away, not thinking to ask for the camera.

A windup monkey he got for her at one of those funky sidewalk tables on 14th Street—their first date. A balsawood airplane she bought him in celebration of his first real published story, a piece in *New York* magazine on the old Idlewild Airport. Wood-backed rubber stamps of Brooklyn landmarks (did she buy those or did he?). Joke birthday presents they once shared, now gone stale. And at the bottom, a batch of loose photos. She searched until she found a good one, and ran her fingers over it to move the dust.

The two of them, standing close under tall gingko trees somewhere deep inside Brooklyn's Prospect Park. Flashes of yellow;

early fall colors. From when they were first living together. But who took the picture? A passing stranger probably. Taken with her old Canon SLR. “This is how you focus and press here, that’s the shutter. Take more than one, please?” Paul has her father’s binoculars slung around his neck. He loved those stupid things, would drag her to the park all that fall to peer at nature. He seems so happy. Such a contrast to her own expression. She couldn’t remember what she was feeling—it was a time when holding a secret she needed kept seemed to color everything—but she could almost smell the ginkgo; see the Asian ladies—small gangs of them—bending to collect the stinking orange fruit that had fallen around their feet.

She reached into the box again until she found the binoculars and tucked them under her arm.

If she had compiled a checklist of what she most desired in a mate Paul probably would have failed to meet even the least stringent criteria —and of course she had, the neatly rendered two-column chart secreted away between the pages of her tenth grade diary.

What is it about a guy’s voice that can turn a girl around so completely?

Maybe it was because his father was a professor, but his speech had just enough of that *Nu Yawk* thing so you could pinpoint him to a particular place yet, at least to her ear, it didn’t come out sounding *too* ethnic—and thankfully, nowhere near as ugly as that perverse city/suburban hybrid she was constantly exposed to, the *Lawn Guyland* yowl.

And there was another thing in Paul’s favor, added to her list sometime later with a big fat checkmark: he *wasn’t* an art student. The art kids always poked fun at her Warhol obsession (“Not quite factory-ready," they'd tease) and were too cool to be into designer clothes—or just about anything in the sartorial spectrum that wasn't black. And they listened to music that was intentionally non-commercial: late 70s punk, gangsta rap, hardcore, industrial. For Jeanine, these cultural signifiers had the opposite effect of what her classmates intended. They didn't represent artistic rebellion as much as a kind of twisted urban conformism. And she half-suspected that many of them wished they could enjoy and even praise some of her more mainstream tastes.

And, sometimes—perhaps most hurtful of all—she was made to feel as if her prettiness was actually a defect. Back then she could sense that guys were attracted to her, the way all attractive girls have that sixth sense. But they refused to take her seriously. Even some of the other less attractive girls were complicit in this.

Paul wasn't like that. He was so accepting of everyone, and especially of her. With Paul she could relax and almost be herself. She relished their all-night sessions then; plenty of sex and cuddling, sure, but also long talks about art, movies, religion—the *future*. She told him she would probably never be a famous artist but she didn't care. She would settle for being a great graphic designer and do commercial work. Maybe at an ad agency or someday have her own design firm. She liked that Paul respected her for having the confidence to admit to not wanting to be an artist with a capital "A," especially since he said he knew so few people who were like that.

So she made a commitment to herself to love him, to be with him.

And she loved the city then, considered Paul inseparable from it. But after almost ten years of navigating motherhood and work and gentrification and then 9/11, the city wore her down. She was already contemplating a move back to the East End when her mother Doris decided to sell the house and move to Florida. At age sixty-five, Doris had told her, "I've buried one husband and divorced a second. It's time."

Jeanine announced to Paul that if he wanted to be part of the move that would be great too.

"It sounds great Jeanine but we can't just pack up and leave the city," Paul had said.

"We will never get an opportunity like this again. To be able to buy a place in the village for that price!" she said.

"You're probably right. But what's wrong with renting? We can always stay at my dad's place in Sag Harbor if we want to visit your brother, and I can use my dad's car."

"I love Isaak, I do. But really Paul, this would be *our own* place. And it'll be better for Connor. I loved growing up out there."

"Is it because you have some sentimental attachment to the house?"

"I thought about that, maybe, I don't know! It is weird to think of someone else living there. My great-grandfather, George Edward Moore, built that house." Jeanine couldn't stop herself from using her immediate ancestors' first, middle *and* last names whenever referring to them, as if she were engraving their names in an official book of the Town's history.

She tried every angle she could think of—the schools, the fresh air, the beach, the economics—and still, she couldn't convince Paul to leave. But she had one more arrow in her quiver. One she had been saving until it was absolutely necessary. She sent Connor down to Florida to stay with Doris, took a few days off from work, and gave herself to Paul—wholly, affectionately. Without condition.

She gave him backrubs, foot massages. Blowjobs. Slow,

concupiscent ones. Making-sure to-lock-her-eyes-on-his ones. Sometimes without the use of her hands (it took all she had not to touch his ears, an obsession she'd always hid from him). She made him pancakes—*blueberry* pancakes. And, after years of telling him no, she didn't even wait for him to ask, simply redirected its aim and trajectory and relaxed her muscles until she could make it fit.

He caved.

After the move, the best she could do was get a little work on the side, art directing ad layouts and bookkeeping for a local real estate firm. Meanwhile, Paul would commute back and forth to the city working on whatever stories he could get and crash on friends' couches, sometimes staying at his father Isaak's apartment in Brooklyn. She'd often complain to Paul that her coworkers, some of them former high school classmates of hers who couldn't possibly be as clever as she, were pulling in these large sales commissions. He'd listen patiently and tell her it was no big deal, they didn't need much, they'd manage on his freelance work, maybe pick up some jobs for the local paper.

So she went and got her real estate license.

Within two years she was one of the top producers at her firm, now owned by White and Reeves, a New York City-based real estate powerhouse and, after several acquisitions of old-line shops, one of the largest on the East End. She only had to sell a few properties a year—especially those in the coveted areas "south of the highway" and nearer to the ocean—to make more than anyone working for Paul's newspaper (by then he'd settled for a full time job there after the freelance jobs dried up), more than pretty much anyone else making their living off of the local economy.

Jeanine had found a calling, a way to put her previously untapped talents to use: the walk, the wink, the sexy smile, the seemingly heartfelt gesture. She discovered she had a knack for convincing people to do things they otherwise had no intention of doing. But once she became successful she'd also discovered one thing she couldn't control that she'd always taken for granted: where and within whom Paul chose to put his dick.

She found some packing tape in one of the custom-made drawers, sealed up the box along with the picture of her and Paul, and went upstairs to find a gift box to put the binoculars in. Standing at the end of the gallery that was her dressing room, she stared at her reflection in the three-sided mirror and absorbed time's passing. What do you wear to a divorce signing? She'd missed that particular article in the cheery brides magazines she'd been poring over the past few months. And why not include it? Like everything else doesn't a marriage necessitate a beginning, middle and end? This constant packing and unpacking? She could use some advice on the baby thing, too. Ever since they'd set a wedding date, she and Butch had been dancing around the subject of her getting pregnant again. And in the past two days he couldn't seem to talk about anything else.

For her meeting with Paul she decided on a sleeveless linen dress, ruched waist, more silver than gray. Simple. Sexy—but not too. Holding the dress up to the mirrors and turning sideways she tried to imagine herself fitting into it at three months, five, seven. God, how long would it take her to lose the weight? She could barely remember.

Chapter 4: Friday afternoon

Paul had already been waiting outside Virginia Woo's office for over an hour when he caught her sneaking off in the direction of the third floor lobby. He'd only had a few encounters with Woo in the past, none of them terribly successful. Maybe she was still trying to prove something. It had only been a year since the East End of Long Island, comprised of the five towns on the North and South Fork—East Hampton, Southampton, Riverhead, Southold, Shelter Island, plus the Shinnecock Reservation—had officially seceded from the rest of Suffolk County. "Au Revoir Hamptons," was *Newsday's* snarky headline, along with an illustration of a gold-braceleted hand breaking off the twin forks like a wishbone.

For high profile cases the new Peconic County forwarded all press relations to Woo, whose responsibility was mostly to keep senior police officials from putting their foot in their mouth, and especially to withhold any information from the press that might make the still-forming institution look foolish. Whatever criticism you might have of these new county officials, you had to give them high marks for their use of technology to create a wedge between themselves and the community they served: whenever Paul tried calling the past two days he'd been directed to a short, carefully worded post on the press page of the County website via a voicemail message related in Woo's typically brusque style. But Paul's editor, Grace Monahan, refused to print his missing girl story until he confirmed the facts with Woo. So his only choice was to attempt an in-person visit. And wait.

When it appeared that Woo was about to leave the building, Paul jumped up to block her way to the elevators.

"Virgina! What a pleasant surprise!"

“Oh, Paul. It’s you,” she said. “Were you waiting for me?”

Woo’s preference for crisp white blouses and gray summer-weight wool suits had her standing out in a building where the dress code typically ranged from khaki prep to poly-blend schlump. She was also one of the few people in the department who’d gone to college outside of the state (in her case, Yale). And although she showed a commanding presence in those skirt suits, Paul thought God had positioned her ample rear end a bit too high up her otherwise slim back, making it appear as if her feet were moving faster than the rest of her. Like a jockey set high on the back of a racehorse.

“Virginia, you haven’t answered any of my calls.”

“I didn’t know that was part of my job description,” she said.

Paul followed Woo onto the elevator. The doors rumbled to a close. It was just the two of them now. She stood with her hands on her hips and pretended to gaze up at the slow digital countdown above their heads.

“This ‘exercise’ I was told about down in Wainscott yesterday. I saw probably a dozen of your guys combing the beach. I know for a fact that a local cop called in something about finding a body. What the hell is going on Virginia?”

“You tell me. I thought you were the expert investigator.”

“C’mon.”

“I only know what I’m told, Paul. The department does these exercises all the time.”

“Sure. And you’ve been in this job what, six months?”

“Five.”

“And they’ve done how many of these? And in the summer? By the way, I spoke to a detective who was there that morning.”

“Really?”

Though the AC in the elevator made it feel like the frozen food isle, he thought he noted a small bead of sweat forming above Woo's upper lip.

"Tall guy, shaved head. Drives a black Crown Victoria. I can give you the plate number." He reached for his notebook.

"And what did this detective tell you?"

"Honestly, not much. Why don't you give me his name? Maybe I can do a follow up."

"So you can put it in your story? There's no story here Paul. Sorry." The elevator doors opened, flooding light in from the ground floor lobby. Latino guys in coveralls were painting white trim around the tall floor-to-ceiling windows while a cloudless summer day beckoned outside. He followed Woo around the lobby's perimeter—in the center more workmen were busy laying tile depicting the new county seal, a sort of angular green Pac Man about to swallow one of five blue stars representing the county's five towns. When she got to the revolving door she placed her hand against the metal bar to stop it from rotating. "I'm going to lunch. And I wasn't planning on company," she said.

Once outside in the parking lot, Paul continued to follow close behind Woo (he was sticking with his racehorse analogy; the low heels of her black pumps clicked and clomped as they made their way across the blacktop). He blocked her way before she could open the door to her car, a jaunty-red Mini Cooper.

"Tell me, Virginia. Tell me you don't care that there might be a girl out there who is missing? Who might be dead?"

"We'll see," she said and leaned past Paul to open her car door. He was close enough to feel the warm, stale air escaping from the front seat. "Have a nice day, Paul. And I mean that. Try to enjoy it."

We'll see, she said. This trip to Riverhead just may have been a victory after all. A small one for sure, but he was willing to accept whatever he could get at this point.

Paul walked out to his truck in the back visitor's lot. He thought about leaving a note on the detective's car that matched the license plate, if he could find it. Maybe the detective would be willing to talk now that he had a chance to reflect. But Paul changed his mind once he saw a fierce looking security guard fronting the fenced-in police vehicle lot.

When he got to his truck he slipped the key into the ignition and turned.

Rat-a-tat-tat-tat-tat-tat-titititititit.

"Damn."

One of the few occasions when the hand crank windows of an old F150 come in handy: when you're unable to start her up. He rolled down the driver side window and waited for a breeze, however slight. Just then, two uniformed county cops wandered by on their way to the official police lot located about thirty yards away.

"Sounds like trouble," the younger one, a guy in a blond buzz cut, yelled out.

"Yeah, I think it's the battery," Paul yelled back, hopeful for the attention.

The other cop couldn't hide his smirk. "Hey, what's the offense for battery?" he asked the buzz cut loud enough for Paul to hear.

Okay, that joke doesn't even make sense, Paul thought.

"I don't know but I hope this guy's got Triple A," the first one said. The two of them chuckled, took off their night-blue patrolman caps and tossed them into the front seat of their cruiser. As they were crouching to get in, Paul spotted the detective—the one with the shiny head and the bad attitude. He was climbing into his own cruiser, the Crown Vic, about four spaces down from Beavis and Buzzhead. Before disappearing into his front seat, the detective gave a chin jut to his fellow officers then turned his head quickly toward Paul.

"Hey! Detective!" Paul yelled out. But the guy had closed the door and was already backing his Crown Vic out of his spot and driving out of the lot.

Paul searched his wallet for his Triple A card and dialed the toll free number. While waiting on hold, he reached across the front seat to roll down the passenger side window but forgot that the window was still stuck; he hadn't gotten around to fixing it. He settled back into the driver's seat, stuck his head out of the hot truck and waited through the voice menu. After several voice prompts and credit card number entries to pay his expired membership, the system put him through to the next phone tree of possible choices.

"And where is the location of your vehicle?" the woman asked once he was able to reach an actual human being.

He told her where.

"You sure you're at the *police* lot? Hmm. And there's nothing they can—"

"—listen, it's a long story," he said and gave her his callback number for the towing company.

Yep, a real victory here today.

~ ~ ~

Ave Maria (1)

She often woke late, usually the last few minutes of morning before the noon hour would announce itself. She learned to appreciate this quiet time when it seemed like the rest of the world was on hold, the constant Muzak of life playing in the background until someone important eventually returned to the line. The cars rolling by outside her window formed a kind of comforting sameness; anonymous as the smooth pebbles she would sometimes collect during her long solitary walks along the beach.

Things she told herself not to take for granted: that shamefully expensive moisturizer for her sensitive skin she found online; opaque colored contact lenses; her ass looking great in no underwear wrapped in skinny jeans; coffee lite—take out—always from the Spanish place; and the pretty summer dress with the spaghetti straps and bright red and pink flowers she managed to find on discount. She was a two but the size zero turned out to be a better fit. Only women could be a size zero or even aspire to be, she thought; like disappearing. This would be the dress she'd wear when it was her turn.

Going back over her list it was clear that, unlike a lot of other people, she didn't need much to make her happy and this pleased her.

Chapter 5: Friday evening

"Really Butch, can't you put that thing down?"

"I'm checking to see when the Yankee game starts, it's usually sometime after seven." Butch was hoping to catch at least some of the Friday night home game before he and Jeanine were stuck at a table too distant from the bar—and the bar's two flatscreen TVs. The Yanks were playing Cleveland at the stadium.

"And, that thing in your ear: *not sexy*," Jeanine said, referring to the slender plastic Bluetooth device wedged inside Butch's ear canal. She knew he *needed* to wear the damn thing. But the pale violet Ralph Lauren sweater draped around his shoulders? That was at Jeanine's urging; he knew he didn't need that.

Their waitress, a blonde teen who could have easily passed for a much younger, hipper version of Jeanine, appeared with appetizers and set them on the table: a tray of sliders and fried calamari. Butch looked up at the waitress and back down at the food. *Always look your waitress in the eye. Better service that way.* The stress was making him hungry.

"Jessica, is that you?"

"Oh, hi Ms. S."

"I almost didn't recognize you—you look so grown up. How is your mom?"

"She's good, I guess. I haven't seen her much. She's been really busy."

"Well, it is a busy time of year." Jeanine turned to Butch. "Honey, you remember Julia Manning, an agent at the firm. This is her daughter Jess. She's in Connor's grade. You transferred to Pierson right?" she asked the girl.

Jessica Manning nodded.

"Sure," Butch said. Julia Manning. One of those divorced women of a certain age he'd seen at parties around town. Pretty women, squeezing each additional pound for every year from the time of their thirty fifth birthdays into a pair of Spanx, their expensive blonde highlights framing heavily made-up eyes that couldn't help but betray a hint of desperation. Or maybe she was one of the lithe muscular types, middle aged cougars turned pseudo-gymnasts training for what, a chance to show off their newly "cut" biceps for chummy male personal trainers half their age? Holding oversized glasses of Chardonnay and chatting conspiratorially near the crudités while scoping the room expectantly, as if they weren't looking over the same half-dozen or so sorry-assed unattached men they'd seen at every other party. That Julia Manning?

"And I'm not Ms. S anymore. I go by my maiden name now: it's Moore. But you should call me Jeanine. This is my fiancée, Butch."

When he found out that Paul had never given Jeanine a diamond, Butch made sure to buy her one big enough to show up on satellite photos taken from space. Yet here she was, turning her engagement ring so the large rock was facedown on the tablecloth. Why would she feel the need to hide it?

"Sure Jeanine. Can I get you guys anything else?" the girl said.

"No. We're good. Tell your mom I said 'Hi.' With the two of us out showing all the time I rarely run into her these days," Jeanine said, releasing her.

Jessica Manning turned her pert little head and skipped away toward the other tables, her left hand perched on impossibly slender hips, her elbow swung back like a cheerleader running back to her squad. Butch followed her tight little rear end with his gaze until the teenager disappeared into the crowded restaurant. Then he removed his earpiece and set his mobile on the table.

"So, did you close on that house on Cedar?"

"Not yet. The buyers are still sending us conditions. I've never seen anything like this, Butch. I miss the days when we had, like, two or three people in bidding wars up to the last day of contract. God, I can't believe I'm already talking about the good old days. I haven't been doing this long enough for that."

He picked up one of the sliders from the plate. The miniature hamburger practically disappeared inside of his large fist before entering his mouth. He devoured it whole, making him feel a bit like the giant from Jack and the Beanstalk fame but with better table manners.

He felt for the napkin on his lap.

By any measure it had been a tough week. He'd received a note from his bank mentioning its intent to recall a loan he had on several spec houses that had been sitting unsold in the Village of North Haven. This was forcing him to delay construction on other projects he had already lined up for the summer. Worse yet, he had work crews waiting for the okay to start breaking ground on already cleared property in a mostly wooded area north of the highway in Sagaponack under his new "Olde Stone Estates" banner. If he missed those deadlines, he would either have to pay his workers to do nothing—mostly out of his own pocket—or run the risk of them moving on and getting work on another job.

Things used to be a lot simpler. After his two years at nearby Stony Brook College he got a job as a carpenter, worked his way up to project manager and then general contractor, building homes designed and paid for by other people. At every step the other guys underestimated his abilities because of his good looks. Pretty Bobby they called him, especially the older Bubs. *Maybe he'll charm those boards straight.* But when he was finally able to scrape together enough money to build his first spec house—although he hadn't designed it he was responsible for every board, shingle and nail that went into it—he was struck with such a deep feeling of accomplishment he couldn't part with the place. Some evenings he'd find himself sneaking out on his wife Jill with some lame excuse so he could park in the drive, the cold slipping away from his beer, and sit and stare at his magnificent creation. It was a simple house, a "Classic Cape," two up and two down, front door leading to a center stair, doghouse dormers on the second floor, and a little extension for the kitchen in a shape that mirrored the main house. Ask a child to draw a house and that's what she'd draw: a solid thing, a place that lets the neighbors know, *a family lives here.* And yet it also provided the owner unlimited possibilities; you could customize it to look like anything you wanted.

Once he got around to selling the house—it took him less than two weeks from the date of listing and he managed to pocket half of the realtor's fee—Butch decided to make it a business.

His timing couldn't have been better. As new houses were built, the proceeds of each successive sale were used to purchase more land and invest money in the building of the next project, and eventually investors were brought in to spread the risk. But building a home on spec was more than simply knocking together some materials to create shelter. It was about perfecting the game, learning how to serve the market's two hungry masters. For potential second homeowners he was selling the dream: glossy brochures promising the Hamptons "lifestyle," grand spaces and high-end surfaces. For investors his pitch was more prosaic: the art of cutting corners—spreadsheets and PowerPoints demonstrating new combinations of affordable and easily reconfigurable materials and furnishings that had the appearance of wealth, prestige and expert craftsmanship, and the hiring and managing of human capital, mostly recent Latino immigrants, purchased at bottom line cost. With the housing market chugging along at a steady pace for several years (sometimes his spec houses would sell for 25% more upon completion than the estimated selling price at the start of construction), these were profitable lessons to learn and Butch was an eager student. It didn't take long for him to grow the company to the point where he was risking more and more money for the construction of larger and larger projects.

But after that the housing bubble burst in '09, all of the old rules had changed. And it was scaring the piss out of him.

"Hey, where'd you go?" Jeanine asked, waving her hand in front of his face.

"Huh? Nothing."

She leaned in close and whispered, "Julia told me her daughter came home one day with one of those tramp stamp tattoos on her back. I can't imagine Connor wanting a tattoo. Thank God I never have to deal with that."

Butch found this last comment a bit curious but chose to keep quiet. Jeanine was only a few weeks from becoming stepmother to his two 'tween girls, both of whom most certainly would have the means, if not yet the gumption, to run into the city and get one of those tattoos. He had always hoped Jeanine would enjoy the girls. And she seemed to have genuine affection for Paige, his athletic eleven year-old who loved riding horses—hunters for now but soon progressing to jumpers. But Jeanine hadn't warmed to the older one,

Bailey, even admitting that the girl frightened her. Taller than most of the boys her age (at thirteen she was already a statuesque 5' 9" in flats), over-confident, too often acerbic, Bailey had on numerous occasions been disciplined at school for her unrepentant cyber bullying. She could go from sweetness to meanness in a matter of keystrokes. "I could only imagine what that girl says about me online to her little friends," Jeanine had commented to Butch.

"Hey, did you call my guy about the new rugs?" Butch asked, purposely changing the subject.

"Not yet. I've been crazy with the wedding arrangements."

"What do you mean? The hall is all taken care of—as it should be, I friggin built the place—we picked out the food, the guys got fitted for the white summer suits. The girls finally decided on their dresses. What else do you need to worry about?"

"I don't know, there are a lot of details," she said, looking somewhat distracted.

"I don't get why they don't put tomato in these. Hey, you haven't even touched your appetizer. You usually love the calamari. They do it great here."

"I guess. Just not hungry."

"Look at this place; the sunset, the boats. Can you ask for a more perfect day? This is what it's all about, Babe. You and me ..." He began to sing a simple melody of love but stopped when he saw the look of disapproval on her face.

"Yeah, I'm still trying to figure it all out. It's not every day you get divorced." She looked into her drink and twirled the thin straw around the inside edge of the glass.

"We're not going to have that discussion again are we? I think it's exhilarating. It's like we're getting a chance to start over again. Have you thought about what we talked about last night?"

"Butch, I don't think I'm ready—"

"—you're not getting any younger, Babe. I thought I had your agreement on this."

This all could have been avoided if she had only said yes twenty years ago, the summer after Jeanine graduated college, Butch thought. They'd first hooked up that Memorial Day weekend and were back where they belonged. Paul was back in the city working, where he belonged. He and Jeanine would meet up every chance they could that summer, usually at Jeanine's house, her mother Doris acting as willing coconspirator. When Jeanine got pregnant he knew the baby was his even if she wouldn't admit it. And although he could easily coax her into bed, he couldn't convince her to leave Paul. It was her decision then not to have the baby—*his* baby. And that was that.

"That's the point, Butch. I'm not getting any younger. In fact, I'd like to keep this body for a few more years before I become totally undesirable to you."

"Hon, you are beautiful now and you will look especially beautiful pregnant."

"And after that?"

"After that you'll be radiant! And we'll have an amazing baby that's *ours*. You'll get your body back, I promise. Besides, you can always get a boob job—you know, not an enhancement, just a little lift to bring things back to normal. This is what we've always wanted!"

"You mean this is what *you've* always wanted. You know, Hon, I'm starting to think this whole baby thing is like another one of your building projects."

"Yeah, and how's that?"

"You want to keep making things without thinking things through."

Butch bristled. His voice dropped a full register.

"What exactly are you saying?"

"What I'm saying is that you seem to be pushing this baby thing really hard without thinking through the consequences. You do that sometimes." She nervously rubbed her forefinger across her teeth—a habit of Jeanine's Butch used to find sexy.

"And that's how I also conduct my business?"

"Sometimes."

His two hands were pressed down on the tabletop. It took everything he had not to go at her full throttle. "Sometimes? Where the fuck do you come off telling me how to run my business?"

Their fellow restaurant patrons, including several members of Butch's yacht club, were trying desperately not to rubberneck in the direction of their table.

"Robert, please use your *inside* voice," she stage whispered to him. "I'm not trying to *tell* you, I'm just—"

"—Godammit, Jeanine, *sometimes* you can be a real bitch!" He slapped his hand on the table, accidently flipping the empty plate of burgers into the water glasses. It sent a report that reverberated through the restaurant.

They were back in high school again, all eyes in the cafeteria on them.

"What have I done? Oh, I know what this is. You *love* turning me into the bad guy don't you? If I'm being a bitch then that excuses everything you do. And whenever you don't want to hear something you make it impossible for me to say anything. You see everything as a criticism. Well, you should learn to be a little less thin skinned," she said.

"Really? And you're going to teach me?"

"That's not what I—"

"—c'mon, show me how to take it like a man." He reached across the table and grabbed her forearm. "Show me, Jeanine. Show me how to take it. I really need to know."

She took back her arm. "Stop this."

He pulled out his mobile and started punching the keys.

"What the hell are you doing now? Would you put that thing down?"

"I'm looking up tips on how to take your criticism. I obviously suck at it," he said.

"God, that is so fucking passive aggressive."

"Oh, you prefer aggressive?" Butch leaned in over the cooling calamari, the grease congealing on the plate. He whispered but too loud: "Fuck you, Jeanine."

Jeanine looked around the crowded restaurant. People were still trying not to stare. She took the napkin off of her lap, placed it on the table and carefully folded it into quarters. Then she looked up at Butch. In a clear, loud voice she said:

"You want a baby? Then go fuck yourself, Butch."

Jeanine leaped out of her seat, grabbed her clutch and disappeared in the direction of the restaurant's hard gravel parking lot. Butch made a motion to get up from the table to follow her and apologize but sat back down. Maybe she would take a walk around the pier or go to the ladies room to let off some steam and come back eventually with an apology of her own. He needed another drink. Where the hell was that waitress? He fingered a small piece of paper he had been carrying in his front pocket. Using these same thick, calloused fingers he typed a note to himself into his mobile, then walked over to the bar and took a seat to watch the start of the Yankee game.

Chapter 6: Friday—same night

"Isn't that Mary Poppins?"

"Where?"

"Far corner, right, sitting with the grandkids." Paul made a gesture toward their table, chin over his shoulder, so as not to look. His friend Jeff followed his gesture and stared blankly.

"Yeah. But I think you mean the actress who played Mary Poppins," Jeff said.

"Right. She is no longer Mary Poppins yet she always will be Mary Poppins. Disney's Paradox."

"And technically she never was Mary Poppins, just someone who was pretending. Not into the game, huh?" Jeff asked.

The two of them were sitting in Rowdy Hall, their occasional Friday night hangout, in front of their third round of drafts and a big flatscreen TV.

"Nah. Isaak used to tell me the ancient Greeks invented athletics. At first, the winner would get a crown of leaves. But once they introduced prize money—around 500 B.C.—you know, it just got corrupted," Paul said.

"500 B.C.? I thought it was free agency and billion-dollar cable TV deals that ruined baseball, but I stand corrected."

The place was packed with weekenders who had driven out from the city or had just gotten off of the 4:07 p.m. Cannonball, finally getting to rest their ever-humming mobiles next to a nice, tall cocktail or beer. The bartender was in the far corner of the bar watching the game and talking to what appeared to be some regular. Paul recognized the barman from his winter tennis league but the name didn't come. It was Jeanine who got Paul into tennis.

Whenever they played mixed doubles, it was guys like this who'd be constantly staring at her hiked up little *skorts* or whatever they were called.

"I still don't get it," Paul said, muttering to himself.

"It's easy, you've got these nine guys on a field shaped like a diamond and —"

"—ha, good one, Mr. SportsCenter. No, I mean this dead girl thing that came over the radio yesterday morning."

"Yeah, you get any updates on that from Woo?"

"It's weird. You've got a cop who calls in a dead body and then when everybody shows up, there's no body. But here's the thing that's really bothering me. There are like six Peconic County cars parked there, East Hampton cops, EMTs. Detectives are walking the beach with German Shepherds. And when we try to get anything from the county, Woo tells me it's nothing, false alarm. We should forget about it. It doesn't make sense."

"Did you get a chance to talk to the cop who called it in?"

"Nah, he must've left before I got there. I managed to get his name though when I overheard one of the other guys talking about it into his cell. When I tried to question this detective he told me to fuck off, wouldn't even give me his name. I swear, I think cops pick up these bad habits from watching TV. And forget about interviewing Clifford now—that's the cop's name, Will Clifford."

"I know the name. Old local family."

"Yeah, came over on the Mayflower or something. Anyway, he's under some kind of gag order. They probably got him at an 'undisclosed location.' The only real lead I got was from this young woman from the Res who was there when I showed up. But she wasn't really giving me any information either. There was something about her though."

"What's that?"

"It was like she was connected to what was going on but somehow not. I can't describe it," Paul said.

"Follow every lead and ye shall find the truth, brother—especially when there is a good looking woman involved," Jeff said.

"I didn't say she was good looking. I mean, she was somewhat attractive, but how did you know that?"

"Lucky guess. Maybe it was that wistful tone in your voice."

"And your quote. That sounds familiar—I mean the first part. Who said that? Isn't that from the Bible—New Testament? Matthew maybe?"

"Is that your final answer?

"Yes."

"I thought I made it up."

"Hmm."

"How come you know so much about the Bible?" Jeff asked. He sipped his beer. "I never took you for the religious type. Although now that I think about it you do have too few vices. Religion could be good for you."

"Most of it I learned at the dinner table with my parents. My mom was a believer. She used to call me 'St. Paul' whenever I did something remotely good—she named me after him. It was Paul who invented *sola fide*, the idea that if you have faith you get absolved of all your sins. Not bad, right?"

"A 'get out of jail free' card."

"Yeah, you sound like my dad. He thought of those books as being written by the philosophers of their time—guys just trying to figure stuff out rather than rules to live your life by. He used to call it 'the beautiful lie,' you know, employing fiction in the service of a larger truth. I think he loved my mom's willingness to buy into that. Maybe he was a little jealous too."

"Uh oh," Jeff said.

"What? Did I offend you?"

"Hardly. But the subject matter is veering into drunk talk: religion, sex. Speaking of which, Happy Birthday. Tomorrow right?" Jeff raised his glass in a toast.

"Yeah, thanks. You know Elvis died at forty two, the poor bastard."

"Really? That young?"

"Thanks for saying that. It's funny. But I bet he always knew."

"What's that?"

"Priscilla. I bet the minute he laid eyes on her he knew he wouldn't be able to keep her."

"Wasn't she like fourteen or something?"

"That's not my point. I mean a girl that beautiful."

"But now you're free," Jeff said.

"Yeah. So why do I feel like the turd all the other turds find repugnant—no offense."

"None taken. I think."

"I was trying to come up with an appropriate analogy for this and all I could think of was Lyme disease. Half the people out here have gotten it: first the rash, then the joint pain, the antibiotic treatments. But I managed to never get it. Whenever someone would tell me 'oh, I've got Lyme disease' I could sympathize—wow, that's too bad, whatever. But I couldn't *empathize*, you know? I could never get it that the poor schmuck who has Lyme spends nights lying in bed thinking, 'there are tiny spirochetes burrowing into my cells and hiding out. The little fuckers are working their way up to the attic—my brain—where they're going to sneak ankle deep into my cerebellum and lock themselves in.' Only, the spirochetes don't go crazy up there in the attic, no, the poor schmuck who is hosting them is the one going crazy as they mess with his memory, his neurological functions, his cognitive functions. With divorce, instead of spirochetes it's these little gremlins that get locked up in there, messing with your ego. They are constantly tearing you apart, needling you, telling you"—Paul tries his best imitation of a spirochete-like gremlin—"Man, you blew it. You had this beautiful woman who was willing to fuck you and cook for you and listen to your boring stories. Someone who maybe didn't always treat you great but was on *your fucking team*, you know what I mean? And now she is fucking a guy on another team ..."

Paul noticed Jeff's attention starting to drift, and each time he said the word "team" Jeff would glance up at the TV. He couldn't help staring too.

"... and meanwhile, the other guy is hearing about all the embarrassing stuff that you and your wife used to go through and she is probably saying to the new guy"— Paul tried to imitate a female voice but it comes out sounding a lot like the spirochete/gremlin voice—"'I can't believe I put up with that shit all those years. Now, you, new guy, you *really* get me. You really understand what I've been through.' Like your whole marriage was a trial or something that she had to endure and now this new guy is the hero saving her from this horrible fate? Oh, and did I forget to mention: she is fucking him? Like probably right this minute."

"You did mention it, yes. I get that you don't like the guy but you've got to admit he's got some fine skin. For a guy."

"You're kidding right?"

"Flawless, that's all I'm saying. No straight guy should be allowed to be that good looking. But, let me address your Lyme analogy. I know some people who have *died* from a deer tick bite. My dog died from Lyme disease. You, my friend, got dumped—and, for sleeping with another woman who should've been taking a creative writing class instead of sleeping with and then sending salacious emails to a low paid journalist—no offense."

"None taken."

They clinked glasses.

"You will live another day, friend. You don't have to do I.V. antibiotics or go to the vet to be put down like Silkie. You just need to find someone new and get yourself laid."

This is the problem when you go out for a beer with the guy who edits you: always picking apart your story.

"Wait, your dog was named *Silkie*? That is a fucking ridiculous name! Silkie? Really? Okay, okay, not a great analogy but you have to admit that Lyme and divorce both *suck* and they occur at about the same incidence, at least out here."

"I'll give you that."

Just then they heard a loud noise from one of the restaurant tables. A bunch of Wall Street types in polos with popped collars arguing and laughing at their waitress who was struggling to scrape up the mess of food at their feet using the shards of broken dinner plates.

"You know what I'm thinking?" Jeff said. He let out a loud belch.

"What?"

"I'm thinking, fuck those guys. You know, *smucks* like them and your friend Butch." Jeff kicked back another swig of beer.

"Yeah, but don't fuck them too hard because we want them to keep building and buying and renting those houses listed by the people who pay for the advertising that pays the paper that pays for our measly salaries. We wouldn't want to disrupt the fragile ecosystem. Besides, I don't want them to feel like we don't appreciate everything they do for us—hey, wait, did you just say '*smucks*?' Man, you suck at trying to sound *Nu Yawk*, bro. It's *Shh-mucks*, like *shit* combined with *mucks*."

"Wow, did I say "*smucks*?" Hold on a second." Jeff turned around on his bar stool toward the packed tables in the main part of the restaurant, raised his beer glass and yelled out to all those humming mobiles and cocktails, "Hello, I want to thank all of you *SCHMUCKS* for paying us to write stories about your stupid property boundary disputes and building code violations. We love you!" Then he whispered to Paul, "How was that?"

The bartender, whatshisname, the *skort* looker, was giving Paul a look that said, *I'm cutting you guys off, like now,* but Jeff was still turned away from the bar and missed it.

Paul, ever careful not to offend—even in this pissed state—grabbed a hold of Jeff's arm and motioned for them to leave.

"Hey, let's take a walk or maybe check out Sam's and see if we can get a table," Paul said hopefully, although he wasn't particularly hungry, having gone through three large bowls of spicy Asian mix at the bar.

Paul paid the balance of the tab and he and Jeff tumbled out into the cool evening air through the alleyway toward the light at Newtown Lane. While waiting to cross they spotted an attractive looking woman in a nearly see-through top and short, white linen skirt rushing toward them against the light. Cars weaved and honked as she pressed forward across the four lanes of traffic, her left leg clop-dropping with each uneven step. When she reached the curb she grabbed onto Paul's shoulder and bent over to examine her broken heel.

"Shit! You don't want to want to know how much I paid for these. Paul, it's so funny to see you!"

It was Jeanine.

"Jeanine, what are you doing? Where is Butch?" Paul asked.

"That fucker?" She was holding the mangled shoe and waving it in the air.

"Whoa, are you okay, Jeanine? You look, like, totally smashed," Jeff blurted out.

"Paul, take me home," she commanded.

"And, where is Butch?" Paul asked again.

"I left him with his big stupid boat and took a cab here to get a drink. I may have had too much. Can you drive me, please?"

Jeanine was only inches from Paul's face and still hadn't released her grip. Her breath held the scent of alcohol—vodka most likely—but underneath he recognized something hot and intimate that was distinctly hers. He tried to fight the memory of it.

Jeff gave Paul a look that said, "I'm okay, I'll let you handle this" and started to say his goodbyes. But Paul refused to let Jeff drive home alone. Of the three of them Paul figured he was the least risk to other drivers on the road. Paul found his Ford pickup in the Town lot (he managed to get it jump started earlier and made an appointment to fix the window) and they all piled into its front cab, with Jeanine taking the middle spot on the bench seat. The three of them rode in uncomfortable silence toward Jeff's house.

"It's brown," Jeanine said all of a sudden, laughing.

"What?"

"Your truck. I always hated it but now I get it. Of course it's brown," she said, her hands slapping the dash.

They pulled into Jeff's drive.

"Okay, this is me," Jeff said. He slipped down onto the hard gravel and a flash of light shot across the front porch, forcing Paul and Jeanine into consciousness. They sat and listened to the muted voices of Jeff and his girlfriend Penny, his "Sorry, I'm so drunk," and her "It's okay, Baby, let's go inside." Then, the slap of the screen door slamming shut, the buzz of the porch light flickering out.

Paul backed out of the driveway and turned in the direction of Jeanine's house in Northwest woods. As they drove through the winding unlit streets, Jeanine eased her left hand over to Paul's thigh and held it tightly. He caught himself fanning his fingers against her thigh each time he shifted gears so he could better sense the smooth surface of her skin.

They turned the next corner and started picking up speed when a large buck materialized from the low-lying fog. It began running alongside, its tall antlers jabbing the air, as if challenging them to a race. The deer shot ahead, paused momentarily, and then leaped in front of their truck. Paul gripped the wheel, slammed the brakes, and instinctively thrust his arm across Jeanine's chest to shield her from the impending crash. The Ford creaked to a full stop, the buck mere inches from the front bumper, unharmed. Instead of running away, the thing stood there, taking its time to move its two gleaming white eyes toward them, as if bored by the whole encounter. Paul and Jeannine sat monk-still, transfixed, watching the large animal's chest rising and falling with each massive breath. It stayed like this for several seconds, staring them down through the illumination of

Paul's headlights. Then, as quickly as it made its appearance known, the deer turned its head and loped back into the woods.

Jeanine turned to Paul and began sobbing. In all their years together, even during the worst of their fights, he'd never seen her cry with such abandon.

"Look, Jeanine—"

"—don't. I mean don't take me home. Take me to your place," she managed to say between sobs, this time her request more of a plea.

As he steered his truck now in the opposite direction, towards *his* house, he felt as if he was no longer driving but being driven by a force outside of his control.

After some effort, they managed to push themselves through Paul's front door (he never locked his; she always locked hers so she absentmindedly tried to use her own keys). Holding hands, they headed straight for his bedroom in the rear of the house.

Jeanine shimmied out of her skirt and, kneeling in front of him, began unlooping Paul's belt. She stared up at him with sleepy eyes and smiled but then stopped abruptly.

"Shit. Connor."

"Sleeping over at Nick's."

Once removing the rest of her clothes and tossing them on the floor, the bluish moonlight casting a cool glow on her now naked silhouette, Jeanine took his hand and in a small, almost detached, little girl voice said: *we're divorced*. She repeated the phrase several times, like a mantra—*we're divorced, we're divorced*—until their bodies fell gently onto the bed.

As Paul and Jeanine moved toward one another, rediscovering their shared lust after three long years of separation, Paul couldn't get the idea out of his head that Jeanine had probably hooked up with Butch that summer after college while he was back in the city working his ass off as a lowly editorial assistant. He'd considered confronting Jeanine about it several times over the years, but never had the courage to bring it up—even avoiding it when the subject of his own infidelity became a central part of their relationship.

This'll have to do.

And as he would write later in one of his spiral notebooks:

> *At that moment, I could feel the mutual distrust and blame that had defined our recent past falling away and there, staring up at me was my wife's face, familiar but strange, revealing a look of vulnerability I had previously believed was impossible for her to possess.*

Jeanine rolled over on her side and buried her face in his extra pillow.

We're divorced...

Such a deceptively simple two-word admission.

We're divorced.

"Oh man, I'm so sorry to hear that. You guys were great together!"

"Yeah. Whatever."

We're divorced.

"Aww, don't do that! Do you know how hard it is to meet someone else?"

"No. Tell me."

We're divorced.

Soon he would find himself tumbling clumsily between the shapes and contours of these two formidable words until drifting off to an uneasy sleep.

He awoke in the black, unsure of where he was. Like one of those

Old Testament prophets, half-starved under an endless sky, that dark vault strung with lights far out of the reach of mere mortals. After his eyes adjusted, he looked over at Jeanine's jackknifed form. She was still naked, her warmth turned away from him. He left his bed to clear his head and take a pee, then down the hall in search of Connor's computer (he hated bringing his own computer home from work. It reminded him of work and of the work he wasn't doing—the kind that might bring him pleasure—like the book he was never going to finish).

Finding it easily, he lifted the lid and settled to the edge of Connor's bed. The notebook's artificial glow filled the empty room with news of unemployment lines, wildfires, food recalls. Californians "defending" marriage (ha!).

He slid the pointer over to the last page Connor had left open. There, in Connor's news feed, amid the raw video clips, profane hip-hop music files and inane teenage patter was an unusual pair of photographs. Taken at a beach jetty. Like those "selfies" girls that age were always posting online. Only these two were different. The contorted nakedness, her expression blank as a death mask. She wasn't posing for us. Paul clicked to expand the two photos until they filled up the screen.

Their meaning couldn't have been any clearer.

~ ~ ~

Ave Maria (2)

She never took issue with the mirror. After all, it had been part of her training, hours upon hours in those mirrored practice rooms, her own reflection a wholly revealed aspect of herself. A constant reminder of whether she was getting it right. And she knew she was pretty not only because of that reflection. She was told constantly, every interaction with a stranger—male or female—an opportunity for someone to say, “You are so beautiful,” and she never got tired of hearing it. He would tell her that too. Until he stopped.

What was it like *not* to be pretty? Sure, someday her looks might dim along with other aspects, but the concern never entered her thoughts. As hard as she worked on everything else in her life she’d never have to work hard at that. And it would take her places she otherwise wouldn’t have been able to go.

Chapter 7: Saturday morning

"Hey," he said, shaking her awake.

"Oh, hey." Jeanine pressed her sticky lips together and apart, rubbed her right index finger along her teeth, and opened her eyes. She didn't bother pulling up the sheets gathered around her waist, instead pushing them down to let the air cool her skin. "Was that you up in the middle of the night?"

"Yeah."

"I thought I heard a scream. Coming from Connor's room."

"So what are we doing?"

"I don't know about you, birthday boy, but I am getting up and making some coffee." Jeanine smiled, swung her sylphlike legs to the floor and launched herself naked out of the bed.

Paul couldn't help but stare at her skin, the way it took on a light dewiness in the unairconditioned bedroom. God, that magnificent skin, how he missed it. Like milk glass; it glowed, *glistened*, an effect that seemed to shed years off of her true age. A skin that somehow managed to reveal no perceptible body hair, save the light downy covering on her arms and thighs and that slim, honey-blond median she kept neatly groomed between her legs. As he watched her glide through the house toward the kitchen, it awakened feelings within him long suppressed; he still hadn't gotten past not having her.

Here it was, all coming back. The things he tried to forget. How she hated perspiring except maybe at the gym or on those 5k runs along the beach she took three times a week (and this time of year especially, each glimpse of a blond ponytail swishing windshield wiper-like against a jogger's lightly tanned shoulders another opportunity for regret). How she couldn't live without air conditioning, always kept it a cool sixty-eight degrees even though there were maybe five days a year when the weather was hot and sticky enough to even justify owning one. The times he'd sneak up on her and massage the little raised goose bumps on her shoulders and neck. "It's not too cold, I'm just extra sensitive," she'd say, unaware that her sensitivity rarely stretched beyond the boundaries of her own disposition. And her preference for light things —her coffee, her toast, the movies and books she consumed. Even the little paintings she made back in college—her "sketches" she called them. Still lifes mostly in subtle Morandi hues: pale blues, washed grays, faded strokes of orange and yellow, the bone-white gesso peeking out from the borders. How this lightness extended to her social drinking too: white wine mostly, mixed vodka drinks. No "browns." Never tequila. She'd say, "Babe, pull me aside and take me home if I've had too much, will you?" Yet he couldn't think of a time when he had to. Which made their previous night together that much more out of character for her.

All these things he knew about her now seemed beside the point.

Paul got up and followed Jeanine into his galley-like kitchen. The room was narrow and dim, and had no window, only an aluminum-framed sliding glass door at the end. Outside the kitchen was a tiny cement patio on which sat a rusted metal table and two turquoise clamshell-shaped metal chairs he'd picked up at the town dump's "community exchange." The chairs stood uneven; you could see the weeds poking through the open wounds in the concrete underneath. As he surveyed the sorry looking kitchen and yard, he'd almost forgotten how easily Jeanine's being there would cause him to view things through her filter, as if overnight everything had become worn and faded or fallen into a state of disrepair.

From this viewpoint behind the glass door, Paul could see straight into the yard of his elderly neighbor, Mr. Hayes, who was probably enjoying the sight of a naked woman half his age on a Saturday morning. Jeanine slid the door open to let some fresh air into the kitchen and started rummaging through the half-filled cabinets. Paul, having sensibly put on a pair of boxers, leaned past her and narrowed the yellowed vertical blinds.

"You don't have any of that good coffee we used to drink? What is this?" she asked, taking out his can of off-brand ground coffee from the IGA and shaking it like a maraca. "You're turning into one of those sad bachelor types aren't you? I'll have to pick you up some."

"Look, if you don't like the coffee why don't you get yourself something on your way to work," Paul said. He was anxious to get to work himself.

She moved toward him and placed a gentle hand on his back, making sure to brush her bare breast against his arm. Her tone was sweeter now.

"You know I have to have my coffee before I can wake up. Besides, things have been slow and I don't have any appointments this morning."

"Well, I've got a bunch of stuff to do and I'm on call at the paper this weekend. What about Connor? Isn't he volunteering on the farm or something today?"

"That's Sunday. Shit Paul, you don't even know your own son's schedule. How many years have you been spending with him on weekends?"

The day before, sitting in her real estate office signing their final divorce papers, the two of them had mostly stared at one another from across the table without exchanging a word. Then, with their representatives out of the room, she leaned in and whispered to him. "Friends?" "Sure," he whispered back.

"That's not fair. You know I make all the school-related stuff. And, he stays here when you and Butch take your stupid real estate junkets or whatever you call them. Last week he even told me he wanted to move in with me."

"What!?"

Now it was her breasts that were doing the shaking. Although they weren't particularly large—especially compared to the increasing number of counterfeits paraded by the supposedly sophisticated women he encountered—Paul thought they still looked pretty damn good. Maybe too good. He began to feel a slight rise in his boxers. Moving out of the kitchen, he tried pushing his projection down with the side of his wrist. She followed close behind him.

Gesturing toward the garage sale sofa and mismatched table and chairs in the tiny dining room, she said: "Sorry Paul, but Connor is not moving into this... house. Our son can wait until college to live like a slob." He turned to face her. She stared down at his boxers. "Is that a woody you got there?"

"Not anymore."

She laughed, walked over to her spilled-open purse, grabbed a cigarette from a half crumpled pack of American Spirits, and lit up using a lighter she had stuffed into the cellophane. The first flick of ash fell on her arm and she blew it off with a long, smoke-filled breath.

"When did you start smoking again?"

"Don't try to change the subject, Paul."

"Look, I'm sure—"

"—it's only once in a while. It calms me, okay? You don't mind if I use this as an ashtray?" Without waiting for a response, she pulled a large clamshell from a glass vase sitting on a nearby table and expertly flicked an ash into it. She crossed her arms over her bare breasts and took another puff, holding the shell in her left hand like an offering.

"It's just I haven't seen you smoke since before you were pregnant with Connor."

Jeanine said nothing. Instead she stared at Paul as if he was a dear but clueless friend from her distant past who hadn't quite caught up with this new improved self she was projecting.

"What the hell was last night about then?" he asked her, finally.

"Last night I needed you."

"And this morning?"

"I was hoping we could fuck. But, you know, if you have stuff to do..."

Another flick of her ash. She moved her gaze to the now flattened front of his boxers.

"Jeanine. Look, I get it. You had a fight with Butch and now you're working out some kind of revenge fantasy. I'm starting to feel a little uncomfortable taking part in it, even if I do think the guy is a prick."

"Yeah, he's *my* prick. And do you actually think I'm going to tell Butch about this?"

"Huh. So I guess cheating isn't worth breaking up your relationship?"

"You could've stopped it. You know you wanted it last night too."

"I was drunk," he said.

"Wrong answer. Or does being drunk give you permission to fuck any girl who throws herself in your path. Oh yeah, I forgot. You've done that."

"Like I said, I was drunk. You were lovely. And now—"

"—and now what, I'm hideous, right?" She rested her arms at her waist and dared Paul to look at her, to try again to hold back his arousal.

"Jeanine." He reached out to touch her but she pulled away.

"Maybe it was my turn," she said. She took a long drag of her cigarette. "Why are you the only one who gets to?"

"Was I the only one who got to?"

Her face flushed.

"This was a pretty shitty thing to do," she said, turning away from him. "And Connor's not moving here. You can forget about that." She snuffed out her cigarette and started toward his bedroom.

Paul grabbed Jeanine gently by the elbow, stopping her.

"Wait, you said something the other day, about it being the right thing to do, us moving here together," he said. "Did you mean it for me too?"

"I was probably trying to give you a pep talk. I thought you needed one."

"Sure, Jeanine. Okay. You were always good at telling me what I needed."

"Happy Birthday, Paul. Consider last night your birthday present."

Paul picked up some clothes from the bedroom floor, grabbed his shaving kit and left Jeanine to get showered and dressed. He carried his stuff—much of it advertisers' swag and other freebies from his magazine writing days—into the guest bathroom down the hall.

As he watched his urine stream out and splash over the sides of the bowl he tried to figure out how he had arrived at this precise moment in his life. It wasn't that he lacked an understanding of the individual events leading up to it; he'd spent plenty of restless hours obsessing over each poor decision and missed opportunity. It was the sweep of it that eluded him, the interconnectedness meant to form some kind of conceivable narrative. He was realizing only now, after three long years living alone, that his desperate need to write down even the most mundane facts about other people's lives was his way of avoiding the facts of his own—he'd settled for being a collector of other people's stories while ignoring his own story.

But now for the first time in a long time he had something no one else had, something of real value, at least within the narrowly defined expectations of his current professional life. And the crazy thing was that this valuable something came to him—pretty much fell into his lap—in very much the same way the revelation of his failure as a faithful husband had come: by poking around where he didn't belong.

After two days of torturing himself to get anything on the story, there she was, this girl who he was told wasn't supposed to exist, staring back at him from the rocks. Reduced to a glint from the news feed on his son's Facebook page.

Posted by some kid named Dylan.

As he began lathering up his shaving brush Paul stopped to consider the reflection staring back at him in the bathroom mirror. He spied his faded doppelganger behind the layer of fog, cleared away a spot with his hand and then marked it with his hot breath before clearing it away again. It wasn't OCD, more of a habit, a game he invented years ago to see if he could uncover something new. Some tiny revelation about himself that might slip through the space between seeing and not seeing. Time had been unusually kind to his face, giving it a not unpleasant softening in middle age. But he did spot something: a few gray hairs sneaking into the areas flanking his too-small ears. After watching the last of his beard stubble snake its way down the drain, he fished out a pair of old scissors from a bottom drawer and performed some selective trimming. He continued with his eyebrows until they no longer looked like the tail of a feral cat—more like a couple of fuzzy black caterpillars racing across the top half of his face. He laid down the scissors and could swear he caught a sly smile reflecting back at him. He hadn't been this clean in a long time.

When he emerged from the bathroom he called out for her. But Jeanine was already gone.

Chapter 8: Saturday morning

Paul wasn't taking any chances with his truck, not this morning. He got on his battered yellow bicycle—an old Motobecane 10-speeder Connor had jokingly nicknamed "Mellow"—for the short ride to his office at the *East End Times*. The office was located on the second floor of a nondescript cedar shingled commercial building well off of East Hampton's tony Main Street, in the shadow of the town's two-story propane tank. The space was typical for a small town newspaper: large, clunky desks with cheap oak veneer peeling off of the sides, creaky vinyl-backed swivel chairs, a few mismatched rugs covering scuffed wood floors, computer cables running everywhere. On the walls were pictures of seascapes and fishing boats, music posters—a parting gift from the last remaining record store in town that had gone out of business, bulletin boards filled with reminders, invitations to events long-past mixed in with a few personal photos, and maps with pins stuck into them showing locations once important for some story but now long forgotten. The paper had recently set up an online network so reporters and editors could log in from different locations, check their email, and upload (or download) their stories and photos back to the main office.

Paul preferred the new location to the main office in Southampton for its relative quiet and easy camaraderie. Four desks were arranged haphazardly in a single large room with no cubicle walls to divide the workspaces. The paper's small staff included Paul and his friend Jeff, the freelance photographer Esra (short for Esperanza) Reyes, and the occasional visit from Grace Monahan, his senior editor, who spent most of her time overseeing the rest of the paper's staff in the main office in Southampton.

There was really no good reason for the paper to exist. But its publisher, Bert Plank, a man of voracious appetite both economic and culinary who owned several papers on the East End, was looking to take on the establishment. The town of East Hampton already had a successful paper going on well past its hundredth anniversary, not to mention numerous glossy tabloids covering celebrity homes and gardens, fashion and the arts. Back when the economy was still red-hot, Bert couldn't accept the idea that locals (and advertisers) had only one choice for weekly news. While big city newspapers were being felled like mighty oaks, "hyperlocal" publications were the rage. Bert saw his opportunity to cash in, and maybe give the other guy a run for his money. Luckily the *EET*, available for free at most shops around town and online, quickly gained a reputation for being a pretty good read.

To save money, Bert chose up to 75% of the editorial content from his existing papers and added just enough hyperlocal coverage to appeal to residents further east. That's where Bert saw Paul as a key asset. Paul's background as husband of a local real estate agent and son-in-law of East Hampton's former police chief—albeit long deceased—gave him local "cred." He was transferred from Southampton to the East Hampton office and had been there ever since.

Paul found a spot on his crowded desk to drop his take-out coffee. Then he went through his email: a few birthday wishes from friends, an e-card from Connor *(Happy Birthday. Fuck you. Ha ha. Just kidding. Love, Connor.*), a brief note from his father Isaak back in Brooklyn about coming out later to celebrate his birthday, and the weekly rundown from Grace on some stories and town meetings to cover for the coming week. But there was one email sent at 12:13

a.m. that caught his eye. It was from the woman he had run into in the Beach Lane parking lot where the dead girl had gone missing two days before. It had been a long time since an email had the potential to offer something worthwhile, a sense of order, of things falling into place.

> Hey Paul
> Great meeting you again although I wish the circumstances could have been better! There is some stuff we should talk about that I forgot to tell you. Come by that BBQ place on Town Line later tonight. That is, if you don't have any other plans. I know it's your birthday. I'll buy you a drink. Meet you around 7:00?
> -Merika

What "circumstances" was she alluding to? He thought about what she had said about the dead girl: *Love is so fragile.* Like she was trying to tell him something beyond the strangeness of everything else that happened that day. And now she was checking up on him, even knew it was his birthday.

He brought his nose up to his computer screen and typed a response. As he typed, his next thought was that she might get scared and change her mind. He tried to keep it short...

> Merika, I'm so glad you reached out to me. I'll be at Townline. Can't wait to see you there later tonight.

Then he hit Send, wrote down this kid Dylan's street address and raced out the door.

Chapter 9: Saturday, later that morning

Dylan's house in Sagaponack was one of those super-sized English Country shingle-style cottages built in the last ten years or so, its tall cedar gate equipped with the now customary high tech security system wedged between a tall, perfectly trimmed privet hedge running the length of the property.

Paul parked Mellow against the high hedge, wiped the perspiration from his face and walked around to the front.

Pushing the call button, he noticed the gate was open.

He waited through two more pushes of the button. No response.

He slipped through the gate, strolled up to the massive oak door to the house and knocked. A second knock, louder this time. Summer. Lawn culture. People spend their time outside right? He walked around the back and started searching the extensive property for some of that culture. Past a four-car garage, two bays open, and matching his and hers European rag tops. A luxury SUV sat parked at an odd angle in the drive, windows open—clothes, towels, and other brightly colored stuff spread across the backseat. Fresh mud and sand marred the SUV's otherwise shiny lower body.

Somebody's home.

He soon found another hedge, this one not quite as tall, and behind it an exquisite hardscaped swimming pool, with dual winding marble stairways leading parallel up a slight berm. Atop this raised area was a good-sized pool house shaded by a big Japanese maple, and between its verdant branches he spied a clue: a white satellite dish, its lollypop roundness forcing its way up from the red-tiled roof. Paul approached the pool house quietly and rapped on the door. Again, there was no answer. But a quick peek into a side window and he could see what looked like the aftermath of a pretty good party.

Despite a cool breeze blowing from the direction of the ocean, the sweat continued to pour off of him, staining the front of his buttoned-up dress shirt. Somebody was home and he wasn't leaving without talking to that somebody. He drew a deep breath and turned the egg-shaped brass knob. The door pushed open easily. In the corner of the room he could see two bodies curled up under bright white sheets. They lay there motionless, their shapes forming a stylized letter "D." The studio-sized room, which now appeared much tighter from the inside, was a mess of clothes, empty beer and soda cans, ashtrays, a large rainbow-streaked glass bong, plastic video game sleeves, take-out food containers, and other trash strewn about the floor, chairs and tables. A huge surfboard with one of those yin/yang symbols hung over the bed with the words "WET DREAMS" in large capital letters painted vertically down one side.

Once Paul figured out which of the two bodies belonged to Dylan, he tapped the bottom of the kid's foot with his notebook.

"What the fah—dude, who are you?"

Dylan sat up and tried to focus his eyes on the intruder who, despite being of average height and build, was casting a considerable shadow.

"Hey. I'm here to ask you some questions," Paul blurted out.

"Are you some kind of cop or something? And, dude, why are you so...sweaty?" Dylan opened his eyes wider to get them adjusted to the light, a sharp angle streaming through the open door, making a slice right through the middle of his bed and up to the glossy surface of the surfboard above his head.

"I'm not a cop—"

"—then isn't this breaking and entering?" Dylan gestured toward the open door, "I mean, at least *entering?* Dude, that's not right... wait; you're not a cop. I know all the cops in town. But you do look familiar. Are you here to buy some weed? It's kind of early."

"I'm a reporter for the *East End Times*. We're a local paper here in East Hampton," Paul said. Then, as if this explained everything: "I rode my bicycle over here."

"So?"

"So, I'm here to ask you about some pictures—"

"—yo, Woodstein Bernward is here for a scoop," Dylan announced to no one in particular. He checked himself now, as if to ensure the three-hundred-plus thread-count sheet still covered his naked figure, at least from the waist down. The kid had a slinky, androgynous look, his long dirty-blonde hair twisted into Rasta braids, and intense green eyes that girls—and guys—his age probably couldn't resist. Paul noted that Dylan didn't even bother to look over at the slender mass curled up inches beside him as the two of them spoke.

"You mean Woodward and Bernstein, and I'm surprised you even know about those guys."

"My dad used to publish books for one of them – I forget which. He *knew* those guys personally, may they rest in peace."

"But they're not dead. You should know that if your father worked with them."

"Ah, but they might as well be. No offense but investigative journalism is dead, haven't you seen the papers? Oh yeah, no one reads the papers, I forgot. Ha! So what can I do for you now that you've ruined any chances of me getting my required nine-hour sleep regimen? We young adults require lots of sleep, you know. Good for the serotonin levels."

As they were talking, Paul studied the body curled up next to

Dylan. She was lying perfectly still, although every now and then he caught a slight rhythmic rise and fall of the sheet. This girl at least was still breathing.

"Look," Paul said, "I saw the pictures you posted on Facebook last night of the dead girl."

"What? Really? How did you get them?"

"It's not important how I got them. But you have to know—."

"–damn, son! We were so *blaszed* last night. I almost forgot about that. Me and some of my friends were here talking and feeling really bad for that East Hampton cop who found the girl. Used to buy from me. He's 'aight. Although I heard he didn't treat his last girlfriend too well."

"You know about Will Clifford?" Even after his visit to Woo in Riverhead, Paul was told by Grace to keep the story about Clifford claiming to find a body on lockdown.

"Yeah. Anyway, he never hassled me and I wanted to do him a favor in return, y'know? I was getting sick of people making fun of him, saying he made the whole thing up. Although it was kinda funny."

"Well, since you seem to know so much maybe you can give me a little information as to where you got the pictures. Did you take them?"

"Nah, I was asleep when those were taken, I'm pretty sure. Let's just say they were taken by a friend. I guess you've seen my Facebook page. I have a lot of friends."

"Who is your friend?"

"Ah, therein lies the rub. I don't think I should answer that."

"Shakespeare. Do you know the next line: 'For in that sleep of death we know not what dreams may come?' Anyway, why can't you tell me? I'm not working with the cops. I'm only looking out for the girl and her family—if she has one."

"Nice."

Paul wasn't sure if Dylan was saying it was "nice" that he could quote the next line of Hamlet or if the kid was just stalling.

"Well, if what you are saying is true then my friend is going to be in some serious trouble. When he took them he probably thought he was getting a souvenir, y'know what I mean? Like bragging rights at being there first before the whole thing blew up. Who knew that a dead girl could get up and walk away?"

"So you don't think your friend had anything to do with the girl, beyond taking pictures I mean?"

"I'll tell you this much: if he did, he didn't tell me. But I doubt it. He's like the chillest guy I know."

"Chill huh? Is he a surfer?" Paul looked up at the board above Dylan's head.

"Dude, you are good at this! Here I am protecting the innocent and you are asking some *very specific* questions. *Very* nice."

"So he *is* a surfer. He surfs, like around Montauk, maybe that part of Wainscott where the girl was? That would make sense given the early hour when the girl was found."

"Whatever, dude. This conversation is over."

"Well, if I were you I'd be getting my story straight. In a few hours the whole world is going to know about this. About you. Consider my visit a friendly wake-up call," Paul said.

"Sounds more like a threat," Dylan said, without the slightest bit of malice in his voice. Then, muttering under his breath, "I can handle those local cops, no worries."

"You don't seem to get this. Those pictures are all over the

Internet by now. Forget about the Town cops. Within a few hours you're going to have Peconic County guys here, maybe even the FBI. You are very likely about to be the center of a murder investigation. If I were you I would think about getting a lawyer."

"Okay, okay. I get it. I messed up and should call my dad. Hey babe," Dylan poked the girl next to him in the ribs. "Jes, c'mon girl, wake up! We gotta go." The girl let out the slightest moan and turned over on her stomach without opening her eyes. The edge of the sheet slid down just below her waist, exposing the graceful slope of her spine and a large tattoo; angel's wings etched into the part of her back where it met her dimpled buttocks.

Paul started making his way toward the door.

Dylan shouted out to Paul as he was making his exit, "Hey, reporter guy, what's your name?"

"Paul. Paul Sandis."

"Paul Sandis. Huh. You sure you don't want any weed? Hold on." Dylan leaned over and pulled out a large plastic bag from under the bed. He slid open the Ziploc closure and took out some of the clumped buds to put in his bong.

"No thanks. It's been a while."

"Hey, I know where I know that name, 'Sandis.' Isn't your kid the science fair nerd? He won first place for some state science award or something. Plants right?"

"Yeah, third place, but close. And yes, plants. That was a couple of years ago."

"Your dude's cool," Dylan said, nodding his head.

"How do you know him?" Paul asked.

"Like I said, I'm friends with lots of people. Peace."

Paul's last glance of Dylan was a right thumb resting on the flint wheel of a classic Zippo lighter as he moved his lips toward the bong's wide mouthpiece.

By 11:30 that morning there were a half dozen official looking vehicles parked outside the gate of Dylan's father's house. The gate was locked and there was nobody home, leaving the summer residents of this manicured cul-de-sac with only the crackle of police radios and a blocked intersection. The pictures of the dead girl were summarily removed from Dylan's Facebook page but it was already too late. Within minutes of their posting, they had been passed around the Internet faster than flu germs at a playground.

Chapter 10: Saturday afternoon

"Connor!" Paul was yelling into his cell phone over a steady, pulsing beat. Some new rapper named Cassius Claim that Connor was always going on about.

"Yo, Dad, what's good?"

"Connor, can you turn down the music?"

"Sure Dad. Hey Nick, I gotta turn it down a minute."

"Where are you guys?"

"Um, at Nick's in Sag Harbor, with Nick and Morris. What's up?"

For several years, Paul and Jeanine had concerns about Connor fitting in at school. He was an intense, shy kid, smart—maybe too precocious for his own good—which made him stand out at an age when fitting in was tantamount. His interest in narrow areas of science, botany in particular, had a way of putting off other boys whose own interests typically laid elsewhere: sports, video games, surfing, skateboarding, girls. But in his sophomore and junior years he had managed to gain a newfound sureness and was able to establish some regular friendships, even mentioning to Paul that he was now "hooking up" with girls. Although generally supportive of this social development, Paul was surprised at Connor's choice of friends. Nick and Morris were nice enough kids, but they didn't seem particularly smart or ambitious. And whenever Paul tried to engage them in conversation they rarely seemed to be *present*.

"Connor, I had a talk today with this kid Dylan about some pictures I discovered on your Facebook page."

"Dylan? What pictures?"

"The pictures of this dead girl that washed up in Wainscott the other day."

"I saw that. Is that for real?"

"That's what I'm trying to find out."

"Whoa, when you talked to Dylan you didn't mention my name to him?" Connor asked. Somebody put the music on "mute."

"No, but he seemed to know you when I told him mine. I find it interesting that the biggest pot dealer out here knows who you are."

"Weed."

"What?"

"Weed. Trees. Only old hippies call it 'pot,' Dad."

"Anyway, we'll talk about that another time. But first, I think you owe me an answer to a question."

"Sure," Connor said, sounding relieved to change the subject.

"Tell me, do you know a girl named Jes or maybe Jessica, blonde, some kind of angel tattoo on her back?"

The three teens were cracking up. At this point Connor had Paul on speakerphone so they could all listen in on the conversation.

"Dad, are you perving on me? Why do you want to know about Jessica Manning? And it's not a 'back tattoo,' it's called a 'tramp stamp.'" More giggles.

Paul tried to ignore their continued laughter at his expense.

"Just tell me what you know about her."

"She's a junior ... at Pierson." There was a sudden quiet at Connor's end of the line—a lost connection? "She's untouchable, Dad."

"What do you mean, 'untouchable?'"

"She doesn't hook up with other high school kids, only older guys."

"Huh. Do you know any of the names of the guys she hangs with? Maybe guys who are also friends with this Dylan kid?"

"Hmm, let me see. There's T'Kwame Jackson: he graduated from East Hampton like two years ago. He used to be her boyfriend. Patrice, the prep school kid from the city that hangs with them sometimes. Dylan you already met. And, oh yeah, that Fredy kid who dropped out of East Hampton after junior year, whatshisname?"

"Gomes!" Nick and Morris yelled in unison.

"Yeah, Fredy Gomes. Tall, skinny dude. Lots of tats."

"Tats?"

"*Tatoos*. Jeesh, Dad."

"Interesting... is he a surfer?"

"Yeah, big time *brahhhh*," Conner said, drawing out the "ah" sound to mock the exaggerated way surfers and skateboarders addressed each other as "brother." "He works at Orange Crush, that hipster skate store in the Village."

"This is great," Paul said, writing the information down in his notepad. "And, what about a guy named Will Clifford? Do you guys know anything about him or his girlfriend?"

"Clifford... let's see: lifeguard, jock, he graduated last year or the year before I think. His parents have that big farm in Wainscott near Beach Lane. Used to come by Sugar Rose with his father sometimes to talk to Ellie about organic fertilizer and stuff. I don't know who he goes out with. What else ... you guys know anything?" Connor asked his friends.

"Dude is weird," Morris said.

"You think everyone is weird," Connor said.

"If they are."

"What does that even mean?"

"Weird. That's all I'm sayin'."

"Hey guys, thanks. I think I got enough. And don't worry. I always protect my sources. I won't mention how I got any of these names. Connor, don't stay out too late. You're sleeping at my place tonight right?"

"Nah, I'm gonna sleep over Nick's again tonight. We're headed to a party in Bridge later and I'll probably have to be the designated driver. Anyway, I'll text you."

"Okay, but make sure you come by before noon so we can celebrate my birthday. And text your mom so she knows where you are."

"Sure Dad, peace," Connor said and hung up.

* * *

Once he was sure the phone connection was disengaged, Nick turned up the music again. "Dude, what's your dad scheming on? Is he like Sherlock Holmes or something?"

Morris was on the sofa cross-legged. Texting, oblivious.

"Yeah, he used to be an investigative reporter when we lived in the city."

"I saw those pictures," Nick said. "Creepy. Wait, do you think Fredy'll find out we gave his name to your dad?"

"Nah. No worries. My dad's cool."

Morris, now half listening to their conversation, announced: "Dude, this sucks. Nick, you said you were gonna bring the new Death Battalion."

"Word, I forgot," Nick said.

"Connor, did you at least bring some weed?" Morris asked.

Connor handed Morris a neatly rolled joint that he immediately lit up. Then Morris used the same disposable lighter to pop the cap off a bottle of Corona he'd retrieved from the mini-fridge. After taking a hit, he passed the joint over to Nick.

The three of them weren't at Nick's house in Sag Harbor. They were at the Cave. In Springs.

April, a few months before, Morris had discovered the house while skateboarding around his neighborhood. A nondescript 60's-style contemporary with vertical wood siding. There was the old gray Volvo wagon, stolid in the gravel drive, its rear windows plastered with years of town beach stickers. The lonely pile of oil delivery receipts collected inside the storm door. The unlocked Bilco leading to the basement. The fake security system. It was just too tempting.

"Everybody in this neighborhood just puts up the signs without paying for the system. You can get them on eBay for like ten bucks," Morris had told Connor while lifting the cool metal door handle and entering the basement for the first time.

The place had everything. A neatly furnished room with all the amenities: sleep sofa, small kitchenette with refrigerator, a full bathroom with shower, a heater with its own thermostat, and a wide-screen television equipped with the newest PlayStation video game console. The furniture was simple and IKEA-spare; if they broke something it probably could be easily and cheaply replaced (by somebody). Once they'd surveyed the room, Morris and Connor tiptoed up each of the polished-wood stairs and tried the door that led to the rest of the house. But it was locked from the other side.

Morris made no attempt to force it open.

"Dude, don't you wanna see what else is in this place?"

"Nah. This is perfect. If we mess with the door then it's breaking and entering right? But if we stay here in the basement, it's like we've been invited."

How Morris derived at this logic Connor wasn't sure but he deferred to his friend's ownership of the place.

And there was one other thing the house had that sealed it for the boys. Morris had discovered it that first day while rummaging through the wall of built-in cabinets opposite the sofa.

"What are you looking for?" Connor asked Morris when he saw his friend poking around in one of the cabinet drawers. Meanwhile, Connor was busy flipping through the cable channels on the TV. Evidently, whoever owned the house kept paying the cable bill even though there was no one there to watch.

"Holy shit!"

"What?" Connor said.

"Dude, you're not going to believe this: they have like every video game known to man and boy here."

After three uninterrupted hours of turning zombies' heads into exploding reams of confetti, pulling crack-whores out of smashed-up Ferraris, and role playing Taliban fighters shooting at American soldiers from behind bombed out Mosques, the two adventurers formed a pact then and there to make the place their own secret retreat.

Struggling to come up with a suitable moniker—"Let's go to that place near your house" just didn't have the right ring to it—they settled on "the Cave." Since the boys didn't plan on going beyond the basement room, the name had a certain air of inevitability to it. Besides, it had a long "ay" sound that was fun to draw out, as in: "Dude, let's go to the *Caaaaaave.*"

Before long, the Cave became their regular place to chill after school and during long spring weekends. And the perfect place to invite girls.

“Yo, what was up with that Daisy chick the other night?” Morris asked Connor while the weed was being passed around.

“Whaddya mean?” Connor said. “They’re supposed to come back tonight I think.”

It was Connor who had set the thing up: two sophomore girls from St. Cecilia’s, East Hampton’s only Catholic high school. Connor hooked up with a Spanish girl named Daisy he had met online the week before. Daisy had brought her friend Glenda for Morris at Connor’s request.

“Every time we do this the girl you fix me up with is totally busted,” Morris said.

“I thought Glenda was nice,” Conner said. “Hey, wasn’t that the name of the good witch in *Wizard of Oz*?

“The good witch was named *Glinda*. Dude, there are no Mexicans in Oz.”

“She and Daisy are Guatemalan not Mexican. And Glinda, Glenda, whatever. C’mon, you have to admit she was hot in that movie.”

“But she was still a witch. And why’d she wait until the end of the movie—*after* her rival witch was dead—to tell Dorothy how to get home? That’s cold.”

“Hey, I figured out the name of our first album,” Connor said.

Connor and Morris had been kicking around the idea of starting a band, a blend of hip-hop and indie—“urban attitude meets spoiled white kid irony” Connor had called it.

“‘That’s Cold?’”

“What’s cold?”

“The name!”

“No. I haven’t even told you the name yet.”

“Nevermind.”

"That's a Nirvana album! We can't use that."

"Why would we want to name it after a Nirvana album?"

"That's what I'm saying. Now would you let me tell you what it is?"

"Sure. But why the big buildup?"

"*Let's Go to the Cave*. That's the title," Connor said.

"Lame."

"Why are all my ideas lame and yours are so brilliant?"

"Cause they usually suck, dude. It sounds like something Robin would say to Batman if he wanted to take him to a gay bar: 'Ooh, my Dark Knight, let's go the Cave!' Lame. And definitely gay."

"Whaddya mean? We say it to each other all the time—ahhh, fuck you, Morris—although now that you mention it ... okay, what about *Harbor Kill*?"

"What about it?"

"For the album title, dickhead."

"That's pretty good. Although *Dickhead* is also good. Write that one down before we get too blazed and forget it." Morris took another hit of the joint.

"Hey," Connor said, starting to feel the effects of the weed.

"What?" Morris had gone back to playing whatever videogame was already cued up.

"Nick's right. This dead girl thing is kind of creepy. What if Dylan had something to do with it?"

"No way. Do you think your dad will find something out?"

"I don't know but I should really get going. You can keep the rest," Connor said, handing Morris the remainder of his weed. "Nick, can you drop me at the farm?"

Nick didn't say much but he was good to have around for rides.

And he had a jeep you could drive on the beach.

"The farm is so gay, dude. Let's hang here for a while," Morris said. "I thought you didn't have to be at the farm until tomorrow."

"I don't, but there's something I need to do there today."

"Well, I'm staying. Hey Connor, if you can't stick around maybe I can invite your mom over. She can try out my joy stick," Morris said, thrusting his hips up and making an "oh" face.

"Fuck you, Morris!" Connor reached over from the other side of the sofa in an attempt to punch his friend in the crotch.

"C'mon, you have to admit she's a total MILF," Morris said.

Nick was barely in the conversation, having started Player 2 within the same videogame.

Connor began flinging lit matches onto Nick's lap to get his attention. After the fifth or sixth one stuck, Nick said,

"Ow! *Alright*, I'll drop you in Bridge."

"Word," Connor said, muttering the socially accepted form of "thank you" used by his peer group.

"But Morris is right, dude. The farm is pretty gay."

* * *

When Paul returned to the office, he made several phone calls but failed to locate Fredy Gomes at the store or at his parent's house. He decided to type up a story based on what he had so far and sent it, along with the pictures he'd downloaded from Connor's Facebook news feed, to his editor Grace Monahan. The story's lede mentioned Officer Will Clifford finding the body and the body disappearing immediately after—sometime between his leaving the scene, calling it in on his police radio and returning to the jetty (Paul had concluded this much from being at the parking lot that day). The article then went into detail about how pictures of the girl had been posted online, and mentioned an "unnamed source" who confirmed the pictures' veracity. After struggling with the suggested headline, Paul decided to go with something simple that wouldn't put too much blame on the part of the officer. He enjoyed the headline's inherent contradiction, likening it to his recent marital situation:

Dead Girl Found in Wainscott; Still Missing.

After sending the story, Paul got on a three-way conference call with Grace and the publisher, Bert Plank, at his editor's request.

Bert: "Why are you guys bugging me on a Saturday? My kids are freaking out here at the miniature golf. This is my life now by the way: *miniature* golf."

Bert, like a number of his late middle-aged peers, was on his second family, which included a set of matching tow-headed five-year-old twins.

Grace: "Bert, if I may, Paul has a story that demands serious consideration. If what he is writing here is true, this gives this fella Will Clifford's story some credibility and opens up what may become a murder or possible missing person's investigation. However, if these pictures are just a hoax—let's face it, you can't trust what people post on the Internet— then this is going to make the paper look really bad."

Bert: (reading the story aloud now on his mobile) "Paul, I'm reading here that you've got one unnamed source and probably not a very reliable one, a surfer kid." Bert said this between bites of what Paul guessed was a Puff 'n' Putt hot dog sloshing around in his mouth.

Paul: "I know it looks thin but I can tell this kid who posted the pictures is telling the truth and the cops will make his story public soon enough."

Bert: "And updates from the East Hampton police, the Peconic County guys? And, what about the kid who took the pictures?"

Paul: "As I mention in the piece, no comment from officials so far. This whole thing is incredibly embarrassing for them. They're keeping it close until they do their own investigation. I mean, either they've got a young, alleged drug using beach cop who makes up wild stories or they got a missing dead body. Either way it doesn't look good for them. And, as for the second question, I'm pretty confident I've found the kid who took those pictures. I'm working on a confirmation now."

Grace: "Bert, I recommend that we get more police sources on this and wait to run it in the paper on Wednesday. Let's hold off putting anything up on the website."

The *EET* was a weekly newspaper, with a deadline of Tuesday night for Wednesday publication in order to beat out the other major East Hampton paper, which came out a day later, on Thursday. Despite the usual chaos on Tuesday afternoons, stories could often be worked over and checked for a few days before they got published, especially when stuff happened on or immediately prior to the weekend. That is, until the last few years when readers started expecting to find updates of stories online. Now if you had a truly breaking story, you had to collect your facts, do your interviews, get the article written, edited, and ready for uploading to the website within a few hours. And, with the recent introduction of a national online news site that was covering the same "hyperlocal" news, there was even more pressure to get stories posted as quickly as possible.

Paul: "Grace, it's not only this most recent source. I was there right after it happened. I heard the cop on the radio. He definitely saw something—*someone*—that day."

Grace: "Then why are the Peconic County police burying this? Word from them so far is that Will Clifford made up this story. No one's sure why. They're treating it as an internal matter. That's why we haven't run anything on it yet. No one else has picked up this story yet either."

This information about Will Clifford was new to Paul. He had been unable to get *anything* on or off the record from Virginia Woo or anyone else at Peconic since that day. Grace had apparently decided to withhold this bit of information from him.

Bert: "Grace, I understand your concern but I only see an upside here. Paul's the only one out there with this *other* story as far as I can tell. Let's put it up on the website. I'll get emails to my friends at the *Post* and *The New York Times*. I'll make sure they mention us as the source. Do you realize how many hits we're going to get?"

Grace: "Okay, but you're not running the pictures."

Bert: (his voice rising now) "Are you kidding me? The pictures *are* the story. I want both of them in. Let's put the dead girl's face on page one, the tattoo on two. Maybe we can get an ID on the girl from someone out there. I'll get permission from the Chief to put up an email address and phone number."

Grace: "But they're low res j-pegs," she said, pleading.

Bert: "So?"

Grace: "So the pictures don't meet our publication standards; they are low resolution digital files, probably taken with a cell phone camera. And look at that strange blurring around her head in that one picture—it's all out of focus. Regardless, Bert, this is a family paper. We've never run anything like that tattoo photo before."

Bert: "We're sitting on what could be the biggest story out here in years and right now we're the only paper with the pictures. We can't get hung up on quality issues. Besides, if we don't run them I know those bastards across town will get them off of the Internet soon. We'll have Alex do some creative cropping. Just make sure to put in enough "allegedly's" and "according to's" in the article to cover our butt. And, Grace, don't worry, I'll take the heat if anyone has a problem with this."

This was classic Bert. Grace Monahan was a twenty five-year veteran reporter and editor who had worked at pretty much every newspaper on the East End in some capacity. Besides editing two weekly papers for Bert—western and eastern editions—it was her job to be mediator, den mother and fixer. And, even though it fell under Bert's job description to manage relationships with advertisers, when the folks from the Village Home Improvement Society or the Long Island Mallard Decoy Collectors Association wanted to drop off their $80 checks for a measly display ad, it was Grace's desk they sought out. It wasn't unusual to find her making time to sit and have tea with these "lovely ladies" as Bert called them (both the women and the men)—even if she was backed up with three or four unread stories on deadline. The previous summer when Grace was on personal leave for a few days, Bert Okayed a story written by an intern about the huge drop in the real estate market without making sure to include the rosy side of the picture. It was pretty much standard editorial practice to always include some kind of optimistic comments when running this type of story to appease the paper's largest advertisers. Upon her return Grace faced a shit-storm of protest and was obligated to spend the following week meeting with representatives from all the major realtors on the East End to unruffle feathers while Bert was off playing golf somewhere in Cape Cod.

Grace: "Okay, it's your paper Bert."

Bert: "Nice job, Paul. Keep working your sources and send us any updates so we can post them online. I think I'm going to enjoy this. (They could hear the sound of children screaming, and Bert's voice directed away from the phone) Boughton! Stop hitting your brother with the putter! (His voice back to the microphone now) Grace, let's meet for a few minutes later today when you come in to the office and we'll discuss strategy on this. Meanwhile, have Alex get this up on the website ASAP."

Grace: "Okay. But may God help us if we get this wrong."

Chapter 11: Saturday, later that afternoon

Paul stood astride Mellow in front of the Orange Crush store in East Hampton Village, looking for a spot to chain her up. A small clothing boutique, Orange Crush sold sneakers and hoodies for roughly two to three times the price you'd pay at a typical mall store. Although a number of shops in the Village had reopened after a long winter hiatus, once again breathing new life into this rarified retail-shopping corridor, there were still too many empty storefronts. At one time a typical small town Main Street with hardware, 5&10 cents store, tailor, barber shop, and cobbler, the old style mom and pop stores and small owner-run boutiques were mostly gone, priced out due to ever-increasing rents that only the largest corporations and high end specialty shops could afford to pay. Sure, there was still the town movie theater, a pharmacy, and overpriced candy store—and some of the smaller shops had found places a few blocks north on Newtown Lane. But Main Street was now dominated by luxury brand satellites that wanted to be able to advertise "East Hampton" on the side of a drawstring shopping bag—regardless of whether they turned a profit there. Even the Village-owned landmarks had gone Fifth Avenue retail: the old post office, its quaint gray-shingled entryway now welcoming Ralph Lauren shoppers; the great white Masonic Hall with its broad stair and neoclassical columns and which once housed four bowling lanes and a bar, now a place to pick up a fifty-thousand dollar Patek Philippe watch or other small gift for that generous weekend host. Other luxury brands might open a "pop up shop"—a temporary outlet that operated for two to three months during the summer—leaving a desolate storefront the rest of the year. Orange Crush was one of the few owner-operated stores that managed to remain open year-round, although technically it was off of Main Street adjacent to a small village parking lot.

Four o'clock on a warm Saturday afternoon. The boutique was empty of shoppers, its front door swung wide open. A teenage girl, looking about seventeen, was sitting on the curb out front smoking a cigarette. Her eyes were circled in black mascara and dark eye shadow like a raccoon; her hair dyed charcoal black with streaks of purple and red. She had on black fishnet stockings and a pink chiffon dress that looked like a little girl's idea of a ballerina costume. Over the top half of her dress she wore what Paul took to be one of the store's graphic T's: across the front the word "modernist" written in small lower-case Sans-serif type.

After locking up his bike, Paul walked over and sat down on the raised curb next to the girl so he was shoulder-to-shoulder with her facing Main Street. They watched as two over-tanned, smartly dressed middle aged women with heavy shopping bags stood chatting and waiting to move into the crosswalk on the other side of the street. There was a prominent yellow sandwich board-type sign announcing to the oncoming cars that they were bound by state law to stop for pedestrians at this crossing. But each time the women took a tentative step into the intersection the hurried drivers would pretend not to notice and whizz right past. It would be at least another two weeks before the peak summer season began and the Village police stationed a white-gloved traffic control officer to man this and about a half dozen other intersections within the Village. But for now the ladies were on their own.

After almost a full minute staring silently at the game of high-stakes chicken playing itself out on Main Street, Paul addressed the girl in the T-shirt.

"So, how's business?"

"Look around, though I'm not complaining. I get lots of cigarette breaks," she said, taking another puff and keeping her gaze forward. "Nice bike."

"I like your shirt," Paul said, trying to find a way into a conversation that didn't involve him having to explain why he was riding around town on a 10-speed clunker, an aluminum clip strapped to his pants leg. He leaned over to remove the clip from his ankle and noticed the silver ring protruding from her nose. If she turned her head just so, a ray of sunlight would reflect off of its shiny metal surface, casting strange shadows across her cheek. Her lips formed a permanent pout that barely moved when she spoke.

"Shirt's from the store. I think we have your size. What are you, like a Large?"

"No thanks. It's okay. I'm not really sure what it means but it looks good on you."

"Thanks. Me neither but they make me wear something from the store," she said, cocking her head toward the empty shop.

The girl snuffed out her cigarette on the curb and blew a final puff of smoke over her shoulder, away from Paul. As she continued to speak she moved her sneakered feet rhythmically back and forth on the dark pavement, letting the tips of her toes tap together.

"Looking for something in particular?"

"Is Fredy working today?"

"Nah, he called in sick today. Are you his dad or somethin'?

"Friend of the family." Lie number 1. "My name is Paul."

"I'm Amy." She squinted at Paul but made no movement that would infer a handshake was imminent.

"Amy, have you noticed Fredy acting strange lately—anything out of the ordinary?"

"Wow, yeah. I was here working stock a couple of days ago and he was buggin' out about something, leaving the store, making calls to people. Seemed pretty upset. I thought maybe he was having trouble with his girlfriend again, y'know? But he wouldn't tell me."

"Was this on Thursday maybe?"

"Yeah, Thursday I think. I know we both worked that day."

"We've been worried about him too, his family I mean." Lie number 2. "Do you know where he is staying these days? We haven't been able to find him."

"At his girlfriend Tiffany's house I guess, up on Springs Fireplace."

"Hmm, right, I always forget which house that is." Lie number 3. He was getting too good at this.

"Oh, that's easy: it's the purple house with the little white fence out front—on that side street across from the sand and gravel place? I get confused on that stretch of Fireplace Road sometimes too. I live in Amagansett, y'know? But I take my car to one of those auto repair places up there. Sometimes drive right past it." She paused a second. "You do have a car don't you? I mean, it's cool if you don't." She stared at the metal clip in his hand.

"No. A truck. I mean yes. But not right now. I'll find it."

"Oh."

"Hey, thanks Amy from Amagansett. You've been a great help." No lie there.

"You sure you don't want to try on the T-shirt? I get a commission," she said.

"No thanks. I'm not sure I can live up to it." Paul got up to leave and put the clip back on his pants leg.

"Hey, tell Fredy I hope everything is okay," she said.

"Should I be worried that everything isn't?"

"I dunno, but you look like the kind of guy to fix it," she said. "Good luck!" Her sad, kohl-rimmed eyes had somehow brightened, her lips forming an upward turn almost resembling a smile.

* * *

Paul was used to riding this stretch of Springs Fireplace Road, a section of East Hampton once known as Freetown. It was said that the land had been set aside by the patriarch of the Gardener family for a handful of freed African American slaves back in the mid 19th century. The same Gardeners who were bequeathed their own private island by King Charles I back in 1639, the first settlement in what would become New York State. Workers living on the mainland would light fires at the water's edge to alert the Lord of the Manor of their presence prior to crossing by boat to Gardener's Island, giving the street its name. But were the fires lit for the benefit of the Gardeners or for the workers back in Springs? *Here we are*, they must have been saying as they sparked their torches. *Here WE are.*

The current Freetown was one of those neighborhoods you were unlikely to find on tourist postcards. Mixed in with the mostly small, dilapidated houses were corrugated metal buildings used for light industry, auto repair and body shops, a large gravel pit and the town dump.

Paul found the little purple house and knocked on its worn aluminum front door. He could hear the blare of a television inside. A tall, spindly kid with spiky brown hair and muscled, tattooed arms came to the door and opened it a crack. He was naked from the waist up; a pair of extra-long board shorts in a bold flower print slung below his waist, the wide bottoms rubbing at his shins. Frankie Avalon meets Sid Vicious.

"Fredy?"

"Yo, wassup? Wuddya want?" Fredy Gomes demanded, adjusting his eyes to the outdoors and looking past Paul to see if there was anyone else there with him. He seemed especially annoyed at the sight of Paul's bicycle splayed in his driveway. "You Jehovah Witness?"

Paul peeked in past the front door and could make out the silhouette of a young black woman about Fredy's age. She held a toddler on her lap and didn't move from her place in front of the TV. The voices escaping from the television were yelling something at each other about a real estate transaction gone bad. A made-for-TV judge got the voices to quiet down with a cutting remark that seemed to please the studio audience.

"Hey, my name is Paul. I want to talk to you about some pictures you took—don't worry I'm not a cop—can you come outside a minute so we can talk?"

Fredy moved quickly out of the house, pushing Paul aside and slamming the front door. The two of them stood on the untended postage stamp-sized lawn, the cars whizzing by on Springs Fireplace Road a few yards away. The white picket fence that divided the house from the road was a caricature, barely two feet high, and had fallen down in several places. Its effect was like looking at a row of uneven, ulcerated teeth.

"Look, I wrote an article for my paper about a missing girl. The pictures have already been posted on our website. I think you took them. I don't want to get you into any trouble. I just want to ask you some questions."

The kid revved like a perpetual motion machine, fidgeting with the drawstring of his board shorts with his left hand while pushing up the side of his head with his right as if trying to squeeze out all of his bad thoughts. Paul noticed Fredy's right hand was bandaged, dried blood soaking through the shredded gauze.

"Look dude, I don't know what you're talkin' about," Fredy said unconvincingly.

"Hey, I know you're scared. The cops are probably talking to your friend Dylan right now and they're going to put the pieces together soon. If you give me a statement I can tell your side of the story."

As Fredy absorbed this last bit of information, Paul could practically see the hologram of the kid's unending summer days and evenings surfing and chilling out along the East End's beaches begin to evaporate.

"Wait, you know Dylan?"

"Yeah, I know him. The question is how well do *you* know him? Do you consider him to be a good friend?" Paul asked.

"Wha-whatever ... I don't know."

"My experience has been that guys like Dylan look out for themselves. Let me ask you this: do you know where the girl is now? What happened to her?"

Fredy seemed to give the question his full consideration. He looked over at the shabby house that had been his refuge. Then, without any warning, he turned back around and swung his bandaged fist at Paul's head, clipping him sharply on his left ear. The force of the blow was enough to send Paul hurtling to the ground, where he landed face down in the dirt. After absorbing the shock, he righted himself and stood back up to face Fredy. The kid arranged his half naked body into a fighter's stance, and was now breathing heavily and weaving side to side. The two stared each other down for a few empty seconds that for Paul seemed like an eternity. Then, without so much as a word, Fredy jumped into his truck and started backing up full speed out the driveway—and smack straight over Mellow. He slammed his brakes on impact, pulling frame, gears, wheels, and leather seat under his oversize tires until the old girl was barely recognizable. When he came to a stop, Fredy craned his neck as far as he could in the direction of his rear tire and peered down at the remains of Paul's mangled yellow bicycle. He gazed back up at Paul with an expression more scared than sorry. Then he shifted back into reverse until his front tires slowly rolled over the speed bump of the bicycle's remains, turned his truck south on Springs Fireplace and sped away down the street.

~ ~ ~

Ave Maria (3)

Her feet were killing her. How funny that expression was. Her sweet, tender feet, manipulated starting at the age of five to conform to the rigors of classical ballet poses. Those damn arabesques. First, second, third, c'mon ladies you know that last one. Wasn't it actually she who was killing her feet, not the other way around? Ever since she was little, she got in the habit of soaking them in the sink. With five younger siblings it was nearly impossible to rely on the bathtub being available, morning or night.

How she longed to watch her own tub fill with warm water, add hyacinth or maybe some sage oil and dip her tired feet in for a nice long soak. But the apartment had only a slow dripping shower, the echo of its cheap plastic stall a constant reminder of life's unplanned limitations. Sitting on the closed lid of the toilet with its fuzzy pink cover, her leg swung over the edge of the low bathroom sink, first the right for ten minutes and then the left, one foot at a time, her knee poised at a forty five degree angle toward her head–she could rest her cheek on her thigh and stretch her hamstrings while she soaked, sometimes catching a glimpse of herself in the mirror. At least she had her routines, rituals like these she could count on.

Chapter 12: Saturday night

Paul got himself a beer and a gin and tonic for Merika and the two of them took a seat at a small table in the back near the restaurant's only pool table. The place, a down-home Texas BBQ joint with reclaimed barn-wood beams and steer head trophies for decoration, was only half full, unusual for a Saturday night in early summer. Choosing this particular table was unintentional. But the flying elbows and cue sticks of the youngish hipster-amateur-pool-sharks nearby forced the two of them to sit especially close.

"I'm glad you wanted to meet," Paul said.

"Me too. Happy Birthday!" She raised her glass and smiled. The intensity of her stare made him uncharacteristically shy and unsure of himself. He usually preferred to do the staring. In fact, he couldn't take his own eyes off of her lips, which appeared even fuller with a dose of red lip-gloss. Her long hair was tied at the top and fell gracefully over her left shoulder.

"Thanks," he said, raising his own glass and taking a sip. A small bead of foam settled on his upper lip. "I've been meaning to ask you, how did you know it was my birthday?"

"I have my ways," she said, and took another sip of her drink. "Actually, I looked you up online. That's how I got your email address."

"Really? I guess I should Google myself sometime. Anyway, I don't use a computer much outside of the office. I borrow my son's sometimes when he's at the house. Still wedded to these." He reached in his pocket and showed Merika one his little spiral bound notepads.

"You have a son?"

"He's sixteen. He stays with me some weekends but he's at a

friend's tonight."

Paul was hoping she wouldn't be too disappointed about his part-time father status but Merika seemed unfazed.

"Oh, so have you gotten any good birthday presents yet?" she asked.

"Hmm, well I definitely got one that was a complete surprise. But it's not worth talking about."

An awkward pause.

"You know," he started again, gesturing toward her drink and trying another tack, "I never got used to the taste of tonic water. When I was in college it seemed like everyone was drinking gin and tonics. What is *tonic* anyway?" Merika laughed at his, as if recalling a particularly funny story. "What did I say?"

"Nothing. It's just that it sounds like one of our quiz questions. Some of my friends, mostly teachers at the Moss Academy, we come here on Thursday nights when the place has its weekly trivia contest. Have you ever done it? If you did, you would remember us. Our team won the last three times we played."

"I hadn't heard about it. But I bet I'd be pretty good competition," he said.

"Really? So, my reputation is on the line here. Let's see ... tonic water ... is made with quinine. The British in colonial Africa would drink quinine to ward off malaria. They added gin to it to make it go down easier."

"Africa huh ... and, did they share this secret with the locals?"

"Good question. I'm not sure but I suspect the Brits had a limited supply. Me, I guess I'm used to the bitter taste of it. And, the gin gets me drunk," she said, taking another sip of her drink.

"I'm impressed. And that part about the supply: very diplomatic answer! So, you hang out with teachers. Are you a teacher too?"

"Yeah, early childhood, but I don't have a full time teaching gig right now. I'm mostly helping out at the daycare center on the Res such as it is and I do some part time stuff. I also sing. I'm a singer."

"Really! I love teachers! My mom was a teacher. My dad, who you'll meet later, is a teacher—a professor actually."

"You're funny," she said, casually placing her hand on his. He could sense their bodies relaxing, drawing closer.

"Why?"

"Because most guys I meet, when I tell them that, they almost always go right for the singing part. Like, 'Oh, you must have a beautiful voice, girl! Where can I see you sing?' —guys who think they're players anyway."

"I guess I'm not much of a player," he said, sipping foam from his beer.

"That's a good thing. I like that about you—I mean I could tell you weren't trying—listen, Paul," she started in a more serious tone, "I'm sorry I didn't answer your questions that day we ran into each other at the beach. It's just, I did see something but I didn't want to say anything at the time. I didn't want to have to make a statement, get involved with the police and all that. I've been through that before and I can tell you it sucks. And then you were talking to that detective. Anyway, I didn't really see anything detailed like a body. I was too far away. But I think I saw other people near the jetty after that cop Clifford took his dog back toward the parking lot. If there was a girl there she definitely didn't walk off the beach on her own. Someone took her."

"I thought there was no one else on the beach at the time. How did the cop not see you?"

"I wasn't on the beach. I was in one of the *houses* up on the bluff in Georgica. That's why I was too far away to really see anything definite. Anyway, you can't tell anyone I told you this. I don't want anyone to know I was there that day."

"Why not?"

"Let's just say that I was not supposed to be in Wainscott that morning."

"Were you playing hooky from work or something? Look, if you need an alibi I'd be glad to cover for you."

"You would lie for me? That's sweet," she said, closing her hand around his and moving her face closer.

"I like to protect my sources," he said, his eyes now locked with hers. Their faces were only inches apart.

"And if I wasn't a source, would you still protect me?"

"Sure. But I'm starting to get the feeling that you can take care of yourself." Merika leaned in toward him and closed her eyes.

"Hey Bub, how is the birthday boy?" a voice interrupted.

There was Paul's father Isaak, standing over them with a huge grin on his face. He was wearing his usual summer outfit: white button down Oxford shirt loosely tucked into faded blue jeans, Docksiders, no socks. On his right wrist were a series of twisted leather bracelets—end-of-the-school-year gifts his students had given him over the years. His still thick, silver-flecked hair was cut close to his scalp and he sported a few days of gray stubble. Isaak managed to stay in pretty good shape despite his habit of drinking two cans of Budweiser every night while reading before bed. His latest passion was Shakespeare. He told Paul he was reading every one of the Bard's plays in chronological order, starting with "King Henry VI" ("I'll always make room for history's magnificently flawed Kings—

Shakespeare's and the King of Beers," he told Paul).

Paul stood up and Isaak gave him a big hug and kissed him on both cheeks.

"Isaak Sandis. Nice to meet you," he said to Merika, extending his hand.

"Nice to meet you too," she said. Isaak took her hand and kissed it.

"Dad, Merika. Merika, Dad. What can I get you to drink, a vodka martini right?" Paul got up and started to move toward the bar. "I'll leave you two to get acquainted."

"Straight up, Bub. Have him make it a little dirty—and three olives." Paul was already halfway to the now-crowded bar to order the drink.

Once the crowd had absorbed Paul, Isaak turned to Merika.

"It's nice to see my son sitting with a beautiful woman on his birthday."

"Oh, is he not getting much action these days?"

"He hasn't mentioned."

"I think he was about to kiss me. Is he always that forward with his interview subjects?"

"I guess he likes you. So, Merika the Beautiful, how did you get that wonderful name?"

"It's pronounced "Mer-*eek*-a," she said, elongating the middle syllable. "I am black, you know."

"I didn't mean—"

"—I'm just playin' with you Isaak! I have a Shinnecock name too—it's a mouthful, Nakoowa Kekutoo, 'one who hears the whispering pines'—but how I got my first name is actually one of those funny sad stories."

"I love stories. And I've got plenty of time."

"You really want to hear this? Okay, I was born after my mom had several miscarriages so my nana, who has deep Shinnecock roots, was like, "Eureka! We should call her "Eureka." She must have thought it was Algonquin or something. By the time of my nana's generation most people had forgotten the traditional language. Anyway, my mom preferred the name Meredith, after the English poet George Meredith. So they compromised: Mer-eeka."

"Your mom likes English poetry?"

"Don't be so surprised. Meredith was known for his poems about nature and the sea and all that. There is one in particular that my mom used to recite to us when we were kids. It's called "By Morning Twilight," I think:

"Night, like a dying mother,
Eyes her young offspring, Day.
The birds are dreamily piping.
And O, my love, my darling!
The night is life ebb'd away:
Away beyond our reach!
A sea that has cast us pale on the beach;
Weeds with the weeds and the pebbles
That hear the lone tamarisk rooted in sand
Sway
With the song of the sea to the land."

"That's lovely," Isaak said.

"Isn't it? The 'dying mother' part used to scare me when I was little. It took me awhile to figure out what the poem meant, but I guess it describes life on the Res pretty well—the weeds and the pebbles, that lone flowering plant rooted in the sand, the song of the sea."

"I have to admit, I never heard of that particular plant," Isaak said. "And, I don't mean to correct your nana but Eureka is a Greek word."

"Yeah, so I must be part Greek then—"

"—Wow, you two seem to be hitting it off," Paul interrupted, having returned to the table with fresh drinks for everyone and feeling like he'd missed out on something again. "Dad, are you onto a Greek thing *already*? You guys just met."

"Are you kidding, Bub? I've already made Merika an unofficial member of our Greek fraternity," Isaak said.

"Only *unofficial*? How do we make it official?" she asked, taking her drink from Paul.

Isaak smiled that big smile again. "Oh, what the hell, let's make it official. But first you'll have to drink like a Greek. Isaak held up his glass.

"*Yiamas*!"

"*Yiamas!*" she repeated and they both took a sip of their drinks.

"So Paul, tell me about this story you've got going. I read it on the bus ride out. The best kind of mystery. A beautiful girl, not quite a girl, or is it a woman, not yet a woman, found dead and then disappears? And in Wainscott. We used to go to that beach sometimes with your mother, remember?"

Paul threw Merika a knowing look.

"Yeah Dad, Merika and I were just talking about it. So far the cops don't really know anything. All we have is the pictures. Probably taken by some surfer kid."

Isaak turned to Merika. "And, you know something about this too or just an interested party?"

"Hey, did I tell you my dad is a philosophy professor?" Paul said to Merika, deliberately changing the subject.

"Sounds deep. What do you teach?"

"It is. My concentration is Beauty and Aesthetics," Isaak said.

"There's a philosophy for beauty?"

"Uh oh," Paul said, his eyes rolling into the back of his head. He'd seen this movie too many times before at countless dinner parties at Isaak's house. Isaak forged ahead, clearly enjoying the thoughtfulness of this attentive new student.

"Paul, behave. Who knows, this just might have some relevance to your dead girl story. Okay, let's agree that we can't understand beauty without it being attached to an object—a sunset, a piece of music, a poem, a young woman"—Isaak made a graceful hand gesture toward Merika—"we have no language to describe it when it's divorced from a particular thing. Plato understood this and we accept this as true. Now Kant argues that judgments of beauty are sensory, that is, they derive from the senses. But they are also emotional and *intellectual*: in order for something to be beautiful we have to use our critical judgment. Follow me so far?"

"I think so," Merika said. "It's like that expression: beauty is in the eye of the beholder, right?"

Paul continued to hide behind his beer.

"Excellent! Obviously what we might consider beautiful will be largely determined by our social experience. Now some philosophers believe this is the only thing that determines beauty. But I would argue that the act of experiencing beauty presses us towards the good and can also be a *universal* experience. Beauty is divorced from the everyday—that's why we seek it out. Beauty can be experienced as pleasure, but it is not connected only to sensory pleasure. The pleasure derives from the experience of this *harmony* of the sensory, emotional, and intellectual that I mentioned. And, it is an expression of the mind's uniquely creative capabilities—how each of us fill in the blanks—rather than a direct reading of the object itself, which would be rather boring. Ultimately, our perceptions of beauty are inextricably tied with our *humanness*. It's what makes us who we are—not the other way around."

"Wow, I never really thought of it that way," Merika said.

"But of course there is a dark side," Isaak cautioned, using a toothpick to hold up one of the olives in his drink.

"What could be bad about beauty?"

"Ahh. The dark side is this: because beauty often represents a desire that cannot be fulfilled—it is a characteristic inherent in our *perception* of the object but not the object itself—some of us make the mistake of thinking we can possess it."

With that Isaak popped the olive in his mouth.

"What he means is that not being able to hold onto something we find beautiful or merely being in the presence of beauty can sometimes make people do crazy shit," Paul added.

"I can definitely see that," Merika agreed.

"Thank you, Paul, although your articulation was less than artful," Isaak said.

After a few more drinks, spicy wings, and a wedge salad for Merika, Isaak paid the bill and said his goodbyes before heading for his home in Sag Harbor. Merika made an attempt to chip in, having promised to buy Paul a drink as a birthday gesture, but of course Isaak politely refused her generosity.

"Next time you'll buy me a drink and read me some more poetry," Isaak said, still flirting.

Paul took Merika's arm and led her outside past the restaurant's parking lot and soon they found themselves alone under an unfurling cape of stars. There were no streetlights here, only the glow from Cassiopeia and her kin. The air was cool and tinged with brine and Paul was feeling lightheaded and loose, and not just from the alcohol. Like he was on his way to something, though where it would take him he still wasn't sure. When the two got to Paul's truck parked along Town Line Road, Merika stopped and swung her butt playfully into his side.

"Paul, your dad is amazing. I really like him but man the guy can talk."

"He means well," Paul said. "Well, I guess this is it. Is it okay if I email you again, you know, if I have any more questions?" He leaned in to kiss her on the cheek but she pulled away.

"Paul, I'm a little too drunk to drive myself."

"Oh, do you want me to drive you? You can leave your car here—"

"—I won't let you drive me all the way back to the Res, it's too far. Maybe we can go to your place for a while until I'm sober enough?"

"You sure?"

They got in Paul's old Ford pickup and started driving toward his house along an unusually deserted Montauk Highway. She filled in the details for him about her conversation with Isaak while he was away getting drinks, adding greater detail about her nana, her nation's traditions. He loved her energy; the way she moved her hands as she talked, her wrists and fingers conducting a small symphony in the space between them. She used these fingers to scan the music on his MP3 player (Al Green and Maxwell: "Interesting"; Aerosmith: "Not so much"; Alicia Keys: "Yes!"). The ease and flow of their conversation struck Paul as so natural and unforced. Still, he was reluctant to press her for more information about that day at Beach Lane. Instead he tried to imagine what it might have been like to meet Merika in college. A sort of alternative universe in which the two of them were the same age, both young and looking for that somebody who could help them realize who they were supposed to be. He would have fallen hard for her then. But deep down he knew that wasn't true. In fact, he probably would never have seen her. He was barely twenty-one when he first fell for Jeanine. She was his Bond girl, all cool surface and restraint. He wasn't looking for anything real back then.

But now, in these small, intimate moments driving with Merika by his side, he was experiencing the thrill that could only happen with someone new, someone who could satisfy his longing for genuine connection. Someone who could provide him with that rare elixir he so desperately desired this late in the game: *possibility*. And yet as he gazed over at her face illuminated by the intermittent glow of yellow streetlights, he could just as easily convince himself that the two of them were already a long-established couple, had actually been young lovers in that alternative universe of his making had he been smart enough then to realize what he needed.

"Wait, wait, pull over!" she said, grabbing his leg connected to the gas pedal.

They were at the entrance to the village, the corner of Woods Lane and Main Street.

Paul slowed the Ford and parked up on the grass edging along Main Street. She bolted out of the car and he followed her past the swans and ducks on the Village pond, across Woods Lane to the front lawn of a large shingled house. It was the site of an old homestead that once stretched from this corner all the way to the ocean at Main

Beach but was now a remnant, a historical oddity tucked within a neighborhood of old-line summer estates.

A small plaque out front announced the name in tarnished bronze letters. It read, "Junket Hill."

"Why are we stopping here?" Paul asked.

"Take off your shoes."

"What?"

"C'mon. Socks too." She reached over and started pulling at his laces. Once they were both barefoot, she took his hand and together they ran up a grassy hill alongside the house. As he made his way up he could feel the wet blades slicing at his toes and the tops of his feet. A sharp pebble wedged at his heel and he had to limp the rest of the way.

When the two reached the top, they faced south in the direction of the ocean and gazed out at the low iridescence off in the distance.

"Wow, nice view up here," he said. "I had no idea—"

"—shhh. Just look."

He stared silently at the water, it's rippling surface answering the sky in a gray-black call and response. Then he turned to her, unsure of what came next. He felt a desperate desire to kiss her.

Before he knew what was happening she was tackling him around the waist and knocking him to the ground. She wrapped her legs around his and they fell over and down the steep hill, their bodies spinning over grass, rocks and dirt. The centrifugal forces pushed him out and away from her insisting she pull him closer, and then just as fast, its opposite realized every other turn as she swung out and away and it was his chance to pull her back in.

After a few runs like this they rolled over on their backs exhausted and holding hands at the bottom of the hill, staring up at the night sky. He pointed to a tiny blinking red light off in the distance as it moved between the glints of white, across the great dark expanse bending end to starry end.

"Sometimes I look up and spot one of those planes and wonder where it's going, if I should be on it. Not tonight," he said, still trying to catch his breath.

"I don't see it. All I see are the stars," she said.

"Probably better that way. Why'd you pick this spot, of all places?"

"It's the only hill I know around here. Where I live it's flat, flat. Kiss me." She eased her body across his and they kissed. After, they lay still for a while and together continued to stare up at the sky.

"This is the old Cliffords homestead," he said, gesturing toward the house. "Used to be anyway. Village cousins of that guy Will Clifford who found the dead girl."

Just then a light came on in the old house and a silhouette of a man appeared in an upstairs window. Seconds later, rows of blinding spotlights ignited the lawn's parameter. The two of them sat up together, their arms swung around each other's shoulders. Paul half expected to see a guard posted at a tower with gun pointed, peering through his scope.

"People live here?" he said.

"I guess so." They turned toward one another other with the same thought, grabbed their socks and shoes and high-tailed it for Paul's truck.

Once at Paul's house, they sat together on his sofa in the dark and made out softly and gently like two practiced high school kids, exploring warm skin under shirts, neither of them forcing things to the next level. She stopped for a moment and considered Paul's face, as if searching for something there.

"Why does Isaak call you 'Bub'? You guys don't seem like long time locals to me."

"It's our little joke. Ever since I moved out here. My ex is from an old Bonacker family. Guilt by association, I guess. And it's what we called the Jewish grandmothers in our old neighborhood back in Brooklyn. The Bubbies. Isaak thinks it's funny, the juxtaposition of those Jewish grannies with the dyed in the net locals."

"You still have a Bubbie?"

"Unfortunately, no. Isaak lost his parents in Greece during the Second World War. In the camps. My yiayiá—my mother's mother—lived with us for a while in Brooklyn but Isaak stopped talking to her after my mother died, when I was eleven. She died a few years after that."

"You must miss her, your mother I mean."

"She had a gift for loving things as they are, rather than how they could be. I miss that." Merika had her arms around him and he felt her squeeze a bit tighter. "My place looks kind of Bonacker though, don't you think?" he said. He was half joking; there wasn't enough light to really see much of it.

"I don't know. I like your place."

"Really?"

She rose from the sofa and walked into the narrow galley kitchen, flipped on the light. Paul heard the tap running as she helped herself to a glass of water.

"Hey, what's this?" She was pointing to a dark metal box on a shelf over the sink. The front of the box had several buttons, knobs, and red indicator lights, and an antenna sticking out of its back. The word "Regency" was spelled out in stylized script on its front.

"That's an old 70's-vintage police scanner. I guess you can say it's what brought us together," Paul said.

"This thing?" she said, picking it up and inspecting its odd contours and little cloth speaker.

"That day we met up in the beach parking lot, that's how I heard the cop call in an emergency on his police radio."

"So this is the little matchmaker, huh?" She fiddled with the knobs for a few seconds in search of the sound of a human voice but all signals were clear.

When she returned, Paul finally got the courage to ask her something that had been on his mind all night.

"Yep. Hey, when you said before that you saw people on the beach that day, can you tell me anything else about them? Were they men? Women? What were they wearing? What were they driving?"

"Paul, I told you I was far away and I couldn't see them. But there was a pickup truck ... a dark color. And one other thing..." she started hesitantly but then refused to continue.

"What? Tell me."

"I'm afraid to tell you. If I do, you cannot repeat it to anyone. You have to promise me. This is off the record complet-ely." She stumbled on the last word, slurring it a bit.

"I promise. Now you *have* to tell me after that kind of build up."

"Okay," she started again, taking her place back on the sofa next to him. "I couldn't tell if they were men or women but I got this weird impression, a feeling really. It was how they moved. There was something ritualistic about their movements."

"What do you mean by 'ritualistic?'"

"Just that. Like they were performing some kind of ritual."

"Wait, you don't mean—"

"—I didn't say it was an *Indian* ritual, only that their movements were very precise, like they had done this before. Paul, if you repeat this I swear I will kill you, I'm not kidding. I am not implicating any of my people. I am only telling you what I saw. That's why I didn't say anything that day."

"And you being there that morning?" he asked.

"I still don't want anyone to know that either."

"You are very mysterious, girlfriend." He kissed her and held her to him, wanting her to feel that everything was going to be all right, that he could keep this information to himself.

* * *

"Hi, I'm looking for Peter Draken's place," she said, leaning out her window and squinting into the light from the truck's headlamps. The guard, a slight Latino who couldn't be older than thirty, exhibited no sign of welcome or rejection. He just looked tired. "I'm Merika. What's your name?"

"Me? Alejandro. It's okay. You can go in. You're on the list."

"Alejandro, you have to sit here all night?"

He seemed surprised at the question or perhaps that anyone coming through would bother to ask him anything about himself.

"Yeah. No problem. I get to sleep most of the time. And I have a book."

He held up a copy of the Bible—dog eared pages with slips of torn paper marking particular passages.

"That's a good one," she said. "But don't give away the ending."

She was entering a place once called the "Georgica Settlement," built in the late 19th century by a handful of Yankee academics steeped in Emersonian Transcendentalism who wanted to create a private retreat where, in the words of one its early residents, they could be "free to think, read, write, and amuse themselves with sport and fellowship without outside judgment or interference." She would learn all of this later, of course. Perhaps too well. But right now, idling in the dark under a sign that read "Private Property," it looked to her like any number of gated homes or communities located along this familiar stretch of beach that was off limits to most folks.

She drove through the Association's dark, winding main thoroughfare in the direction of Georgica Pond until her car's high beams found a wooden sign with the name "Draken" at the foot of a long, pebbled drive. At first she thought it was the large multi-cupolaed house facing the ocean—people on the East End threw around the term "cottage" pretty loosely. But soon she found a more modest one-story shingled house, lights burning, located down another narrow driveway on the property. The house was perched on a bluff surrounded by tall beach grass, overlooking the pond. She checked her lipstick in the car's rearview mirror, fastened the second button of her blouse and then unbuttoned it again letting her hair fall over her exposed skin, walked up the broken stone path and knocked on the door.

"Hey," she said.

"Hey." Peter led her inside and immediately handed her a beer.

The cottage consisted of a large, open living room with a fireplace, a small kitchen with outdated appliances, one bathroom, and two small bedrooms located down a narrow hallway. The main rooms were simple and understated. Everything seemed to be made of the same type of wood except for a few pieces of upholstered furniture with an old-fashioned floral pattern that also matched the curtains.

On the walls hung small paintings of seascapes with similar-looking seafront cottages, and lovingly drawn prints of ducks and hunters hiding in duck blinds. One unique feature of the living room was the abundance of musical instruments strewn about: electric guitars and amps, an old upright piano with a few chipped keys, and a drum kit set up in one corner. There was enough starlight outside the windows to reveal framed water views of the type Merika had only previously seen in those thick, glossy real estate brochures that fell out of the local newspaper during the summer. The back of the house faced Georgica Pond to the east, and from the front you could see the big house and the ocean beyond.

"Nice place. Where is everybody?" she said.

None of her co-workers from the restaurant had come. It was just her and Peter. She was about to leave, make up some excuse about needing to get home.

"Stay," he said. "Finish your beer at least."

She suggested the two of them take a walk along the beach. They freed themselves of their shoes and socks and ran down to the ocean. The night was clear, stars mostly, the beach empty of people. She took hold of his hand as they walked along the shoreline toward the jetty, and together they let the legs of their dark work slacks get soaked in the surf. Peter would stop every few feet in search of a flat rock to toss into the waves. Once near the jetty they warmed themselves at a small fire that had been left on the beach, its embers still burning. Their bodies huddled close but didn't touch. Peter pulled out a joint from his shirt pocket and they smoked it as they watched the water lap up against the rocks. The warm smoke felt good against her throat.

"High tide. Look. What's that out on the jetty? It's moving. Over there." Peter pointed to a place out toward the rocks.

"What? I don't see anything."

"I'll show you." He ran over to the jetty and climbed barefoot over the large rocks until reaching a place along the bulging middle. He bent to pick up a large horseshoe crab and held it aloft by its spiky tail. The thing was huge, bigger than Peter's head.

"Hey, I caught a dinosaur!"

The prehistoric creature wriggled its legs and swayed violently in its shell to get free. Peter struggled to hold onto its tail and dropped the crab into the water.

"Oh no," she cried.

He yelled back to her and waved, "It's okay!" Then, he looked down at his feet, and in the next second fell to the rocks and disappeared into the crashing surf.

Merika emptied her pants pockets, sprinted over to the jetty and dove into the water. When she reached him, he was standing, but only barely, the waves threatening to knock him over. He put his hand on her shoulder and coughed up a mouthful of seawater. She eased his arm around her waist and guided him in to shore—like leading a child she would remember later. They stood there on the beach, both soaking wet in their heavy clothes and shivering from the cold.

"You're bleeding." She touched a slight bruise on his forehead.

He let out a nervous laugh, flipped open the phone he had stored in his front pocket and stared down at it. The screen was black.

"Let's go back," he said. "It's friggin' freezing out here."

After gathering up her things from the beach, they walked back to the cottage to change out of their wet clothes. He offered her a big blue cotton robe with the initials "PTD" embroidered on the front that she wrapped around herself before slipping out of her wet slacks and top. Peter went off to one of the bedrooms to change. She sat on the sofa, the big, heavy robe past her ankles, her knees up and arms wrapped around her legs. She was about to get up and take a tour of the room when her eye was drawn to some hand-carved pieces sitting on a low end-table; and one in particular, a small antique scrimshaw box carved from a single piece of whalebone. Intricately carved whalebone pieces of this type were now illegal and difficult to find (vendors at the powwows she attended had no choice but to sell replicas made of cheap plastic). The lid of the ivory-colored box was etched with a lovely beach scene: a sailor saying goodbye to his beloved, and behind the two lovers, a tall ship waiting offshore in the distance. Merika rubbed her fingers across its engraved surface and before even realizing what she'd done, slipped the box into the pocket of her robe.

"You have a hairbrush? I left mine in the car." she yelled to him. She checked the pocket to make sure the box didn't show.

He came back with a brush and two more beers and handed her one.

"That's my grandmother's."

"Huh?"

"The hairbrush. I hope it's okay."

"Oh. Thanks." She felt a little buzz slip through her as she took her first sip of cold beer. "This place is like a hotel. You know, the robe and everything." She let her robe slip open slightly as she leaned forward and brushed her wet hair. "You don't have your grandmother's body stashed away somewhere I should know about?"

"Huh?"

"Psycho. The movie?"

"Oh believe me. My grandmother is very much alive."

She pushed her hair to one side and pointed to the embossed lettering above her left breast. "Hmm. And do all your clothes have initials on them?"

"Um, just the ones I give to other people. That way they always remember to return them. It's a little damp in here isn't it?" He walked over to the fireplace and carefully placed rolled up newspapers and small pieces of dry wood in to ready a fire.

"Why hadn't I thought of doing that? And the "T"—what does that stand for? Thomas, Theodore, Thurgood maybe?"

"I'd rather not say."

"C'mon, we're among friends," she teased.

"Okay, since we're among friends," he said, smiling and looking around the empty room. "Actually it's my mother's family name. Thornton. I come from good New England stock." He announced this last bit sheepishly, as if admitting to some embarrassing secret.

"Why be ashamed to tell me? I do too. My great grandmother was Mashantucket Pequot—from Connecticut. Lots of us on the Res' got some New England blood."

This information seemed to pique Peter's interest but Merika offered no further explanation.

"What's with the instruments? I thought you were a lawyer," she said.

"Law student."

"That's what I meant."

"But what I really want to do is play. I mean play guitar. I play jazz, some blues. I had this band that gigged around while I was at school, mostly small clubs. Do you listen to jazz?"

"Sure," she said. She thought of the geeky white boys in freshman dorm with their Miles and Coltrane obsessions. "Why jazz?"

"Are you kidding me? Jazz is about improvisation, making it up as you go. You get to get lost and then, if you're good enough, you find your way. There are rules but you're expected to break those rules, to make order out of chaos, create your own chaos and then find order again."

"Sounds exhausting."

"Yeah, well, that's what I want to do but my grandfather has other ideas. It sucks. It's like they got you, y'know? They give you all this freedom and then they just pull it out from under you, y'know what I mean?" Peter's eyes flared and he paused, as if letting his words catch up with the rapid firing of his thoughts. "It's like my grandfather pretends he doesn't already have my whole life planned out for me. Law school, work twenty-four hours a day for his firm, make my way to partner, all that. He won't take my music seriously."

"That does suck," she said. "What about your parents?"

"My parents are dead. My grandparents raised me."

"I'm sorry," she said. She felt ashamed suddenly for teasing him and closed the front of her robe.

"Yeah, well sometimes it feels like I was adopted by strangers. By the time I was fourteen I was sneaking downtown, going to shows, meeting these really cool guys and playing. My friends at Brearly thought I was making stuff up until they saw me play. I hated that whole Manhattan private school thing anyway, you know, they're all out here in the summer. At least at NYU you probably got to get away from that."

"Sure." *RWPP*, she added under her breath.

Rich White People Problems.

"What's that?"

"Nothing. It kind of sucks for me too. I grew up on the Res with my Mom, my brother and little sister, here in Southampton. Once I got into a good college, there was all this pressure to get perfect grades, to be the role model for the other Res girls—"

"—yes! Exactly. That's what I'm talking about. That whole bourgeois thing. That shit will kill you. Hey, you're easy to talk to. I have to admit something. When I first started working at the restaurant I was afraid to approach you."

"Really?"

"Yeah, you can be a little intimidating."

"*Really?*"

He stared at the brush in her hand. "And you seemed to spend a lot of time on your hair. I was kind of afraid to get between the two of you."

"Huh." She handed him the brush, then passed him her wet jeans and shirt. "What do I do with these?"

"I'll put them next to the fire once I get it going and dry them for you. We don't have a washer or dryer here."

"That could take awhile," she said.

"Let me play something for you then," he said and went over to pick up his guitar.

By early morning, she would transfer the small scrimshaw box from the robe to her purse and take it home to her mother's house, giving it a prominent place on the bedside table in her tiny upstairs bedroom.

After their first night together, Peter started calling Merika "the Duchess," after a lady guitar player he once saw in an old music video.

That's when Merika started calling him "the Drake."

"Sorry, but 'the Duke' is already taken," she told him.

A few weeks later they agreed to arrange their work schedules so they could spend two full days together at the cottage. They spent most of their time in the living room, their sanctuary a mattress they'd dragged in from one of the bedrooms. He played his guitar for her and she would sing if she knew the words, work out a few of the notes of the melody on the piano. They used the fireplace to heat up any food they could scavenge from the kitchen: baked potatoes, popcorn, frozen pizzas—even fish sticks that they thawed and clumsily pierced with some rusty skewers. It all felt unrehearsed, wonderfully spontaneous.

"What are you doing?" she said at one point, laughing. The question was meant to reassure her that he was listening, to hear the sound of his voice in response to hers.

"Don't make fun of me, Duchess. This is how we do fish. It's a very sophisticated process," he said, rotating the lumpen rectangles of breaded fish meat over the coals. The two of them were sitting cross-legged on the floor next to their little campfire.

"We?"

"We what?"

"You said, 'we' do fish."

"Yeah, you and me," he said.

"Oh, okay. Let me try then." She grabbed the hot skewer from him but let the fish get too close to the fire. It flamed until it turned a sticky black. For some reason this made her laugh. The look of shock on Peter's face triggered more laughter.

"Girl, what the fuck! What am I supposed to do with this?" He grabbed hold of her wrist and thrust the burnt fish carcass toward her face.

"Ow! What are you doing?" As she struggled to get free he tightened his grip. She looked up into his piercing blue eyes to check if he was kidding, to see him crack a smile to let her know it was only a joke.

"Let. Go. Of. Me," she said.

"Why should I?"

"You're hurting me!" She twisted her hand free and stood up. "So the 'we' isn't us. It's you and your people. That's what you meant." She was rubbing her sore wrist.

"What?"

"What are 'we' anyway?"

"*We* were having a nice time. Until now," he said.

"Is that what this is about, you having a nice time with the black girl? Your little Duchess?"

"Do we have to have this conversation again? You burned our dinner and I got upset. So what? Get over it, and stop being a little bitch."

"You don't get to call me a bitch. Ever. Fuck you, Peter!"

She pushed him onto the rug and ran into one of the empty bedrooms and slammed the door. There was no bed she could throw herself onto so she sat on the floor in a corner and cried. But not too loudly—she didn't want Peter to hear. She stared at the faded wallpaper, the yellowed trim, the awful little pictures in their awful ornate frames, their flat painted surfaces revealing nothing yet speaking volumes. Alone in this dark little room, she began to think of the cottage as separate from her, a heavy, breathing thing, a kind of friendly-sad monster from a children's book. Weighed down by its former occupants' memories, their secrets. But she wasn't a child and this house wasn't a monster. And right now, at this late hour, there were probably dozens, maybe even hundreds of young women like her sitting in houses like this along this beach who were perfectly content to be where they were.

It was the world outside the window that was truly hers. She watched as the moon's reflection moved in tandem with the waves across the great expanse of ocean, out toward the long tail of the rock jetty in the distance. She opened a window and let the salt air fill her lungs. She drank it in. After what seemed like forever but was maybe fifteen minutes she heard him creeping outside the bedroom door.

"I didn't mean it," he whispered.

"Go away!"

"C'mon baby. I'm sorry. You're not a bitch. Come out and let's eat. I made a new one for you. I'm all better now."

"You sure?"

* * *

Paul noted an abrupt change in Merika's mood.

"Are you okay?"

"I'm feeling a little dizzy. Paul, I think I need to lie down," she said.

Paul gave her a pillow and made room for her on the sofa, then excused himself to use the bathroom. When he returned, he found Merika asleep under a small handmade throw blanket, a present from his mother-in law that Jeanine insisted he keep after their break up. He wrapped Merika in the blanket and carefully picked her up, making sure not to wake her, and carried her through the darkened house. He liked holding her this way; the weight of her, the way she surrendered to him in his arms, her head nestled gently on his shoulder. He placed her on the bed in the guest room down the hall from his own bedroom, turned out the lights and got ready for bed.

Chapter 13: Saturday night

Paul was nudged awake again, his heart quickening. He could hear someone walking the house. The digital alarm read 2:35 a.m. He tried adjusting his eyes in the gloom.

“Who is it?” he called out.

Silence. The figure seemed to draw closer. He heard something fall off a shelf onto the floor.

“I said, who is it dammit??”

A shadow of a figure appeared in his bedroom doorway.

“It’s me, Connor.”

“Damn, you scared me.”

Connor gave off a foul scent, one you’d expect after an evening crowded together with other teenagers practicing at being adults: an unfortunate mix of cigarettes, beer, Axe body spray, and a skunky odor that Paul found too familiar of late.

“Sorry to wake you up.” Connor approached the bed and Paul could see that his son was smiling. Too much like his grandfather, Paul thought.

“What is it? Connor, why are you home? You were supposed to be sleeping at Nick’s.”

“Nah, he dropped me off. The party was lame.” Connor stretched his arms above his head, yawning. “Dad, there is a woman sleeping in the guest room. She looks pretty hot too.”

“Did you wake her up?”

“I don’t think so. Who is she? I didn’t see another car.”

“Look Buddy, just go to sleep and try not to wake her. I’ll tell you everything tomorrow.”

“Sure Dad, but pretty weird. I’m not sure I approve.”

"Yeah, well, you smell like shit."

"Yeah, a bunch of girls were smoking at the party. I only had, like one beer, I swear."

"Okay, go to bed. Love you, g'night." Paul's voice trailed off.

"Love you too," Connor said and scurried off to his bedroom without brushing his teeth.

Paul got up and went to check on Merika. She was sleeping quietly, her bare legs stretched out beyond the small throw blanket, luminous against the plain white sheet. At some point during the night she must have slipped out of her jeans. He wanted to climb into bed next to her, to experience that sensation again of skin against skin, but instead he replaced the throw with a proper cotton blanket, kissed her on the cheek, and headed back to his own bed.

* * *

Party *was* lame. Until the end.

But did what just happened really happen? She—Jessica *fucking* Manning—looked so hot in that 70s-style halter-top. After four beers Connor finally got the balls to go up and speak to her. Almost as a joke. Told her how hot her top looked, how he picked up on the hipster way she paired it with super-skinny jeans and jelly shoes ("You know what jellies are? What guy knows that?"—"If they pay attention," he said). That's when she yanked up her top and showed him her new tattoo. Chinese characters, stacked in a vertical on the side of her upper torso, the stylized logograms practically licking the curve of her right breast. Means love is the *only* thing, she said. That's what started it. Next thing they're playing that thumb wrestling game only using their tongues and she—Jessica *fucking*

Manning—is leading him down a brightly lit hallway into a little kid's bedroom, the bed covered in Disney characters, the walls covered with posters of children's books—Harry Potter glaring down at him with those goofy glasses—and his knees are rug-burning on the Belle coverlet, their clothes spread all over the room and his hands are going everywhere, her hands going somewhere. He was smart enough to know (even after four beers and a few hits on that huge blunt Nick brought) that Jess was only using him for something or someone. Her raising her hot little blonde head and perking up her perfect little ears every few minutes to tell if someone was looking for her. Like she was *hoping* that someone would walk in on them. But if this was some kind of trick she was playing for someone else's benefit, he was more than happy to be the magician's assistant. More than more than happy. Until he remembered exactly who the trick was meant for.

This was the thing keeping Connor awake and what Nick said about maybe it wasn't such a good idea giving his father so much information about his friends when his mobile chirped with a Morris text.

Morris: Dude she has a blog

Connor: Who Jess

Morris: Who? Ha ha ha no. Your spanish gf

Connor: WTF Daisy?

Morris: I'll text u the address

Connor: Are we in it

Morris: Just read it dickhead

* * *

Por/Que: Daisy's True and False Blog

Where Daisy tells you what's what and por/que
(Because "porque" means because and "por que" means why that's why, mis locas)

"An Excited Latina"

True: *C.S. is hot.*

-Por/que? He's shy and incredibly handsome (although a little skinny-I'm not complaining). He invited me to some place called "The Cave." Will have an update soon ...

True: *The Cave is cool.*

-Por/que? Because, mis locas, I got invited. A bunch of cool juniors were there. My friend G. who I made come with me thought it was lame but I think it's because C. and I were too busy kissing and I couldn't pay attention to her. I won't say what else we did but you know we didn't hook up all the way. I'm not that kind of chica.

False: *All white guys are assholes*

-Por/que? C. is not an asshole although technically he may not be a white guy since he's part Greek and part Jewish or something. Anyway that's what he told me.

False: *His friend M. is cool.*

-Por/que? Because he kept bugging me and putting his hands on me whenever C. went to the bathroom or was outside with his friends. What's up with that? My friend G. thought M. was creepy too.

Obvious: Some white guys—even some cool ones—think I'm hot: okay I am very CURVY (curvy is sexy no matter what you skinny white bitches think) and i got a little extra in the trunk but a lot of white guys like that I think.

Also Obvious: My mom would totally freak if she knew I was with a *guero*. Shhhhhhhhhhhhhhh.

<3 <3 <3 <3 <3 <3 <3 <3 <3 <3 <3 <3 <3 <3 <3 <3 <3 <3

Por/Que: Daisy's True and False Blog
Where Daisy tells you what's what and por/que
(Because "porque" means because and "por que" means why that's why, mis locas)

"A Wise Latina" *(inspired by "Invisible Man" by R. Ellison)*
Note: Although I didn't get all of the symbolism of "The Invisible Man" we are reading in English class, the main dude sounds a lot like a Latino to me. Actually, G. said that out loud when we talked about the part where the narrator gets the job in the boiler room and that guy Lucius thinks he's coming to take his job.

True: *Suicide rate is up for Latina teens.*
Says *The Daily News*: "15 percent of Latina teens in New York City

have tried to take their own lives."

-Por/que? Could it be because Latina women are so often portrayed in the media as stable, successful people or because when you Google "Latina teen" looking for a role model all you get is porn sites?

True: *Latina teens get pregnant at a higher rate than African American or White teens*

-Por/que? You can't tell your mami you want contraceptives because that means you are admitting that you are having sex. Our culture tells young women to be virgins and men to be machos. So who do they think is having sex with all those horny machos?

False: *All Mexicans are gardeners or housekeepers.*

-Por/que? Pa-leez. They are also poets, painters, lawyers, scientists, actors, gangsters and writers. And even if they are gardeners or housekeepers, a lot of times they don't have any other choice in this land of the free.

Obvious: Speaking of housekeepers, why would Arnold Schwarzenegger *NOT* want to sleep with one of us?

And, speaking of wise Latinas, my mom ...

1. Is a beautiful, smart, strong Latina woman and a great role model

2. Has no fashion sense. Nada. Really. It's embarrassing sometimes — okay, only EVERY time she tries to take me shopping and ~~every time she puts on clothes~~.
3. Thinks I'm still eleven years old. Also see #2 above. I know, mis locas, she wanted to throw me a big, ghetto-fabulous, quinceañera last month even though I didn't want one so she knows I'm fifteen but you know what I'm talking about.
4. Changed her name when she came to America because she thought no one would be able to pronounce it. She was right: Ixchel – is it "ee-chel" or "eesh-ell" or "Ish-tell" or why not just call her "Seashell" like my sister Sylvia and I do sometimes? When I ask her she says, "Daisy, listen to the Beatle's song "Michelle" (it's Paul or John I can't remember) and take off the "M"." Thanks for the advice, "ami."
5. Doesn't know I write this blog. Or that I got invited back to the Cave with C. tonight. Shhh. Seashell might hear us.

<3 <3 <3 <3 <3 <3 <3 <3 <3 <3 <3 <3 <3 <3 <3 <3 <3 <3 <3

* * *

Connor: K she likes me so what

Morris: She said some shit about me not true btw

Connor: This from last week? Get over it mo

Morris: And all that stuff about her mom was weird

Connor: Sweet

Morris: ????

Connor: I thought it was sweet. She likes her mom and the Beatles so what

Morris: So fuck those bitches. I told u

Connor: Whoa chill

Morris: No. F.T.B.

Connor: Whatever. Go to sleep.

Morris: Peace.

Chapter 14: Sunday morning

Paul got up around 8:00 a.m. and missed Merika, who was already gone via taxi to pick up her car at Town Line Road. He forgot to ask for her phone number and so resolved to email her later when he got to the office. Connor wouldn't be up for another couple of hours so he decided to get a few things done before they had a late breakfast together.

His first chore was to visit that great leveler, the Town recycling center. Each week he'd go there to haul his pre-sorted bundles of take-out containers, frozen dinner packaging, avocado and orange peels, miscellaneous bottles and cans, and of course, newspapers and magazines. Most of the summer people had their trash picked up by private hauling companies. Still, you were more than likely to run into a few Wall Street types and blue haired society ladies spiriting their trash from the otherwise spotless trunks of their luxury SUVs. The past winter he even glimpsed a befurrred TV blonde in heels dropping a bag in the bin. The one from that HBO series that featured four women who were always having sex, not having sex or talking about the sex they were having or not having. The actress reminded him of Jeanine but only a to a degree: the character the actress played was a lot tougher.

As he was dropping his own trash into the proper bins marked "*Glass*," "*Plastic and Metal*," "*Mixed Paper,*" and "*Non-recycling*" Paul overheard two local guys talking about the pictures of the dead girl that had been posted on his newspaper's website the day before. He tried to eavesdrop but could only make out a few random comments over the din of the trucks and screeching seagulls circling the bins: "That's a sweet tattoo," "She's some kind of Mexican I guess," "Probably another whore, so what?"

He was tempted to go over and speak to them but made a point of not engaging personally with people about the stories he wrote. Instead, he cheerlessly finished his chore. Before he could get out of the unloading area and the accompanying stench, his cell phone rang. It was Olivia. They hadn't spoken in months and it'd been even longer seen they'd seen each other.

She was short of breath, talking in between gasps.

"Paul, oh my God I'm so glad you picked up."

"Olivia, what's wrong?"

"Paul, last night at a dinner party someone was talking about the article you posted online about that dead girl in Wainscott. I hadn't given it a thought until early this morning and took a look at it myself. Oh my God, Paul. I know that girl."

"What? What do you mean you know her?"

"I know who she is. She used to work for me cleaning my house."

"Olivia, are you sure it's the same girl? What's her name?"

"Clara. Her name is Clara. She worked for me until last year. I thought she was stealing from me so I had to fire her. Oh my God Paul, who would do something like this?"

"Olivia, try to calm down. What is the girl's last name?"

"I don't know."

"She worked for you and you don't know her last name?"

"Don't be mean Paul. I paid her cash. She may have told me her last name but I don't remember... Rodriguez, Ramirez, I don't know. Maybe it doesn't start with 'R.'"

"You must have her phone number somewhere. Did you save an address? Maybe you saved a holiday card from her? Do you have *any* evidence that shows who she is?"

"I don't think so. I was so mad I threw out all traces of her. But I know that it's her from the picture. She has that same beatific face. Like a Modigliani. Paul, the girl in the picture, she looks so... fragile."

"Olivia, search around the house and see if you can find any evidence, anything she may have left that gives us a clue as to who she is. And, don't call anyone else okay? You need to be sure before you start talking to people. Have you talked to anyone else about this?"

"Not yet."

"Good. I'm at the dump right now. I'll try to come over there later after I shower and see if I can help you find anything."

"Thanks Paul. I knew you could help."

"Oh, and one more thing ... your Clara, did she have a tattoo like the one in the picture?" He was referring to the blue star tattooed north of the dead girl's pubic mound, just below her panty line.

"Paul, if she did I wouldn't have seen it. What are you *thinking*?"

After stopping home to shower, Paul drove back to the office and sent Merika a quick email asking her for her phone number and checked his email and voicemail. His inbox bulged with messages. His voicemail account had run out of space and included several calls from the East Hampton Police Department, some Peconic County guy from Woo's office screaming obscenities, and a slew of newspaper reporters from several national publications. *The New York Times*, *New York Post*, *Daily News*, *Newsday*, and papers from New England to California to Toronto, even *The International Herald Tribune*—all requesting more "color" to add to their own stories for their Monday edition. He was half-hoping Goldberg—or one of his other buddies at *New York*—had messaged him and then cursed himself for even thinking it.

He was contemplating whether to return any of the calls when his phone rang.

It was Captain Tom Cole from the East Hampton Police Department, one of his regular sources at the department and a long-time friend of Jeanine's family. Cole usually didn't call Paul at the paper unless he was upset about some factual error or if he felt the department had gotten a bad rap in one of his articles about the Town Police's handling of a case.

Tom Cole was also one of the first local people Paul got to know when he and Jeanine began spending summer weekends on the East End together. Every July 4th Cole and his wife Becky, and a number of other young families—cops and volunteer firemen mostly—would stake out a spot on one of the beaches on Gardeners Bay, drive their pickup trucks up to the water's edge, fire up the barbeque and stay until dark to watch the Devon fireworks. Paul usually had fun but Jeanine *hated* it. Whenever she and Paul would be invited to one of these tailgate-barbeques, she would spend most of the day complaining about how "unevolved" her people were, how this guy or that woman was a clueless Bub—"Do you know there are people out here who have never even been to the city? *Maybe* to see a Broadway show. Once."

The first time Paul had a chance to talk to Tom Cole was during that first July 4th beach picnic after college. Jeanine and Butch, who was often in attendance at these gatherings—at least in those early days—had gone together on a beer run, leaving Paul alone to talk with Cole at length about his ambitions for moving up in the police department, his love of fishing, his newborn daughter, and other subjects that left Paul mostly nodding his head with little to say. Cole would ask him about the usual safe guy topics: what was he working on, what sports teams he followed, how could he and Jeanine stand to live in such a small apartment in the city, etc. These conversations took on a familiar repetition each year, the only difference being the activities of their respective children once Connor came into the picture, and the names of the people Paul happened to be interviewing for his freelance magazine assignments. But, what really stuck with Paul was a conversation he had with Cole at one of these events years later, after he and Jeanine had decided to move to East Hampton full time. It was something Cole did *not* ask him: *Why did you move here?* It was a question their city friends never failed to bring up, usually asked with the phrase *full time* tacked on the end, as if living on the East End in the off season was some kind of punishment. As he and Tom Cole watched the dazzling stream of fireworks light up the summer night sky, their bursts of light and color reflected off of the smooth black surface of Gardeners Bay and the even smoother surfaces of the four-wheel drive vehicles of the local families parked up on the beach, wasn't it obvious why the question needn't to be asked?

"Paulie, I hear you are a busy guy these days."

"Captain Cole. I got your voicemail but haven't had a chance to call you back."

"How is your lovely wife or should I not ask that?" Cole asked anyway.

"She's fine. Our divorce was final on Friday so you may have to ask someone else next time."

"I heard. Butch Weeks. Great guy. Wow, handsome too. Sorry."

"Yeah."

"You know her father, that was a wonderful guy. Did I tell you he used to take us fishing on that crappy tub of his when we were kids? Guy pulled in some big ones in his time. Too bad you never got to meet him."

"I know. I heard he was a man among men. So, to what do I owe this honor?" Paul asked, trying to move things along.

"Paulie, I'm calling to thank you personally for your article."

"Really?"

"Hey, we're allowed to like some of the things you guys write. Those pictures, I'm still not sure how you got a hold of them, but they totally corroborate our guy's story. The description he gave us from that day matches perfectly—the hair, the dress, the tattoo."

"I'm glad, Tom. I'm sure Officer Clifford is a decent guy. And it sounded like he followed procedure that day. I did have one question about him though."

"Shoot."

"Do you know anything about a girlfriend of his?"

"Sandis, are you trying to connect Will Clifford to this dead girl? Because if you are this is going to be a very short conversation. And here I was calling to thank you."

"It's just that I heard something about him and an ex-girlfriend."

"Well, whatever you heard, you can forget about it. The guy is shook up as it is. He doesn't need you poking around into his private life."

"Okay, okay. But, tell me, what's going on over there with the cone of silence? Why can't I get anything from the cops on this case?"

"That's part of the reason I called. Paulie, I'm not supposed to be telling you *anything* but since you did us this favor I can share something—strictly off the record of course. The Counties are keeping a tight lid on this."

"Of course."

"Truth is they got nothin' on this girl. I mean it. They checked every recent missing person's report for three hundred miles that matches our guy's description of her. Coast Guard doesn't have anything. They've tried to question people who may have been on the beach the night before and that morning. Peconic has even asked us to check local surf rentals, boat rentals. Nothin'. This girl is either a mermaid who stopped to sun herself or she doesn't belong to anybody. She's like a phantom. I've never seen anything like it."

"Wow, so you guys didn't have the pictures?"

"Other than the few local inquiries I just mentioned, our department was told not to investigate further. That is, until you posted your article. Any time there's a possible murder or missing person's case it becomes the county's baby and you know they are pretty slow."

Tom had a point. The blue and green painted crest on the re-fitted Peconic County Sherriff cars barely had a chance to dry before the department found itself driving headlong into one of the most curious missing person cases ever to show up on the East End.

"Sure, Tom. And, what about this kid who posted the pictures? They must have got him by now."

"The Facebook kid? Thought you'd ask me about him. Already lawyered up. He's not saying anything. And we haven't found anything we can charge him with," Cole admitted.

Just then, Jeff walked in and sat down on the edge of Paul's desk. Paul pointed to the phone's headset and wrote the words "Five-O" on a piece of paper and held it up for Jeff as he continued his call with Cole ("Five-O" being gangsta rap slang—and Paul and Jeff's shorthand—for the police).

"And you don't know who actually *took* the pictures yet?" Paul asked Cole.

"Nope. Is there something you're not telling me, Paulie?"

"Well, since I got you on the line... I did try to talk with this one kid, Fredy Gomes, but he bolted when I asked him about it. He was acting pretty guilty about something. Before he took off, the kid clipped me with a nice right hook."

"Gomes huh? Spell that one for me." Paul abided and gave Cole a recap of his conversation with Fredy in Freetown, ending with that right hook and Fredy's bandaged bloodied hand. He left out the part about his bicycle.

"So, I just gave you another lead. You got anything else for me?" Paul asked.

"That's it." Cole said. "But one word of advice: be careful with this thing. You don't want to be too far ahead of these investigators. There is already some talk of reining you in. You haven't been very popular down there. And these new county guys don't like surprises."

"Thanks for the advice. And, *Tommy,* thanks for being up front with me," Paul said, cracking a smile and looking over at Jeff.

"Huh? Did you just call me 'Tommy?' Nobody calls me that except my big brothers. You're weird Sandis. A good reporter but weird. I'll catch you later. And say hello to your ex for me."

Paul chuckled, hung up the phone, and turned his chair to face Jeff's desk.

"Bower, what are you doing here on a Sunday? I thought I was the only one on call this weekend."

"Well it appears you got a new angle on one of the biggest stories this town has ever seen and you've been hiding it from me. Is it something I said? I know I was pretty drunk the other night."

"Just doin' my job, brother." Paul couldn't help smiling.

"Speaking of Friday night, I hope you didn't take advantage of that nice lady you drove home. Because she looked more wasted than me and I was wasted enough that *I* probably would've slept with you."

"Thanks for creating that picture in mind," Paul said.

Since taking the job at the paper, Paul considered his younger friend a kind of mentor in the ways of small town journalism. Jeff was a good reporter and knew the area well, especially the minority neighborhoods in town. When Bert was staffing the East Hampton office he chose Jeff to run it over the objections of Grace, who believed him too young and irresponsible to handle the position (choosing Paul wasn't even on the table). She finally agreed under the condition that she maintain a presence in the office there. Although there had always been friction between Grace and Jeff, she did have a point. Jeff's erratic work habits were well known. Ever since moving in with Penny, his longtime girlfriend and mother of his young son, he would sometimes take off for days at a time, only to show up at the office and spend forty-eight hours straight working stories, crashing on a ratty old sleeping bag he kept in the coat closet next to his stash of herbal tea and Doritos. Come summer, Jeff would spend nights in the cabin of his tiny sail boat moored in Three Mile Harbor and arrive to work the next day bleary-eyed, sleeping through important morning meetings. His work area was always a disaster, which drove Grace and Esra crazy. But once Jeff had made the move to East Hampton, the bosses in Southampton didn't seem to mind his many quirks as long as he could continue to meet his quota of stories written and edited each week.

"Seriously man, what's up with this dead girl story? Alex told me the site went down three times yesterday because the server couldn't handle the traffic," Jeff said.

"Wow. That is very gratifying. But I'm purposely avoiding going to the website, as much as I love reading all those deeply insightful comments from our online readers. Hey, can I complain about something else for a second? I just told Tom Cole that I got punched by some surfer who might be a prime suspect in this dead girl thing and he didn't even show a speck of concern."

"And this is strange because?"

"Never mind. But I have to tell you something: The kid who hit me is a murderer."

"What are you talking about?"

"Mellow. He killed her. Death by auto. I can't even provide her a proper burial. I left her in pieces."

"Poor girl. What am I saying? Poor *you*. I am so sorry to hear that." Jeff walked over to Paul and put his arm around him in a pretend gesture of comfort. "I hope they catch this kid. If only for that reason. I really do. Maybe after work we can go to the Build-A-Bear place together. I hear that's good therapy."

"I know you mean that sincerely. Thank you." Paul squirmed out of Jeff's embrace. "By the way, our friend Grace in Southampton, how is she doing?"

"Funny you should ask. Freaking out, as usual. I just came from there. In fact, she sent me here to talk to you. I think she's afraid her head will explode if she speaks with you directly."

"Maybe I should call her?" Paul formed a new picture in his mind: Grace's gray matter splattered over the sailboat pictures in her tidy office cubicle.

"Basically the message is that she doesn't want us to report on any new information that doesn't come directly from official police sources," Jeff said.

"*Us*? She's got you working this story too?" Paul was beginning to feel his one shot at glory slipping away.

"Don't worry, brother. She wanted me to cover the fallout, you know, do a piece on the public reaction. Totally separate. What do the JoeHampton55's and BeachGrrl22's of the world have to say about it, that sort of thing. This dead girl has obviously hit a nerve out here. It's your story as far as covering the case as it unfolds. And between you and me, I would ignore that message I passed on about official sources."

"I already did. Anyway, I've decided that I'm working for Bert now."

"Ooh, I like this new Paul I'm seeing. Hey, I wanted to remind you that you've got to cover that Town Board meeting tomorrow morning. It should be interesting in light of what's going on," Jeff said.

"Whaddya mean?"

"The house overcrowding thing in Springs. The Town Board is taking it up at the meeting tomorrow at 9:00 a.m. You may have a mob scene there. I'm almost sorry I'm going to miss it."

"Yeah, well I'll let you know how it goes. Hey, do you know if I'm supposed to answer all those emails and phone calls from the other newspapers about this story? I kind of have to go do something."

"Oh yeah. I almost forgot. Don't bother. Grace is handling all the press relation stuff. It may seem sexy to call the guy at the *New York Times* for a chat but face it—he or she doesn't really give a damn about you. These guys from the national press, they only want to steal from you, and then they'll twist what you say to make it sound like they've got some unique angle. Go slay your story, man."

"Thanks. Let me know if you come across anything in your travels that might be interesting and I'll do the same." Paul gathered up his stuff to leave.

"Will do. Hey, I know they say this in the movies but I mean it: be careful out there. You didn't tell me where you were headed."

"To see Olivia."

"Olivia? In that case be extra careful," Jeff yelled as Paul raced out the door.

Chapter 15: Sunday, later that morning

"Something's different," Paul said. He was looking out onto Olivia's vast property facing Acabonac Harbor. Past the orchard, the outdoor garden rooms, the chicken coops. Though he wore sunglasses to shield his eyes, the low angle of the sun forced him to squint at the reflection off of the water in the distance.

"I've been replacing the last of the non-native shrubs. Oh, and I started growing lemons. See the trees, over there," she said.

"That must be it."

The two of them took a seat on Olivia's back porch under one of the many arbors she had designed. Paul reached into the back pocket of his jeans. "Okay, here are the pictures we posted on the paper's website. Now, if you can get that picture you found, we can compare them."

"Wait here," she said.

She scooted on bare feet to a small room off of her kitchen and came back with a picture she managed to find of her former housecleaner, Clara. In the photograph it is a sunny day. A young Latina is squatting in a brightly colored dress as she feeds one of Olivia's chickens, her unsmiling face looking reluctantly toward the camera. Olivia's house and lush garden rooms are in the background, providing a strangely bucolic counterpoint.

"That's Clara—and Mingus," she said, pointing to the picture. "God, look at the light—isn't it a marvel? So luminous. Like today."

"Mingus is the chicken, right? I just want to get this straight."

"Paul!" She smacked him lightly across his head, grazing his still tender ear and almost knocking off his sunglasses.

"Okay, I'm already seeing differences," he said. "Clara's hair is much shorter and darker in your picture. Her eyes, they're closer together and rounder than the other girl."

"No, no. Paul this is the girl. I can feel it. There was always something tragic about her. Besides, how many of these girls just disappear?"

"I'm sorry, Olivia, but I have to disagree. Look, there, Clara has a small mole on her cheek." He pointed to a spot above the girl's right jaw line. "And look at the eyebrows."

"Hmm, maybe you're right," Olivia admitted. "Did I say Modigliani before? Now that I see this I recall thinking of Clara as more like one of Milton Avery's women, his portraits of his wife Sally in particular. She was always so *serious*."

"Okaaay ..."

"Really, Paul. Surely you can see why I would mistake Clara for this girl."

"Of course. But are we in agreement that this is not the same girl?"

"I guess. Only if you are sure."

"Maybe we should leave it to the cops to figure out who this dead girl is, okay?"

"Okay," she sighed. "Hey, have they replaced your computer yet?" She began stroking his arm lightly with the tips of her fingers.

"Ha. Yeah, but I had to be very creative in explaining to my bosses why I needed to."

"Paul—

"—I know."

"No. It's just, I am sorry for all of it. I couldn't help myself then. We did exchange some pretty good emails though. If I was Jeanine and I found them I guess I would have done the same thing."

"Divorce me?"

"No, God no. I mean to your computer."

"Oh. And how is the invisible man?"

"My husband you mean? Peripatetic, as usual. He's got a new girlfriend. Evidently there was a picture in a magazine of the two of them snuggling at some fabulous resort. He's been doing a terrible job as the invisible man so I can no longer call him that. Until I can think of something more fitting, I've been calling him 'the bastard,' as in, '*the bastard* hasn't called or emailed me in three months.' Why are we talking about him again?"

During this last brief exchange, their bodies had managed to move closer and closer together on the wooden porch swing until they were practically on top of one another. She was wearing a slip dress not unlike the one she wore when they first met, only lavender with black trim bordering a deep V-shaped neckline that revealed the perfect sweep of her cleavage. Paul felt a familiar sensation, a certain gravitational pull taking hold.

"You're doing it," he said.

"What?"

"You're doing that thing. Trying to suck me in."

"Paul, you think too much of yourself."

"Then why do I feel this intense urge to jump you right now? Your force is too powerful. You're like a Siren in one of those Greek fables my dad is always quoting. It usually doesn't end up well for the *Siree* as I recall."

"Now you're just trying to flatter me."

"I mean it. You've got to turn it off sometimes."

"Okay, I'll stop." Olivia removed her hand from him and straightened herself by patting her long, elegant fingers down her sides. She then slid her slender rear end over a few inches from Paul to give him a little space. “Sorry Paul, it’s been awhile. Not just us, but since I’ve had any man. I miss it.”

“You deserve to have everything, including your man. But you know I’m not him.”

“Yeah, yeah. When did you become so practical?”

“Actually, I met someone. I mean, there is someone—”

“—have you fallen in love? Paul, this is exciting!”

“I don’t know. We’ve only been together once. We haven’t even slept together yet.”

“Wow. That sounds like love to me. Tell me about her.” Before he could answer she reached her hand toward his face and carefully removed his sunglasses, an intimate gesture he couldn’t imagine allowing anyone else. That is, until now.

“Look, you don’t want to hear about this. I appreciate your interest in my love life but— it’s funny, I almost feel like if I talk about her it won’t be real anymore.”

“This *is* serious.”

“Maybe. I don’t even have her yet and I’m afraid of losing her already. How is that even possible?”

Chapter 16: Sunday afternoon

Paul returned home from Olivia's house around noon to find Connor standing over the stove in his pajamas: loose-fitting yoga pants and an oversized T-shirt he picked up at a secondhand store. On the shirt was emblazoned a large four-leaf clover with the words *Kiss me I'm Irish*. "It's vintage," Connor said the first time Paul asked him about it, as if it was a fine wine and not something a drunk might have puked on at a past Montauk St. Patrick's Day parade. Paul studied Connor as his son finessed a series of cracked eggs into a pan. With his fair complexion, delicate features and athletic build, Connor was his mother's son. Paul barely recognized himself in him. And wasn't it only recently that he'd gotten off the train from the city and was swinging Connor up over his head and atop his steady shoulders? There was an expiration date on that sort of thing, he knew. But lately Connor seemed almost too heavy, immovable. Yet Paul was also envious of Connor's passion, his ability to immerse himself so completely in whatever excited him.

"Hey buddy, sorry I'm late," Paul said.

"No worries, son. You're just in time for my Spanish eggs," Connor said. "I told you I'd make you breakfast for your birthday."

After Paul made a fresh pot of IGA coffee, the two of them sat down at the dining table and dug into the feast Connor had prepared.

"This is really good, spicy but good," Paul said between mouthfuls of fiery eggs and cheese.

"Three kinds of chilies, cayenne, a little cumin. The chilies are from my garden at Mom's house. You're a man, I know you can take it," Connor said.

"Thanks for the vote of confidence."

Connor's phone chirruped with an incoming text.

"Could you not get that right now? I'd like to talk to you about something," Paul pleaded, looking over at Connor's mobile screen. "And who is Daisy? Is that your new girlfriend?"

"Just some girl," Connor said, putting his phone back in his pants pocket.

"Listen, you know your mom and I finalized our divorce on Friday. You and I haven't really had a chance to talk about it."

"What's to talk about? It's not like I was lying awake at night praying that you two guys would work things out and get back together. It's just a piece of paper right?"

"Well, that and the fact that your mom is now legally free to get married to Butch in a few weeks."

"Butch is okay, I guess. Mom's got him wrapped around her little finger. He's harmless."

"Is that how you measure him, in terms of how much harm he can do to you? That's a pretty cynical way of looking at it."

"How else should I look at? Dad, I'm sixteen. The guy is not gonna be telling me what to do. He can barely control his own daughters. They're a couple of spoiled brats."

"I thought you were getting along."

"Putting up with them is more like it. They're sweet little kids but their values are like totally fucked up. All they care about is clothes, jewelry, all that stuff. You and mom were never like that."

"At least we got something right, I guess," Paul said, gulping down his third glass of water in an effort to put out the fire in his mouth. "What would you say your mom and I care about?"

"I don't know but not *stuff*. If I had to think of something I guess I'd say you guys are more grounded or whatever. Although Mom seems to be going over to the dark side. What were you gonna to say?"

"I would say that we care about you and try to give you every opportunity to realize your talents, whatever they may be," Paul said.

"Did you read that in a parenting magazine or something? Is this what happens when parents get divorced? If it is, please make it stop."

"C'mon, this is me trying to be sincere. How is the music thing going?"

Lately, Connor had been spending hours locked in his room studying rap music, L.A. hip-hop in particular—stuff created by African American skateboard kids barely out of high school. Connor would analyze how these artists incorporated meter plus rhyme plus simile plus attitude, the same way he might tackle a science or math problem. Then he'd create his own songs based on these elaborate formulas using the music software on his computer. What often sounded to Paul like a cacophony of angry proclamations and discordant notes was to Connor a lovely geometry with its own unique set of rules, textures and shapes.

"You wanna hear a new rap I did for Morris? It's pretty fresh." He pulled up a music file on his computer and cued up the backing track, a slow looped drum and bass beat with repeated samples of children screaming and backwards guitar riffs. Paul expected the fever-pitched cadences of the rapper Cassius Claim to start in but what he heard instead was the syncopated moan of his sixteen year old son, throaty and sinister sounding.

Yo, I'm gonna show, u I got game, ur goin down in flames
my rhymes so fresh they're gonna make you insane,

using only your first name ...
Morris, u think u kickin styles for miles like Chuck Norris
But when u play your Flyin' V it aint fly, u just bore us
Suckin' dicks aint no way to get the bitches to adore us
Like Michael Jackson, all the hottest girls ignore us
—is ur mind porous?
I keep droppin' u the cue but u always miss the chorus

"That's all I got so far."

"Hmm. I like the backing track," Paul said, impressed with his son's vocal prowess and not knowing what else to say.

"Yeah, I gotta work on it some more. Hey, did you tell mom I want to move to your place before school starts? You won't even have to take me in the morning. I can get a ride from Nick or whoever's driving."

"I would love to have you move in with me. We don't get to see each other enough. But your mom may take some convincing. She wasn't too hot on the idea when I brought it up the last time I saw her."

"Dad, you didn't mention it at the divorce signing did you? Bad timing, dude."

"No, I wouldn't have done that. I mentioned it to her after."

"Really, when?"

"Um, we kind of ran into each other later that night. Look, it's not important. I think she'll come around. She's got a lot on her plate with the wedding and all. She'll be distracted. I'm sure you can wear her down."

"Cool. Hey, I almost forgot. I have a present for you." Connor went back to his bedroom and came back with a cardboard gift box the size of a hatbox.

"Happy Birthday. A day late but whatever."

"Wow, thanks. Did you buy this?"

"Just open it, *son*!" Connor demanded.

Paul opened the box, which Connor hadn't bothered to gift-wrap. Inside was a pair of old field binoculars in a cracked leather case. Paul carefully removed them, inspected their weight, and then tried focusing the lenses.

"These were your grandfather's. Did you have permission to give these to me?"

"Do you think I stole them? Don't be a dick. Mom suggested it. She thought you would like them. I thought it was a nice gesture on her part, you know, considering."

"I don't know what to say."

"Thank you?" Connor said.

"Of course, thanks."

* * *

"What are you looking at?"

"There's a girl down there and she's pretty sexy ... wait, let me focus ..."

The two of them were busy unpacking, but mostly Jeanine. That fall after graduating college, Paul managed to find them a one-bedroom in an under-supered pre-war building in Brooklyn on one of the few tree-lined streets off of Myrtle—their first shared apartment. But what in late spring held the promise of an exciting new beginning, by summer's end felt more like a compromise. They were a couple. School had ended and they both wanted a place without roommates. Of course they were going to live together. Yet in the final days before the move, Jeanine especially was often moody and tense; Paul wasn't even sure she still wanted to live with him.

He helped her hang her Warhol posters. She emptied boxes full of their few belongings into a tiny, shared closet and secondhand dresser, and arranged their books on the bookshelf by subject, then author. Now they were going through the last of it strewn over the unmade futon.

"Hey, those were my dad's binoculars! They're not for peeping at other women."

She tried snatching them from Paul's grip.

"I don't think your dad would mind. He would probably say I was being a healthy, red-blooded American boy. One who stole his shiksa daughter that is."

"Paul, stop. I don't want to think about him that way."

"Okay, okay. Just teasing. Hey, these things are great. I feel like Jimmy Stewart in that Hitchcock movie. You can be Grace Kelly and we can watch for bad guys on the street before they come up to our apartment and rob us."

"Great. And you'll protect me when they come to steal my womanhood?"

"Ah, but that's already been taken." Paul tossed the binoculars aside, grabbed Jeanine by the waist and rolled her onto on the mess of stuff she had yet to put away. Pretty soon they had their clothes off and were initiating the futon, the binoculars resting precariously at the foot of the bed.

Jeanine stopped abruptly and pushed him off of her.

"What's the matter?"

"Nothing. I wasn't feeling it. Do that thing." She climbed atop

Paul and cupped her hands around his miniature mug holders. Since they'd been together Jeanine developed an unhealthy attachment to his ears.

"What?"

"You know."

"Really?"

"Please."

"Okay. I lufyoo Jeanine Maw."

"Say it louder. Like you mean it."

"I lufyoo Jeanine Maw!"

She tightened her buttocks and was rocking back and forth now, knees bent cowgirl style, pinning his wrists to the bed with her elbows, her thumbs and forefingers rubbing the outside of his earlobes.

"Again."

"I lufyoo Jeanine Maw!!"

She leaned forward until her swollen nipples were barely touching his chest, pressing her lips to his ear.

"That's it, baby," she whispered. "That's what I want."

* * *

Later, while Paul was scraping the last of the spicy egg off of the dishes into the garbage, Connor came into the kitchen and gave him a hug.

"Dad, it's going to be alright. Divorce sucks. We'll both be all right."

"Hey, did you just call me 'Dad?'"

"Yeah, *son*."

"Funny."

"Okay, so who was that woman sleeping in the guest room last night?"

The question wasn't all that strange nor was it the first time Connor had asked it. Paul had invited a few women through the revolving door of his modest home since he and Jeanine split—one or two who may have even stuck around for breakfast.

"She's a lady I met while doing this dead girl story. Her name is Merika. We had some drinks with Isaak last night and she was feeling too sick to drive home. That's why she slept over."

"Community service, huh?"

"Not exactly. But I hope you can meet her soon. You'll like her. Actually, I need to borrow your computer again. I sent Merika an email earlier this morning—I don't have her phone number—and I was hoping she emailed me back by now."

"Dad, you've got to start bringing your work computer home again—at least get a mobile with email. The divorce is final. You have to stop pretending your computer broke up you and Mom's marriage. And, it's kind of creepy having you look at my personal stuff. Besides, you have nothing to worry about now. No one's going to be reading your emails."

"You're right. But just let me use yours right now."

Paul grabbed the computer from his son's bedroom, walked it into his own bedroom and logged into his work email. Sure enough, there was a new email from Merika among the dozens of unread emails he'd received since the day before, most of them relating to the dead girl story. He felt a rise in temperature as he clicked the little icon next to her name, then his throat closing tight around his Adam's apple as he read her message:

> I can't believe you could betray my trust so easily Paul. I was vulnerable last night and what you did was unforgivable. Please don't call me or try to send me an email. I will only delete it.
> -Merika.

For a few seconds Paul literally could not take a breath. He read the message again but couldn't comprehend it. Each of the key action words were sparklingly clear: "betray," "trust," "vulnerable," "unforgiveable"—all words that had been tossed at him deservedly, perhaps too often, during the worst days of his breakup with Jeanine. But coming from Merika? It just didn't make any sense.

He ran into the kitchen and tried the telephone directory. There were lots of Jones' in Southampton, but no Merikas and her mother JoAnna's name wasn't listed either. He looked up the main number of the Shinnecock Nation's Tribal Office and tried it.

Of course there's no answer—it's Sunday you idiot.

He yelled to Connor, who was at the other end of the house.

"Connor, aren't you helping out on the farm today?"

"Yeah. You gotta take me in a few minutes," Connor answered.

"Okay. I'll drop you off. I'm heading over to the Reservation after," Paul said, still a bit shaken. "Do you need to be picked up later?"

"Nah, one of the guys will drive me back to Mom's."

"Great. I'm not sure how long I'll be out anyway."

Chapter 17: Sunday, later that afternoon

"Hey, babies."

Connor squatted and counted the blades on each successive fan leaf. Three, five, seven, nine. All of them, the most beautiful color green. And no traces of yellow.

Love.

He was in the far eastern corner of "Ellie's End," the commercial area of Sugar Rose and usually safe from the intrusion of farm co-op members and most volunteers. He had chosen this spot deep behind the farm's tall, arching blackberry bushes for its high cover and optimal, sustained sunlight. The blackberry bushes, some of which grew to more than seven feet, were now thick and fragrant with the bloom of white flowers.

Before exiting his grow area, he peeked through the tightly packed maze of brambles to make sure there was no one coming down the path. He was about to emerge when he spotted a friend who had no legitimate business being here. Yet there he was, pacing the path next to the blackberry bushes on the opposite end of where Connor was standing. He waited until his friend had his head turned before jumping out into the path, and then started toward him.

"Hey Con, there you are. How is the crop going?" Dylan asked, as if he could always be found loitering here.

Connor had been going over in his mind how he would explain to Dylan why the guy who had ambushed him in his pool house the day before might have known to go there. And there was that thing about last night.

"Yo, Dylan. What's good? Whaddya doing here?"

"Not a lot is good right now. I just spent the last twenty-four hours avoiding cops and running up a lawyer tab that my dad is not too happy about," Dylan said. "But wait, *your* dad probably could tell you about that."

"Look, Dylan, it was an accident, I swear. My father got up in the middle of the night to use my computer and saw the pictures. I hadn't even seen them."

"I see. Hey, no worries son," Dylan said. He proceeded to remove his long blonde dreads from in front of his face and tucked them behind his ears and into his wool cap. It was amazing how he could keep that wool cap on his head all summer long and not get fried. "There's a rumor going around that you hooked up with Jess last night. I thought you were seeing that Spanish girl."

"Yeah, I mean, no. We went to this party in Southampton with a bunch of other people but we didn't hook up. I'm not seeing Daisy anymore though. I kind of fucked that up."

"How was that party? I heard the cops busted it up when some Res kids crashed it."

"Yeah, it kinda sucked."

Dylan seemed blasé about the whole Jess thing, as if he was discussing what vegetable varieties to plant and not the girl he'd been sleeping with the past six months.

"Sucked, huh? Yeah, Jess is a good girl. I'm sure you're right. Anyway, since we're in business now maybe I'll just use this opportunity to let you do me a small favor," Dylan said.

"What's that?"

"Well, I've got this friend, you know that guy I told you about from up-island who is gonna buy all that weed you're growing? I told him to meet me here in a few minutes."

"Wait! You *didn't* tell the guy where I'm growing the stuff! We made a deal that it was just you and me who would know. I can get into some deep shit here."

"I wouldn't have told anyone but the dude has been pressing me. He wants to make sure we are legit. Let's call it payback, if you want. Anyway, he's real interested in how things are progressing. I thought since he's a partner that maybe you can give him a little tour."

"Dylan, fuck, dude. If we get caught—"

—"*we* won't get caught. Anyway, no worries, dude. This guy is cool."

"How do we know he and his boys won't just come and steal the plants once they're mature?"

"That's just a chance we'll have to take. Anyway, you've got sky-high fences around this place. It's more secure than a Saudi virgin's pussy around here. I told you these guys are paying one-third up-front to get first dibs."

Just then a short, stocky kid of about nineteen passed through the open deer fence gate that separated Ellie's End from the rest of the farm and began walking toward Dylan and Connor. The compressed lower half of his body would have you believe that a small child was approaching: he had on wide, baggy black jeans hanging below his boxers that almost completely covered day-glow-orange skateboard shoes; his over-extended pant legs dragged comically along the ground as he walked. But this lower half stood in stark contrast to his sculpted upper body, shrink-wrapped in a sleeveless wife-beater and showing off an extensive collection of brightly colored tattoos. The swirling shapes, text and rainbow colors covered almost every inch of his exposed skin, including his neck up to both his ears. His dark hair was twisted into dreadlocks that were much shorter and tighter than Dylan's, who typically wore his partly hidden under his wool cap. To top it off, he had several piercings including a silver ring on his left eyebrow and a large metal stud protruding below his lower lip.

"Yo, wassup my nigga?" the kid said to Dylan.

"Luis! You found the place. Isn't it beautiful—fresh air, sunshine, *la madre naturaleza*—right?" Dylan executed some kind of elaborate handshake with Luis that Connor didn't recognize. "Hey, this is Connor, the kid I told you about."

"Wassup," Connor said, more as a statement than a question, and nodded toward Luis.

"What is this place?" Luis asked.

"It's a community farm. I'm just volunteering here so we have to be cool," Connor said, looking around to see who might be watching them.

"So where's the grow area?" Luis asked Dylan, not paying attention to Connor's response.

"Um, it's somewhere hidden, here on the farm. There really isn't much to see now. The plants are just starting their growth," Connor said.

"What he say?" Luis said to Dylan.

"Connor, Luis came to see the plants. He and his friends are putting up some serious money," Dylan said.

"Who is this little kid? *No me chingues*," Luis said to Dylan. "Don't fuck with me," he repeated in English this time, still ignoring Connor.

"Dude, you remember the stuff I got you last year? It was fucking amazing, right? He's a kid but he knows how to grow this shit," Dylan said, referring to the weed that Connor had grown on the back of Butch's sprawling property the year before and had shared with some friends.

Connor's first attempt at an outdoor crop the previous summer had been mostly successful. Although he lost a few plants to foul weather and critters, he managed to turn out some wicked bud on those that survived. It had a nice fluffy, sticky texture. And when lit, the draw was smooth with a little tingle that hit the tongue, the smoke sweet—almost mangoey in flavor—and the high was, well, incredible. Those who tried it were convinced he was using a popular strain known as Kush, or *Cannabis indica*, found growing wild and cultivated in the foothills of Afghanistan and Pakistan, and famous for its powerful high. His friends were correct but only partly. This was Connor's own strain, created by experimenting and crossbreeding several indica varieties under grow lights indoors before planting them outside. Connor had spent several months experimenting with the desired traits (resistance to insects, flavor and aroma, early maturation, etc.) and manipulating the genetic information that all plants needed for transmitting from one generation to the next—pollen of the staminate parent and ovule of the pistillate parent—until he came upon a strain that would "breed true" for the particular traits he was looking for. The rest was a lot of trial and error. His biggest challenge though, like that of many Northeast growers, was to acclimatize high-THC strains originally grown in Equatorial areas to the cooler summers of the East End once he moved the plants outdoors. The second biggest challenge was to make sure his plants didn't grow too tall and be discovered. Strains containing indica were preferred since the plants tended to be shorter and more compact and produced greater yields.

This year Connor tried something more ambitious with a new strain he had developed and that required a more controlled environment. The deer fencing and relative quiet of Ellie's End would afford him the perfect combination of security and camouflage (although you were unlikely to see a deer lighting up, they sometimes liked to chew on the leaves of young marijuana plants). The business arrangement was this: Connor would grow the plants to adulthood, harvest them and sneak the buds out in batches in his backpack at the end of each day. Connor would, of course, keep a small stash for himself and his friends but hand the bulk of the crop over to Dylan. Dylan would sort and weigh the final harvest to assess its value and determine the final wholesale price. Once Dylan handed it over to Luis, Luis and his crew would perform the laborious task of trimming the leaves and drying and curing the cleaned buds to ready it for street sale. Connor was a grower not a dealer and told himself that he wasn't in it for the profit. However, he was looking forward to using some of the money he earned to put toward a greenhouse he planned on building on a friend's property. Continuing to use Butch's place to start the young plants was becoming too risky.

Luis, likely filled with fond remembrances of smoking Connor's superior bud from the year before, finally addressed Connor directly.

"Show me," he said.

"Trust me, the plants are secure. I can guarantee you that my stuff will be really good, even better than last year," Connor said, still trying to stall.

Luis reached out his right arm, squeezed Conner's shoulder with his powerful hand and smiled, exposing a gleaming gold tooth. Sweat glistened off of each of his elaborate tattoos, including one that Connor was noticing for the first time on Luis' upper arm: a blue five-pointed star. Luis stared Connor down menacingly. And after a few moments of restrained silence, Luis tightened his grip on the back of Connor's neck and said,

"You show me yours and I'll show you mine."

Luis then lifted the front of his T-shirt with his free hand to reveal a large marijuana leaf tattooed on his ripped lower torso.

"Try to keep your arms close to your body; you'll get fewer scratches," Connor advised, as he guided Luis and Dylan through the prickly shrub in the direction of his inner sanctum. They reached a small clearing where about a dozen small green plants were lined up in neat rows, their bright leaves turned eagerly toward the sun.

"Careful, you have to walk on this side so you don't trample them. These are only a month old but we had some lucky weather. They'll definitely be ready by late September."

Luis bent down and examined several of the young plants. His movements were uncharacteristically gentle as he ran his fingers over the tiny leaves. Then he stepped back and counted the plants in Spanish: *uno, dos, tres, cuatro,* etc.

"They look good. And they better *be* good. I'll see you in September," Luis said. Then, squeezing Connor's shoulder again he said,

"And don't forget: *Soy machín.*"

"Soy matching?"

"You can look it up, Dexter, if you don't know what it means."

After checking to make sure the path was clear of people, the three of them marched back out in a straight line through the thick bramble. Luis and Dylan were picking the last of the brambles out of their hair when Ellie Steadman, the farm's director, came jogging down the path and greeted them. Though Connor was used to seeing her as just Ellie, she struck most people outside the farm as a kind of new age hippie-pirate. With her long beaded and braided hair, brightly colored head-kerchief, ankle-length pleated skirts, and laced-high work boots she wore even on the hottest day of the year. Connor thought Ellie smelled nice too—patchouli (Pogosteman, of the mint family).

"Hey Connor, looks like we have visitors today, huh? Nice dreads guys," she said, referring to Dylan and Luis' natty locks. She showed them one of her own brightly colored beaded creations from inside her tangle of braided strands.

"Uh, thanks. I'm Dylan," he said reaching out his hand for Ellie to shake. "This is my friend Luis. We were just talking to Connor about maybe volunteering for the farm."

"Cool, guys. We could always use a few more strong men around here," she said. In other areas of the farm, volunteers were busy planting tomato, onion, pepper and eggplant seedlings and starting Brussels sprouts and pumpkins in one of the three greenhouses, and there was a lot of hoeing and weeding going on. She wiped her brow with one of her gloves, reached into an apron pocket and handed the three of them a handful of ruby red radishes. "This weather has been just incredible. We've got plenty of picking to do: asparagus, strawberries, the lettuce is coming up. Connor, why don't you get your friends a couple of applications and drop them off with Sherry?" Sherry was Sugar Rose's co-director and Ellie's wife. "Do you two guys have any farm experience?"

"My grandfather has a farm in Ecuador," Luis said, apparently inspired into conversation. "I spent a few summers working there when I was younger."

"Awesome! *Podemos usar un poco de ayuda con experiencia,*" Ellie said to Luis. Then, distracted by a sudden burst of activity in an adjoining field, she excused herself and said, "I hope to see you guys again." Then she ran off to help with one of the thirty-seven varieties of tomatoes that members of her staff were beginning to plant.

"Fuck. That was close. Hey, I didn't know you worked on a farm, Luis," Dylan said.

"Yeah, my abuelo had six acres, mostly marijuana. Until the US government sprayed paraquat and killed off everything back in the day. Now he just grows chilies on a small plot and barely gets by. I tried growing my own plants there a couple of summers ago but it wasn't as good as this weed—that is, if this is as good as what you gave me last year. Shi' why am I tellin' you this? It's time to go."

Luis turned to Connor and said,

"Don't let anyone else near those plants. *Ay te watcho.*" He thrust his fist toward Connor's chest but stopped before making contact. Connor flinched and Luis let out a cruel laugh.

As Dylan and Luis made their way out of Ellie's End, Connor could hear them arguing.

"Wait, I thought the paraquat spraying thing was done to Mexican weed," Dylan said.

"Yeah motherfucker, I'm Mexican. That's why I *said* I was from Ecuador. And why did you tell that bitch my real name?"

"No worries, dude. She'll probably forget our names in like the next five minutes."

"Sure, sure. And you better hope it, bro." Luis held up the radish he'd taken from his pocket and waved it at Dylan. "Hey, you guys really eat these?" He took a bite, squinched up his face and spit it out.

The two of them were almost at the next gate when Dylan turned around and yelled out,

"Hey Con, by the way, Jess told me everything. Peace, *Vato.*"

~ ~ ~

Ave Maria (4)

All week she had been looking forward to painting her toenails a new deep green color called "Envy" she'd picked up on her last visit to the drug store.

She dragged one of the kitchen chairs into the bathroom and propped her foot on the lid of the furry toilet seat. She then placed the tiny folded-over cotton squares strategically between each of her toes as she worked, starting with the paintbrush slightly away from the cuticle and filling in the area next to the skin, then drawing three parallel strokes out toward the front of the nail. Pushing out a small stream of breath over each toe, her plump lips formed what might look to a stranger spying through her window like a prelude to a kiss. The liquid's toxic signature made her queasy, an olfactory alert that went straight to the neural pulses within her brain. Still, she continued brushing.

Was it really worth the trouble—all the filing and painting and primping?

Who knows? But she loved the color.

Envy. What a silly name for a nail polish. It was an emotion she tried not to get too caught up in, although she did sometimes feel it from others. When she completed painting the tenth toe she stretched out her legs and leaned forward to review her handiwork. Maybe one more coat?

Chapter 18: Sunday morning

Neither of them saw it coming.

First two, three, four, then seven “black and whites”—county Sheriff cruisers—sped past bittersweet-tangled oaks on their way down Middle Gate Road, lights flashing, followed by two unmarked Crown Vics packed with detectives. It was a show of force that hadn’t been visited upon the Shinnecock since the massive drug raid several years before that resulted in the arrest of a dozen young men who had been dealing cocaine and heroin out of homes and businesses there. That case involved the coordinated efforts of multiple federal, state and former county agencies and police departments, over one hundred state police officers, mobile response teams and helicopters. The scale of this morning’s raid paled by comparison but these new Peconic County cops weren’t taking any chances. A total of nine cars carrying twenty-one peace officers were sent to bring in one man. The prime suspect in what was now considered a murder and kidnapping investigation: Andre Little.

The detectives, with heavily armed sheriffs as back up, moved in swiftly and quietly to their target, located in a wooded area near the end of Little Shore Road. Two of the patrol cars positioned themselves at forty-five degree angles to block traffic in both directions. Four uniformed men got out and waited by their vehicles in the street. Four more ran stealthily down the flag lot and along both sides of the house in pairs of two to cover the back door. The remaining dozen or so officers fanned out in a V-pattern out front, among them two senior uniformed officers who stood ready, guns drawn, in case the suspect decided to flee. Five of the officers, two plain clothes, stood on the sagging front porch ready to enter the house.

The lead detective knocked on the door.

After a few long seconds of summer quiet, birds chirping, a young woman answered the door in pink bathrobe and koala slippers.

"What!?"

"We're looking for Andre Little. Bring him out or we're going in. *Now*," the lead detective, a man named Quinn, said. Quinn pulled at his goatee. He was wearing a bulletproof vest under his windbreaker, just in case.

The woman looked anxiously past the detective and the other officers and police cars gathered out front.

"You gotta be kidding. *Really*?" She craned her neck toward the back of the house. "Heeeyyyy, Andre!"

"Whassup, Babe? Who the hell is here this early?" a man's voice answered.

The detectives didn't wait. They pushed open the door knocking down the young woman. It was only a few steps to the small kitchen in the back of the house where they reached Andre Little sitting at a small Formica-top table. The five officers drew their guns.

"Don't move and keep your hands on the table!" Quinn yelled out.

There was the suspect, Andre Little, but he wasn't alone. He had a toddler in his lap. All eyes in the room went to the small boy sitting in front of a bowl of Cheerios. His tiny hand holding the spoon. The oaty rings clinging to his milk-soaked chin. The applesauce painting his cherub face and Sponge Bob bib.

The boy lifted his wide-open gaze at the tight cluster of detectives, defiantly thrust out his spoon, and shrieked a single,

"NO!"

Andre Little held the boy close and covered him with his head.

After holstering her gun, one of the female detectives picked up the boy and handed him to the woman, now shaking at the doorway. The three uniformed policemen lifted Andre out of his chair, pulled his thick arms behind his back and placed his wrists into handcuffs. He was still wearing the clothes he had slept in the night before: gray sweatpants cut off below the knee and a baby food-stained T-shirt depicting a rifle toting Indian that read, *My Heroes Killed Cowboys*. Unwilling to give the officers eye contact, Andre stared down at his coffee cup sitting beside the bowl of soggy cereal he'd been sharing with his girlfriend's son.

"C'mon, man. At least let me finish my coffee," he said.

One of the other detectives who led a search of the rest of the house walked in and addressed Quinn.

"All clear," he said.

Detective Quinn mumbled something about an outstanding parole violation and read Andre his rights.

The others moved with the now handcuffed Andre en masse toward the front. Quinn hung back with a female officer to make sure the girlfriend didn't try anything foolish. Once they'd all reached the front door, Andre shouted,

"D'Nize, tell my moms to call our lawyer."

The procedure, from entry to exiting the house with their plus one, took a total of five minutes.

By the time the policemen escorted Andre outside and into one of the unmarked detective cars, a small group of tribal members—mostly older residents—had already gathered at the start of the gravel driveway. A few of them shouted questions at the police.

—"What are you doing down here?"

—"Why don't you leave this man alone? He hasn't done nothin'."

—"You have no right. Do you know where you are?"

—"Where are you taking him?"

But their shouts and questions fell on deaf ears. The full police contingent, their suspect now in custody, left the Reservation much as they had entered, lights flashing, and kicking up clouds of dust and pebbles on their way out to the old Montauk Highway.

Chapter 19: Sunday afternoon

Paul wound his truck through the flow of hard candy-shell luxury SUVs and sun-dappled pedestrians crossing Southampton's Main Street, down Jobs Lane and onto Hill Street west toward the Shinnecock Reservation. This stretch of Hill Street represented the northern border of one of the oldest and wealthiest summer enclaves in the country, Southampton's "estate section." In the past few years, many of the old estates here had been torn down and replaced with something new. And that "something new" was unlike anything seen before on the East End. It wasn't enough any more to keep houses with five, ten or even fifteen thousand square feet for a single family's use a few weeks during the summer season. Paul had seen real estate listings from Jeanine's firm for properties topping out at twenty thousand feet or more featuring twenty-plus bedrooms, Olympic-size pools, children's entertainment centers with skateboard half pipes, petting zoos, movie theaters, golf greens, racket ball courts, eight-car garages with hydraulic lifts, multiple elevators, complete spa facilities and even a discotheque. The motivation behind the building of these colossal summer estates had gone beyond mere desire, beyond ego even. The only explanation, Paul reasoned, came down to the old joke about why a dog licks his balls: *Because he can.* And damned everything else—the village, the neighbors, or the area's natural habitat.

Traffic on Hill Street slowed. Now he was stuck behind drivers rubbernecking to catch a glimpse of people gathered under a multi-speared tent set up for some kind of fundraising event. Everything about the scene gleamed white: the silken tent fabric, the table cloths and linen-backed chairs, the ladies' billowing dresses, the men's trousers; the giveaway bags full of goodies waiting to be carried off. People were standing around drinking from champagne glasses and chatting, the sound of their voices forming an enchanting whisper.

But Paul was in no mood for enchantment. He flipped the Philco dial to the local public radio station to hear some jazz. Instead he got an earful of the theme from *Media Marvels—Special Sunday Edition!,* a show hosted by the silken voiced Ronnie Price. Ronnie moderated a weekly show where editors from the local press came by for a recap of the week's news. And who was her guest this week? Paul turned the volume up.

"We are here with Grace Monahan from the *EET*. You guys've got a big story over there. Tell us about it," he heard Ronnie gush.

Somehow Grace managed to talk a lot and not really say anything in particular. It was all, "the dead girl" this and "the dead girl" that. Without a name for the victim, the moniker had stuck—even among the press. And Grace was careful not to criticize either the local police or the county, even giving them credit for their "ongoing investigation." And, Paul noticed, not once did she mention his name as the reporter who broke the story.

He switched off his radio.

Finally, less than two miles from the center of town, he was riding the Old Montauk Highway, its south side making up the northern border of the Shinnecock Reservation: the Shinnecock Museum, a farmer's market and several trading outposts selling takeout food, tax-free cigarettes, jewelry and other Native paraphernalia. Probably the only place in the Hamptons—or maybe anywhere downstate—where you could drive up to a window and buy a cheap pack of smokes, a pair of mocs, a hot dog extra relish, and a Coke without ever having to get out of your car.

Much of the tribe had worked the land and lived north and east of here, in Shinnecock Hills, out toward the Village, Sagaponack and beyond prior to 1859. It was during that year the Shinnecock were force-marched down from the hills through the neck of the peninsula to the site of their current territory. A result of New York State legislation enabling the Town Proprietors of Southampton to abrogate a thousand year lease negotiated and signed in 1703 in exchange for a deed of land that covered only a fraction of the Shinnecock's original holdings. The only problem was that the Town Proprietors were not the holders of the original lease; they abrogated a lease to which they were not even a party. As a tribal member would later conclude after several failed petitions to the State of New York and testimony before the U.S. Senate Subcommittee on Indian Affairs in the year 1900,

"I guess they stole it fair and square."

The tribe's current land consisted of eight hundred flat, marshy acres along this narrow peninsula—a misshapen arrowhead jutting out into Shinnecock Bay and situated between Southampton's estate section across a narrow channel to the east and the middle class Tuckahoe and Shinnecock Hills neighborhoods to the west and north on the other side of Old Fort Pond. Three separate entrances or "gates" accessible from the old Montauk Highway led visitors onto the Reservation's grounds. These gates, having once been used by local white settlers to keep the Shinnecock *in* under strict curfew, now had notices at their entrances warning unwanted visitors to keep *out*—"No Trespassing" signs that on this occasion Paul found particularly wounding.

After entering the gate, he rode past spare but comfortable-looking homes, with deep lawns separated by broad patches of deciduous trees. Cars—some flashy some not—were parked at the end of long drives, a few work trucks scattered among them. Exposed Tyvek wrap on some of the larger houses reminded him of the tribe's common land ownership: there were no Fannies or Freddies allowed here, no taking advantage of historically low home equity loan rates that helped wreck the rest of the country in the last few years. The only real housing speculators were children and grandchildren who hoped to one day share a piece of their elders' property to build their own house someday.

After driving midway down East Gate Drive toward the first major crossroads, Paul encountered a hopeful sign: Aaron-Achak Prince's Chevy pickup bumpin' old school rap and kicking up clouds of dust in the direction of Cuffee's Beach. As the two men approached each other in their respective pickups, Aaron lowered the music's volume and slowed his vehicle. Paul came to a stop alongside him.

"Hey Aaron, how are your *Oys-chers*?" Paul yelled out across the transom, purposely employing the bastardized pronunciation used by Aaron and his crew to make fun of outsiders.

"Ha! Hey Mr. Reporter! You know me, still doing the chunkoo dance, still trying to learn all the steps. But since we spoke I believe we found the sweet water off of Cuffee's. It's all about *terroir*, my friend. We'll be finishing our biggest spring harvest over the next few weeks."

Ter-wa? Maybe aquaculture required more sophistication than Paul originally thought.

"Sounds great! You'll have to save me a couple." Paul said.

"Hold on a sec." Aaron's right hand disappeared into a white bucket resting next to him on the front seat, pulled out an adult oyster—*Crassostrea Virginica*—from the cold water and in one effortless motion pried open the hinge with his favorite wooden-handled oyster knife, cut the adductor muscle to open the shell and then slipped the knife underneath the oyster to further cut the muscle and loosen the tender meat from the cupped bottom shell. He then passed the pulpy treat to Paul through his open window.

"Wow, thanks!" Paul carefully accepted the gift, making sure not to spill its precious contents. He slurped the briny liquid and knocked back the oyster whole. "Hey, that doesn't even need sauce. It's perfect the way it is."

"I like it with a little lemon. Sorry I didn't have one for you on the truck," Aaron said behind a big laugh.

"You got a name for these yet?" Paul asked, knowing that a trademarked oyster could mean significant money for the tribe once it became popular.

"Not yet. Let's just call them 'Real Local Oysters,' Aaron said. "So what brings you out here on this beautiful day, surely not to talk about oysters?"

"I'm here to visit someone. Merika Jones."

"Oh, Nakoowa Kekutoo? Sweet girl. I guess you heard what happened this morning," Aaron said.

"Aaron, to be honest, I'm not sure I know what's happening. But I thought I'd talk to Merika and see," Paul said.

"You can probably find her at the rec center or the pre-school. I saw her down there with a bunch of the kids earlier. Hey, I gotta go take this crew back out," Aaron said referring to the two guys sitting quietly in the bed of his pickup truck among the jumble of cages, nets and floats. Paul hadn't even noticed the other men until Aaron had pointed them out.

"Good to see you again and good luck," Aaron said, and drove off toward the beach to tend to his floating farm out in Shinnecock Bay.

"Great to see you," Paul yelled back, and meant it.

Paul continued toward a cluster of low-slung communal buildings on Church Street, parked in the lot next to the Reservation's white stucco recreation center and made his way toward the entrance. As he approached the front door of the building he heard footsteps coming from behind. Before he could turn around and see who might be following him, he felt a large fist connect with his right ear. His sunglasses flew from his face. His left leg buckled and he fell to the blacktop.

Paul blink-opened his eyes. Everything hurt.

"This is him, right?" a large guy in his twenties wearing baggy jeans, green NY Jets jersey, and baseball cap was saying to a couple of other equally large guys his age.

"Yo, du'e, you know you are on private property, right?" the same guy yelled out as one might to a slightly deaf person. Paul looked up toward the three men who were forming a towering semi-circle over him. The fear that had lodged itself in his gut when he was first hit now coursed through every cell in his body.

"Wassup with this guy? Doesn't he know he's asking to get his ass fucked up by comin' down here?" one of the other men said.

"Du'e, I didn't hit you *that* hard. Look, he ain't movin'," another one said.

"Why did you have to hit him?" a voice sounding like Merika's pulsed in Paul's wounded ear. She moved from behind the men toward him. "Paul, this was a really bad idea. I told you not to contact me."

Paul rubbed his sore right ear, which felt as if it had doubled in size. He rolled slowly onto his back to face the glaring sun. His left shoulder ached, having taken the brunt of the fall to the rolled pavement. Small drops of blood dribbled from his lower lip. He squinted up at Merika but almost didn't recognize her. She was wearing no makeup, a college sweatshirt over jeans. Her hair was tied tight in the back, business-like.

"You said not to call or email you. This is a personal visit. You never said anything about coming in person."

"Whoa! We got ourselves a wise guy," the largest of the men said, raising his fist. He was wearing an XXL black T-shirt, baggy cargo shorts, and a doo rag wrapped tightly around his closely shaved head. His size fourteen-plus Nikes were inches from Paul's own aching noggin. "Do you seriously want me to get all Quentin Tarantino on your ass?"

"Don't let him scare you, Paul. Lucrecious can be very protective but he would never *purposely* hurt anyone—would you Luc?" Merika said.

"Merika, when I got your email I had no idea what you were talking about. At least give me time to explain what it is you thought I did. Just give me five minutes," Paul pleaded. He tried crab-walking his body away from Lucrecious' over-sized shoes.

"The cops came here and arrested my brother Andre early this morning. These are Andre's friends," she said, gesturing to the three large men. "All that stuff I told you about last night. I can't believe you would share that. I really wanted to trust you."

Paul was absorbing this new blow, worse than the one he had just received to his ear. At least now he understood why they felt he deserved to be knocked down after showing up unannounced.

"I did speak to my source in the East Hampton police department this morning. But I definitely didn't tell him any of the things we talked about. Merika, everything you said to me was strictly between us. You have to believe me."

"Then why did the cops think to come here?"

"I don't know but let me make a call and see if I can find out what's going on. I can try to reach my guy in East Hampton who talks to the Peconic cops. He'll explain it."

Paul made a gesture to stand up. The other men offered to help him but he politely waved them off. He took his cell phone out of his pocket and began dialing Tom Cole's number.

Merika and Andre's friends broke out in huge grins.

"What? *What*? No cell service, right?" The four of them were laughing. "Is there a landline we can use?"

Merika led Paul past the rec center to the other side of the Presbyterian Church into a modest, cedar-shingled building the size of a small house. Andre's friends stood guard just outside the door.

"This place is cute," he said.

"Yeah, it used to be our schoolhouse before kids started going to the public schools. This is where I spend most of my time. We do morning preschool, after-school tutoring, weekend activities for the kids. It's too cute. We've been trying to raise funds for a proper building. An early learning center."

She took Paul into a tiny office in the back that barely fit a small metal desk, push button phone, and a chair. A cork bulletin board behind the desk was papered with family photos: shots of kids' smiles with rows of missing baby teeth, a crowd of colorful bridesmaid dresses, a family gathered around a tall Christmas tree, and large groups of people dressed in traditional Indian regalia at an outdoor event. The women and girls in the large group picture, with their simple tan smocks of buckskin and beaded headbands were no match for the men, posed in elaborate layered cloaks of indigo and vermillion decorated with sunbursts, stars and eagles, and medallions of turtle shell and silk, their multi-feathered headdresses rising high above the women's heads.

Merika pushed the telephone toward him.

"Is that one you? That's how you looked the first time I met you and your mother." He was pointing to a big group portrait.

"Yeah, from our Labor Day powwow a bunch of years ago. When I was Miss Teen Shinnecock. That was a year before we first met."

"Miss Shinnecock. Wow. Is that like Miss America—swimsuits and all that?"

"What?"

"Kidding. No, really I'm honored. What does a Miss Shinnecock do?"

"A bunch of stuff. Like performances. At our powwow here and at other tribes. What?"

"Nothing. It's nice to see you."

"This is the Early Childhood director's desk. That's her family there," she said, pointing to another picture.

"Not to take anything away from your boss' family but you look adorable in that other picture."

"Really? I think I look kinda goofy—hey! Paul, stop stalling. Is this guy you're talking about for real or were you just trying to get me alone?" She tried her best to appear annoyed but Paul could detect a slight smile creeping into her voice.

She handed him the receiver and waited with her arms folded for Paul to make the call. He held the earpiece slightly away from his sore left ear and dialed. Once it was ringing, he invited Merika to bring her own ear close to listen in. Despite his nagging physical pain, Paul was excited to have her be this close to him again.

"Tom! Thank God I caught you."

"Who is this?" Cole asked.

"It's Paul Sandis. Tom, sorry to bug you again on a Sunday but I have to ask you about a new development in this dead girl case."

"We're cops. We don't have regular weekends like you guys. What's up?"

"I heard the Peconic police arrested a guy on the Res this morning. Andre Jones—" Merika whispered, "not *Jones*—Andre *Little*" in Paul's other ear to correct him—"huh, Tom, I mean Andre Little. What can you tell me about him?"

"Sandis, I warned you not to get ahead of this and you're already calling me about information that has not been made public yet. You must have some very good sources. Maybe you should come and work for us," Cole said.

"I'm down at the Res in Southampton. The arrest is no secret here."

"Fair enough. Okay, let me check my paperwork." Cole put them on hold.

Paul could feel Merika starting to relax, the trust beginning to flow back to him. They sat on the edge of the desk for a few empty moments, looking straight ahead yet keenly aware of each other's breathing. Although they didn't need to, their bodies—and their ears—remained close together as they listened to a distant-sounding Muzak version of Billy Joel's "New York State of Mind" coming through the phone's little speaker until Cole returned to the line.

"Got it. Hey, this conversation is off the record until the press conference," Cole said.

"What press conference?"

"The one the County is going to have in an hour. You can't share this until after that, got it?"

"Yeah, no problem." Paul held up a finger to his lips as if to say to Merika, *we can't get caught*. "Tom, how come I didn't know about the press conference?"

"Woo's office from Peconic sent out the email announcement earlier today, didn't you get it?"

"I guess not," Paul admitted. *It must have been buried in all those stupid unopened emails.*

Cole read from his report:

"Andre Little. Male, twenty-five years old. Peconic County detectives made the arrest at 8:15 a.m. this morning in Southampton. Being held as a person of interest, blah, blah. Had a girlfriend matching the description of the missing girl found in Wainscott. The girl disappeared a few weeks ago and has yet to be located."

"That's all they got? Missing girlfriend? That can't be enough to hold the guy."

"Paulie, he's got a couple of priors. They're holding him on a technicality, an old parole violation, while they gather more evidence. I guess they think he's a flight risk. Hey, you may remember that case a couple of years back in Montauk. This guy Little messed up his sister's boyfriend pretty good, ended up with a suspended sentence for assault. He and his Res buddies beat up some rich puke. Probably deserved it." Paul threw a quick glance over at Merika. He was now forced to consider how harmless Lucrecious and the rest of Andre's crew might be. Merika closed her eyes and brought her hand up to cover her mouth.

"Anything else?" Paul asked.

Paul looked out through the open door of the small office into the main play area. He could see a large mural on the opposite wall depicting several scenes of Indians harpooning whales from dugout canoes, lighting fires next to small straw huts, and collecting shells on the shoreline. He tried to imagine himself within this tableau and then thought better of it.

Cole said, “Okay, this one is totally off the record until we can confirm. I’m only giving you this because I still owe you one for that Gomes kid, who by the way we have yet to locate. This will not be mentioned at the press conference until we can get confirmation: our guys tell me they have a positive ID on a blue Toyota Tacoma that matches the one that Little drives, seen on the day the dead girl went missing. I got a witness who saw the truck spinning wheels down the beach east of Wainscott around that time but no plate number. The witness—an elderly lady—was so startled, her little Pomeranian almost shit. I hope she had one of our doggie mitts to clean it up. That’s my baby you know, the doggie mitts, had them installed on all the public beaches. Anyway, it’s looking pretty bad for this guy.”

“Where they holding him, in Riverhead?” Paul asked.

“Yeah. At the lockup there. Sandis, don’t you go down there bothering the county guys with this information until after the press conference. I don’t even want to know what led you to the Res but I don’t want any of this to get back to me.”

“No problem. Thanks, Tom.” Paul’s heart sank below his knees for a second time since Spanish eggs. There was not a good feeling in his stomach either.

“Oh, listen Tom, I just want to confirm something: other than the info on that Gomes kid, have I told you anything else about this case? I’m just going over my notes,” Paul said, pretending to flip through his ever-present notepad.

"No. Not that I recall. You got something to share, share it," Cole said.

"Not right now. I'll let you know when I do."

Paul thanked Tom Cole and hung up the receiver. Before he could say anything to Merika, a little girl, looking to be about four years old, skipped over to the two of them. Other children were starting to trickle into the main play area of the building and pick up art supplies from a small table in front.

"Mommy, where did you go? I couldn't find you," the girl said, tugging on the end of Merika's sweatshirt.

"I just went to make a quick phone call, baby. This is my friend Paul. Paul, this is Natasha," Merika said, holding back tears.

"Nice to meet you Natasha," Paul said, and offered his hand to her. Natasha gave him one of those little-kid handshakes; pulling his hand down rapidly and swinging it back up again just as fast and then letting go. She could have been her mother's younger twin but for her eyes. They were much brighter, deep blue-green with flecks of light brown at the edges.

"Honey, go back and play with your friends. I'll be with you in a few minutes," Merika told her.

The girl did as she was told and skipped back to join the other children, flip flops flapping the wood floor, her long braided hair swaying side to side. Merika turned to Paul and said simply,

"I'm sorry."

"It's okay. You guys should go down to Riverhead and see if you can put some pressure on the cops to get him released. Do you have a lawyer?"

"We have a guy who does stuff for us but we haven't been able to reach him. My mom's been trying since this morning."

"Well, maybe you and your mother should go down to Riverhead anyway. See what the cops will share with you," Paul said. He and Merika walked back outside into the sunshine. Andre's friends were in the same spot where they had left them outside the door. It occurred to Paul that it was probably a beautiful day at the beach for someone, one of those perfect-ten days when the sky loses its familiarity with even a passing cumulus cloud.

"You're not going to write anything about Andre are you? I mean after the press conference is over?" Merika asked.

He was hoping he wouldn't get this question.

"I don't want to but I have to. Once they have that press conference everyone else will know about it," Paul said.

"But, everyone is following *your* version of the story. Please Paul. You've got this big audience," she pleaded.

"Merika, I know you don't want to hear it but this is much bigger than either of us at this point. It's going to be a big story that goes a lot further than our little paper's website. There is nothing I can do. If Andre didn't do it, they'll only hold him for a short time and then I'll make sure to update my story immediately."

"*If!!?* Paul, did you say "if" he didn't do it?" She was starting to get hysterical.

"I meant "when!" *When* they figure out he wasn't involved." Paul's head was spinning.

Merika's voice went cold. "Paul, you need to leave now."

Lucrecious, perhaps sensing the abrupt change in Merika's mood added, "Yeah du'e, *one*."

"We out. That means you out," said the Jets jersey, in case Paul hadn't gotten the message.

Lucrecious handed Paul his broken sunglasses. The three large men then escorted him to his truck. He turned to catch a last glimpse of Merika but she had already gone back into the schoolhouse.

With the buildings on Church Street fading in his rearview mirror, Paul looked out his window at the people he passed and they back at him. Some of them offered a smile and a curious wave hello. Others, not so much. Relaxing in lawn chairs, doing yard work, or standing and chatting in front of their homes on a breezy Sunday afternoon, these were people whose lives were not all that different from his own, he thought. People likely familiar with the comfort of disappointment and heartbreak.

~ ~ ~

Ave Maria (5)

She had been told too many times by her aunts and older female cousins that she was "small boned, like a bird" (she took after her mother in that respect). If it were indeed true, why the predilection for powerful, muscled men, their hands too large and clumsy to adequately satisfy her carnal desires? Why not settle for a shy, diaphanous type like so many of those same cousins had done?

But that's the thing; if she followed their advice it would feel like *settling*. And settling wasn't part of her nature. Compromise? Sure, everyone had to do that but it wasn't the same thing. Settling was what other people did who weren't as strong or capable. Settling meant giving up, giving in—*losing* your sense of self. And that was a choice she couldn't bear to make, even if it meant taking on the hurt it took to refuse it.

Chapter 20: Wednesday, Beach Lane – The Lovers

The texts kept coming in all day, sometimes in twos and threes. Like a ghost in the machine.

Unknown: Please come over. It's just me. Come to the cottage
Unknown: Let's talk.
Unknown: Please, I beg you.

Finally, she thumbed a terse response:

Merika: K I'll come.

On the second day of their non-stop lovemaking marathon on the mattress in the living room of that cottage—after she locked herself in the bedroom and made up her mind to give him another chance—Peter told Merika about his decision to go back to law school. He also told her that he loved her. Lots of guys had told her that before but she felt like this time here was a guy who really meant it. She would have done anything to be with him then, to get him to *stay*. And, was she the one who had whispered, while surrendering to that dreamy, nebulous present-state that lovers will tell you feels like a blissful eternity but in retrospect can seem as fleeting as the flicker of an eyelash pressed against their lover's cheek, "it's okay, you can come inside me." After which he had said, "are you sure?" and she had replied that, *yes*, she was sure? Or was it Peter who initiated the exchange? Memory, like love and other entreaties, can be a slippery thing.

The weekend after she saw that little blue plus sign appear she told Peter. He tried to talk her out of having the baby but Merika wouldn't listen. She told him she loved the idea of making a baby, *their* baby. It'll all work out, you'll see, she said.

Then he disappeared.

"How could you not know that the outside world doesn't care about our people, especially our women? We are only trash to them to be used and discarded," her father would tell her. And who was he to talk? Growing up she rarely saw the man who had sired her and her half-siblings even though their lives were circumscribed within the same eight hundred tribal acres. Besides, Peter wasn't like that—he wasn't anything like her father. She and Peter were in love and love was supposed to conquer all things. She actually believed this then.

Months of watching what she ate, watching her belly swell. An at-home birth planned with the tribe's sole midwife. Like her mother and her grandmother before her. The baby, breech. Downward Dog, Merika on her knees. Pushing. Screaming. Crying. The cool feel of a washcloth pressed against her forehead. The warmth of her mother's caresses, her quiet prayers. The bleat of the fetal monitor, in sync with tribal music from an old tape machine. A song she sang her own verses to at "forty-niners," powwows past:

I went down to the water to meet my man /
Oh hay ya away hee ha, oh hay ya away hee /
He said he'd be there to hold my hand /
Oh hay ya away hee

More pushing. And finally, a breakthrough. First, her baby's vernix covered foot. A leg, another leg. The swollen belly. It's a girl!

An attempt to turn her. The room silent but for the bleating of Doppler against drums, out of sync now. The baby stuck. Her sister Aiyhana pointing a flashlight, telling her, "You look like shit, Mer." Her screaming *fuck you!* Her mother's prayers growing more intense. *Sweet Jesus.* More crying, pleading, *Why is this happening? I. Can't. Do. This.* Half her baby, still dangling from her. Mottled skin tinged blue. Her little sister slipping on a pair of surgical gloves. Her slipping into silent prayer:

Half is not enough. God, the Creator. Half is not enough.

Then, a shift in position. Four hands reaching, turning, pulling. *Working.* A bigger, more miraculous turn. Her daughter falling through her, through the ether, through the ages. And then gently onto the soft blanket. A tiny, muffled cry and her baby—her baby!—attached to her waiting breast. A mother crying, then two. Her sister screaming, "woot, woot." The heady scent of burning sage. Of smoke. Of *life.*

Wuniish. May it be beautiful for you.

Wuniish, Nasháne. My in-between spirit.

She was still angry and hurt, sure, less raw after all those years but still not ready to open old wounds. What could he say to her that would make any difference now? Was she afraid of owning up to her role, of admitting to something she still hadn't fully admitted to herself? And what about Natasha? There was no way she would take her daughter to see him. Whenever Peter's name would come up—and Merika made sure that it rarely did—it was shooed away like an errant bird that slipped into the house. But she never stopped thinking about him or what her life might have been like had he stayed. And deep down she felt like she owed him something—if not an explanation then maybe the slightest amount of her attention. So she went. But she wasn't going to mention her plans to anyone. Merika would tell her mother that she was going to visit an old college friend in the city, that way she could return home late and be sure that Natasha was cared for.

Despite it being almost five years since her last visit, the guard at the gate, Alejandro, recognized her immediately. *Good old loyal Alejandro.* Seeing him reminded her how much time she had spent in Georgica that summer, how much of her she had left behind in that cottage that was never really hers.

She called out to him, "You finish that book yet?"

He smiled, deep lines collecting around his tired eyes.

Evidently he had no clue she wasn't to be allowed in. That the Drakens had taken an order of protection out on her and Andre since the beating. That she was persona non grata beyond this invisible line that separated the rarified world from, well, another part of the rarified world. Both of those parts having once belonged to her and her people. Alejandro simply waved her in like the guy at the Southampton Recycling Center who sits in the little booth. *Just dropping off the trash, Alejandro.* Maybe her father was right after all.

"Hey," he said as she walked through the door, as if time and his prolonged silence hadn't carved an insuperable chasm between them.

He looked too good. His bleached blue eyes, still clear and intense. His sandy hair, worn just long enough to make him appear anti-establishment. She had secretly hoped he had been scarred in some way, half a face ravaged by fire maybe. A leg lost in some gruesome accident. Not as revenge for what he'd done but a reasonable enough excuse for pulling away from her, for disappearing when she needed him most.

Despite the early evening sunlight illuminating its interior spaces—magic hour golds and purples—the cottage seemed smaller and shabbier than she remembered. She moved over to the sofa and sat down, keeping her body rod-straight, evening out the folds of her dress with her outstretched fingers. The old piano was still there. But the guitars, the drums, the other musical equipment on which they both played that summer—all of it gone—and giving the place an even lonelier vibe than it warranted.

Finally, after what seemed like several seconds of silence, she spoke his name.

"Peter."

"I'm sorry, Duchess," he said.

The stiffness of her body ensured that he not attempt a move toward the sofa. She narrowed her eyes at him.

"Okay, okay. *Merika.* Let me start from the beginning," he tried again. "After that weekend when we last spoke I went home and told my grandfather about your plans to have the baby. I guess I don't have to tell you he was incredibly upset. It was almost funny in a way. All that summer he and my grandmother were so concerned I'd do something to the cottage—host wild parties and break up the place or have my grandmother's precious antiques stolen—you would think it'd be a relief that it was only a baby we were talking about."

"Peter—"

"—I know. I'm sorry. I'm sorry." He repeated this several times, pushing the flat of his right palm against his forehead. "I tried to convince them this wasn't your fault but they wouldn't listen. God knows they blamed me too. You don't understand. My family is used to getting their way. My grandfather said, 'In my day, we had ways of taking care of this,' meaning the family would just pay the doctor, a family friend. He wasn't prepared for having your people get involved. He threatened to cut me off completely if I tried to contact you."

"My people? You are so full of shit, Peter. You were twenty-three. You could have told them to go to hell if you really cared about me or what I was going through."

"Peter got a girl knocked up. But not some rebellious WASP or a nice Jewish girl whose got her gynecologist on speed-dial. No, Peter had to get a dark-skinned girl from the Res knocked up. This is the stuff they were saying."

"So this is your way of getting me to like your family? You still could have called me or emailed me, even if it was to say 'fuck off.' That would have been better than what you did."

"I was ashamed of everything. My behavior, my family's, of leaving you like that. Too much time had passed. I didn't even know how to approach you."

"Uh huh. And what about now?"

"Enough time has passed that I thought you might be able to forgive me. Please."

Peter moved toward Merika but she put her hand up and refused to look at him.

"I should have known just looking at these paintings that I didn't belong in this house," she said, referring to the water-stained duck portraits and cheerless landscapes. "It was like your family's ghosts were watching us the whole time."

"What? The cottage?" He let out a nervous laugh. "My family's never stayed here. This is where the staff stayed."

In all their time together Merika never saw anyone except the maintenance crew set foot in the big oceanfront house, let alone the cottage.

"Oh." She suddenly felt out of sorts, the once familiar room strange, otherworldly. "So why are we here? Now?"

"I wanted to see my daughter. I was hoping you would bring her."

"Whoa, *your* daughter? You want to see *your* daughter?"

Rallying, she pulled out her mobile from her purse to show him pictures, brandishing an initial image of Natasha like a weapon.

He stared at his daughter' face, an unmistakable composite: Merika's broad cheekbones and full lips, her unruly hair, his dimpled smile and light eyes.

"That's all you get," she said after a few more pictures. She put her phone away.

"She's beautiful."

"You don't have to tell me."

"Look, I know I deserved everything. And I don't blame Andre for what he and his friends did that night. But you have to believe me when I say I miss Natasha. I can't stop thinking about her. That's why I had to see you."

Up until now coming here seemed like a cruel game, as if she and Peter were arguing sides on behalf of their long past, forgotten selves. But hearing him say her daughter's name shocked her into the very real present.

"You're not going to see her, if that's what this is about. And, I don't even understand what you're saying. You can't miss someone who was never yours."

"Then at least let me give her some money. I should be getting money from my grandmother's estate soon. Very soon in fact."

"Sure, that will solve everything. And, yeah we could use some money. But she won't be told it's from you."

They talked like this for the next several hours, Peter pacing the living room while Merika sat on the dowdy flower-patterned sofa where they shared their first kiss. Every once in a while he would walk over to the window and peer at the view of the jetty where he fell that first night.

One of those times, apropos of nothing, and talking to himself more than Merika, he said, "You could do that back then. If you had enough money and influence you could control nature. My great grandfather had those giant boulders dumped out there as protection. As if the rocks would be able to absorb anything terrible the waves might toss at us."

When she cried, he tried to comfort her. But she wouldn't allow Peter to touch her; she receded from him each time he drew close. Part of her needed that comfort, to allow him in again. She could see he was in pain. But if she let him she was afraid she'd have to admit to *wanting* to get pregnant that summer, to wanting something better than maybe she deserved, to feeling that what they were doing back then was more than just sex between two people who had no business being together.

Merika managed to keep Peter at arm's length throughout the night and early morning until he stumbled into one of the bedrooms and fell asleep. Even after he was out she was too on-edge to put her head down. With the darkness of early morning still pressing against the windows, she kept herself busy by taking inventory of everything they'd done, said, hadn't done or hadn't said in that cottage five summers before. Back when her life was just beginning and it still felt like they belonged only to each other and this place.

After checking in on Peter to make sure he was still asleep, she removed the small scrimshaw box from her purse, returned it to its place on the end table and waited for the sun to come up. Soon she found herself slipping in and out of consciousness, her carefully compiled inventory of past events morphing into a flotsam of conversational fragments, slights and promises of what may or may not have occurred that summer, spooling in her head like a strange Zapruder film of their broken relationship.

A few hours later she went into the kitchen to make some coffee. She happened to be looking out the window—at the same view that so obsessed Peter only hours before—and saw what had to be Andre's truck parked on the beach behind a tall pile of sand. *How could he know I came here last night? Did he follow me?* Reflexively, she moved away from the window even though there was no way anyone could see her from such a great distance. When she dared to return to the window a few moments later she saw two figures wrapping something large in a blanket and lifting it from the rocks. Bending low, the figures carried this burden purposefully along the jetty to their truck. She then watched as they placed it in the back and drove away. The movements of those distant forms filled her with a foreboding as deep as the ocean that lay just beyond her view. She decided then that she had to leave the cottage. She stopped for a few minutes at the gate to say a final goodbye to Alejandro. And as she was driving out of the Georgica Association she noticed two police cars, lights flashing, turning onto Beach Lane and heading toward the beach.

When she got to the parking lot she was relieved to find no sign of Andre or his truck. Several county cops soon pulled up in black and white cars marked "Sherriff" and began what looked to be a search along the beach. There was someone else there too. An almost-handsome guy who had arrived immediately after, a reporter who had written a profile of her mother several years before who said he remembered her. It was good to see a friendly face.

The reporter, a guy named Paul, described to her what the cop had said over his police radio, about finding a dead girl on the jetty. She wouldn't allow herself to even consider who the girl might be or how she had gotten there. And why had he told her this? Weren't reporters supposed to keep that kind of information to themselves? But she was even more surprised at what she had revealed to him: "Love is so fragile." Why would she say that? Sure, she was tired from not having slept, emotionally exhausted, but what would cause her to reveal her feelings like that to this man she barely knew? He must have thought she was crazy. And yet, when he heard her say it, he didn't treat her like she was crazy, in fact quite the opposite.

"I know," he said, but in a way that made her believe he truly did.

"Don't go," she told him. And so he stayed—for a while at least.

Soon after Paul left, she saw what appeared to be a young local cop in a blue windbreaker talking with county police. Clifford, she guessed. The one the detective mentioned on his call. The young cop was visibly upset, on the verge of tears. He was explaining something to the other officers and pointing in the direction of the beach. Then, as Clifford was being put into the back of an unmarked county cruiser, he glanced over at her and their eyes locked for one intense moment. It was a look she could only interpret as a cry for help, as if the two of them were now in possession of a terrible secret. Then he lowered his head and the door of the cruiser closed behind him.

Chapter 21: Sunday afternoon

On a glorious East Hampton Sunday afternoon, Father Edward de la Rosa stood at the pulpit of St. Cecilia's below the church's circular stained glass window, spectacular streams of early summer sunlight filtering through the outlines of the cross and single white dove emerging from a five-pointed star, and told the story of St. Margaret Mary Alacoque.

"Margaret Mary all those years ago would experience '*una gran aparación*,' Edward told his congregation. "While she had many visions throughout her life, this apparition came during the octave of the Feast of Corpus Christi, a celebration of the body of Christ. Jesus appeared to the young nun and asked her to ensure that a new feast be celebrated on that day to recognize the sacrifice He had made for all of mankind.

"Now here is the tricky part," Edward said. "Christ himself, or at least a vision of him, was asking that his heart be celebrated, which, on the face of it, sounds like He's being a bit self-centered."

Where is she? Rachel would have smiled at that line.

In a dramatic gesture, Edward raised his left hand toward the pentagram in the window above his head.

"But what He was asking was that the feast, which in past traditions celebrated the *physical* heart of Jesus tied to the Five Wounds of Christ, would now celebrate His Sacred Heart as a *symbol*—a profound symbol of the love He has for everyone who would deem to accept it."

How could she not show up—today of all days?

"The lesson we take from this story is that it is okay to ask for things—even Jesus did this sometimes—if what you are asking for is in some way tied to your love of God. Free yourself of petty desires for material things and sordid temptations of the flesh and instead ask how you can find love in Jesus. Now let us pray." Amen.

She must have been too scared to come.

"Dominus Vobiscum," Edward repeated at the conclusion of the late afternoon Mass as his parishioners filed out of the white clapboard church.

"Et cum spiritu tuo," they each answered in turn.

Edward both loved and often regretted this part of the service, its bittersweet conclusion, as he blessed his flock with the Latin, "Go with God." Of course he was glad to see the joyous faces of his parishioners and felt secure in the knowledge that each of them had, perhaps to varying degrees, found some solace during the brief hour he got to spend with them in God's church. But there was always something that would gnaw at him, some aspect of his performance as a spiritual leader that would lead him to question his abilities once he was alone again, tucked away in his tiny office retreat in the adjoining rectory. His regrets taking the form of one or more of the following admissions: *I wasn't clear enough. I didn't love enough. I failed to demonstrate Christ's love enough.* And, this week in particular, he might have added: *I wasn't persuasive enough.*

It had been a particularly trying few days. Since the pictures of the missing girl had been posted online the day before, much of his Spanish-speaking congregation was abuzz.

—"Who is she?"

—"Do we know her? She looks like Benny's niece, whatshername, Nilda, you know the pretty one from up-island."

—"Did you see that halo around her head in the picture? Just like the Blessed Virgin!"

—"¡Dios mío! Who would do something like this to such a beautiful young woman?"

Indeed, it was this last question in particular that was being asked over and over again by many of Edward's Latino parishioners in the past two days. And he could tell by the tone they employed in the asking that the question was more than a predictable human response, more than a plea to God to help them better comprehend this tragedy. For there was a shared understanding lying beneath its surface, as though they were also looking to Edward to acknowledge—or perhaps even assuage—one of their worst fears: that whoever did this was someone outside of their community. Perhaps someone who might harbor ill will against them. He was thinking about this and what he could possibly do about it as he stared at the small painting of the Sacred Heart hanging in his office—the only personal item he had brought with him three years before from his parish in the South Bronx.

Three years, and he was still in the storage closet. Next to the stacks of pink copy paper for announcing church events, the ink cartridges, the 40-gallon Super-Flex trash liners, the votive candles. How could the parishioners who came to visit there think of him as anything but a failure? Second rate? Staring at the impervious gray metal shelves behind his desk, the workplace safety posters tacked over water-stained plaster? When he arrived on the East End to serve the increasing number of Spanish-speaking Catholics in the area he was promised these accommodations would only be temporary. Only a year they said. Then he would be moving into a new office in a new church, they said.

The diocese had the plans, the public support, and importantly, they already had the land. A small parcel in Sagaponack North purchased on the cheap, located in a mostly wooded area far enough from the beach and near enough to the airport and its incessant helicopter noise.

But it was becoming increasingly evident that there wasn't going to be a new church anytime soon, if ever. He would have to continue to hold his Spanish language services at odd hours of the day in deference to his fellow priest with whom he shared the pulpit. In fact, he'd be lucky to keep his little office in the storage closet.

"But we all have to carry on, don't we? God wishes it so," his bishop said after breaking the latest news to him. "And we will say nothing of this to the congregation."

"Yes. Yes, that's what we do. It is God's wish," Edward replied.

But this new crisis regarding the dead girl was beyond anything he'd ever faced. In fact, it was the first time he was having trouble deciding what God wished of him. And this time he couldn't count on having Rachel by his side to help him.

Was his obsession with Rachel unhealthy? Lustful even? She was married, after all. Part of a sacred bond. Yet he still blushed whenever she dropped the *Padre* and called him by his first name. *Edward*, she'd say, as easy as all that, oblivious to the effect it had on him. At the pulpit he would look out into the crowd for her expectantly for any changes of expression, anything that would give him a clue. Was she really listening? Was she *feeling* the same things?

When they were together he tried to control the urge to tell her everything about himself, yet she shared almost nothing.

This is what he knew:

She was born and raised in a small Mayan village in southern Guatemala at a time when the country was going through an intense civil war, a war that would take most of her family, including both her parents and her sister by the time she was twenty one. On the verge of giving up hope for any kind of meaningful future, she managed to flee her village with the help of a rebel army soldier and found a job in a Mexican hospital that was looking for skilled midwives. In Mexico she would eventually meet and marry her husband Miguel. When Miguel's cousin asked if he could help him with his home repair business on eastern Long Island, the young couple managed to find one of the few honest *coyotes* to get them safe passage over the border into the U.S. Soon after, she bore him two daughters. The family had been living on the East End ever since.

She was reticent about sharing details of her time in war-torn Guatemala especially, even downplaying their importance, as if the circumstances surrounding the loss of her family were merely part of the price of growing up.

"*Yo no hice mi pasado*"— "I didn't make my past," she would say and leave it at that.

"Quizás nuestro pasado nos hace," Edward would reply— "Perhaps it is our past that makes us." To which she would simply shake her head.

Someone who'd suffered and lost so much could have simply buried herself in her grief. But Rachel chose a different path: she decided to fight instead. And she saved most of this rebellious energy for causes she considered *una injusticia social*. She was trouble, and although everything he knew that was right told him to beware, he couldn't control his desperate desire to please her.

The last time he recalled Rachel making trouble for him was the year before—the summer of the anti-immigrant rallies. And one tense week for his congregation in particular. There'd been a scuffle between white protestors and Latino workers at one of those protests that sent a parishioner to the hospital. Sure enough, there was Rachel at the door of Edward's little office, broadcasting her earthy essence like a rare flower and setting him into a fit of nerves. She looked more beautiful to him than ever in her acid washed jeans and prim buttoned up blouse, her hair tied tight in a neat ponytail. Her fierce, determined expression.

"First they won't give us our own church and now this," she said. She threw down a copy of the *EET* onto his desk. An article about the recent clash at the train station was splashed across its front page with the headline, "Protestors Say 'Immigrants Out!'"

"One has nothing to do with the other," Edward said.

"Having our own church means respect in the community. *Acceptance.* We were promised last year. And the year before that. The archdiocese has got to have the money. The bishop's ring alone is worth—I mean, it's going to be a beautiful little church right?"

"Rachel, believe me, I am as upset as you are about the new church," Edward sighed. He stared at one of the work safety posters hanging behind her, a cartoon ladder with the words *Take your next step with care* running up the side. "But this situation at the train station—I've given it some thought. I'll go over there today and see what I can do. I'll be heading out there around noontime after I finish some things here."

"Will you, Father? Then I'll go too." She approached his desk until she was standing close, breaking the formal distance expected between parishioner and priest.

"That's probably not a good idea. It'll be too dangerous." There was no way he could allow Rachel to come. Besides, like some of the workers who congregated there, she had questionable legal status herself.

He had to admit; the idea of having her there excited him.

"No, of course. I understand," she said. She then left abruptly to another part of the church to talk with some volunteers.

When she was gone, Edward let go a long breath.

Was that a 'no' you're right, I shouldn't come or a 'no' I understand your concern but I'll be there anyway?

He didn't ask.

When Edward arrived at the East Hampton station sometime before noon he encountered half a dozen protesters there, huddled together carrying large signs on wooden sticks that read "Don't take our jobs!," "Stop the invasion!," "Illegals are criminals!," and "If it's brown, flush it down." Four Latino workers were positioned, as usual, on their own side of the split rail fence waiting. These laborers would sit there, sometimes all morning and afternoon in all kinds of weather, wearing their hoodies, Carhart jackets and baseball caps like so many birds on a wire holding on for the chance to earn some spending money and a little left over to send to their families back in Mexico, Guatemala, Panama, Honduras, Costa Rica, Ecuador, Columbia.

A lone policeman was stationed a few feet from the action toward the street, rocking back and forth on his heels and looking bored.

Rachel, of course had showed up early, and had positioned herself on a bench near the bus stop pretending to read a magazine.

Throughout the weeks of protest, community and church volunteers had been making sandwiches and bringing them to the train station to feed the day laborers. To show his support and help ease tensions between the groups, Edward had a divine inspiration: wasn't the Bible full of missionaries sent by God to talk to people who weren't exactly open to what they had to say? He decided to take his cue from Jesus himself. Why not feed the poor—in this case those with a deficit in judgment? They suffered from a sickness, Edward believed, a sickness brought about by ignorance and fear. And he was confident he could provide the cure.

Edward greeted the workers outside the fence, and then quickly moved into the waiting area where he began handing out sandwiches to the protesters. They initially showed surprise. A few even smiled as he made the rounds and asked them their preference for P&J or Turkey. His parishioners, the day laborers, also seemed especially pleased, acting confused at first but then laughing and carrying on once they'd received their sandwiches and had unwrapped them.

Then things got complicated.

A couple of the younger protesters, men barely out of their teens, accused the priest of trying to poison them and threw their sandwiches in the trash. One of them demanded to see his birth certificate. Edward could have explained that he was a third-generation New Yorker, born and bred in the Bronx, but decided instead that he could reach the protestors more effectively by asking them to join him in impromptu sermons and prayers celebrating the teachings of Christ. But before he could open his mouth to speak, first one, then a few, then all seven of them were chanting,

Go home, go home, go home to where you came from.

As the chants grew in intensity, a tall protestor of about nineteen or twenty with a blaze of red curls and muscled sunburned arms strode over, his broad mouth arranged in a devilish smirk. The youth seemed to be particularly interested in the cross around Edward's neck and reached out his hand to touch it. The chanting continued, increasing in volume.

Go home, go home, go home to where you came from.

The copper-headed youth let go an eerie chuckle. "Forgive me Father for I am about to sin," he said.

Reeking of alcohol, he placed the palm of his freckled hand on Edward's chest, pressing into the large wooden cross. Then he gave Edward a hard shove.

Go home, go home, go home to where you came from.

The young man's friend, another boy his age, unbeknownst to Edward was positioned immediately behind him on all fours. Before losing his balance, Edward flashed on a small scar above the boy's right eye and a colorless brow blending with pink skin. He sailed backwards over the squatting youth, elbows and wrists breaking his fall against the hard pavement. The bible he had been carrying went scattering across the waiting area, pages fluttering in the breeze. Although he had only traveled a few feet, in that moment Edward felt as if he was falling into a deep abyss, backwards through time. To his childhood in Hunts Point and the playground macadam where bullies would single him out for some form of cruelty.

"Eduardo the Retardo. Get up!" the boys called out as they extended a hand and pushed him down again.

"Yo, *de la Regla*," taunted the Spanish-speaking kids, using slang for a woman's menstrual cycle, *"¿dónde está tu mami?"*

There was some awkward laughter from the other protesters, but soon the crowd fell silent. They looked down on Edward, who was now clutching his elbow in apparent pain. Meanwhile, the single cop on duty had his head turned and missed everything; he was busy biting into his second peanut butter sandwich and checking out three teenage girls in skimpy bathing suits loitering in front of the upscale market across the street.

The four Latino workers quickly came to Edward's aid, helping him up off of the ground and handing him his bible. Aside from a few bruises on his left hand and wrist and an abraded elbow that still stung, he was okay. The group of protesters continued to stand there and stare vacantly, unsure of what to do next.

Then the youth who had pushed him made the first move.

He put down his sign, yelled out "Let's bounce!" to his friend, and the two of them beat a retreat to a pickup truck parked at the north end of Railroad Avenue.

Having apparently scared away the most volatile of the bunch, Edward faced the remaining protesters.

For Edward, this odd series of events represented a turning point, one of those unexpected hinges in the course of everyday events he had often read about but had yet to experience. *God has made his presence known here today,* he was convinced. And he was especially glad Rachel had been there to see it.

Rather than leave now with his dignity still very much intact, he dusted himself off and jumped headlong into this opportunity he was sure God had handed him.

"Now, where was I?" he said, addressing the assembled with renewed vigor and opening his bible. The remaining protesters lowered their signs. Edward read this as a different kind of sign.

And so he continued on, first with a quote from the prophet Paul of Tarsus from Corinthians :12 and :13. Then, the lesson laid out in Mark 10:30 10:31 with its origins in the Old Testament—the verse Edward had referenced earlier in the day to try to convince Rachel to show mercy on the protesters:

And you shall love the Lord your God with all your heart, with all your soul, with all your mind, and with all your strength. This is the first commandment. You shall love your neighbor as yourself. There is no other commandment greater than these.

They seemed to really be listening.

To further elucidate the meaning of *neighbor* he recounted the parable of the Good Samaritan, from *Luke* 10:25, an attempt to get the protesters to "show mercy" on those who might be different from them just as the Good Samaritan had done.

Once convinced he had effectively made his case, Edward thanked everyone and left with a promise to return the next day. The protesters soon put down their signs and dug into the remaining food he had left them.

On his way back to his car he caught sight of Rachel at the bus stop and approached her excitedly.

"You came! We are making progress," Edward beamed. His expression changed when he noticed Rachel's look of concern. She appeared visibly shaken, as if she had just seen the dead walking past.

"I almost ran over to help you, Father. But I couldn't. Something kept me. I was like a statue. I couldn't move," she said.

"It's alright, Rachel. I understand," Edward said, placing his hand on her shoulder.

"I know but ... it was foolish of me to come. I thought I had become immune to that kind of hatred but I guess I was wrong. Are you all right, Edward? You hit the pavement pretty hard." She reached out and touched his elbow, rubbing it gently.

Edward.

"I'll be okay. Try not to judge them too harshly," he said.

"I'm still not convinced you were getting through to them but at least you tried. That's something," she said, brightening.

Just then, one of the paper wrappers from the sandwiches he brought blew in their direction. Edward picked it up to take it to the trash. Before dropping it into the bin, he noticed some handwritten words in Spanish on the inside of the wrapper.

"What's this?" he said. "Holy Mother! I didn't see this before."

"What's it say?"

"It looks like, *'para los idiotas'* (for the idiots). The workers watched me hand these out!"

"Now, who do you think would have done something like that?" Rachel said.

After two weeks visiting the train station on a daily basis that summer, his methods either had a profound impact on the protestors or they just got tired of the opposition fighting back with unfair weapons like love and kindness. Whatever the case, the protestors would soon move on once it became clear that the town wasn't going to do anything about the workers gathering there. St. Cecilia was rewarded for his efforts in the form of sizable donations from contractors and other anonymous contributors. Edward felt buoyed by the success of his first real test of community activism. But he had also made enemies along the way, some who might view the defeat as justification for hardening their stance.

It was the potential for reprisal by these unspoken enemies that was weighing heavily on Edward's mind and the minds of his parishioners as they were filing out of the church on that beautiful Sunday during the celebration of the Sacred Heart of Jesus. There were renewed suspicions of more attacks that summer. Including a man from Hampton Bays who was jumped and beaten while walking down the street. However, Edward wasn't willing to surrender to his own worst suspicions, as had others within his congregation, about who might be responsible for the death of the young Latina found on the beach that day.

As it would turn out, these enemies would soon find ways of making their protests known that he hadn't anticipated.

Chapter 22: Sunday night

"Isaak, admit it; the reason you invite us to these silly dinner parties of yours is because we add some desperately needed glamour to the proceedings."

This was Isaak's friend, Russell Thorpe, owner of a small local art gallery who, accompanied by his latest boyfriend Philip, was sitting in Isaak's dining room along with a few other invited guests at one of Isaak's regular Sunday evening dinner parties in Sag Harbor.

The mood at Isaak's dinner party was unusually festive, especially given the hot topic of most of the evening's conversation: the dead girl.

"I prefer to think that I am providing a true public service," Isaak said to Russell. "You two attend too many fabulous parties out here. By coming to my house I'm helping bust a stereotype."

"But we love the stereotype, dear Isaak. Actually, these days we're happy to be invited anywhere—no offense. The crowds keep getting younger and younger at those *other* parties. Thank God I have Philip to bring along."

"Well, I am honored to have you two just the same," Isaak said.

"Why are we talking about us? We should be talking about this dead girl story. I don't know about you but I can't get enough of it," Philip said.

Also seated inside the cramped but tidy mid-19th century whaler's cottage were Isaak's friends the artist Laszlo Lowe, Priscilla Field, a writer and poet, and Isaak's current lady friend Masha Bernstein, a Russian-born professor of women's studies who, like Isaak, taught at Brooklyn College and had a summer house in nearby North Haven.

In honor of Laszlo's new work—sculpture created with non-traditional materials culled from local sources: rotting produce, duck feathers, honey, beeswax—Isaak promised to serve everyone dishes consisting only of local ingredients. The group had already made their way through the sautéed lemon sea scallop and pea shoot appetizer and were nibbling on bits of Mecox cheddar cheese and sipping a dry Pinot Grigio from the nearby Channing Daughters Winery. George Moustaki, the French folk singer, could be heard emoting his way through "Ma Liberte" on Isaak's ancient record player (Moustaki wasn't local but he was one of Isaak's favorite's—and hailed from Corfu, Isaak's birthplace).

"Laszlo had an interesting observation about the missing girl, what were you saying Laszlo? Paul should really hear this. He's coming by later and should be able to give us an update," Isaak said.

Laszlo began, "At first I thought that maybe this missing dead girl was a hoax or even some kind of artistic hybrid: earthwork (out of Laszlo's mouth it came out sounding like *erth-verk)* plus performance, sort of like Smithson's *Spiral Jetty,* except instead of the jetty disappearing, the girl disappears—which means she should be turning up again the next time the tide goes out."

"Please. More matter and less art," Russell said, rolling his eyes at his friend's preposterous suggestion.

Laszlo, unperturbed, continued, "But now I'm convinced the dead girl is something less: a manifestation of every young girl's desire to be openly sexual without thinking through the consequences. The flimsy dress, the tattoo. It's all a result of the culture of self-expression that we started back in the sixties. But back then it was part of a larger cultural movement; there was something behind it, yes? Now it has no meaning beyond pure titillation. Girls barely out of adolescence bumping and grinding in front of millions and for what? I wouldn't be surprised if this girl put an ad on one of those Internet sites selling her wares and something went haywire (hay-*vire*)."

"Although I see this from a *much younger* perspective," Philip strained to point out, "I have to say that I'm with Laszlo on this. Her look is atrocious—God that dress! And, you can tell whoever took those pictures did not style her well," he said.

"You can't make assumptions about her sexuality just because she wears a tattoo. It's her right to mark her body just as it is any man's right. But as soon as a woman displays any aspects of her sexuality you assume she is a whore," Masha said. "It's been a long time since a tattoo on a woman was enough to put her in the whorehouse—or the circus," she added.

Philip pushed up the sleeve of his fitted polo shirt to expose a tattoo stitched over his muscled bicep. A series of Kandinsky-like concentric circles in repeating patterns and colors. "I designed it myself," he said. "Wearable art."

"Point for or against?" Russell teased, in reference to the tattoo's association with whoredom.

"It's no wonder the Muslims think we're all a bunch of Sodomites," Laszlo continued, not paying attention to the younger artist. "Bring back the hijab I say! And, all of this social media business is so antisocial, yes? At least when I was younger and had my first prostitute I knew her name, I knew where she lived. I was able to meet her mother, a lovely woman by the way. She cooked an incredible Puttanesca."

"My dear Laszlo, only you could mention the Muslim veil and reminisce about a whore in the same breath, but you raise an excellent point," Priscilla chimed in. Aside from a recent reissue of an anthology of her early poems, Priscilla had not had any of her work published in years and was unusually circumspect whenever asked what she was currently working on. Priscilla and Isaak had been lovers at one point in years past but had settled into a kind of begrudging friendship. And, although neither of the two women would own up to it, she and Masha had a bit of a rivalry going ever since Masha had taken up with Isaak.

Priscilla continued, "I think this really tells you something about the decimation of the family and community in this country—a breakdown of society and its natural bonds. Where is her mother? Why hasn't her family come forward? She has to be someone's daughter, someone's sister. A mother is crying out in the night and there is only silence and despair." On emphasizing this last point, Priscilla nearly toppled her glass and had to grab hold of its stem to steady it.

Masha stared with disapproval at the bowed crimson imprint left by Priscilla's lip-gloss around the glass' rim.

"God, Priscilla you can be so maudlin," Masha said. "Obviously, she is a victim—excuse me, I know you abhor that word Isaak—a victim of a brutal, male-dominated society that doesn't know how to treat its most precious things. And there is no question that the girl is beautiful. Some man must have felt so threatened by her beauty he felt she had to be destroyed."

"Don't you get any ideas," Philip said as an aside to Russell, his much older lover, who feigned a spit-take as he was taking a sip of his wine.

"That sounds like a romantic notion right out of a Greek tragedy! And, you thought I was being maudlin," Priscilla said.

Masha ignored her, continuing her conversation with Lazlo.

"Laszlo, why do you assume that every young girl who is unattainable is a slut?"

"Now, Masha, let's not get personal. Who says she is unattainable? She looks pretty attainable to me and now, with these pictures, she belongs to everybody," Laszlo said. "And, by the way, why does it have to be a man who is involved? Maybe she killed herself because she couldn't get on one of those reality TV shows. Maybe she was killed by a jealous wife or girlfriend–this has happened before on Long Island, you know. Or maybe she was killed by her own girlfriend, *Girlfriend.* Don't underestimate the power of female rage, yes?"

Priscilla jumped in again. "Laszlo, now *you're* getting into romantic tragedy territory. Isaak, wasn't it the virgin goddess Athena who turned her gal pal Medusa into a snake-haired ogre as punishment for having sex with Poseidon? I'm seeing a whole new side of you, Laszlo," She refilled her lipstick-stained glass and took another sip of her wine.

"But this isn't about gods and mythology. Here on earth, female power is dependent on male acceptance," Masha interjected. "It's not a coincidence that to be a popular female politician in this country she also has to be a babe. She's got to be a cougar or whatever to have mass appeal."

"Hold on, aren't *all* politicians whores? I don't think it matters if they are men or women," Laszlo said, picking up on an earlier thread and biting into his umpteenth cheese and cracker.

"I think we can all agree on that," Priscilla said.

"Absolutely," Russell agreed.

"Laszlo, I'm proud of you. That's the least sexist thing you've said all night," Masha announced, drawing shared acknowledgement and laughter from the group.

There was a brief knock on the front door and the sound of someone entering the house.

"Paul, come in, sit down and grab some wine," Isaak said, getting up to greet his son in the foyer off of the dining room. "I didn't know what time you were coming. We already got started."

After brief hellos were exchanged and a place for Paul was set at the table, including a full glass of Chardonnay—the Pinot had long been drained—all eyes were on Paul as he was expected to join in on the conversation with some new gossip.

"On my way in I overheard you guys talking about whores. Who are we talking about?" Paul asked, trying his best not to look at Masha.

"You caught the tail end of our conversation about the dead girl. We kind of got sidetracked on the whore issue," Isaak said. "Paul, you've been following this story closely—everyone, Paul was the first to post the pictures of the girl for his newspaper." The group nodded their approval. "Tell us if you've heard anything new."

"Well, they have a guy in custody, a young Shinnecock whose ex-girlfriend has been missing. It looks like he may have had something to do with it," Paul said. The weariness in Paul's voice at making this known, along with its matter-of-fact specificity, had the effect of sucking all of the oxygen out of the room. Isaak and Masha took this as their cue to disappear into the kitchen to prepare dinner. Paul shared the few scant details he knew about the case with the remaining guests. The group then moved on to a mostly polite discussion of the fate of the Shinnecock, the inherent racism lying even in the East End's most liberal precincts, and other topics in this vein until dinner was served.

After a main course of grilled striped bass, roasted baby potatoes with rosemary, and fresh asparagus, with local strawberries and rhubarb compote for dessert—a meal that would have appealed to even the strictest locavore—Isaak's guests said their goodbyes and wished Paul luck with his ongoing reporting of the dead girl story. Paul was especially anxious for them to leave so he could have a chance to talk with Isaak privately. The two of them moved to the kitchen to start cleaning up the dishes from dinner.

"Dad, I didn't want to say anything in front of your friends but it's Merika's brother who is now the main suspect in this dead girl thing," Paul said.

"No kidding? I'm sorry Paul."

"And she won't even talk to me. I'm the guy on the outside now and it's killing me," Paul said.

"Well, what do you think? Do you think he did it?"

"I don't know. If I'm using Occam's razor then it points to her brother Andre. His ex-girlfriend is missing, he has a history of assault, and the police have a description that matches his car that was seen on the beach around the time the girl disappeared. It all adds up."

"That sounds like compelling evidence but are you sure you're not just thinking emotionally about this?"

"What do you mean? I've been going over it in my mind since this morning and it all matches up *logically*. Let's look at the other possible suspects. There is the cop, but why would a cop who just killed somebody call the police and then lose the body? And if he is responsible, the local cops aren't disciplined enough to maintain a conspiracy of that magnitude—the kid who posted the pictures on Facebook knew about this Will Clifford guy even though it was supposed to be kept a secret. Then there's this surfer who probably sent the pictures to this Dylan kid. If he did it why would he send pictures of a dead girl to his friend and then hide the body before the friend has a chance to show up and help him? And, if the friend was involved why would he post the pictures? You would expect that only someone who has no fear of being accused would make the pictures public. Besides, we don't have any other information about these other guys that points to a relationship to the dead girl."

Isaak considered Paul's recitation of the known facts and said,

"What I mean is that because you are too close to this that maybe you're not thinking things through. Based on everything you just told me I would say that your reasoning is flawed."

"You can't attack me for ad hominem reasoning. I was prepared for you to point that out. There's more evidence here than the guy's character."

"I wasn't going to fault you for that but I'm glad you did your homework."

"Okay, then what did I miss?"

"Although the case against Merika's brother *appears* persuasive did you ever think that maybe it wasn't any of the three scenarios you mentioned? This case is only a few days old. Maybe there's more that we don't know. Now, if you were to look to Aristotle—"

"—is he still doing PI stuff?"

"Funny. No, but he had something to say about observing the world that is relevant here."

"Okay, let's have it, not that I have a choice," Paul said.

"Aristotle would tell us to look to the natural world. Let's say the answer to this puzzle—who did it and why—is its essence or *form*. Aristotle would argue that it takes time and change to understand something's true form. Just as a tomato seed has the *form* of a tomato, we wouldn't know it by just observing the seed. We have to wait until the seed becomes a plant and then the plant bears fruit."

"So none of these guys did it? A tomato did it?"

"I didn't say that. I'm just saying that we may need to know more about the form of this before we—before *you*—draw any conclusions."

"I'd like to believe that, for Merika's sake."

"And, for the sake of your relationship with her?"

"Yeah."

"And, speaking of relationships, how are you doing now that the divorce is final? We really haven't had a chance to talk about it," Isaak said.

"You should have heard my rant two nights ago when I was with Jeff—or maybe not, I was pretty drunk. I guess I'm getting used to it. I have had a few years to think about it."

And?"

Paul considered telling Isaak about his recent drunken night with Jeanine sleeping over but kept it to himself.

"I still feel guilty for cheating on her—and I miss her. You gave me some pretty lousy advice back then. Advice I could have chosen not to take, I know. But the more I think about it, the more I think the reason I did it was that I wanted to be more like you, if that makes any sense."

"You mean that whole "live in the moment" discussion? When we spoke about it then I didn't think you were asking for permission, I thought you were asking for forgiveness."

"The difference being?"

"You had already cheated. I was giving you my perspective

because I thought it would help you to try to forgive yourself. It was up to you to decide if you wanted to repeat the act. If I led you astray, I'm sorry Paul. Sometimes when your past is too painful and the future scares you, you're only left with the present," Isaak said.

"Why should the future scare you? Things are good, you've got your teaching—"

"—I was waiting for a good time but I might as well tell you: the university has cut my courses. They don't have the funds anymore to support my classes. In fact, they're cutting back on the whole philosophy department—the perils of working for a public college. I guess the New York City Board of Higher Education doesn't consider philosophy a bankable profession."

"But, you're not retiring?"

"God no. I have tenure. They're going to continue paying me when I'm tottering around campus in my underwear and muttering Plato's *Dialogues* to myself. I'm staying. I just won't be teaching any undergraduate courses."

"Dad, I'm so sorry. I know how much teaching means to you."

"It's alright, Bub. I'll miss the students but I guess I'll have more time to write. And I'll have even *more* time to live in the present," Isaak said, smiling and probably thinking of Masha and whether she may be amenable to a visit later in the evening after this discussion was over and Paul went back to his house in Springs.

By now Paul and Isaak had moved to Isaak's living room and were sitting across from each other in a couple of leather club chairs Isaak had purchased at a little Sag Harbor antique store around the corner.

"So what is it called when you're not comfortable living in the past, present or the future?" Paul asked.

"Anhedonia." Isaak sighed.

"Really? There's a word for that?"

"It's the opposite of hedonism. It means you can't take pleasure from everyday things. But I don't believe you're there yet, at least I hope not. You're in the middle of something that you can't see your way out of right now. And, I understand what you're going through, Bub. When you're a kid and you lose a parent it's like losing your whole world, the planet rotates a bit differently for a long time after that. We both know what that's like. But when you lose your spouse it's not the same. You've become an adult and you are supposed to have a better handle on your world. You are more of a *complete* person. But that's also the problem. When you lose a mate, you lose a piece of yourself–you are no longer complete. So when you think about Jeanine, you need to ask yourself: besides having her warm body lying next to you at night, do you really want Jeanine or are you just missing that part of yourself she took with her? Because you can get that part back. The part that can love, that can be tender, funny, caring, forgiving, whatever. You might want to start by forgiving yourself."

"And with Mom, I mean, how do you become complete when the person isn't even around anymore to obsess over or to get over?"

"You don't. You just try to get used to having that piece missing and fill the space up with something else."

Chapter 23: Monday morning

On Monday the weather turned.

Paul could barely drag himself out of bed. He'd been up all night obsessing about Merika. His failed marriage. Olivia. The dead girl. It was going to be one of those muggy, clammy June days when the fog rolls in off of the ocean and just sits on her big fat ass on both sides of the Montauk Highway. And now he was going to be late. After losing a few more precious minutes rinsing off the thick coat of oak tree-pollen covering every inch of his truck, he stopped to pick up a quick breakfast at the Scuttle Bucket across the street from his office. A shitty cup of coffee, runny egg and cheese sandwich, extra pepper. And a copy of that morning's *Long Island Newsday*. The dead girl story made page one of Long Island's paper of record, alongside an article about another local hero who had been killed in one of the country's unending wars. And a sidebar featuring a professional athlete caught up in the latest doping scandal.

"Quite a story," Griffin Rivers, the store's mustachioed proprietor, commented as he handed Paul his change. "They find that girl yet?"

"Yeah, and what's up with this Shinnecock guy?" one of the store's morning regulars asked Paul. "I heard the cops picked him up yesterday on the Res,"

"It's a shame. At least they got the guy," someone else said.

"But who is the girl?" another one asked.

"Yeah, *who is the girl*?" they all seemed to asking.

"Sorry guys. I got to run over to Town Hall for a meeting. You can read my version of the story in the *EET* when it comes out," Paul said.

Customers peppered Paul with a few more questions about "the

Shinnecock guy" and the dead girl but he apologized again and ran to his truck. He raced over to the Town Hall in East Hampton to cover the Board meeting, grateful to get one of few remaining spaces in the back parking lot.

Paul entered the old New England-style farmhouse that was now the main town meeting hall and tried to find a seat. The place was packed, with several people lining the walls and spilling over into the hallways outside. He recognized a number of his neighbors from Springs and what looked to be a bunch of summer people who had come for a show. Paul had never seen this many people at a public meeting at Town Hall before, at least in this new location. After almost giving up on getting a seat, he spotted his next-door neighbor, Mr. Hayes, who offered the empty chair next to his. Yancy Starling, Paul's main rival at East Hampton's other main source of printed news, gave him a brief nod from the other side of the hall. Yancy was a good reporter with a strong competitive streak. Unlike some of his other colleagues who covered local news, she rarely shared her sources. She was also young and painfully attractive, pretty much guaranteeing her easy access to sources. Especially if they were male.

As the meeting was about to start, Yancy caught Paul's attention from across the room. His lip reading skills weren't great but he had no trouble reading hers.

"This is going to be good," she mouthed.

On this muggy, rainy Monday, the massive double sliding barn doors, which usually afforded wide views of Pantigo Road, had been slammed shut and the state-of-the-art-geothermal-cooled air conditioning was on the fritz. In the front of the hall, the town supervisor and four councilmen and women sat high above the assembled in large swivel chairs. So high in fact that only the members' heads were visible from the cheap seats. At their sides sat the town attorney and town clerk at smaller pine desks located at floor level. The walls were heaving sweat in the packed hall as Bob Hartley, the town supervisor, called the meeting to order.

"Would anyone from the public like to comment before we start the meeting? If so, please step up to the microphone," Supervisor Hartley announced.

It was standard practice to invite public comment prior to the Board starting on the day's agenda and, for most town meetings, you'd maybe have one or two people who would come up and make a brief comment for the record. In fact, at most meetings, these would be the *only* people in attendance aside from a few town employees and one or two reporters who bothered to show up. On these occasions, Paul could barely keep himself awake while he scribbled a few notes for a story he'd have to write covering the pressing issues on the day's agenda. But today the anticipation in the air felt as thick as the fog outside those giant sliding doors.

"I'd like to comment, Bob."

It was Lucy Birch, an anti-development activist and grandmother of four from Springs who sat on the local school board and was often forming groups to protest Town projects and spending proposals. At her side was Charlie Conrad— the former Chaim Klineman from Queens—a handsome fortyish local attorney who would often provide legal council to groups formed by Lucy and her friends. Conrad's choice of clients never struck Paul as particularly ideologically-driven. One day he would be representing an environmental group that was trying to stop a developer from building adjacent to a nature preserve and the next he might be arguing the other side for an individual homeowner wanting to build a dock or house expansion on their waterfront property. Despite this apparent lack of focus in his law practice, it was suspected that Conrad had strong political ambitions. The attorney's pro bono legal work had been instrumental in the successful secession of Peconic County. And there were rumors around town that he was looking to run for the newly created County Supervisor position in the next election—a job he helped design. Paul had also heard from a reliable source that Conrad had recently hired a New York City-based media consultant to help him strategize ways to gain attention on key issues facing East End voters. Issues like illegal immigration, for example.

Conrad appeared agitated as he watched his client barely reach the microphone to make her comments.

"Bob, members of the Board, I represent a number of concerned homeowners in Springs who would like to see the Town start applying the multi-resident laws in the hamlet," Lucy Birch began. Her voice sounded more chipper than the subject seemed to require. "To get things started I have brought a list of addresses of single-family houses we have compiled that we believe have multiple families living in them illegally." Birch then walked up to the tall podium and handed the list to one of the councilwomen seated.

"Thank you Lucy, we understand your concerns," Supervisor Hartley said from his perch before Birch could return to the microphone. "The Board and I are still considering a number of options, including raising the cap on the number of legal apartments allowed in each school district and designating some of the larger single family homes as multi-family residences to bring them up to code. As I mentioned at a prior meeting, we just don't have the manpower to investigate every complaint of overcrowding."

"The members of C.H.U.Q.L.S., the Concerned Homeowners

United for Quality of Life in Springs, don't believe the answer is to create new legislation to make more of these residences legal," Birch continued. "The answer is to enforce the laws already on the books. These people are destroying our quality of life with their loud parties, all night soccer games and vehicles blocking the street. They are lowering our home values and putting an undue burden on our ground water. Our taxes have been rising every year within our school district, which is also feeling the effects of overcrowding. It's time the Town did something about it."

"We can't just start knocking on people's doors based on a list of alleged lawbreakers," Len Philpott, the town attorney said. "We need to have proof that people are violating the law before we can proceed. We have to be careful here, Lucy. Otherwise the Town can be subject to lawsuits—especially if it appears we are discriminating against a particular group."

"Maybe we should sue the Town for lowering our property values and raising our school taxes," Birch countered. "This is reverse discrimination. We are fighting for our homes and we will not take it any longer!" she said. A number of people in the audience applauded and stamped their feet.

"I'd like to make a brief statement," Charlie Conrad interjected. He approached the microphone and kindly asked his client—who showed a look of surprise—to step aside. What immediately struck Paul was Conrad's appearance: gone were the rumpled Brooks Brothers suits and haphazardly slicked-back hair of the attorney who would sit fidgeting in the back of the room during contentious zoning board disputes. He looked like he had trimmed off about fifteen pounds as he stood in a slimming charcoal gray Italian suit, crisp white shirt and navy blue and crimson rep tie, his shirtsleeves rolled up neatly just below the elbow. Conrad had what the bubbies from his old Bronx neighborhood would call a *goyisher kop*; his wheat colored hair allowing just a hint of gray and now neatly cropped with a few tufts hanging strategically over his forehead. He appeared to be a man remade in the mold of Robert Redford's dashing baseball player in "The Natural." Well, maybe not "The Natural," Paul corrected himself, more like if Redford and Barbra Streisand's characters in the movie, "The Way We Were," had a boy instead of a girl and when that boy grew up he took a sharp right turn against the liberal political leanings of his mother.

"For those who don't know me, my name is Charlie Conrad and I represent these concerned homeowners. I am also a resident of Springs. As many of you may have heard, a dead girl was found this week on the beach in Wainscott and has disappeared. My sources in the Peconic County police department tell me that the girl was wearing a blue five-pointed star associated with a violent gang called the *Nuestra Isla*. This gang is known to be involved in prostitution, theft, the selling of drugs, and now the possible murder of an innocent child who may have been branded and forced into gang violence."

The crowd fell silent, holding onto to his every word.

Conrad continued, "We suspect that members of these gangs are already living within our communities here on the East End, within "safe" houses, perhaps in large numbers, probably in Springs, which has seen a steep rise in crime in the past year along with the rise in the Hispanic population. I cannot stand before you today and let the leaders of our town simply ignore the facts."

Again there was loud cheering from the crowd tempered by a few boos in response to this new accusation. A small contingent of Latino residents who had come to the meeting to show support for their neighbors were now looking increasingly uncomfortable as they shifted in their blond, straight-back bentwood chairs.

Conrad was getting fired up now, his voice a cross between televangelist and late-night direct marketing pitchman.

"Our town's proud founding fathers, the good, hard working settlers who came down from the Massachusetts Colony oh so many years ago, when they discovered their way of life threatened, they knew how to respond. Back then it wasn't Hispanic gangs but packs of wild wolves destroying crops and livestock. Wolves that were being protected and domesticated by the Indians. These dangerous animals were tearing apart the innocent settlers of this town. It was every man's responsibility to eradicate the evil menace that was destroying the peaceful existence of this hopeful new community. We cannot, I repeat, we cannot, let these people continue to destroy our way of life. Like those early settlers we need to go door to door using any means necessary to root out the evil that has entered our midst. The time to act is now!"

The hall erupted. Town officials begged the crowd to keep calm.

Mr. Hayes, one of the few African Americans in the crowd, and who up until that moment had sat quietly next to Paul through the speeches, shook his head and muttered a single: "Damn."

Philpott, the town attorney, jumped out of his chair and attempted to turn off Conrad's microphone.

Supervisor Hartley stood up and yelled over the din, "Order, order, please! Mr. Conrad, these accusations are outrageous! Everyone, please calm down."

Conrad turned to look at a stunned Lucy Birch, smiled a million-dollar smile, and walked out of the hall. Birch followed him at a safe distance, covering one side of her face with the rest of the printed speech she had carefully prepared but now looked as if she would never give. As the noise of the crowd began to die down, an undersized thirtyish-looking man wearing a black suit and familiar starched white clerical collar made his way up to the microphone and tapped it a few times with his index finger.

"Hello. Hello. My name is Edward de la Rosa and I am a pastor at St. Cecilia Catholic Church in East Hampton. I am here to speak for the residents of this community who are being so wrongly singled out."

The crowd quieted down further to hear the priest, whose voice was registering just above a whisper in the cavernous hall. Hartley asked Father de la Rosa to please speak louder, and the microphone was turned back on.

With the hall still straining to hear him, de la Rosa began by quoting St. Paul and segued into the story of the Good Samaritan, only rather than referencing the traveling Jew and his apathetic cousins as Paul remembered it, the priest changed any reference to Jews so the story was about "immigrants" and the Good Samaritan was cast from the hard-working local white population. The priest then tried to provide some additional perspective to the assembled crowd, carefully choosing each word from his prepared comments.

"Whether you believe in the teachings of Jesus or not, you have to believe in statistics. The Springs community is now more than one-third Hispanic. The vast majority of us are here legally, we fully participate in this community and we pay our taxes."

A chorus of cheers was heard from the Latino section of the crowd, led by a dark, smallish middle-aged woman in faded blue jeans. Her tight ponytail swung around as she stood and encouraged the others.

"Sit down!" someone yelled—either at the priest or perhaps the woman standing.

She turned toward the people seated in her section and began to lead the group in a chant. They repeated the call, which grew successively louder.

Estamos aquí, y estamos quedando. Acostumbrarse a él!—We're here, and we're staying. Get used to it!

Their chants were soon met by loud boos from other members of the crowd until the hall turned into a cacophonous babel.

The priest walked to the Latino section and whispered something to their leader, his face clearly pained. The chanting stopped and the rest of the crowd quieted down. The Father then returned to the podium, circling back to his prepared remarks.

"We understand the concerns of our neighbors about overcrowding. But many of the people in these homes have a tradition of living with extended families under one roof. And housing is very expensive, as many of you know. The work our people do plays an important part in the lives of everyone here and few complain when we serve your food, take care of your children, and help build and maintain your homes and gardens. People need to appreciate that we want the same things as everyone else: to live and work in a safe community in which we can bring up our children. Yet many home owners are being harassed, sometimes with threats of violence, and are living in constant fear. All we ask is for some patience and understanding. Let us remember that we are, each of us, angels with only one wing, and we can only fly by embracing one another. May God bless us all."

De la Rosa left the microphone to more loud cheers from the

Latino section. Perhaps because he mentioned God and blessed the congregation, no one dare boo him too loudly at the conclusion of his remarks.

With no other speeches from the community forthcoming, most of the crowd snuck out of the hall while the Town Board moved on to the detailed drone of the proposed zoning plans and other items on their agenda, and the meeting wrapped early.

Outside, the fog was now so dense you could barely see past ten feet out into the parking lot. Yet just outside the glass entry doors, Paul caught sight of the woman who had led the cheers. She was animated, gesturing wildly as she spoke to the priest. Their body language seemed peculiar, revealing an intimacy unusual for a priest and his parishioner. Like watching a bickering couple, Paul thought.

Before he could get through the door to speak to them, Yancy Starling collared Paul in the muggy glass and steel enclosure outside the main hall.

"Sandis, some weather huh? Hey, do you believe that guy?"

Even Yancy was perspiring in her sleeveless top and form-fitting Capri slacks.

"Which one—the priest or the asshole?" Paul asked, still peering out into the parking lot. The Father and the woman were beginning to move further away from the glass doors.

"Forget the priest with all that love-thy-neighbor crap," Yancy said. "Conrad is the gift that keeps on giving. The guy is incredible. I'm going to tell you my headline now so you don't steal it: 'Conrad equates Hispanics with wolves; says root them out!' This has got to be his kickoff for public office. Man, he played the crowd like a real pro."

"He may be a pro but the game he's playing has real

consequences," Paul said. He searched again outside for the woman but she had already disappeared into the fog.

"And, it looks like he just scooped your dead girl story, Sandis. You might want to check your sources on that. I'm going back to the office to do some research on the wolf thing. That was priceless," she added.

Paul finally removed himself from Yancy and ran outside. The parking lot was virtually empty. The woman and her priest were gone.

Chapter 24: Monday morning

"Where's your cuz?"

"Working, bro. I thought we could chill here for a while. He promised to come back around noon with the money."

"New cabinets?"

"Yeah. My *homes* redid the kitchen. Check out these drawers." A sleek new kitchen drawer floated air pocket-like over expensive looking hardware. When pushed closed, the drawer slid effortlessly over its rails then hesitated ever so slightly before gently kissing the cabinet frame.

"Damn."

An overhead cabinet was opened, and three glasses set down on a shiny granite countertop. A plate of cookies was prepared. One percent milk poured. As they sat down to eat, one of the members of the group dropped his split Oreo-half on the sparkling clean linoleum, white-side down.

"*¡Ah, chingado!*"

The exclamation was answered with a hard slap to the back. "Hey, you got to pick that shit up! Don't leave no crumbs!"

The friend bent down, picked up the cookie, blew over the top and ate it. He glanced past the kitchen toward the fenced-in yard in the back of the house.

"Swimming pool. Nice."

"Gunite."

"No shit? Your cuz got it down, bro."

The three youths, still holding chalky half-filled drinking glasses, slipped through the kitchen's sliding glass door to the patio and stared down at the pool. Its shimmering surface was barely visible beneath a thick layer of morning fog. They set down their glasses, removed their sneakers and socks and sat at the deep end, dropping their legs in. Their tattooed calves read as otherworldly magnifications beneath the water as they swung their feet.

The most muscular of three removed a small metal pipe from the pocket of his cargo shorts, pushed some bud down into the bowl and lit up. After taking a hit he passed it over to one of his friends.

"You should have seen the look on that kid's face yesterday, bro."

"Ha ha, yeah, but what about the weed?"

"No worries. This Dylan guy is for real. He'll make it happen. That stuff the kid had last year was *asombroso*."

"Ha, yeah, well I don't trust him. This thing, posting the girl's pictures—" he stopped to take another hit from the pipe—"that's fucked up. How could you let him do that, bro? Too much attention."

"I told you. I had a talk with him about it. He knows what he has to do."

The friend shook his head as he pushed out the last plume of smoke from his lungs. "I can't believe you got us buying weed grown by some fuckin' high school kid."

"I said, don't worry. Shit's under control. If anything goes wrong I'll take care of it."

"Yeah, you are always taking care of things, Luis."

Chapter 25: Monday later that day

Back in school, racing to lunch after sweating through his Advanced Calc quiz, Connor's mobile trilled.

Morris again.

Morris: UR not gonna believe what that bitch wrote

Connor: U at school? Didn't see u

Morris: Nah

Connor: Who wrote

Morris: Your spanish gf. Pull that shit up!!

Connor: Calm down

....

Connor: Is this true?????????????

....

Morris: Yeah well c-man im fucked. Text her and tell her to take that shit DOWN. But prolly too late

Connor: Damn. She's right u R an asshole. I mean u and me both.

* * *

Por/Que: Daisy's True and False Blog

Where Daisy tells you what's what and por/que

(Because "porque" means because and "por que" means why that's why, mis locas)

"An Angry F-kg Latina"

True: *C.S. is an asshole.*

-Por/que? He left me alone with his friends in the Cave after inviting me again (this time G. didn't come with me) and I heard he went to a party and hooked up with that skinny slut J.M. with the stupid angel tramp stamp

True: *I think M.T. raped me.*

-Por/que? Okay, I am using the Women's Law Project definition (I Googled it) because the official legal definition is totally *pendejata* (wonder if white guys are behind that, ya think?). A guy doesn't have to use his penis 4it2b rape you got it?

After C. left, I had a little too much to drink (but didn't smoke any weed, you know I don't smoke!) and M. came over to "comfort" me. After I calmed down we kissed a little bit (I told you I had too much to drink) and then he kept grabbing my head and trying to put it between his legs. Like that is *SO* sexy. After I said "NO" several times he slipped his hand down the front of my pants. They were of course still buttoned I swear! And then he put his f-kg finger in me. Hard. And it hurt. A lot. I cried until he finally left and I got out of there.

False: *Some white guys are NOT assholes (revised)*

-Por/que? C. is an asshole for leaving me alone with M. How could he f-kg do that?

M. has graduated from asshole and passed through creep into rapist.

False: *The Cave is cool (revised)*

-Por/que? See below.

Obvious: I am only fifteen and can no longer trust men (especially in enclosed spaces). I'm depressed, mis locas. Very DEPRESSED. But I WILL SURVIVE.

I know I should tell Mami but...

1. She will freak.
2. Will she think it was my fault?
3. She used to be a midwife so she should understand. But she had a lot of horrible things happen to her when she was a girl and young woman in Guatemala and I don't want to remind her of those horrible things.

<3 <3 <3 <3 <3 <3 <3 <3 <3 <3 <3 <3 <3 <3 <3 <3 <3 <3 <3

* * *

Connor's phone shook. This time, a text from Dylan.

Dylan: Yo good meeting. Luis liked you. Jess liked you. We all like you.

Connor: Ha

Dylan: Don't fuck this up. Peace.

Chapter 26: Monday still later

"You look like someone just ran you over with their Range Rover. How was the meeting or shouldn't I ask?" Jeff asked when Paul walked through the door.

"Don't ask," Paul said. He dropped himself into a chair and started squeezing the little rubber "stress ball" with the *EET* logo sitting on Jeff's desk. Bert Plank had given the balls out at the last Christmas party hoping they would be put to good use. So, upon returning after the Christmas holidays, Paul and Jeff created their own stress-release game. They made a target out of Grace's portrait and tacked it to the wall, with the highest score a bull's-eye dead center of her eyeglasses. Whenever they got bored during those long non-Grace visitation days, out came the target and balls. That is until they almost got caught—when Grace walked in announced. Anyway, it was difficult to tell exactly where the ball hit so they'd spend more time arguing about the score than playing. Esra once came by in the middle of one these heated post-game debates asking why the two of them were going on about their shared desire for "sticky balls," which, of course, they both refused to explain.

Paul threw the little rubber ball at Jeff, just missing his head.

"That's how it's going," Paul said.

"Okay then. I'll just get back to editing the police bulletins for the week," Jeff said, retreating.

"I'll give you Yancy's lede, with my spin," Paul said finally, picking up the rubber ball and squeezing it tighter. "Charlie Conrad takes over the meeting and claims the missing dead girl was killed by a local Hispanic gang called the *Nuestra Isla*, and then uses this tidbit as a battle cry to break down the doors of Latino families in Springs."

"Holy shit! Yancy was there? How is she looking these days? Was she wearing the blue thingie with the swooping neckline or the red one with the tight—"

"—c'mon Jeff, this is serious. That Conrad guy is dangerous. I felt like strangling him with the microphone chord. At least the priest from St. Cecilia's was able to give an impassioned speech on behalf of his community. Although I'm not so sure that it mattered."

"And our friend Lucy Birch, did she make an appearance?"

"Yeah, she brought Conrad with her. She was his warm up act."

"I've seen her perform. Did I ever show you these?" Jeff opened an email window on his computer and clicked on one sent to the paper from Lucy Birch with "CHUQLS" in the subject heading. Jeff clicked again on the column header and about twenty additional emails lined up underneath with the same subject heading.

"I get one of these every couple of days. Just about everything that happens out here—school budget issues, school registration, housing violation issues, it's all filtered through her animosity toward one particular population but couched in language that claims strict adherence to the rule of law and 'fairness.' She's got a cc: list of about fifty people and it all gets posted on her CHUQLS (Jeff made it sound like "Chuckles") Facebook page where everyone gets to pile on with their own racist commentary."

Paul pointed to the most recent email from the group.

"Hey, here's the list of homes she is targeting. Print that out for me," he said. The list was arranged alphabetically starting with "A"—*Alvarez.*

"Done," Jeff said, tapping the little icon and setting the old workhorse printer in the far corner whirring. "You know I kind of feel sorry for her."

"Why's that?"

"That first address on that list, the Alvarez house, I know that place. There are too many cars and trucks parked out there. I'm sure it gets loud with so many people living close together like that. Every time Lucy drives by those homes full of 'shady' people it's a reminder that her world has changed profoundly."

"There are other ways to respond to change, you know."

"Such as?"

"Walk over and introduce yourself. Bring over a Bundt cake or whatever it is people bring these days and get to know their new neighbors," Paul said.

"You've been in your house for what, almost three years now? How many of your neighbors do you know on a first name basis?"

Paul took a quick mental inventory of the houses on his block. Most of them he'd have to label "anonymous"—summer places left empty starting the day after Labor Day, the remaining ones inhabited by tradespeople whose trucks he knew better than the person sitting behind the wheel.

"Mr. Hayes next door, we're buddies."

"And his first name is?"

"I see your point. So what can you tell me about the notorious *Nuestra Isla* gang?" Paul asked, happy to change the subject.

"Nada. Why don't you Google it? Wait a minute, actually you should try Grace."

Paul winced.

"I'm not kidding, man. She worked on a story about gangs for one of Bert's up-island papers awhile back. Hey, maybe they're like Latino Robin Hoods, you know, badass but kind of loveable. That would make a good story," Jeff said.

Paul moved over to his computer and started looking for anything he could find about the *Nuestra Isla.* After several minutes searching he was getting nowhere.

“Everything is in Spanish. And, I’m getting what looks like vacation websites,” he whined.

“Search it again with the word *‘pandilla’* or *‘ganga’* next to it,” Jeff said, and then spelled out each word for Paul.

“How do you know this stuff? Okay, I’m finding a few things with a ‘translate this page’ tag next them but the articles are behind a pay wall—I can’t believe I’ve got to pay to read this?”

“Hey, don’t complain, Paco. There’s a rumor going around that our glorious little hometown paper is getting one of those pay walls real soon. Maybe Bert will raise enough cash to allow us to keep our lousy *trabajos.* And, if we’re good maybe they’ll even let us view our own articles without having to pay the subscription. C’mon, it’ll take forever to find anything online. You have the resources of a great metropolitan newspaper at your fingertips! Call Grace. She won’t bite, I promise,” Jeff said.

Paul dialed Grace’s number half hoping she wouldn’t answer. She picked up after two rings.

“Grace. Hi, it’s Paul. I just came from the East Hampton Town Board meeting.”

“Any interesting news to report?” she asked.

“The usual, you know, pretty boring stuff.” He glanced over at Jeff, who would be editing his Town Board meeting story prior to sending it to the paper’s main office and Grace’s desk. “Listen Grace, what can you tell me about a gang called *Nuestra Isla*?”

“Who?”

“*Nuestra Isla.*”

"Sounds like a vacation spot. Are you thinking of doing a piece on them? I don't remember us talking about that." Grace said.

"No, it's just that someone referenced them briefly at today's Town meeting. Jeff told me you might have done a piece on gangs in Suffolk County. I was just looking for some background."

"Oh, sure. Actually, I helped do some research on local gangs for a paper Bert has some ownership stake in near Huntington but the story never got published. Most of the stuff was about the Latin Kings. I don't recall that other name you gave me though. Do you want me to send you what I've got?"

"Thanks, Grace. That would be fantastic. Thank you so much."

"Paul, how is your story about the missing girl going? Any updates I should know about?"

"Not really. But while I have you on the phone... you don't happen to have spoken to any of your Peconic County police sources lately? They seem to be taking your calls but not mine."

"No Paul. That's your story. You should try them again," she said.

"Will do. Thanks again, Grace."

"Okay. I'll send that stuff over right away. Bye."

Paul gently put the receiver in its cradle and then smashed it back down a few times.

He stepped back from his desk and let out a blood-curdling scream.

"Feeling better?" Jeff asked.

"Why don't I feel like she is being straight with me?

About an hour and several clicks later Jeff looked up from his desk.

"You find anything?"

"Yeah. The star. They've got a five-pointed blue star as one of their gang markings. Conrad mentioned something about that."

"That is something. Wait, do you think our girl is a gangbanger?"

"I don't know. Maybe. But, the rest of it doesn't seem to fit. Says here they are classified as a 'stoner gang.' They wear marijuana leaf tattoos. And here is my favorite bit:

Members of the Nuestra Isla are inspired by but do not accept all of the tenets of Jamaica's Rastafari movement. Tenets they have in common include a spiritual embrace of marijuana and rejection of mainstream, white society.

"Pot heads with a Tejano soundtrack—Hispanic Rastas! I mean, how badass can they be? That last sentence describes half of my high school class in Brooklyn—and that's just counting the ones who graduated. These guys are probably stoned half the time to do any harm," Paul said.

Jeff started to sing, "*Rasta-man vibrations, si!* —hey, you sound disappointed."

"Maybe."

"They already got someone in custody—that Shinnecock guy you wrote about. You nailed that story. I would think you'd be happy to have this gang thing be a false lead. Especially since it discredits our buddy Conrad."

"Um—"

"—wait a sec, this isn't about that woman you told me about the other night?"

"Maybe?"

"Paul, c'mon, tell ol' Jeff all about it. No secrets here, brother."

"Okay, okay. 'That woman' I told you I met the day the dead girl disappeared—her name is Merika. The guy the cops have in custody,

Andre Little, is her brother. And, oh yeah, she spent Saturday night at my place."

"Oh."

"Yeah. Would I like the cops to pin this thing on some gang I never heard of and write a story about that? Sure. But these *Nuestra Isla* guys sound like a joke, that is, if there are even any out here."

"I see your point. But maybe they're branching out beyond the pot thing to more hard-core stuff to draw new members. You know, diversification is important. Diversify, diversify," Jeff chanted.

Paul decided again to try Virginia Woo at the Peconic County police department. To Paul's surprise, after several unanswered calls, Woo must have felt it time to take pity on him and picked up the phone.

"Virginia, how are you? It's Paul Sandis from the *East End Times*. I'm just checking in to see if you guys have any update on the case of the missing dead girl in Wainscott."

"Oh Paul, yes, well I don't think we have any updates since the last press conference. I posted the information on our web page. I can send you a transcript—"

"—I am asking specifically about a recent charge that's been made that Peconic police detectives are looking at the possibility that this was a gang-related crime."

"We are looking at every possible lead in the case. The investigation is ongoing."

"So are you confirming that?"

"As I said, we are looking at every possible lead."

"Virginia, let me ask it this way: could the death or disappearance of the girl found in Wainscott be gang-related, yes or no?"

"Paul, you know I can't answer that."

“Off the record?” he asked.

“Off the record, we are not happy with the publication of evidence that may be material to cases important to our department without running them by official sources first.”

“Ah, I got you. But you have to admit the pictures were pretty. And Grace Monahan from our Southampton office?” Paul asked.

“What about Grace?”

“Since we’re off the record? Grace, my boss, seems to be getting certain information from your office about this case that is, let’s say, *partial.*”

“Paul, I have no idea what you’re talking about. My advice is to keep your internal issues within your own house,” Woo said.

“Got it. One more question.”

“Sure, I’m here for you,” she purred, without a trace of irony.

“You are currently holding this guy Andre Little as a ‘person of interest’ in connection to the missing girl. Any chance he’ll be charged with something or released soon? Especially given this new information about a possible gang connection?”

“So far he has not been charged with any crime relating to this case. You’ll know if there’s an update when everyone else knows. And, I’ll ignore your comment about the gang connection. Is that it?”

“Yep, thanks Virginia. I feel like we’ve made some real progress in our relationship today.”

“Very funny, Paul. Enjoy the rest of your day.”

Jeff looked over expectantly as Paul hung up the phone.

“Not getting much love today, huh?” he said.

“How’d you guess?”

“I was searching some stuff for you and thought you’d be

interested in this." Jeff had the local TV news website up. "Check out this video of your friend Conrad from earlier today."

"Please. Not the town hall meeting. I'm not watching that again."

"No. He was over in Riverhead afterward, doing an on-camera interview. They just put it up."

Jeff pulled up the video full screen on his monitor for the two of them to watch.

There was Charlie Conrad, this time with his suit jacket on, standing in front of the courthouse in Riverhead, again with a TV-ready smile. He was being interviewed by Long Island Channel 17 TV News' star reporter, Rebecca Loeb-Farrar.

"Hey, it's Long Island Channel 17 TV News' star reporter, Rebecca Loeb-Farrar," Jeff announced.

"Shhh," Paul said.

"I stand by my support of the good people of Springs and am firmly against laws that continue to support and aid illegal immigration. However, these recent accusations of racism on my part are deeply unfounded and untrue. My statements at that meeting were clearly taken out of context," Charlie Conrad said.

"Ha!" Paul interjected.

"Just watch Rebecca work her magic," Jeff said.

"Mr. Conrad, you made a reference regarding a Latino gang who may be active here on the East End in relation to this story about the missing girl in Wainscott. Can you elaborate on that?"

Rebecca pushed her microphone in Conrad's face with great determination.

"I just came from a meeting here at the courthouse and have been asked not to mention anything further about this ongoing investigation. Police officials here are doing an incredible job and

I'd rather not comment."

"Can you elaborate on what you know about this particular gang?"

"That's all I'm at opportunity to say on the matter, for now."

"That's because I know more about them than you do and I never heard of them before five minutes ago, you idiot!" Paul screamed.

"And, what about this quote that's been attributed to you?"

Rebecca then read from a note she seemed to have jotted down in the palm of her hand.

"'We need to go door to door using any means necessary to foot'—I'm sorry that's 'root out the devil—that has entered our midst.' What did you mean by that statement?"

"I don't recall saying that."

"He said, '*evil*' not '*devil*' you bimbo! Read the damn transcript! You just let him off the hook. Ahhh." Paul held his hand in front of his eyes, pretending not to watch.

Rebecca continued, maintaining the same bright smile and cheery tone she used when interviewing girl scouts about their cookie sales.

"Mr. Conrad, is this a call for citizens of Long Island to put aside the rule of law and take actions into their own hands in regards to illegal immigration?"

"That's up to the citizens of Long Island. And, as I said, I don't recall making that statement. However, I will say this, Rebecca, there are more and more reports of people coming to Long Island from other countries for the sole purpose of giving birth to their babies free of charge, and then their families using the child as a means to stay in this country—these so-called anchor babies are real and they are bankrupting Peconic County. Let me give you an example of how it's putting pressure on hospitals right here in our

proud new county. Tuckahoe Hospital's maternity ward is being forced to close because they cannot deal with the sheer number of anchor babies being born there. Right here in one of the richest communities in the nation! They are going to have to close the only maternity ward on the South Fork. How long are we as citizens going to continue to look the other way, to live in a nation ruled by people who have no respect for the law?"

"Okay, that's news," Jeff said.

"Don't bother fact checking any of it. I'm sure he made it up," Paul said.

Jeff moved to Paul's computer and started fact checking it.

A pregnant pause in the interview as Rebecca looked down at her hand for the next question. Most likely, due to her naturally occurring perspiration and the muggy weather conditions, her palm-written notes had started to blur.

"Interesting! I mean that's terrible. You know, babies are important. They are our future. You know what I mean... On another note, Mr. Conrad, are you ready to announce your intention to run for County Executive in the upcoming special election?" Then, in a light singsong voice...*"There have been rumors..."*

Conrad grabbed the microphone from Rebecca and spoke directly into the camera.

"I will be announcing my intentions soon. Thank you and God bless the good people of Peconic."

Fade out. The video looped to a commercial for a local Ford dealership. Girls dancing a can-can dressed in bright red lobster costumes. Didn't people know that only boiled lobsters (i.e., very dead ones) are that color?

"You're right. Conrad made it up," Jeff said, looking up from the computer. "Maternity is like the hospital's biggest profit center. Totally false."

"Well thank *you*, Mr. Bower, for making my day," Paul said.

Chapter 27: Monday afternoon

Por/Que: Daisy's *New* True and False Blog
Where Daisy tells you what's what and por/que
(Because "porque" means because and "por que" means why that's why, mis locas)

"A Confused Latina"

Note: I apologize to all of you out there who had to search for my new URL. See explanation below.

True: *My sister is a jerk.*

-Por/que? My sensible sister Sylvia (I WILL keep calling her that bc it drives her crazy. Good.), who is older and "wiser" than me, told my mom about my last blog post. I know, está muy pinche, mis locas.

Here is what my mom did when she read it, in order (as much as I can remember):

1. She yelled at me. Screamed really, mostly in some crazy Guatemalan-dialect Spanish that she never uses around the house, so I could only make out some of it. But I could tell what she was saying wasn't flattering to either of us (I stole that last thing from her—she always says that whenever I do something she thinks is stupid).

2. She cried. Then I cried. We cried together (that may be all we girls

got but sometimes it feels good).

3. She told me I was beautiful and that guys are assholes but I shouldn't think that just about white guys. Is Papi an asshole too I asked her? Sometimes, she said but he gets a pass. Mexican men get too many passes if you ask me.

4. She grounded me and made me shut down my blog and delete all of it. But I just got my computer privileges back, mis locas!

False: *It gets better with time.*

-Por/que? I'm still pissed. And, now I can't even go out with my friends (and G. is pissed at *me).*

Obvious: There is no way I am telling anyone official at school or beyond about what happened and my mom agrees with me. Except she said I should talk to Father d. about it "when I'm ready." But isn't he an asshole too under your definition, Seashell?

Not so obvious:

1. My mom has been acting crazy loco this weekend. Something's up besides my thing but I can't figure it out. She and Papi have been very QUIET and then acting STRANGE and leaving the house together without telling my sister Sylvia or me where they are going. I think they even went to_

"Daisy, you little shit! I can't believe you are writing another blog after what happened. You are ridiculous."

Sylvia had just walked into Daisy's room and caught her little sister typing on her computer. She leaned over Daisy's shoulder and pushed the front of her thick glasses against the bridge of her nose to get a better look.

"You're just jealous, big sister," Daisy said, barely turning her head around.

"Mami is going to kill you—if I don't do it first."

"Yeah, what's up with everybody? Mami and Papi are acting *crazy* the past few days. And I don't think it's just about me."

Sylvia lowered her voice to a whisper: "I can't tell you. It's grown up stuff," she said. Daisy couldn't tell if this was anything to worry about. Her sister had a tendency to take everything way too seriously.

"But is everyone alright? I mean no one is sick or anything?"

"No. No one is sick, Daisy. Maybe you for writing those stupid blogs that nobody reads," Sylvia said.

"Shut up! Hey, have you heard anything new about the dead girl? That girl is obviously a Latina and she's so obviously sexy. All the girls in my class have been talking about it. Glenda can't stop talking about it, anyway—at least when she was still talking to me."

"Yeah, some seniors think it's a big deal, I guess. A few of them are saying they know who she is but I think they're just making it up to get attention."

"You don't seem so excited about it," Daisy said.

"I just rather not think about it right now. And I think you should not post any more comments about the family online. What if someone actually reads this thing?" Sylvia pointed to Daisy's computer screen at her latest post. "Hey are you talking about me online? We don't want everyone to know our business."

"Okay, okay." Daisy closed the lid on her computer as if this simple act would make these recent bits of digital detritus disappear.

"Have you talked to that boy Connor?"

"I texted him and told him he was an asshole but he hasn't texted me back. I don't think he wants to talk to me. I still can't believe he hooked up with that little Jessica bitch. God! She's such a slut."

"Maybe it's all for the best."

"That's what Seashell said. You're starting to sound just like her."

"She's right and don't call Mami that," Sylvia said.

"Wait, Mami hasn't been talking to Morris' parents has she? Please tell me she hasn't. That would be so embarrassing. I might as well kill myself now."

"Don't worry, she wouldn't do that. Papi would definitely not let her do it. Have you talked to Father d. yet?"

"No. Not yet. I don't understand what he's going to do to help me anyway—tell me to say two Hail Marys and three Our Fathers? I don't have anything to confess, Sylvia. That jerk Morris raped me. He's the one who should be asking God for forgiveness."

"You don't have to do it as part of confession. And, he's a smart man. Father d. may have something to say that can help you. And what that Morris kid did was terrible but he didn't rape you, Daisy. You have to be careful about what you say—"

"—if you want to help me you can leave me alone and let me figure it out. Talking to a man—even if he is a priest—is not going to help me. And why won't anybody believe me that the guy raped me?"

She started to cry.

Daisy felt her sister's warmth bridge the space between them and leaned in for a welcomed hug. As much as she was trying to push her big sister away and be her own person, she was craving Sylvia's attention and acceptance now more than ever. She was the baby and although sometimes ashamed of her behavior she felt it was her right. Besides, her sister had always been there for her, had listened to her stupid problems when no one else would. Daisy was the pretty one but Sylvia was the smart one—that's what everyone always said—although they were sometimes jealous of Sylvia's beautiful long hair.

She couldn't be as smart as Sylvia but she could at least try to understand the world. Recently, she made a promise to herself that she would *make* herself smarter. Maybe if she just spent more time online, reading and clicking on every hypertext link until it led her to more hypertext links and when she ran out of links she could underline the words she didn't know with her mind and move her mouse to that little box on the top right hand part of the page, type in the search term until she started the process all over again, reading and absorbing and clicking, reading and absorbing and clicking, reading and absorbing and clicking, until she could make sense of the world and her place in it. Daisy began stroking her sister's long dark hair—it really was beautiful and soft, much softer than her own coarse frizzies sticking out in all directions. Softer even than the fake pony's hair on the dolls Daisy used to collect and obsess over only a few years before, the ones she was forced to put in a cardboard box and give to her mother's friend who worked at the women's shelter. She was angry at her mother for making her give away all of her beloved toys but Sylvia told her not to worry, that she would soon forget about her toys and grow out of them once she discovered boys. And somehow she did but look how that was turning out. She couldn't even remember now why she loved those stupid ponies so much, why she had wasted so much time fussing over them, combing their rainbow-colored hair and giving them dumb Anglo girl names like Madison and Taylor and Britney. As she gave herself to her sister's embrace, Daisy's sobs grew louder and more intense, coming from someplace deep inside that scared her and yet somehow made her feel safe at the same time. Right now all she wanted was to climb under the covers like when they were younger and have Sylvia wrap her skinny arms around her and tell her funny stories until they both fell asleep laughing in each other's arms.

Could the Internet explain all of the things she was feeling right now?

"Oh, *mi hermanita. Lo siento, mi amor,*" Sylvia whispered, holding Daisy close and kissing the worry lines of her forehead. "You have no idea what kind of trouble we are in."

Chapter 28: Monday, later that afternoon

"Hold on, yes, how can I help you? Shit."

No knock, just the door opening and someone barging in. When Paul looked up from his place behind his desk there was Butch, towering over him, clenching his perfectly contoured teeth.

"'Shit' is right. Where did she sleep the other night?"

Butch must have run up the stairs, two at a time, because he was having trouble catching his breath.

"Hey Butch, can't a guy get a 'hi, how are ya, how is everything?'"

"Sandis don't get cute. Did you sleep with Jeanine Friday night or not?"

"Cuckoldry's a bitch ain't it?"

"What?"

"Nothing. What did Jeanine say happened?"

"She didn't come home that night and she's not saying. What good are these stupid phones if no one answers you?" He was pointing to the mobile attached to his belt. He had one of those little plastic thingies curled around his left ear.

Butch certainly cut a menacing figure from this vantage point—but only to a degree. Gone was the macho contractor uniform of jeans, T-shirt and steel-toed work boots. His new "builder of dreams" image demanded a different look: pressed dress shirt with requisite company initials (*OSE*) embroidered over the pocket, pleated khakis, and paper-thin dress socks tucked into Italian loafers. The precision Swiss timepiece strapped to his wrist bulged; it was a wonder he could lift his left arm. Still, Paul would have preferred the distance he typically enjoyed between himself and this much larger man. Like on those occasions when he had to pick up or drop off Connor and he got to stay in his truck, idling by the curb while Butch sat in central-AC comfort somewhere inside his large house, most likely occupied in front of one of his equally large flatscreen TVs.

"So, yes or no, just tell me, did you sleep with her?" Butch demanded.

"What is it with you two? Very demanding lately."

"Sandis."

"Okay, okay. I ran into Jeanine Friday night and she was *very* drunk and in no shape to drive home. I offered to give her a lift. She asked to come home with me instead. She passed out at my place and left in the morning."

"That's it?" Butch appeared relieved but skeptical as to the lack of specifics. "Did she say anything about me?"

"That's all I can remember, anyway. Oh yeah, in the morning she complained about the decor and didn't like my coffee."

"That sounds right," Butch said, betraying a slight smile. He sat down in a chair facing Paul and picked up the little rubber stress ball on the desk. "What is this?"

"It's meant to relieve stress. Very soothing on the nerves. Try it out. It might be good for me."

"Don't you mean, 'good for you?'"

"No, right now I mean, 'good for *me*.'"

Butch stared at the little red ball in his hand as if it were a strange, foreign object and placed it back down on the desk. He heaved a super-sized sigh.

"I'm losing her," he said.

"What's that?"

"Jeanine. I feel like I'm losing her."

"C'mon—"

"—I don't mean that she wants to go back to being with you. That's *not* happening. I mean I feel like she's having second thoughts. About us."

"You mean you're *afraid* of losing her."

"Yeah, I guess that's it. Is there a difference?"

"Why are you telling me this, Butch?"

"You and me, we never talked about her. Two guys talking. I know you don't like me but, I mean, we must have a few things in common."

"Less than you know."

"But more than you think. I love her. I think you do too," Butch said.

"Then go get her, cowboy. I have work to do."

Paul pulled his chair closer to his desk, turned his attention back to his computer screen and started typing.

Butch stood up and leaned over the desk. He picked up the stress ball and was squeezing it hard now, his large fingers swallowing the ball whole.

"Look, Sandis. Give me one reason why I shouldn't hit you right now for sleeping with my fiancé?"

"Let's see ... number one, you are in my office and we have a strict 'no hitting' policy here. We in the fourth estate are very traditional that way. Number two, I've already been hit twice this week by other much more interesting people, and you hitting me now would be highly unoriginal. And three, you won. Congratulations. You get to have her, for the rest of your life probably. Take my word for it: being afraid of losing someone and actually losing someone are not the same thing."

Not that Paul had much experience dealing with jealous

boyfriends but now that he was over his original fear he noticed something odd about Butch's behavior. His old nemesis didn't seem to be fully invested in this tough guy act. It was as if Butch's swagger had been slowly drained out of him. If it were liquid it would be pooling at his feet. And he looked tired. What the hell had Jeanine done to him?

"You're right, Paul. I win," he said, unclenching his fist and putting down the ball.

Butch turned toward the door but instead of leaving walked a few steps over to a small conference table where Paul had left pictures of the dead girl on top of a stack of papers. The big man hesitated slightly, drew in a deep breath and rather than pick up the pictures gestured toward them instead, as if touching them might be too intrusive an act.

"So this is the girl everyone is talking about, huh?"

"Yeah. I'm working on a related story right now, in fact."

"Really? Any updates?"

"None that I can share with you right now."

"Huh. I heard they got the guy already. Some Shinnecock from the Res."

"Could be him."

"So it's not definite?"

"Let's just say there is some speculation. *That's* the story."

"Hmm."

Butch was silent for a long moment before continuing. You could almost hear the gears in his head turning. Paul had seen him do this before, this pause for effect, and was almost certain of what was coming next: one of Butch's carefully chosen bits of wisdom, likely taken from one of his favorite pop songs. Paul liked to call these little phrases of his “Butchisms.” He’d sometimes ask Connor to relay any new ones his son may have heard around the house (they included gems like “Luck ain’t lucky; you got to make your own breaks” and “Hey, I’m just keeping the faith,” which Butch would offer up in response to any criticism Connor might throw his way).

“People believe what they wanna believe, I guess,” Butch said.

Bingo.

“Listen Paul, I just wanted to say... I know Jeanine doesn’t want you at the wedding but if it were up to me ...”

“Yeah, I know. You wouldn’t have invited me either. Take care of yourself, Butch,” Paul said. Then he watched as Butch’s hulk-like figure slowly made its way out the door.

* * *

Paul sent his finished Town Board story off to Jeff and was getting ready to leave when his phone rang.

“Pa—you—g-t—”

“Jeff, I can’t hear you—you’re dropping out—what’s going on? Did you get my Town Hall story? It’s past five o’clock already. Where the hell are you?”

“Wains—Beach La—. Come—here—as you—” Jeff’s voice quavered through the cell phone’s little speaker and cut out again.

Chapter 29: Monday, even later that afternoon

When Paul turned the corner at the start of Main Street in Wainscott he came upon a six or seven police cars near Beach Lane, their lights flashing, and cops on foot directing traffic. Tons of small, older-model Japanese cars and trucks had parked themselves on each side of the road and continued a full half-mile to the beach.

Scores of people, mostly Latina women, were walking in the direction of the ocean, chatting in Spanish, a giddiness to their talk. Paul begged a policewoman for permission to park on the grass next to a small farm stand and squeezed his truck into a spot behind one of the patrol cars. He then jogged down Beach Lane as fast as his body would let him. The day's fog had started to dissipate but traces of moisture could still be seen in the form of an eerie white mist. Too bad, because about a hundred yards from the parking lot he missed a true spectacle: a glistening multi-color blanket of wildflowers—an explosion of red, pink, and white cosmos spreading all the way to the western boundary of the Georgica Association.

When he finally got to the end of the parking lot there were hundreds of people walking toward the jetty, and a large crowd had already gathered at the site about a mile down the beach. The crowd was at least three or four times larger —and considerably more diverse—than the one that had showed up to see the right whale that had washed up on Main Beach the summer before. He noticed too that several sojourners were carrying flowers, candles, copies of the dead girl's picture, prayer beads, and what appeared to be small household items and religious figurines. Some of the younger women, who Paul took to be about the same age as the dead girl, were holding handmade signs that read *Te queremos Estrella* and

Volver Estrella—with the English translation—"We love you Estrella" and "Come back Estrella"—on the flip side.

Once at the jetty, he saw older women in long summer dresses standing on the jagged rocks in prayer as the spray of the ocean washed over their bent figures. Paul could make out the familiar cadences of the Ave Maria, though spoken in a language in which he was unaccustomed.

Dios te salve, María, llena eres de gracia ...

Others gently laid the items they had brought on the jetty's far edge, risking a slip on the rocks' slick surface. The younger among them had their mobiles out and were snapping pictures and videos and likely forwarding them to friends. A sizable assemblage of flowers and other gifts had already accumulated, with some of the smaller items slowly drifting out to sea and then rolling under and over the waves back to shore again. Each roll of the waves created a new opportunity for a photograph, and with each photograph another opportunity for continued sharing.

Jeff was there with Esra Reyes, who had been conducting interviews in Spanish and taking pictures of people holding the items they'd brought. The two of them were talking to one of the younger women, a chubby teenager with short dark hair framing her round face, a silver ring protruding through her left eyebrow. She too was holding one of the Estrella signs. After they finished, Jeff and Esra spotted Paul and ran over to greet him.

"Holy shit, man. Can you believe this?" Jeff said. "It's beautiful, isn't it? They've been coming in droves. We've got some great interviews so far, although my and Esra's Spanish are not the best."

"Speak for yourself, *Vato*," Esra said and nodded hello. "Hey Paul, yeah, people have been coming from all over—some as far away as

Queens! The crowd seems to be split between Estrella fans and those who believe this is a sighting of the Virgin," she added.

"What?" Paul asked, still a bit overwhelmed by the scene.

"The Virgin Mary, man!" Jeff said. "And not just *any* Virgin Mary but the Virgin of Guadalupe herself. It's mostly the older ladies. They keep telling us, '*Es una aparación, es una aparación'* and pointing to her picture. They think the white light around her head in the picture we posted is a halo. You know what this means, brother? When the Virgin of Guadalupe appears a miracle is going to happen. How cool is that?"

"I get that. But what is the 'Estrella' thing?"

"Those people not in the Virgin camp have given her the name 'Estrella,' based on the star tattoo. It seems to have really caught on," Esra said.

"You have to admit that it's a nice name. Better than 'dead girl,'" Jeff said.

"Yeah, *we* should probably stop calling her that," Esra said, making a face that could easily be interpreted as, *why do you guys always have to act like such dicks.*

"Estrella. You brought her to life, man. You should be proud," Jeff said, patting Paul on the back.

"I'm not so sure about that."

Just then Rebecca Loeb-Farrar of Long Island Channel 17 News came running down the beach and started setting up the camera and mic for a "stand up" next to the jetty.

"And now she's a rockstar," Jeff said, motioning toward the news crew.

"I guess all it takes to be famous nowadays is for a girl to pull up her dress and flash a tattoo," Esra said, sounding jealous.

"That and being dead," Jeff joked. "Anyway, if that were true, they would be setting up the cameras for you, Esra."

"Very funny, asshole!" Esra said as she sent Jeff a rolled up fist to his solar plexus. Jeff and Esra, both in their early thirties, would often carry on this way like a couple of battling siblings, although there was an unmistakable element of flirtation that went beyond their usual platonic banter.

"Hey, I almost forgot. Did you get my Town Hall story?" Paul asked Jeff.

"Yes I got it. It was good but—"

"—but what?"

"It needed more emotion, brother. You may have been a little too evenhanded with it."

"Really?"

"Sorry, but we are trying to sell newspapers. Or display ads or whatever it is we do online."

"Tell me you didn't."

"What?"

"Give that Conrad guy more ink."

"Grace is making final edits. You can check it out when it's up and give me shit about it later. Hey, did you find out any more information about that *Nuestra Isla* thing?"

Before he could answer, Paul heard a familiar voice calling his name from the crowd of people walking east toward the jetty.

"Paul, there you are."

It was Merika. She ran up to Paul and his colleagues.

"Merika!"

Paul took a step back in order to convince himself that it was really her. He then introduced his coworkers to Merika. Jeff shot

Paul a knowing look.

"Paul, I want to apologize. I acted really shitty yesterday. I was so stressed out. I'm sorry I didn't believe you. I know that you were trying to help. I hope you didn't get hurt too bad," she said.

"Don't worry about me. What's happening with your brother?"

"We went down to Riverhead—you were right about this being a big story. There were swarms of reporters trying to interview anyone who they thought might be from the Res. Like we all could impart this great wisdom about our fallen brother or something. But seeing people from the tribe down there I think put some pressure on the cops to hear us out. Anyway, my mom and our lawyer had this detective contact Andre's old girlfriend Elena who had moved back home to Ecuador. Elena sent over a picture of herself, her passport with a stamp showing when she left the U.S. Even a signed statement saying the last time she saw Andre was a couple of weeks ago. She was really sweet about it."

"That's good news," Paul said.

"And get this," she continued, "they send the picture of Elena over from the Quito police and the captain is on the speakerphone and he's like, in perfect English, 'This girl doesn't look anything like your dead girl. Why are you holding this guy?' My mom stared down the Peconic cops with this look that was priceless. The police are planning on releasing him this afternoon. They had to let him go."

"What about the ID they had on his truck? Did they talk about that?" Paul asked.

"They didn't mention it. I guess they didn't think it was conclusive or something," she said.

"Hey, how did you know I was going to be here at the beach?"

"I called your Southampton office and they said you would

probably be down at Beach Lane."

"You were looking for me?"

"Whaddya think, dummy? What's going on? I haven't seen this many people since the tribal elders held a prayer for that beached whale last summer. I had to walk like a mile just to get to the parking lot here."

"These people are here to celebrate our dead girl," Jeff said.

By this time a large crowd had formed ten-deep around the jetty. The atmosphere had become increasingly animated as more and more people started to arrive, including packs of school-aged children and their parents. It was as if a whole community of people usually content to blend into the background of daily East End life was having a great big coming out party.

"Not 'the dead girl.' *Estrella*," Esra corrected him.

"They know her name?" Merika asked.

"Not exactly. It's the Spanish word for 'star.' That's just what some people are calling her," Esra said.

"Hmm. I guess it's fitting since we're made of stars," Merika said.

The others looked at Merika quizzically.

"Oh, I mean that literally. That's why we're always looking to the heavens. Everything we humans are made of—carbon, oxygen, iron—those elements all existed out there first. The only thing that separates us from the distant galaxies is time—and maybe a few big explosions. That's why all these people are here with their prayers and offerings, taking pictures. When I was a little girl I'd look to the sky and imagine reaching up, grabbing a star and holding it in my hand. But later I learned I didn't have to. I bet these people are feeling that same physical connection. This girl reminded them."

"I have to admit I never thought of it that way. You're quite the empiricist," Jeff said.

"I don't know. It's really not that different from our Shinnecock creation story, all those stories I was taught growing up," Merika said. "Whether it's a giant turtle or the Earth Mother or God the Creator, it all goes back to the same thing. Even the Bible refers to Jesus as 'the bright and morning star.'"

Paul fell in love all over again.

"Jeff, I want to go post this update about Andre on the website and get the article started for Wednesday's paper. You've got a great story with this Estrella thing, brother. I'm jealous," he said.

"You're leaving?" Merika asked.

"Yeah, why don't I walk you back to your car? Unless you want to stay..."

Merika took Paul's arm for the walk back to Main Street. As they made their way toward the parking lot the two of them passed several more people walking in the opposite direction toward the jetty.

"I guess Estrella really has become a star," Paul said.

* * *

Once they were a quarter mile or so from the beach entrance, Paul stopped and pointed to one of the old farmhouses on the block.

"What is it? Why are we stopping here? My car is further up."

"That's the Clifford farm house. That's where that cop lives," Paul said.

They were standing at a rusty black mailbox at the end of long gravel drive. The mailbox belonged to an old two-story farmhouse with faded green clapboard siding. Further up the drive sat two muddied white pickup trucks, a rusty red tractor and more modern-looking farm equipment. An oak tree stood tall out front, anchoring the house to the center of a broad, open field of grass. The bright green of the front lawn put up no defense against the stubborn layer of fog still hanging, cloud-like over ground. Normally, little Wainscott Pond could be seen a short distance away across the street but that view was obscured as well.

Paul and Merika tentatively approached the front door of the house.

"There's no bell," she said.

Paul knocked lightly on the screen door and waited. He knocked again, this time rapping louder on its worn wooden frame.

She whispered, "I thought you were supposed to leave him alone. Isn't this going to get you in trouble with your policeman friend?"

"I guess not. It doesn't look like there's anyone home."

They waited a few more moments out front, even peering around to the back of the house to see if there was anyone there. As they started to make their way back down the long driveway, Paul tried explaining to Merika about his conversation with Isaak the evening before and why he failed to give Andre the benefit of the doubt.

"Look Paul, you don't have to apologize—Oh!"

Merika jumped back unexpectedly, clutching her chest.

"What is it?"

"I just saw something moving. In the window above the garage."

"Where? Are you sure?"

"Don't look, silly!"

Trying his best to attend his gaze to the row of cars parked along the block, Paul managed to steal a glance up at the window. He could only make out a still, dark curtain.

"Weird. I guess he's not receiving guests just yet," he said.

"Maybe your policeman friend—what's his name...?"

"Cole, Tom Cole."

"Yeah, have you considered that maybe your friend Cole isn't telling you *everything*?"

"What do you mean?"

"Just that," she said, motioning toward the Clifford house.

Her suggestion hung.

"Hey, this place is creeping me out. Can we get out of here?" she said finally.

"Come with me then," Paul said, pulling her in the opposite direction from where her car was parked.

"Paul, stop. Where are you taking me? You've got to go back to work."

"I don't want to let you out of my sight right now, if that's okay."

~ ~ ~

Ave Maria (6)

Summer had yet to officially arrive but she could sense the change of season. The warm air heavy with moisture in her lungs yet somehow lighter, the sun angling itself into a less severe plane of sight. On days like this she felt as if she could look directly into its flare and it would still protect her, despite its power for harm.

She couldn't tell you what all of the things she came upon in nature were called but she understood their capacity to awake the senses. The budding trees and shrubs she passed on the way down to the beach aching to burst again with their heady fragrance after an extended abeyance. The distant call of the birds flying overhead. The sea grass scratching her shins and ankles. The shells, scattered across the beach and looking to her like so many of nature's leftovers. And then, down to where the sea meets the shore, that initial sting of cold on exposed skin, and the hard scrub of sand and pebbles crunching underfoot. Knee-deep was her limit. She had yet to experience the joy of being fully immersed, buoyant in the ceaseless movement of the waves.

If you were to ask her why she walked so tentatively toward the water's edge and never beyond, she would simply say, "Y'all know I can't swim, silly." Then she would smile and repeat a joke her father used to tell about his fear of heights, only giving it a different spin.

"My Daddy'd say, 'I'm not afraid of falling. It's the landing that scares me.' But, you see, with the ocean it's the opposite. Once in over your head there's this vast emptiness and no hope of ever reaching solid ground. And that emptiness, when unbroken, well that's the scariest thing ever."

Chapter 30: Monday still later that afternoon

Will Clifford peeled back the curtain and peered out of his upstairs apartment window.

It was her. The dark haired woman who showed up at the beach that day. For a second, he considered coming down—maybe if she had been alone? He was tired of hiding. It was bad enough being forced to take that ride to Riverhead in the cramped backseat of Quinn's county car. His bare knees knocking together like a child's the entire trip. Staring through the windshield, that familiar strip of Montauk Highway narrowing to a tunnel while Quinn repeated his questions about the dead girl.

So you didn't know the girl? Why so nervous? You don't know who killed her do you?

Kill. He couldn't stop saying it, thinking it.

Sometimes when he and his crew were totally blazed, somebody would shout out a word at random—*golf*, say—and they'd repeat the word over and over, moving it around in their drying mouths until they were on the floor laughing hysterically.

Or *farm.* He spent his whole life on one. Must have said the word every day. To his parents, teachers, the workers. But say that word out loud, isolated and suspended in a haze of Oxy and marijuana smoke, and it became absolutely ridiculous. *Farm.* Fucking hysterical.

But this word was different. No matter how many times he repeated it, somehow it still managed to retain its meaning. Its weight. It wasn't as if he was unfamiliar with the concept. He'd killed before, bow hunting in the dense woods north of Town Line Road. You'd camo-up, climb into your tree stand and wait for the kill. You lived for the kill. The kill was what the whole damn thing was about.

But not this.

God this was so cliché, like De Niro in that fucked up movie. But ever since it happened he would stand in front of the mirror watching his lips form the word, or the sounds rather. The initial stretching of his cheeks and lips on the hard *k* and *eeei*-sound. All of the action on the roof of his mouth. Then the tongue, forcing itself between his teeth to complete the final *el*.

Kee-ill. Kee-ill.

He thought doing this might take the sting out of it, make it less real somehow. But nothing—not writing it, not thinking it, and especially not saying it out loud could change what he'd done.

He wanted to get high so bad right now.

It'd been five days. Five days and he still hadn't talked to anyone outside of the police. Except for the police shrink, which didn't really count. He called but only after his mother insisted. Almost eleven months sober he told the woman on the phone—ten months, thirteen days, six hours but who's counting? Yeah, he couldn't guarantee it would last honestly. He'd stopped talking to his sponsor a long time ago. When this thing blows over you'll come in and we'll talk, she said. We'll get you some help then. For now you can visit this website. Some exercises to help you deal with your problem. That's the word she used, *deal*—another ridiculous word. Like it was a negotiation he had to have with himself that he had any chance of winning.

He tried the website the shrink recommended. It wasn't long before he used up all of its tricks and phony affirmations (*God, yeah, it's me, Will. Listen, if you're not too busy can you grant me the sincerity to accept the things I cannot change? No? Okay, I'll try again later then.*). It was five days already. Five fucking days. Too much time for someone like him to spend at home alone. His thoughts rattling around like broken shells inside his head.

He did manage to sneak out a few times with his binoculars though, to the backyard, in the early mornings when he thought no one would notice.

He had to see what his birds were up to.

Since spring and early summer he'd counted at least thirty species. Lots of the smaller birds in the mudflats around little Wainscott Pond across from his house. Killdeer, bobolinks, bitterns and horned larks, a few piping plovers whose breeding grounds would soon be closed off along the ocean beach. Larger waterfowl too—snowy egrets, Louisiana herons, blue herons, all kinds of ducks and mallards. He even spotted a few tundra swans that must have stayed over from the winter.

But the great white or "common" egret, that was a special find. Maybe it was something about the bird's unique proportions. Its graceful movements while in flight. The long spear-like beak. Its broad wings spanning almost five feet that seemed to magically disappear while standing. And its reed-like legs it kept perfectly still while waiting to attack its prey.

Or maybe it was the bird's elegant "s"-shaped neck that reminded him most of Caridad. His breath would quicken each time he caught one streaking across the sky or lazing close among the reeds.

And now all he could see was people. Lots of them. All afternoon he had to watch them walk by his family's house, laughing and singing and carrying stuff with them down to the beach. Part of him wished he could join in too. Pay his respects, like the others. Maybe even bring the truth out in the open. But that would have been a really bad idea, especially with the news cameras and reporters down there. And he was tired of doing really bad things.

"*Caridad*—her name is like a song," his mother once said. But they never prepare you for when the song is over do they?

Chapter 31: Monday evening

The first thing Paul did when he and Merika got to the office was call Virginia Woo. Once again her line went to a voicemail referencing the county website, this time featuring a press release consisting of two terse lines of *officialeze:* the first stating "lack of evidence" for continuing to hold Andre as a "key person of interest"; the second line a veiled apology to the Shinnecock Nation for any "inconvenience this office may have caused." Not a word about any other developments in the case or who the real suspects might be.

He decided to try Tom Cole.

"Cole here, what is it?"

"Tom, it's Paul, Paul Sandis. I'm writing this update about the release of Andre Little—"

"—Jesus. I'm not answering any more of your questions, Sandis," Cole said.

"Hey, what's up?" Paul tried, lightly.

But Cole had already hung up on him.

Armed with this small bit of information and a few other details he'd learned, Paul tried to fashion a story for his paper's online addition about Andre's release and the still unsolved mystery. When he got to the end of his draft, Merika was looking over his shoulder at the blinking screen of text.

"That's it? You're not going to say what assholes they were?"

"Not unless you want to be quoted directly. I'm not comfortable using an unnamed source to attack these guys. I'd like to keep my job."

"I guess there's more nuance to this than I realized," she said. "I was actually thinking that *I* might like to do some reporting, you know, maybe cover the Shinnecock beat."

"We already have someone in Southampton who does that."

"No one who is a Shinnecock. How can they know what's really going on?"

"They try their best. Tell you what, why don't you take a shot at this one?" Paul rolled his chair back from the screen, and put his palms face up toward the keyboard. "Really. Go ahead."

He figured that would end her complaint but instead Merika lifted Paul out of his chair, sat down at the computer and read over the copy again. She shooed him away and then began to type.

"Just don't hit that "Submit" button until I get to read it first," he said, stepping away and moving over to Jeff's desk. He opened the top drawer, pulled out the little *EET* stress ball, and started squeezing, sneaking glances over at Merika every ten minutes or so in between a game of Space Invaders.

When she was satisfied with what she'd written she rolled her chair back from the computer and invited Paul over for a look. The two of them read the revised copy together, this time with Paul peering over her shoulder. Merika had left Paul's factual version of events intact. But with the addition of a few critical sentences she'd managed to weave a bit of emotional truth into the story: inferring the possibility of the police's initial prejudicial approach to its investigation, their willingness to compromise once political pressure from the tribe became too intense to ignore, the subsequent relief of the families involved, and most importantly, a more finely developed portrait of the accused who had been struggling to get his life on track at the time of his arrest. It was a pretty good piece of journalism.

"So?"

"That is like the sexiest thing," Paul said.

"Y'think?"

"I'll prove it to you." Paul placed his arm around Merika's shoulder and spun her chair to face him. She moved toward him for an embrace but instead of reciprocating he reached toward the keyboard, typed the words, "by Paul Sandis and Merika Jones," in the author's space and hit "Submit."

* * *

"Hey, what's this?"

They were back at Paul's house, Merika on the living room sofa. Paul was in the kitchen fetching a beer when she picked up one of his small spiral notebooks from the end table and started flipping through the dog-eared pages.

"C'mon, give me that." Paul reached for the notebook as Merika ran across the living room.

"I was thinking, now that I'm a journalist I should have access to your notes," she said. She continued to scan the pages while Paul tried grabbing it from her. She ran to the other side of the sofa and opened the book to a word-filled page. "Hey, is this your poetry?"

"Some of it ..." He reached again to grab the notebook from her hands.

"Wait a sec. 'By Morning Twilight.' This is the poem I told Isaak about. Paul, you looked it up? That's so thoughtful. And what's this?"

She read aloud from the facing page:

"'Love consists in this, that two solitudes protect and touch and greet each other' —did you write this?"

"I wish. I mean not originally. It's Rilke, the German poet."

"It's beautiful."

"I think so too."

She took his hand and led him into the bedroom. He tried unbuttoning the front of her dress but she pushed his hands away and took a step back. She then continued for him: first the straps of her sundress, one at a time gently pushing them aside with her forefinger until the outside curve of each loop rested on her upper arm, then gracefully lifting her arm through and shimmying the entire garment down the length of her body until it fell softly in a pile; after unhooking the clasp of her bra and freeing her breasts she turned the backs of her hands inward, and leaning forward like a swimmer getting ready to plunge, let gravity slide the undergarment down the length of her arms until it joined her dress on the floor. She ladled the thin elastic band of her panties, this time running her forefinger along the length of her right leg and stepping out of them until they too united with the rest of her clothes. Paul watched with great anticipation, a tent forming in his boxers, which he pulled down along with his jeans in one swift motion and kicked to the side. She helped him pull his T-shirt over his head and took a step back.

They regarded each other now, eyes locked and then allowing their gaze to roam across each other's face, chest, arms, hands, belly, cock, pussy. All at once they became acutely aware of the other's breathing, and adjusted their own until they were both convinced they were sharing the same breath. Paul reached out his hand and brought Merika to him, wrapping his arms tightly around her, his stiffness pushed against the softness her belly, and buried his face in the flare where her neck met her shoulder blade. They remained this way for several seconds; still attuned to each other's breath, until he lifted his head and joined her in a kiss.

She was unquestionably different from any woman he had made love to in the past. It wasn't just because she was Black *and* Native American; he felt enough of a burden trying to avoid the outsized exotic implications of this. Of course he couldn't deny his attraction to her unique redolence, the coarseness of her long cork-screwy hair, the darkness of her nipples and surprising variations of color he discovered on other areas of her skin as he began to explore the contours of her body. But no, it wasn't *just* that. It was her complete acceptance of him—as he brought his mouth to her mouth and then to her breast, his tongue probing her as she arched her back, and later, as she helped him roll on the condom and guide him in. With Merika he was made to understand the absolute appreciation she felt for her own body, with all of its voluptuous curves, folds, and uneven arrangements. And in the sharing of it was an act of utmost generosity; there was nothing selfish or self-conscious about her.

"Hey, I thought you said you weren't a player," she whispered to him breathlessly at one point.

"Huh?"

He lifted his head slowly from between her legs. She reached out her hand to caress his cheek.

"That first night at the restaurant, you told me you weren't much of a player. But you seem to know exactly what you're doing. It's like you're practicing some kind of reverse origami down there. And it's working. Don't stop."

After they did stop, Merika began telling him how she had been blown to smithereens by the men in her life and...

"It's almost as if you were putting me back together again. I know it sounds silly: first the unfolding and then—Paul, are you crying?"

"What? No, no, I'm laughing."

"Really? How come? Am I that funny?"

"No, I'm just happy," he said.

Later, as they lay naked in each other's arms and the last rays of evening sunlight faded, a clattering ceiling fan making its uneven rounds above their heads and cooling their sticky skin, Merika felt comfortable enough to tell her story about Peter that ended with that final morning at his grandmother's cottage in Wainscott. And in the telling, he could sense an unburdening rather than sadness. Perhaps it was because for the first time in a long while she too was feeling truly happy.

"Paul, why are you laughing *now*? I know you're happy but this is not supposed to be a funny story," Merika said.

"I'm sorry, but you used to call your guy 'Drake,' right? A drake is a male duck. That's pretty funny. I keep imagining this guy Peter waddling around the cottage with a fat white tail and a beak," Paul said.

"Y'know I never thought of that. I always considered the name regal or something. But now that you said it, I remember seeing all these duck pictures in that place. They used to kind of creep me out, especially the ones of placid-looking white guys hiding behind bushes, holding those shotguns. But be careful Paul, you won't win any points by tearing down my old boyfriends, especially the father of my child. I'd rather that he just be a blank..." She paused for a few seconds, eyes closed with her head back on the pillow, as if trying to erase Peter from her mind's eye before continuing.

"Hey, you don't think that Mr. Drake—I mean Peter—had something to do with the dead girl showing up in front of his family's house."

"No."

"Okay."

Merika sat up in the bed with a renewed energy.

"Hey, I told you my story, now you need to tell me something about you. But there's a catch. It has to be something you've never told anyone before."

"Why?"

"Because you got to have this hot body. This don't come for free. You gotta work for it," she said, rubbing up against him.

"Damn! Okay. How about this: You are amazing. I never told anyone that before," Paul said.

"Pfft. That's too easy. And definitely not news."

"Too much of a cheat huh? I guess, especially since I will be telling everyone that soon enough."

"C'mon, tell me something you haven't told anyone before. And I want a story, not just 'I think blah, blah' or 'I like whatever.' That's not going to cut it. And, you should know something else about me: stories turn me on," she said.

"Hmm, some real motivation; now we're talkin'. Okay, I have a sad story. Is that okay?"

"As long as it's a story," she said. Then she put her elbow on Paul's chest, propped up her chin in her hand, and gave him a look that said, *Okay, I'm listening; this better be good.*

Paul started with: "I was eleven when my mother died—"

"—wait, Paul, you don't have to tell me *this* story."

"No, let me tell it. It's a good story. Don't worry it gets better. Anyway, I was eleven when my mother died. After she died she was cremated and a few days later my dad brought home my mother's ashes in an urn. He placed the urn on top of the fireplace mantle in our apartment. The fireplace never worked but it had a shelf over it where we used to put all kinds of art projects I'd done and stuff like that. Anyway, my mom was now home with us, so to speak, up there on the mantle. Every year, even though my dad is an atheist, we would follow the Jewish tradition and light a Yahrzeit candle—this is a candle that burns for a full day to pay tribute to the memory of your loved one."

"We have something like that. When someone dies we light a bundle of white sage as part of the funeral ceremony. The smoke is used in a cleansing ritual to see the deceased off into the spirit world," Merika said.

"Yeah, I guess using fire in funeral ceremonies is common practice probably going back to the caveman. Anyway, Isaak and I created our own tradition around the urn. We'd tell my mom stories, light the candle. Sometimes my dad would let me have a drink of wine or beer on the anniversary and we'd get a little drunk. Other times I would talk to her when I was alone."

"That is so sweet," Merika said.

"So this goes on for like five years and then when I was sixteen I came across this letter in Isaak's room." Paul then recreated what he could remember of the letter for Merika.

My Dearest Isaak,

You told me to make a list of all the things that I have ever loved in the world and I told you that I would try, even though it is painful for me. Although I would think it should take a normal person a very long time to write and certainly read a list that long I am afraid that mine is very short. So here is what I remember:

-Rubbing the soft spot on the top of little Paulie's head when he was brand new (I am sorry my beloved to start with our son, I hope you will forgive me)

-The way you would kiss the back of my hands and feet when we made love

-Watching the dust particles dance in the stream of light that shone through my old bedroom window when I was a child back in my parent's house in Greece and dreaming of coming to America (I know that's two but they happened at the same time!).

-The way our family priest, Father Leonidas, would smile at me as if I were the only one he was saving his smile for when he offered the host to me at Mass,

-Our first summer together in Brooklyn before my parents refused to let me see you—the hours we spent lying on the beach in Coney Island, playing in the waves. You were so handsome and I was so foolish then.

-My wonderful students — God knows not all of them — but so many who have grown up and made me proud to be their teacher.

-Music, beautiful music, and dancing —if only I could keep dancing for you my love.

This is so difficult, sweet Isaak, but I cannot think of more to say other than goodbye.

But there is one more thing I need to tell you. It is more of a request than a memory: please bury me in the Catholic cemetery next to the church. Father Stanislaus will give you the details. I never told you because I thought you would think it selfish of me but I purchased a plot months ago with some of our savings when I first became ill. I know because of your beliefs that you cannot lie beside me for eternity and it pains me to think of this. But Isaak, that is my final wish.

Please take care of our son and know that I will always love both of you.

Your loving wife,

Sophia

"Wait, so your mom's final wish is to be buried in the *cemetery*? Wow, how could Isaak not satisfy her final wish and have her cremated? Paul, why are you telling me this? I love Isaak. Was I wrong about him?"

"No, let me tell you the rest of the story. Remember, this is a *story*. You only allowed me to tell you the beginning and part of the middle. I haven't got to the end yet," Paul said.

"Okay, I'll shut up now. But I'm not liking Isaak at this point in the story. What did you do when you found the letter?"

"I'm getting to that. At first I was so angry I didn't know what to do. How could my father do this to my mother? How could he be so selfish and never say anything to me about it? I know I was a little kid when my mother died but still, he usually told me everything that was going on, even if it was painful. He told me about his past, how he had lost his parents and sister during the war. After I got over the initial shock I confronted him about it and he was really upset.

"He said, 'I know, but it's not what you think.' And I said, 'You couldn't give her this final wish? How could you have her cremated? Why was that so important? How could you do that to her?'"

"So Isaak says, 'That's the thing, I did grant her that final wish. She was buried in the Catholic cemetery. It's you that I wronged.'"

Merika looked perplexed.

"I was just as confused as you are. Let me explain.

"Isaak agreed that it was a beautiful letter but he was furious about her request. My mother wasn't a very religious person but she knew she was going to die and wanted to be embraced again by her church. My parents talked it over many late nights—they'd wait until I'd fallen asleep—sometimes I'd wake up and hear them bickering but didn't know why. Isaak called her nostalgic and silly. She faulted him for his absolutism, saying his atheist views were as narrow as any religious zealot. Eventually, she made him realize how important it was to her, that she had found a way to let go, to accept death with grace.

"So Isaak granted her wish—what else could he do? But he wasn't willing to go all the way.

"'I loved her, she was my *life*,' he told me. 'But, I couldn't accept the fact that the same church that took me in and saved me from oblivion could take Sophia away from me.' You see, Greek nuns had hid Isaak during the war while the rest of his family perished.

"He devised a plan. He kept me from going to the cemetery with everyone else that day. We went home right after my mother's service. For years he refused to visit the grave. He even cut himself off from my mother's family."

"What about the ashes?" Merika asked.

"He had a janitor at the college give him some ashes from the incinerator—they still burned paper and other trash back then—and put them in an urn he bought at some store on Flatbush Avenue."

"But why go to all that trouble? Why didn't he tell you the truth so you could visit your Mom's grave? How could he take that away from you?"

"I was all he had left. And he was afraid of losing me if I ever found out that he skipped the burial and kept me from it. And, after some time passed I think the ashes comforted him, comforted *us*. He started to believe it *was* my mother in that urn, each year, lighting the candle, making up our own prayers for her, telling her stories. That day I found the letter he sat me down and said, 'I guess I thought that if I told you the truth it would be like losing her all over again. I wanted her here with us, not in some random plot with a bunch of strangers.' I think he was afraid. Fear is a very powerful emotion. It makes people do stupid things."

"Did you forgive him?" Merika asked.

"Of course. He was hurting," Paul said. "I still believe that he was acting selfishly but he was also trying to protect me, trying to create something for the two of us that only we could share. He made me realize how important that was to him. After that we went to the cemetery together every year. And, we kept the ashes. Isaak still has them in his apartment."

"And, you never told anyone about this before? Even your wife—I mean your ex-wife?"

"I considered telling her but never found the right moment. Maybe I was afraid that she wouldn't forgive Isaak like I did."

"I forgive him," Merika said.

"I'm glad." Paul kissed her.

"Paul, I have to tell you something."

"Uh oh, you know what happened the last time you started a conversation this way. La, la, la," Paul chanted like a child and held up his hands to the sides of his head to cover his pint-sized appendages.

"C'mon, be serious. I'm trying to tell you something I'm not particularly proud of," she said, pulling down his hands and holding them in hers.

"What's that?"

"That day in the cottage with Peter when I saw the truck parked near the jetty, my first instinct was that it was Andre. I thought maybe he had followed me or somehow found out that I was there. That's why I went over to the beach afterward when I saw the cops parked there."

"But you didn't believe he had anything to do with the missing girl?"

"That's just it. I didn't want to believe he did but I wasn't sure. He's my brother. I love him. But he can do some crazy shit, you know. That's why when it seemed like you doubted his innocence I was so angry—because maybe I also had my doubts."

"That's a lot to admit. Thank you," Paul said, climbing on top of Merika and kissing her again, this time with a bit more passion. She pulled away from him abruptly, grasping his arms and staring into his face. "What is it?"

"There is something else," she said.

"What else?"

"My name. That story I told Isaak about the Meredith poem. It isn't true."

"The whole thing?"

"Yeah. It was a poem I memorized in fifth grade for school. My mother just liked the name 'Merika,' but that isn't much of a story is it? I was just making conversation. I didn't think it would become this big thing. I mean Isaak loved it so much I kept it going. Are you mad?"

"I don't know yet."

"It was lovely of you to search it out for me. That was so sweet. It's still something we can share, right?"—Just then a loud siren blared from a not-too-far distance. "What's that?"

"Sounds like the alert for the fire department here in Springs. Hold on a sec." Paul got out of bed, walked into the living room and brought the antiquated police scanner back into the bedroom with him and started setting it up.

"Hey, it's our little friend," Merika said, sitting up in the bed.

"Sorry, bad habit, but I just want to make sure this isn't something serious." Paul turned on the machine and tuned the dial to the frequency the fire department used for their emergency communication. In between the static and fading in and out of crackling distant radios, Paul and Merika could make out a few brief exchanges.

—Fully engaged structure fire—31 Antler Ridge, I repeat: fully engaged—possible ten-thirty one, copy?

—Yeah, this is ninety five thirty one. I'm closing off Antler Ridge at Garden St.

—Thirty-one, this is ninety-five thirty en route. See you there buddy.

—That's a ten four, over.

"This isn't good. That's the same street as that family who was singled out at the town meeting. Jeff and I were just talking about that house earlier today."

"What meeting?"

"Merika, I hate to do this to you but we should go over there and see what's happening. It's not far from here. The dispatcher said, "fully engaged." That means the whole house could be on fire."

"Then let's go."

Chapter 32: Monday, later that evening

Edward was in his small office in the rectory at St. Cecilia's preparing a sermon for the next week when he heard the loud siren warning of a fire somewhere in East Hampton. He was about to make a phone call to one of his parishioners when there was a soft knock at his office door.

"Excuse me Father, I'd like to make a confession," the young man said from behind the half-closed door.

"We have hours set aside for confession. Could you return another time perhaps? I'm a bit busy at the moment," Edward said without looking up from his desk.

He heard the door opening slowly behind him.

"Forgive me, Father, but I need to speak with you *now*, if that's alright." The young man's tone revealed an urgency that Edward couldn't ignore. He turned around in his chair to face the tall youth with flaming red hair now standing inside the office door. Edward recognized him immediately.

"Ah, I see. Um, can you give me a moment? Please, wait for me in the confessional." Edward disappeared into another room adjoining the church to fetch his confessional garb. He returned promptly, rosary in hand and cassock blowing as he hurried to take his place on the other side of the screen within the ornately carved wood confessional box. He was so rushed he placed the traditional purple stole used for the sacrament of Reconciliation in reverse, its white side facing up—white usually reserved for celebratory occasions. Upon stepping into the box, he took note of his error and rearranged the purple silken garment across his shoulders.

"Do I have to kneel, Father? I prefer to sit, if that's okay."

“Of course. Whatever works.”

“I haven’t done this before. I’m not even Catholic. I’m not even sure how this is supposed to go," the young man said.

A fire truck siren whined in the distance and quickly faded. Two more sirens followed. Edward leaned in and drew the small panel to one side, revealing the latticed screen safely separating the two men. It had been almost exactly a year since they were this close.

“Let’s try this again, only this time you talk and I listen.” Edward paused and curled his fingers around the large wooden cross that hung from his neck. “Now, what is it that is bothering your conscience?”

Chapter 33: Monday night

Two fire police cars, lights flashing, were stopped at the corner of Antler Ridge and Garden Street blocking the street from traffic. White smoke cancelled out the dark June sky for blocks. Paul parked his truck on a nearby side street and he and Merika moved quickly on-foot past the roadblocks toward the blaze. By now the day's fog and mist had completed lifted—but not the intense heat and humidity. There were no streetlights in this neighborhood but it was easy enough to follow the path of smoke and flame. People congregated on their front lawns chatting, nervously shuffling their feet side to side—that is, doing whatever it is people do when their neighbor's house is blazing and they have no way to control the outcome. A few pointed Paul and Merika in the direction of the fire as they ran by, perhaps thinking the two of them were in some way important.

They were able to get within a few hundred feet of the burning house when a fire policeman stopped them. The fire cop had closed one lane of the road with a band of yellow police tape in front of his police vehicle, the other lane blocked by orange cones. In the area beyond the tape, there were five large fire trucks and two EMT vehicles, and emergency service personnel could be seen milling around. Even though crews had set up a high-powered light for night viewing, it was difficult to see exactly what was going on from this vantage point. Paul was looking around for Jeff but didn't see his friend anywhere. He had left a message on Jeff's voicemail before he and Merika left the house but was unable to reach him.

"Hey, my name is Paul Sandis from the *East End Times*. This is my colleague Merika Jones," Paul said, showing the fire policeman his press ID.

The policeman was a strapping guy in his sixties with closely cropped dark hair and graying temples. Like everyone else there, the sweat was showing through his T-shirt in the extreme heat. Paul assumed the guy was one of a dying breed, a "good Jake" who took the job of fire policeman when he'd aged out of fighting fires and couldn't give up the life. Since 9/11 the job had become more of a professional position, attracting younger volunteers who were eager to take the extensive training in order to get a badge confirming on them the job of peace officer. Usually Paul would approach one of these newer, more eager volunteers since they were likely to allow him past the public barricades to get a closer look and take pictures. But this guy wasn't budging.

"Wait here. Let me call the incident commander," the fire policeman said.

He stepped away from them to call his chief on the radio and quickly got a confirmation: any journalists who showed up were to be assigned to him and stay put behind his emergency vehicle.

"Can we at least get some information? Do you know whose house that is? How did the fire start? Was anyone hurt?" Paul asked.

"Enough with all the questions already. You're starting to be a real pain in the ass, you know that?"

It was Tom Cole, walking over to them from behind one of the other police barricades beyond where the fire policeman was parked. Paul was curious as to why Cole might be here. He obviously knew a lot of the guys in the Springs Fire Department, including the chief, who was himself a police officer for East Hampton Town. But he couldn't possibly have time to respond to every fire.

"Tom! Look whose looking for trouble. Hey, this is my colleague,

Merika Jones," Paul said.

"Colleague huh? You're not getting writing tips from this guy, I hope. Nice to meet you," Cole said, extending his hand to Merika.

"Tom, what the hell is going on?" Paul asked.

"We got a real shit-mess here Sandis—pardon my French," Cole said for Merika's benefit. "We don't have confirmation yet regarding cause but it looks like the fire may have started in the garbage bins next to the house. House belongs to a family named Burger. Neighbors say they're primarily weekend people. We're trying to get in touch with them now. Thankfully, no one was at home when the fire started and we were able to get everyone out of the nearby houses safely. Guys are working right now to make sure the fire doesn't spread."

As he was jotting this down in his notebook, Paul was puzzled. He took out a folded piece of paper from his pocket that he had printed out at the office earlier that day. The list of homes being targeted by Lucy Birch and her followers she had posted on her group's Facebook page.

"Tom, I'm confused. Take a look at this." Paul handed Cole the list.

"What is this?" He took the paper from Paul's hands and started reaching for the flashlight in his back pocket.

"The Alvarez' address was on that list of homes targeted by Lucy Birch and her friends. Look, there it is, number thirty-one. We heard the guys on the radio call that house number, *that's* the address for Alvarez," Paul said, pointing to the address at the top of Lucy Birch's list.

"I've seen this list," Cole said, scanning the page. "We got a call from the priest over at St. Cecilia's after that Town Hall meeting today asking us if we could do something to protect those homes. Sandis, you know we don't have enough guys to watch a dozen houses around the clock—hey you're not printing this. This is just me talking off the record, got it?"

"Sure Tom, off the record, but who is this Burger? Did the fire department get the house number wrong when they called it over the radio?"

"I don't know," Tom said, apparently as confused as Paul was.

"Maybe this Lucy woman got the house number wrong. She must have listed Burger's address on her page by mistake," Merika said, figuring out the error before the two super-sleuths.

Just then, there was a loud explosion. A large piece of the roof collapsed into the Burger home. Flames and sparks shot up and out toward the house next door, further lighting up the night sky. Tiny flakes of white ash floated down from above their heads; a bitter snowfall on one of the hottest nights of summer. Paul could now see what he guessed were members of the Alvarez family, including several adults and small children, standing at the end of their driveway behind another police barricade. Their house was safe—for now.

"Whoa! Are there any firefighters in there?" Merika asked, after watching the roof collapse into itself. The house wheezed a toxic blend of acrid and sweet.

"We've got about forty guys fighting the fire from the *outside*. We gave up trying to fight it from inside once it was clear the house was toast. And, Miss, please stay behind the barrier," the cop said.

"Tom, you've got some strong circumstantial evidence here. Is it more than a coincidence that this address—whoever's house it is—made the top of what is essentially a 'hit' list?" Paul asked.

As Tom Cole was pondering this, someone approached the three of them from further up the street where the Alvarez family was gathered. As the figure edged closer, Paul could make out the silhouette of a man in a black suit. He was moving toward them slowly, almost gliding along the pavement, taking small, calibrated steps as if the ground in front of him could open up and swallow him at any moment.

"Hello, I am Father de la Rosa. Are you the detective?" He was looking directly at Paul. The priest was sweating profusely in his black wool suit and high collar. Circular stains dampened his jacket in the area under his arms. His face glowed bright red in the heat.

"That would be me. Detective Tom Cole, captain of the East Hampton Police," Cole said, reaching out his hand.

The priest took Cole's hand and shook it, bowing his head slightly. "Captain Cole, yes, we spoke earlier today on the phone. We are all very saddened by this. I can't help but think that—"

"—hold on there, Father. I know where you are going. There is no proof that this fire is related to this list," Cole said, holding up the paper Paul had given him.

"You have the list? Why would you have the list if this is not a concern of the police?" de la Rosa asked.

"*Jesus*—sorry Father," Cole said, glancing over at Paul. "Of course it is our concern. But, let's not jump to any conclusions. There will be an investigation. We will do everything we can to find out the cause of this."

The priest's expression couldn't hide his apparent dissatisfaction with Cole's response. "Of course. Thank you, detective. I wanted to ask you something else. Do the police know anything yet about what happened to this poor girl in Wainscott?"

"Not yet," Cole said and then, without skipping a beat, "But we're getting close. Maybe you can pray for us, Father."

At this point the Burger house was too far gone to be saved. Firefighters were desperately trying to contain the blaze and stop the fire from spreading to the houses next door on either side. What little wind there was earlier in the evening seemed to have changed direction and now flames from the Burger house were extending their fingers toward a two-story contemporary located on the side opposite the Alvarez home. Firefighters quickly moved en masse to the narrow patch of lawn between the burning house and this other house but it was already too late. Flames from the Burger house had started to migrate to a wood-shingled dormer on the second floor.

Paul caught the priest's attention and held out his hand.

"Father, I'm Paul Sandis from the *East End Times*. I saw you speak this morning at the town meeting. I admire what you did in that hall today." He shook the priest's sweaty hand.

"I was just trying to get people to broaden their minds a little and to accept God into their heart. I feel very passionately about that."

"Well, I have to tell you Father, in my job as a reporter I've seen you speak at events before but never with so much conviction."

"Thank you."

The priest, so diminutive at the podium earlier in the day, had a more substantial presence face-to-face. Sort of like an oversized child that demanded you pay attention.

"By the way, who was that woman you were speaking to, the one who seemed to be leading the chanting at the meeting? I was hoping to interview her for my article about the meeting for our print edition."

De la Rosa blushed. "Leading? I'm not sure what you mean. We have some very vocal members in the church."

"No, I'm pretty sure there was one woman who stood out. The lady with the ponytail, bright colored top? I saw you talking with her afterward, in the parking lot."

The question seemed to have hit a nerve.

"I'm sure I couldn't tell you. There was a lot going on," he said. "Well, it was so nice talking with you but I should be getting back. Thank you for your time Captain Cole."

As the priest began walking back toward the Alvarez family, Paul ran up to him and took hold of his arm.

"Listen, Father, can I talk with you for a moment in private?"

"I don't know. What is it?" he said.

"Father, I couldn't help notice that you asked Captain Cole about the dead girl who was found in Wainscott. I was wondering if perhaps your interest in the whereabouts of the girl was more than parochial, if you know what I mean."

"I'm not sure I do."

"Well, I know that you have a sizable Latino congregation and a lot of people believe that the missing woman is a young Latina. *Was*, I should say. Perhaps you know who she was or know someone who might know," Paul said.

The priest looked pained, as if trying to figure out how to get away from Paul without being rude. Although it may have seemed impossible only moments before, his face began to turn an even brighter shade of crimson.

"If I had that information I would definitely let the police know about it," he said.

"So when you say *that* information do you mean to say you may have *other* information that might be relevant to this case?" Paul asked.

"I should get back to the others," the priest said nervously, turning to leave.

Paul grabbed onto the priest's jacket sleeve again before he could walk away. "Father–"

Just then Paul heard a loud cry for help and turned to look at the second house that had now caught fire. Two men–ordinary men wearing no special gear–were running into the burning house.

There had been strange movements at a basement window in the front of the house next door to the Burger house. It looked as if someone was trying to crawl his way out through one of the slender casement windows. Luis Alvarez and other members of his family seemed to be the only ones close enough to the house to know what was happening. "*Mira*! Over here, over here," they were yelling. But the firefighters were preoccupied with putting out the fire on the second floor dormer and the family's cries were ignored.

Someone had to do something.

Luis Alvarez and his cousin Carlos broke ranks behind the barrier and ran toward their neighbor's house whose second floor was now fully ablaze. This caused Carlos' wife Carmen to let out a shrill scream that finally got the attention of firefighters–but it was already too late.

First the two men tried to enter the basement through an outdoor Bilco door but it was locked tight. They quickly moved to the front of the house and, after a few unsuccessful attempts, managed to get past the front door by breaking the lock. Once inside they searched desperately for an interior basement door, unlocked the bolt and rushed down the stairs, the smoke trailing them as they went. When they reached the finished basement room they discovered the teenage boy they had seen trying to escape through the casement windows. He was lying unconscious on a futon. Across from him was a large TV fixed to a first-person-shooter video game, the play paused in the middle of the action. Empty beer cans littered the room. The two men did a quick search to see if there were any others but apparently the boy was alone. They then managed to get his arms over each of their shoulders and carried him upstairs, moving as low as possible to the ground as the smoke began to enter the first floor from above. When the three of them reached the threshold of the front door, firefighters and members of the EMT crew were already waiting with oxygen and a stretcher.

The teen, Morris Tendel, was semi-conscious, most likely in shock, and had suffered from smoke inhalation.

Paul watched Cole run over to the EMT crew as they were putting Morris into the ambulance, the victim's face and arms covered with a blanket. After a few tense minutes, Cole walked back to join the others. They all watched as the vehicle pulled away, lights flashing and siren blaring on its way down Garden Street.

"It was just some stupid kid who got drunk and fell asleep in the basement. But it looks like he's gonna be alright," Cole said.

"Whose kid is he?" Paul asked.

"I don't know. He was pretty shaken up. I didn't get a name. We'll get you all the details later once they get him to the hospital. Those two guys who went in are crazy but crazy enough that it looks like they saved the kid's life—"

Before Tom Cole could finish, two people raced up to where their little group was gathered.

It was Jeff, with Esra Reyes in tow.

They were both out of breath, having run some distance. Paul noticed that Esra had showed up without her camera. Strange since she was always clutching the thing or carrying it in a black bag slung across her shoulders.

They all turned to look at the two burning homes in the near distance. The Burger house was now almost completely unrecognizable, a smoldering charred mass. The fire in the house adjacent was still burning on its second floor but now seemingly under control.

"Holy shit," Esra said, speaking on behalf of most of those present. She took out her mobile and used her zoom to take the best picture she could under the circumstances.

The priest turned to Detective Cole and said, "Before, you asked me to pray for you. Now, I believe I will pray for all of us."

He then left to rejoin the Alvarez family, his black silhouette disappearing into the night and smoke.

* * *

Another night and Paul couldn't sleep. Trying his best not to wake Merika, he crept down the hall to the living room and clicked on the lamp. He began searching the house: the coffee table, kitchen counters, the end table with its stack of junk mail and Connor's seed catalogues. He tried the laundry closet. There they were, sticking out of the back pocket of a pair of jeans crumpled in a ball at the bottom. He pulled out the folded, crinkled pictures and smoothed them on the surface of the coffee table.

Who are you? Why hasn't anyone claimed you?

As a parent, he could look into that angelic face and recognize her as someone's child, a girl who shouldn't be made to know about life's darkest corners. And yet, the picture with the tattoo confirmed her as something more. A sexual being. A creature to be observed, touched, and pleasured. To be explored.

As Paul studied the two photographs again it was if he was seeing them for the first time.

You really are beautiful.

And with it came a realization: he had been so focused on trying to figure out what had *happened to her* that he hadn't bothered *considering her*. Like so many others, he'd found it convenient to simply classify the girl by type—precious victim, corrupted youth, mysterious vixen, careless whore. Now that he was truly *seeing* her maybe he could begin to think of her as someone worthy of love and respect.

Maybe this is what Isaak meant when he said that experiencing beauty presses us toward the good.

Sitting in his dimly lit house in the quiet of early morning, his bruised and battered heart now entwined with that of the beautiful stranger sleeping safely in the next room, Paul tried piecing together what he knew to be true and what he could only imagine. Isaak was correct in thinking it was better to wait until all the facts revealed themselves before rushing to judgment. But what was Paul to make of this new information? What did Father de la Rosa know? And how could he, a man of God, not feel empathy for this girl? The priest was obviously hiding something. But perhaps Paul had been too quick to attach motives to de la Rosa as a protector of whoever might have done something to harm the girl. Maybe it was the girl who needed protecting. Maybe the priest understood the true meaning of beauty as only he himself could understand it: that protecting the girl's soul was more important than everyone discovering the truth.

Chapter 34: Thursday, Beach Lane – The Cop

Will Clifford zipped up his new blue police-issue windbreaker, put Pico on the leash, and headed east down the beach in the direction of the Kilkare house, its 19th century porch jutting out toward the ocean like the prow of a giant ship. Once they got out a few hundred feet or so he let the dog run and fetch an old tennis ball. Pico was fearless, as usual. Leaping into the crashing waves. Disappearing under the foam and rearranging his brute self a few seconds later. The yellow ball clenched tightly between his teeth. Clomping back onto the shore, tail wagging, and dropping the slobbering mess at Will's feet. Then panting with excitement, his head cocked and ready to start the process all over again.

But there was an abrupt change in the dog's routine once the two of them reached the beach near the Georgica Association's graying cedar dressing rooms. This time, after retrieving the ball, Pico dropped it a few feet short. The dog raised his head to better sniff the salt air, and made a quick sprint toward the rock jetty.

* * *

"Listen, Miguel, we have to say something, if only to the boy's parents," Rachel said. She and her husband were scraping their steel-toothed rakes along the sandy bottom at the shallow end of Georgica Pond.

"I know it feels like the right thing to do but it will only hurt Daisy," Miguel said. "She's gone through enough."

"That boy has to learn, Papi. What if he does it again to some other girl? Then what?"

Sylvia, Rachel's older daughter, who was only half-listening to their conversation, spied a man who appeared to be from the Town Police running down the beach after a big black dog in the direction of the jetty.

"Mami, Papi, quick, get behind the hill," she shouted.

Sylvia typically didn't accompany her parents on these illegal clamming trips but today she promised to come and act as lookout, using the small field glasses her father had given her. An avid bird watcher, she had only agreed to come along if she could spend some time birding and not have to wade into the pond with them.

Their blue Toyota Tacoma was parked, hidden behind a tall pile of sand, just west of where Rachel and Miguel were standing knee-deep in the pond. Each October, the town trustees would create an opening between the pond and the ocean to flush out its waters and provide access for the newly born fish to venture out into the ocean. Nature would then fill the opening with sand by early summer. As usual, the pond was opened during the fall, and then closed up again. But that winter the beach had suffered under several Nor'easters. So the trustees sold hundreds of yards of sand to the Georgica Association and set it aside for the wealthy homeowners to repair their beachfront. This sand pile created a sort of man-made dune between the southwestern part of the pond and the surrounding beach. It was behind this tall "dune" that the three of them were parked out of view from anyone who might venture along the beach from the Beach Lane entrance.

* * *

Will called out to the dog but Pico wouldn't come.

He could see Pico's black frame hunched over something on the far end of the jetty and so began to work his way out on the rocks. The dog was over-excited, circling and wagging its tail. Will climbed across the last few stones to get a better look, his Nikes gripping their irregular surface with each step.

Lord Jesus. It can't be.

He leaned over the far edge of the jetty and stared down at her. She looked so vulnerable like that, lying out on the rocks, the waves breaking over her lifeless body.

He looked into her dark eyes and shuddered.

Caridad. I'm so sorry.

Strangely, it made him calmer to keep his eyes on her. It was when he looked away and back at the empty beach he began to panic. This meant taking slow, deliberate backward movements along the rocks. He attempted to walk a few steps this way but it was awkward and he soon lost his footing. As he tried correcting himself, he fell forward and landed directly on top of the girl, smothering her with his six-foot-plus frame.

"Aaaargh!"

He took a quick look around but there wasn't anyone he could see on the beach.

Placing his hands on either side of her now, he rolled himself over into a sitting position and began scooting along the rocks in order to put some distance between himself and the girl. Pico moved past him and continued sniffing around the body.

Will pulled his cell phone out of his red swim trunks, leftovers from his ocean lifeguarding days, and dialed.

No signal. He tried dialing again and again but again, nothing.

"Pico, goddammit no!"

Pico had gotten hold of a piece of the girl's dress fabric in his jaws and started frantically tearing at it, whipping his large head from side to side. Then, using his front paws as an anchor against one of the rocks, the dog attempted to drag her off of the jetty.

Will tried pulling Pico away by the collar but the animal was persistent, showing its teeth and growling. Running out of options, Will raised the dog's leash in his right hand, and began striking Pico on the head and neck again and again in order to get the animal to release the fabric from his grip. Finally, after several beatings, Pico retreated and slunk away to lie down on the sandy beach.

Exhausted, Will had no choice but to head back to the parking lot to his truck and try his police radio. He started the long trek back by placing Pico on the leash and sprinted as fast as he could down the beach toward the entrance.

* * *

Rachel had borrowed her daughter's field glasses to get a better look.

She'd been watching the scene at the jetty unfold from behind the makeshift dune, and waited until the man in the blue police jacket and his dog were out of sight. Miguel was worried that the man would soon return. He yelled for his wife and daughter to get in the truck.

But Rachel had seen something the others hadn't.

Although the large rocks obscured her view of anything below the man's knees, she could tell something was desperately wrong. And each time he raised his head and brought down the strap for another vicious strike, she became ever more convinced. The bright shock of rust-colored hair was too distinct, cut shorter but distinct nonetheless.

It belonged to the *idiota* who had attacked Father de la Rosa that day at the train station.

Defying her husband's order to leave the beach, Rachel left Miguel and Sylvia and walked out toward the jetty. She found it difficult to climb over the uneven boulders but managed to keep her balance by holding her arms out on both sides, and shifting her weight side to side on her bare feet.

"¡Ay Dios mío!"

It was a cry of anguish that should have been heard up and down the beach, if only there was someone to hear. Her past melded with the present. And she heard another cry, this one from her heart:

"Eres mi hija (You are my daughter)."

The girl was sprawled on the rocks, her dress badly torn and pulled up over her, exposing her body below the waist. Her skin was a translucent gray. She must have been dead for some time. And yet—in addition to the blackish bruises on her legs there were what looked like fresh tears in her skin, with traces of deep red blood around the scarred edges.

The dead don't bleed, do they?

Sometimes after death, blood can flow to the lowest parts of the body. If you make a fresh cut, there will be blood. What kind of monster would do something like this?

The dead girl's eyes were opened wide, staring up to God and the heavens, as if searching for an answer.

Rachel called to Miguel and Sylvia who by then had gotten out of the truck and were craning their necks to see what she had discovered.

"*Mira!* Miguel, bring a blanket from the truck. We have to wrap her up."

Miguel told his daughter to stay in the truck behind the dune, grabbed a blanket from the back seat and ran across the jetty as swiftly as he could over to Rachel and the dead girl.

Rachel and Miguel freed the dead woman from the rocks. Then, lifting her gently by her hands and feet, they laid her on the blanket. After wrapping her up, the two managed to carry her back along the ragged jetty, over to their truck and placed her in the vehicle's covered bed.

Miguel jumped behind the wheel, turned the Tacoma toward East Hampton's Main Beach and made a quick retreat.

* * *

"Hey, this is two-two-five from East Hampton Beach Patrol. I'm here at Beach Lane, Wainscott, do you copy?" Will's voice was breaking now, trapped deep in the back of his throat, "I—I'm going to need an ambulance and some detectives out here ASAP. I think we got a dead body."

—"You *think*? Where is the deceased?" a man's voice on the radio answered back.

"On the jetty out near Georgica Pond, copy?"

—"Did you touch the body?"

"Um, no. It's not going anywhere—I mean she's caught up pretty good on the rocks."

—"She? Did you get a positive ID that it's a woman?" the voice asked. Then, the voice faded, and Will could hear the sound of a hand covering the microphone: *"Who is this guy calling in?"*

"Yeah, she's young. I'd say about eighteen or nineteen. And, look I mean she's—"

"—who is watching the body?"

"Listen, I'm sorry, I had to leave the scene to get to my car radio. My cell wasn't working here—"

"—get your ass back down there as soon as you can and wait for detectives."

"Okay, but—"

"—but what?! Get your ass down there! Over."

Will got Pico in the back of his pickup, shifted into 4-wheel drive and skidded off the blacktop onto the sand. As he drove into the low sun, he checked in both directions to see if anyone else had entered that part of the beach. There wasn't a living person in sight.

~ ~ ~

Ave Maria (7)

"I swear that man is a force of nature."

This was her mother's way of describing her father whenever he would bring her too close to the precipice. Growing up, she could never allow herself to fully acknowledge the meaning behind her mother's words, although she could guess why her mother said it. Her father seemed all too human to her, frail at times, belligerent at others, maybe a little crazy. Okay, maybe *a lot* crazy, especially at home. Too crazy to have so many kids around the house wondering, waiting, ever fearful of what he might say or do next. Did her mother mean that God—nature—whatever—made him this way and they all needed to live with it like you would a tornado or hurricane that whipped through your house, most of the time without prior warning? Where was the weatherman when you really needed him? A *force* of nature: wasn't her father also responsible for his own actions like so many of the male figures in the Bible stories she was *force*-fed growing up? Or was this outburst just her mother's way of giving in to the unchangeability of her circumstances, of accepting them as she accepted that the sun would come up each day and then fade into darkness, a darkness she didn't dare fully embrace?

Of course she was drawn to these same kinds of men, these "forces" who seemed to rule the small part of the world they inhabited only to find out later they were just as weak and fragile as she was, only lacking in self-awareness. The heart knows what the heart wants but why set it on repeat? Was it because the heart, that steady, throbbing organ in her chest pushing the blood to her head, her arms, her delicate hands, her aching legs and feet, the heart she would gladly give over to someone who could truly *understand*, was too preoccupied with all of that other business? Maybe the heart didn't know shit. The rest of her had doubts (wasn't that always the way?) but her heart always seemed willing to take that chance.

And now her heart was telling her something else. One very important thing that could mean her very survival.

Go.

Chapter 35: Wednesday before – The Sailor

"That's yours I hope," Jeanine moaned. She felt for his body under the cool sheets.

Of course he'd beaten the alarm. He was standing over the bed fully dressed and after-shaved, buzzing from caffeine and ready for Marty. Marty Cooper. His one indispensible. His go-to. And a major pain in the ass. Marty could work his crews like hell to meet the deadline but lately he'd been forgetting things, important things Butch would likely have to fix or worse, cover up. And, Marty was chronically late. If Marty spent one more late night downing jack-and-cokes and ogling the slumming female tourists at Wolfie's, Butch was going to have to escort his friend back into rehab. He'd scheduled a 6:00 a.m. with Marty out at one of their building sites in Napeague to bust his chops. And maybe talk to him again about getting sober.

"Yeah, Hon. Go back to sleep."

He was almost at the worksite when he realized he needed to first pick up some plans he'd left on his boat. Speeding past the turn, he continued further east from Amagansett along the Napeague Stretch toward Montauk. The high canopy of deciduous trees disappeared abruptly, replaced by the flattened outline of scrubby oak and pine, opening his view of the pre-dawn sky. God, he loved this time of day, before the sun would poke its swollen head out above horizon. And later, when its rays would break through the fog and cast finger-like shadows across the landscape.

He continued north at the circle, past Montauk's famed commercial fishing boats and chowder houses, to the marina. When he reached the entrance he found it strange that the gate would be left open. He went on through, making sure to close and lock the gate, and down to "A" dock out to his private slip. As Butch climbed over the guide rails onto the transom of *Bailey's Pearl,* he heard a familiar ringtone chiming from his pants pocket. Bon Jovi's "Livin' on a Prayer."

It was Marty.

"Yeah, what's up? I'm on my way over to you."

"Can't make it today, boss."

"What? You drinking last night?"

"Listen, I gotta go. Hcch. Hcch. I'll try to come by the site later if I can. The guys know what has to be done."

Marty hung up.

Butch had a choice. He could pick up his construction plans and head back to the worksite—without Marty. Or—he looked out onto the sleepy harbor and knew. Especially on a morning like this.

He set aside the plans, shook off his leather loafers, plucked a pair of Docksiders from a closet in the ship's main cabin and slipped them on. Then to the rituals every captain learns to love in anticipation of the sail: switching on the boat's batteries, disconnecting the shore power, turning on the running lights and starting up the engine. He motored his way through the dark waters of Montauk Harbor past the sturdy commercial rigs tied up to their fish docks, the private sailboats with masts swaying like Halloween skeletons, and wound around the spit of Star Island toward the inlet. Once beyond the tips of the jetties and the green and red flashing towers, he did a quick engine check, ran up the mainsail, unfurled the jib part way from the halyard and charted a 180° course into Block Island Sound.

The mainsail full out took the wind, and heeled the boat heavily to one side. Once he was going, the sturdy craft was gliding through the water at a good five knots. He watched as the tiny lights cast from the other boats onshore began to fade from view. And finally, quiet. The only sound his ship cutting through the waves into open sea.

As he was leaning back in his captain's perch in preparation for a nice solo sail, Butch could swear he heard a knock coming from one of the cabins. Followed by a scraping sound. Some kind of animal trapped below?

He made a move to check out the noise when a young woman emerged from the ladder and pulled herself up to the deck. She paid no attention to him, brushing her long dark hair from her face and crinkling her eyes toward the cold stream of light shining off the front of the boat. Her small frame was enveloped in a paper-thin, strappy tank dress that barely covered the tops of her thighs. She was barefoot, her toes and fingernails painted a matching dark green. She seemed to him a flesh and blood expression of unsullied beauty, as if created to make a lie of the idea that the world could produce anything ugly or debased. Then, as casually as someone might whose presence had been expected all along, she looked over at Butch and spoke in a voice like melted ice cream.

"Are we *moving*?"

The front of her dress clung tight to her shapely figure as the back fluttered in the breeze behind her, mimicking the shape and movement of the sails.

"Yes, we're *moving*," he said. "What the hell are you doing on my boat?"

"I guess I must have fallen asleep." She yawned and stretched her arms into the black as she took in her surroundings. Then she used one of her small hands to grab onto the lifeline cable attached to her side of the boat.

"That's pretty fucking obvious," Butch bellowed from the cockpit, puffing out his chest.

"You don't recognize me do you?" she said.

"Should I?"

"Do you often forget the girls you've slept with?"

"What are you talking about?"

He truly had no recollection of this girl. Yet he made no attempt to change his course further out into the Sound.

"I just got out here yesterday—from New Jersey," she explained. She pronounced it *Noo Joy-see*, but falsely, as if to communicate that she wasn't originally from there. "I came to stay with this girl I used to know. Anyway, I thought she still lived out here in Montauk."

"So?"

"So, I came out here looking for a job, a waitressing job. And I thought I could crash with her."

"What's that got to do with me? And what happened to your friend—should I expect another visitor from below deck?"

"No," she smiled. "But I was asking myself the same thing. Poof. Gone. I had no place to stay and I was really tired after taking the train and walking all the way to her house so I came down here. I remembered being out here with my friend once, at your club having drinks. You invited the two of us out for an evening sail."

He scrolled through the events of his recent past and couldn't recall any evening sail. Not this particular one anyway.

"How did you get on the boat?"

"The gate was open. There are a lot of boats here. Believe me, it was tough finding yours but I remembered the name—it's so sweet—and I remembered that it was one of the nicer ones," she said. "Look, I'm really sorry. Most people only go out on the weekends, right? I didn't think I would run into you. I'm gonna try to find my friend again today but I have a feeling she doesn't live here anymore."

"Are you sure none of *my* friends put you up to this? Marty maybe or Freddy Hayek?" For a minute he was thinking this might be an elaborate bachelor party prank. The wedding wasn't for another three weeks.

"I don't know any of those names," she said.

"Hmmm."

"Is that important? I mean, isn't it something that we ran into each other like this?"

"Well, now that you decided to come aboard, what are we going to do with you?"

He meant this as a rhetorical question, something that an adult might say to a child who had done something naughty. But somehow it came out sounding like he had something very specific in mind.

She let the question hang. He could feel her eyes on him as his hands gripped the wheel. It forced him to look away for a moment at the scene he was leaving behind: the churning wake of the boat reflected in his taillights; the tips of the jetties at the mouth of Montauk Inlet, now tiny fork tines; the red and green lights flashing in the distance.

Finally, she said, "So, what do you do when you're not sailing your boat at the wee hours of the morning? I seemed to remember you did something with your hands..."

"Not bad," Butch said, playing along. He followed the girl's continued gaze, turning his left hand over and staring at his naked ring finger. There was a slight blanching of the skin where his wedding ring used to be. Earlier in the week, when he and Jeanine had gone to the jewelers to pick out their platinum wedding bands, it was the first time he'd really noticed it.

"You're an artist, a sculptor maybe. No, wait; you build things right?" she said.

"Right again. You're good," he said. He was beginning to think maybe he did know this girl. "I'm a builder. I've got a bunch of developments going. In fact, I've got this great thing going right now out here in Bridgehampton that I'm just waiting to start. It's the biggest thing I've ever done. Three million dollar houses. But you don't want to hear about that."

"I knew it! You have to tell me about it."

"Really, it's pretty boring. Just a bunch of houses," he said.

"Those must be big houses! And, I'm sure it's not boring at all."

"Well, I've got it all planned out—we got the best architect out here, great subs—that's subcontractors—the whole thing. I'm just waiting for the final financing to come in."

"It must incredible to live out here. I've always wondered what it might be like."

"It is beautiful—I grew up here, my family is from here. So tell me, what do you do when you aren't looking for waitressing jobs and sleeping on other people's boats? I thought all waiters were really starving artists or actors or something."

"Um, I guess, but I'm a dancer." As she said this, she lifted her arm gracefully above her head and straightened her back.

"A dancer? I don't think I've ever had a dancer on the boat. You'll have to show me," he said.

"Here?"

"It's the least you can do to earn your keep on my vessel," Butch said, smiling. "Everyone has to pitch in when they sail with me."

Without hesitating, the girl skipped her bare feet across the deck to the starboard side and jumped up on the outside edge of the boat. She began by twisting her body into a few ballet poses. First a few slow, deliberate forward movements to get her balance. Then, a swift kick that had her jumping in the air with legs crisscrossing and landing in the same position along the ledge. Just as she was attempting a graceful half turn, the mainsail caught a sudden gust of wind, heeling the boat further to the starboard side. She leaned into the boat and tried to grab onto the taut lifeline cable but it was too low. She couldn't hold on.

Butch ran quickly across the deck and caught her by her slender shoulders. As she fell towards him, he accidently pulled down one of the thin shoulder straps of her dress, revealing her left breast. Time seemed momentarily suspended as they both watched the soft, delicate convexity of her exposed nipple begin to stiffen against the wind.

"Oops. Thanks. *That* was awkward," she said, raising her left arm to pull up the skinny strap and scooping her breast back into the dress. As he held her there in his arms he fought the urge to kiss her. Perhaps sensing this, she smiled and took a careful step back.

For the first time, Butch noticed something amiss: a series of dark bruises on the girl's legs. The marks were drained of color but at this hour, with the light yet to break through the horizon, everything seemed to read as black and white.

"How did you get *that*?" he asked, pointing in the direction of her thighs where they met the hem of her dress.

"What?"

"There on your—"

"—oh this?"

She set her foot up on the bench seat and lifted her dress. With her other hand she pulled down a bit of the sheer fabric of her panties to reveal a small star-shaped tattoo. "I just got it a few days ago. My declaration of independence. It still hurts but it's a good kind of hurt, you know? And it itches." She rubbed the area around the tattoo with two delicate fingers as if to prove her point.

In the pronounced battle now raging between his head and his loins, Butch's conscience was losing badly. Here was this beautiful stranger who was claiming to know him, her legs spread wide, the top lip of her underwear pulled down as she massaged a raised rash that had formed around the tattoo's outer edges. A show put on expressly for him.

"A declaration of independence?" was all he could manage.

"Yeah, I put off getting one for a long time. I used to have this rule that I shouldn't mark my body or get surgery or anything like that. It's not natural, y'know what I mean? Although I did have to shave off a little more than usual for this one."

"Sure."

"But then I thought, what the hell, I'm ready for something different. At first I wanted a star with four points but they were too religious looking. Then when I saw the five-pointed stars I thought: 'now, that that's what I'm talkin' about!'" She giggled and pointed to her tattoo. "This one's called 'azure.' I was gonna get the same color for my nails"—she held out her manicured hand and set one foot up on the ledge to show him her toes, showing off nail polish as shiny as a lime lollypop—"but I liked this green color. It's called 'Envy.' Isn't that a funny name? Do you think it matches?"

"The blue does match your eyes," Butch said. He tried desperately to keep his focus on hers and not on the resplendent area around that tattoo.

"That's what my boyfriend said—my ex-boyfriend I mean," she said, dropping her leg and patting down the front of her dress. For the first time Butch could feel a shift in her casual mien. The girl looked past him out to the horizon just as the first light was trying to seep in where dark water met an equally dark sky. Masked in a layer of thick fog, the light's diffusion made the sea appeared molten, steel-gray, impenetrable as igneous rock.

"Look, I should be taking you back," he said. "This has been fun but—"

"—Hey, I bet you know a place that's hiring. I have lots of experience," the girl said. She grabbed Butch's hand before he could move toward the winches to start turning the boat about. "And you must know a lot of important people."

"Um, I guess. When we get back to the marina I can put in a good word for you at the restaurant there."

"That would be really sweet. I knew that you would help me," she said, brushing her breast against his arm as she moved closer toward him. She took his left hand and pulled him away from the cockpit. Her hands now wrapped tightly around his, she looked up at him and said, "Can I ask you something?"

"Sure."

"You have to give me an honest answer."

"I'll try," he said.

"How free are you?"

"Huh? I'm divorced, if that's what you mean." He could feel the fingers of her right hand closing in on his naked ring finger, entangling it.

"No. I mean, are you *really* free?"

Butch wasn't sure how to respond. But he got the feeling there was more riding on his answer than he was willing to admit.

"Well, it's complicated," he said.

"It always is, isn't it? That's too bad. I like it when things are simple," she cooed, still holding on and leaning closer. "I guess it's all I ever wanted."

This time it was her words that hung there, the only thing separating the two of them. He was close enough now to almost taste her breath. That sweet breath of youth before it all turns stale and sour.

Then there was an itch that needed scratching. The girl was lifting up her dress again with her free hand to get at her rash.

Reading this as his cue to make his move, Butch placed his large hands on her, almost completely encircling the slim outline of her waist. He leaned down and kissed her full on the mouth, tasting what was only hinted at moments before. As he began to fondle all of the wondrous aspects of her body under that dress—her pert little breasts, the gentle slope of her back, her tight rear end, her impossibly silken thighs—there was one descriptor that kept popping into his head and urging him forward: *ripe*.

This girl, this *ripe young thing*—he figured his chances of getting with a woman like that were pretty much close to done. So, while a little voice inside his head was telling him: *way too risky, you are getting married in a few weeks,* every other element of his being was begging him to take this girl below deck *RIGHT NOW*. But why bother taking her below at all? Why not do it right here? And with the sun beginning to peek out from behind the fog line he could get an even better view of her once he got her out of that dress.

"I remember you now," he whispered to her.

She seemed as ready as he was to get this going but now she was trying to tell him something, whispering a completely different word to him. The pleats on the front of his Dockers were about to burst their seams as she rested her small hand over his fly.

"What is it?" Butch asked.

"Condom," she said, looking up and smiling. "Do you have one?"

"Oh yeah, sure. I should have some below. Don't move."

He ran as quickly as he could below deck and looked through the main cabin. After a frantic search of practically every shelf and cabinet, he found a bright silver foil sleeve marked "Super Sheath" hidden under a box of flares. On the same shelf, a framed photograph of him and Jeanine taken the summer before. There was nothing really special about that day. A morning sail from Montauk out to Sag Harbor. They'd dropped anchor for lunch just off Barcelona Neck, just the two of them. Jeanine had brought little finger sandwiches and a bottle of Chardonnay. After they'd finished their lunch he set up his digital camera on a little collapsible tripod. He remembered trying to get her to smile for the shot. She kept looking away from the camera or making silly faces so he had to take several pictures, each time counting aloud the seconds as the timer clicked down. He later printed and framed the best one: her eyes are staring intently into the camera lens, self-assured but with an almost questioning look. As if their day together—a healing sun, a pleasant breeze, a nice bottle of wine shared with her one true love—couldn't possibly be enough to make her content.

He grabbed the condoms and brought them up to the deck.

When Butch emerged from below, the girl was no longer leaning against the cockpit where he had left her. She seemed to have disappeared into the darkness. Then, in the next moment he caught a glimpse of her, walking along the boat's far starboard side. Not walking exactly but, as before, attempting a series of what looked like classical ballet moves. She was now raised a couple of feet above the deck along a narrow ledge surrounding that side of the boat.

"Hey, look—I'm getting the hang of this," she called out, smiling for him. She returned her focus straight ahead in order to better concentrate on her movements. Her arms were extended out front, elbows to the sides in some sort of elegant ballerina pose. Then she placed one raised pointed-toed foot in front of the other, carefully maintaining her balance as she moved along the ledge. Upon reaching the end of the ledge, she swung out her leg to execute an about-face turn.

A familiar creaking sound. The billow at the back of the girl's dress slackened. Then the main sail. The boat began to stall. Butch watched as she halted mid-step and raised her head, eyes closed, as if pausing to savor this rare moment of quiet.

Then came a loud whistling noise. The clatter of ropes over from the port side.

The heavy boom of the mainsail swung violently across the boat over Butch's head, tilting the vessel and everything on it starboard. As the girl tried desperately to maintain her balance on the outer edge of the boat, she must have failed to notice the large contraption sweeping into view. The top of the boom vang or kicking strap—the low-hanging triangular attachment of pulleys and ropes running from the boom to the base of the mast—came crashing into the side of her head. The impact sent her tripping across the low-hanging lifelines. She spilled over the side of the boat and into the Sound.

Butch ran over to starboard. He watched helplessly as the girl's long dark hair spidered across the water's surface and followed her into the deep. As he stared dumbfounded over the now-empty ledge, the boat moving steadily away from her, he played the scene over in his head to convince himself that what he just witnessed had actually occurred. Her lovely movements along the edge. A radiant smile laden with the promise of sex. A moment of reflective silence. And then, a dull thud as the force of hundreds of pounds of metal came crashing into her skull. Those beautiful eyes rolling into the back of her head as she fell. And finally, a splash, the sound of it drowned out by the whap, whap, whapping noise of the full mainsail flapping in the wind as the sailboat pitched and creaked until it righted itself, jibing the boat starboard.

The mainsail.

How could he let this happen? He forgot to set the autopilot. The captain had allowed himself and his passenger drift off-course into a forced jibe, recklessly losing control of his ship.

Butch made a quick move to luff the sails and slow the boat, turned on his engine and steered in the opposite direction in an attempt to retrace his course. He grabbed a spotlight from under the cockpit and shined its beam over the surface of the water but the sun had already started to peek through the clouds and fog, making a mockery of the flashlight's beam.

He tried (God knows he tried) but there was no way to accurately calibrate his prior movements, especially after accidently making that leeward turn—the boom had sent the boat and its captain into a virtual tailspin.

Now, searching the surface of the water for any sign of her, Butch started mulling over his options. Life—*his* life at least—was about options. And, he prided himself on seizing opportunities other guys couldn't recognize or were too scared to grab hold of.

Did anyone see this girl get on the boat? The Harbor Master—was he watching when she slipped into the marina? Unlikely. Had she told anyone where she was going? Maybe her friend doesn't even exist.

Or maybe the girl herself was a figment. As ancient sailors who once captained these waters might attest, perhaps it had all been a trick. An illusion conjured by the drunken haze of early morning. Casting his impotent light over the ship's bow onto an unforgiving sea, he could almost convince himself he was in no way connected to these events, attributing them instead to an unexplainable, dark magic; something beyond his control.

When he first left the yacht club he had motored past all those fishing boats on his way out of the harbor. And, once out in the Sound, he and the girl were all alone otherwise he would have never risked what he was about to do. Any of the guys he might have passed on his way out could testify to the fact that he was sailing solo. If she was gone it was her own damn fault for stowing away on his boat in the first place. She shouldn't have been on that goddamn ledge. If somehow she managed to swim her way to safety or grab onto the net of a commercial fishing rig, sure, she might be able to later identify him. But she wasn't going to find her way back, ever.

These were justifiable truths.

After scanning the water in vain for several minutes, Butch decided to abort his search and rescue mission. He killed the engine and ran below to see if the girl had left anything there. He discovered a backpack hidden under the bunk in the main cabin and brought it up to the deck. Inside were some clothes, makeup, a pair of plastic sandals. He held the sandals in the palm of his hand. They were so small, about the size his daughter Bailey wore, their pink bottoms barely meeting the distance from his wrist to the end of his middle finger.

He pulled out her mobile and checked for any recent activity: no calls or texts made in the past twenty-four hours and none received. There was nothing that might reveal where she was going. No GPS markers. No trace. He reached into the bottom of the backpack and fingered a small red wallet with a metal clasp. Inside was a driver's license behind a scuffed cellophane window.

Noo Joy-see.

There she was, this woman—a girl really—staring back at him in a faded picture taken by some bureaucrat at the DMV. A picture she was probably never comfortable letting anyone see: her dark hair framing an awkward smile, her eyes in a state of surprise at being caught by the sudden flash—more black than the blue eyes he couldn't help fixating on during the few minutes they'd spent together. He checked her birth date and did the calculation in his head. She was past the age of twenty-one, as if that made any difference now. Then he noticed, sticking out from an inside flap of her wallet, a rumpled train ticket stub dated the day before: NEW YORK PENN, NY to MONTAUK, NY, the passenger name typed out in impersonal computer font: MAGANDA, MARIA. Butch rubbed the paper stub with its raised block lettering between his fingers and slid it into his pants pocket. He grabbed a small towel from inside the stowage area in the cabin, wiped off her wallet and cell phone and carefully returned the items to the backpack.

Wait. The condoms.

They were clearly *his*—there was nothing evidentiary tying them to the girl—yet he now viewed them as an accomplice, a mundane yet powerful object lending support to the condemnation of his uncontrollable desires.

If there was dark magic at play it had surely been of his own making.

He searched himself for the crinkled sleeve of condoms. Feeling an unfamiliar bulge in his back pocket, he took them out, wiped them off with his rag, and placed them in the backpack with the rest of her things. He scanned the water one more time to make sure no other boats could see, zipped up the last remaining evidence of her visit, and tossed it over the side. He sat back in his captain's chair, exhaled, and watched it sink out of view. Then Butch turned his boat back around one more time, set sail and took her into shore.

Autumn

Chapter 36: September

They were something to behold—those big, gorgeous, *zaftig* females reaching almost six feet. The spindly hairs on their multi-fingered leaves ripe-red, buds pregnant with intoxicating THC. The flowers packed and ready for harvesting.

Now that Connor was back in school, he was only able to get to the farm—and his grow area—about once or twice a week. It was time for the late September harvest, and the staff kept him busy with other tasks whenever he was there, leaving him little opportunity to tend to his own crop. And, ever since his parents had found out that it was Morris who almost got literally toasted in the Cave, they had been keeping close tabs on him, even restricting the number of days he could spend on the farm. To say that they freaked when they found out about Morris would have been an understatement.

"Dude, it was incredible, I was racking up all these points on Death Battalion and then lost everything. But I made those two guys heroes," Morris said, when Connor visited him in the hospital. "Pretty cool, huh?"

In the past few weeks, Connor barely had enough time to perform the final, critical task required for tending his crop: the topping or pruning of the plants' main stem in order to further growth of the other nodes as the plants graduated through their final flowering phase. He had managed on his last visit, however, to sneak in a pair of scissors and a lens microscope, test some of the trichomes for color, cut a few plants that proved mature, and dry and cure the buds at home. The results were even better than he had hoped.

But now that most of his plants were ready he was frustrated at not being able to harvest more of them. There was way too much activity going on along the adjacent path for him to sneak his backpack in and out of the blackberry bushes as planned.

And wouldn't you know it, marijuana, when you've got a lot of it growing in a concentrated area—especially in full sun—can be one fragrant son of a bitch? Just as his plants had become successfully acclimated to the East End, Connor too had become acclimated to his plants to such a degree, so much time spent that summer within those few precious square feet of his grow area that, like a naive middle school girl who hasn't yet discovered one of puberty's varied gifts in transition to womanhood can be some unmistakable pheromone emissions, he failed to notice how much his cannabis plants had been broadcasting their agreeable but pungent scent to other parts of the farm. A few of the younger members of Ellie's full-time staff noticed it but chose not to say anything. Maybe there was a crop—perhaps one of the many herb varieties or the new broccolini—that was *supposed* to smell like the skunky grow closet they kept in their off-campus share back in college. After all, the fields were bursting with all kinds of life this time of year. But when Ellie discovered the not unfamiliar bouquet originating from an area near the blackberry bushes, it didn't take her long to find the mother lode. And it didn't take much guesswork for her to figure out who had planted them. The next time Connor was able to make it to the farm—but before he could sneak off into his now less-than-secret domain for what he hoped was a major harvesting—Ellie asked him to have a little sit down with her in the tool shed located in the back of Ellie's End. Just the two of them.

"So Connor, how are your friends Dylan and Luis doing? I noticed that they never signed up to be volunteers," she said.

He was impressed that Ellie had remembered their names.

"Uh, okay I guess."

"So tell me: which one of them is selling for you and which one is the buyer?"

Connor nearly fell off his stool. Somehow he hadn't expected this even though being invited to the shed should have tipped him off to something. Perhaps his giddiness at coming this far along in his project had blinded him to this possibility. He scanned the array of metal tools and farm implements attached to the opposite wall. Which one could he possibly use to get himself out of this? His gaze fixed upon a neat row of toothy handsaws hanging from rusty hooks.

"Um, please tell me you didn't cut them down," was all he could manage. He thought of the new leaves that were coming up on Butch's property, the ones he'd planted as a backup. Maybe he'd be able to harvest enough there to put off Luis and not get himself killed.

"Not yet. We'll wait until everyone has gone home first," she said. "And, then you're going to help me do it."

"Dude, are you going to tell my parents? Wait, Ellie, you haven't called the cops have you?"

"Are you kidding? How would that look: thousands of dollars of weed growing on land that is in the public trust under my supervision? I've been doing this too long to risk losing everything we built here."

"Then what are you going to do with it?"

"Well, let's see, we could offer the whole crop to our members—limit six ounces per member? That would be fair wouldn't it? Or maybe we can burn it and risk getting the whole town stoned. I admit it sounds like a fun idea but I wouldn't recommend it. Connor, what do you suggest we do with it?"

"I know you're upset. I'm so sorry." He started to cry. "You see, I kind of promised it to some people who may not be happy to find out that they've put up money for nothing."

"Ah, enter our friends Dylan and Luis, no doubt."

"Uh huh." All of the blood seemed to rush up to his face at once. His knees wobbled below his seat.

"These guys have got you pretty scared," she said.

Connor hadn't mentioned it to anyone, even to Dylan, as if speaking the words out loud would somehow make it true. But at this point, more than anything else, he felt he needed an ally.

"Did you notice his tattoos? Luis, I mean?" Connor asked.

"Vaguely. He had that Cholo thing going, but with some Rasta thrown in. I remember that. Very original."

Connor took a long, deep breath. "He has one tattoo I noticed in particular: a blue star. That's the same one they found on that dead girl." There. He said it. But for some reason saying it out loud didn't make him feel any safer.

"Huh," she offered, more as a 'how about that' than a question. Before Connor could interpret the lack of specificity in her response, Ellie began to unbutton her blouse. She pulled the chambray fabric to one side, exposing a small tattoo above her right breast: a blue, five-pointed star.

"Connor, do you think that I killed her too?"

He slouched in his seat and stared.

Ellie buttoned up her blouse. "So, let's take stock of our situation: you've been given some money—"

"—Dylan, actually. I only got a little so far for fertilizer and some other miscellaneous stuff."

"So, Dylan's been given the money, which from the point of view of your buyers means that *you've* been given the money. And, let's just say for argument's sake that Dylan no longer has this money to give back. And even if he did, your buyers don't want their money back, they want the weed and will assume you reneged on the deal. How am I doing so far?"

"You are not new at this are you?" Connor was visibly shaking.

"Let's just say I'm a California girl who was raised in the '70s and '80s and spent time around *all types* of farms," she said, revealing a sly smile. "So, the only conclusion I can come to is that if you don't hand over the weed these guys are expecting to receive, then you are looking at a world of hurt—whether these guys are killers of innocent teenage girls or not. I would also venture a guess that Luis may be one of the more reasonable minds among his friends. Your parents and the cops may be the least of your worries at this point."

"Yeah, I think you pretty much summed it up. The last time I saw Luis he threatened me. He said "soy matching" or something, which scared the crap out of me—but I have no idea what it means."

Ellie let out a laugh. "Is that what he told you—*soy machín*?"

"Yeah, that's it! He told me to look it up but I couldn't find it anywhere. I didn't even know how to spell it. Why is that funny?"

"He was telling you he's the *baddest motherfucker*. He was playing you."

"Damn! Ellie, I was so close," Connor said, dropping his head into his hands.

"Have you harvested any of it yet—and don't lie to me?"

Connor swung around his backpack, opened the zipper and produced a quart-sized Ziploc bag of some of the bud he had already dried and cured. "This is it—so far."

"Well, I'm going to send everyone home a little early and we'll go take a look at what we got out there," she said. She asked Connor to wait for her in the tool shed. "You should call your dad and tell him you're going to be late for dinner."

Once everyone else had gone home, Ellie locked the tall metal gate from the inside and she and Connor returned to the scene of the crime. After close inspection and a little expert help from Ellie, they were able to determine that almost seventy percent of the crop was ready for harvesting, with the remaining plants having some kind of damage or too young or thin to have adequate levels of THC. They put on their gloves and went to work placing the sticky buds in canvas sacks and cutting down all of the remaining parts of the plants for composting. Somehow they managed to complete their work before the last sliver of light was left in the late summer sky. With the help of a couple of flashlights and an old wheeled wooden cart, they moved the heavy sacks up to the tool shed and sat back down in their respective places for a strategy session. Ellie lit a candle rather than turn on the lights in the shed so as not to alert any of her co-workers who might see bright lights still burning on the farm and decide to investigate.

"Here's the deal. I'm going to let you sell this crop to your friends for two reasons and under two conditions that I set: the reasons are that I believe marijuana should be legal—even though you're too young to be involved in commerce at this scale—and two, I don't want to see you get hurt. I'd never forgive myself if I turned you over to a bunch of gangbangers. The conditions are that any money you personally receive from handing this crop over to your friends goes directly back to the land trust—you will make no profit. Consider it the rental fee for the land."

"Thank you, thank you, thank you." Connor jumped up from the stool and gave Ellie a hug. He was surprised at how good she smelled after a full day on the farm, especially given the sweat they both put into the last few hours. Once in her arms he felt himself relax like a rag doll, giving in to the simultaneously soft and muscular contours of her upper body. As she stroked his back he imagined her whispering, *"Everything's going to be alright,"* and moved his own lips to form the words he wanted to hear. Then he stiffened his body and gave her one long desperate hug before releasing her.

"Hey, before you said two conditions. But so far you only mentioned one."

Ellie didn't answer. Instead, she reached up in the dark to move aside a few clay pots sitting on a tall shelf, revealing a plain wooden box. Using both of her hands, she carefully slid the box down from its perch. She opened the lid and pulled from it a small, shiny glass object, which she held next to the burning candle. And emanating from the center of her outstretched palm, a magical glimmer that gave him the answer.

"'The greatest service which can be rendered to any country is to add a useful plant to its culture'—do you know who said that?"

"No, but I love it."

"Thomas Jefferson!"

"No kidding. Connor, I gotta use that!"

"It's yours, dude. *Whooosh.*"

"Man, this stuff is really powerful. What you got in here?" She choked back a cough and reached out her hand for him to pass the pipe back to her.

"It's my own strain, kind of a secret."

"I heard there are all these new strains of medical marijuana out there, designer stuff with ridiculous names, you know, like Aurora

Borealis, Arctic Sun, Bubble Gum—"

"—Belladonna, Blackjack, B-52. Yeah, and that's only the beginning of the alphabet."

"Well, I hope you weren't going to name yours after Sugar Rose."

"Nah, I was thinking 'Blackberry Blast.' He smiled, and whispered, "Can't we keep a little? You've got this loft area here in the shed that's perfect for drying and we could—"

"—don't push it, kid. Nothing stays here beyond what you already got in your bag there," she said, referring to the contents of the Ziploc.

"Mmm, I thought I'd ask anyway. Hey, how did you know? I mean, how did you find out?" He lit some more bud in the pipe.

"Connor, you did an amazing job with those plants but you forgot one of the most important rules for outdoor growers."

"What's that?"

"You're supposed to place other fragrant plants near your grow area to mask the aroma. You should know by now that nature embraces diversity. The blackberries were good cover but they were too neutral in terms of smell when harvest time came."

"Damn!"

"Don't be too hard on yourself. Y'know, we could still use you in the greenhouse. As much as I am enjoying this—oh my God, did I just taste butterscotch?—you may be wasting your talents on the illegal stuff."

Just then Connor's mobile warbled. It was the fifth unanswered text from Dylan that day asking Connor when the "product" would be ready for pickup.

"Tell him to meet us outside the gate in half an hour," Ellie said. "And let me see that bag again."

Conner texted the information to Dylan and reached in his backpack for the bag of weed to give to Ellie. Another warble. He looked over at the response.

Dylan: I'm bringing a friend.

Chapter 37: September, that same week

After he hit that guy in front of his girlfriend Tiff's house, Fredy headed straight to his cousin Rico's in the middle of Suffolk County to hide from the cops. While the pictures he took of the dead girl were everywhere, he tried his best to disappear. And he wasn't having much fun either. No AC in his cousin's cramped basement apartment. Nights spent sleeping on the couch. No real chance of surfing, not with the cops looking up and down the beaches—heard they had a regular APB out on him. No job. No money. His truck idle for fear they'd run his license plate. No risking contact with Tiffany or his son Elijah, who he missed more than he ever expected to. And no one to hook up with. That is until late July, when he and his cousin hit this pool party out near Ronkonkoma. Was getting with this one girl upstairs when local cops raided the place on account of some sixteen-year-old dude who got fucked up and almost drowned in the pool. And wouldn't you know it, the girl Fredy was with was underage. The weed, Oxycontin and open bottles of Cuervo were in the same house as two losers from out of town over the age of eighteen. Being on the younger side of eighteen, they let his cousin go with a warning. Fredy meanwhile got sent over to Riverhead and Peconic cops who held him for two full days of questioning.

"C'mon, tell us everything you know about this dead girl and we can drop the drug and alcohol charges," the cops told him.

"Whaddya want to know?" Fredy said.

They had this one detective, a guy named Quinn who was riding him hard.

"What about this kid Dylan?"

"I don't know nobody named Dylan."

"We have cell phone records."

"Must have been a pocket call, you know, shit happens."

"What about the girl?"

"Never saw her before. And what if I was taking pictures with my phone?"

"Why take her picture then?"

"Cause I had a fucken camera in my fucken pocket!! Last time I checked it wasn't against the law to take pictures."

"Gomes. Is that a Spanish name?"

"Yeah, rhymes with *homes* so must be, right?"

"Don't get smart."

So they sent in another detective who started grilling Fredy in Spanish.

"Look, I ain't in no Spanish gang. I don't even speak Spanish! I can get my Tata in here to translate if you want."

Despite the best efforts of his incompetent court-appointed lawyer to protect him, Fredy was finally released when it was clear that there was still no sign of a body or a motive or even a crime committed. He'd been fired from his job at Orange Crush—what he did was "too creepy to even think about," the store's owner told Amy, the person who knew Fredy best. But it didn't matter since his summer was pretty much fucked anyway and he couldn't see himself going back to playing the part of the authentic surfer-dude for some snooty rich kids who wanted to buy a pair of two hundred and fifty dollar sneakers. Fredy moved back in with Tiffany on Springs Fireplace and even started spending more time with Elijah.

Since he had nothing else to do he fell back to surfing. And now he could plan his whole day around when and where he could find the best conditions. Montauk or Georgica or Sag Main or the Cut—

anywhere but Beach Lane and the jetty. He'd take his five-eight out to the mostly flat surf sometimes just for a chance to stare back at the coastline. The big waves no longer mattered. And he'd lost his bone reader, stopped talking to Dylan and Jess after what they did. But there was water. A vast rippled plain he could find balance on, float on, race on, do tricks on, drift on, empty out the contents of his brain on, or maybe just chill on and watch the tiny sparkles of sunlight reflecting back. And, whenever he could—like the original soul surfers of his grandparents' generation—he made sure to go out when and where there were no other people around (as soon as a group of crumbeaters would show up with their flashy new Cannibals or Jimmy Lewises, hogging the best waves and talking shit like, "We're shreddin' the gnar, dude," he'd be like, "It's called 'surfing' you fucken' Barneys. Peace. I'm outtee, son," ride back in and hit a different spot down the beach).

By the end of September he managed to get a job on a construction crew. His Tata knew some guy who knew some guy who was starting up construction on a bunch of $3 million-plus spec "estates" on adjoining lots in Sagaponack North, each with pool and tennis court. The project had been postponed for three months and the contractor lost most of his original crew. Some guys had moved to other projects, and some illegals were forced to go back to wherever they were from due to lack of work. So they had an opening.

The builder had purchased most of the remaining land on both sides of a winding half-horseshoe of a road that ran north from the LIRR train tracks and out to one of the main north/south routes that stretched from Bridgehampton to Sag Harbor. The plan was for a dozen Dutch Colonial-style mansions with gambrel roofs, each set on a shy two-acre lot. With the only free lot the builders unable to scoop up belonging to the Catholic Church, a wooded parcel on the northern end of the street that didn't look like it was going to have anything built on it anytime soon.

Anyone traveling this road in the past few weeks couldn't miss the worksite if they tried. In front of each of the planned driveways on both sides of the block, now just a series of muddy cuts snaking in from the road to a denuded landscape, was a large sign reading "Olde Stone Estates" and an architect's rendering of the proposed manse, with shaded figures representing the lucky family who could afford to stand within the borders of this soon-to-be lush, paradisiacal scene. Behind these elaborate signs, work crews were busy most days moving earth with heavy equipment and pouring foundations from huge cement trucks.

Fredy started at the bottom, working on a team of two to dig the foundations and backfill foundation walls once they were set into place. Dave operated the backhoe. Fredy moved the dirt with a shovel wherever the backhoe couldn't go and acted as Dave's eyes and ears on the ground. It wasn't so bad, this job moving dirt. Fredy took to it fairly quickly.

"So, what is the job title? What would you call me?" Fredy was asking the project manager, a slightly pickled middle-aged guy named Marty Cooper, on his first day after being told his overall responsibilities.

"Helper. *Hcch.* You're not union so you can't have one of their titles—or their level of pay. And we don't like overtime. You finish what we tell you to finish in the timeframe allotted, got it?"

"Helper. Sounds good," Fredy said. "I can do that."

"Yeah, well don't think your job's any less important. Those foundations are gonna end up being filled in with finished basement game rooms and they have to be perfect. We don't want to disappoint the customers."

"Aye, aye Captain," Fredy said.

It happened on one of those weird, warm Indian summer days. "Eighty-nine-fucking-degrees in late September? No such thing as climate change my ass!" he overheard Dave muttering to himself. Part of Fredy's job the past two days was to make sure he and Dave stayed precisely within the markers the surveyor had set up to dig each foundation. The parameter of each foundation was marked off with pine sticks sprayed with Day-Glo orange paint arranged exactly five feet from where the outer borders of the hole was to be dug. Normally, any dirt that was dug up would be loaded onto a truck and hauled away to another site or to the sand and gravel contractor's property (sometimes to be sold back to the same project later—the builder would literally be buying back his own dirt). But today the two of them were taking the dirt and making a large fill pile to be moved later in the day to other parts of the site for landscaping. When they returned from their lunch break, Dave and Fredy were sent to start the last building lot that needed a foundation dug. A patch of dirt cleared on the far northern edge of the multi-property worksite adjacent to the woods.

Just as the two of them were setting up their gear to start digging, Fredy came across a strange marker poking up from the dirt. And well within the five-foot parameter of where the shovel was to be put down.

Fredy yanked the small white marker out of the ground and held it up so Dave could see it.

"Hey Dave, what the hell is this?"

Dave cupped his hand to his ear and yelled from his perch in the cab of the backhoe, "That looks different. What does it say?"

"It's got some hand-written letters on it," Fredy shouted back. "D, O, M, the number one maybe—"

"—I don't know what the hell that is but it ain't ours. Move aside." Dave started working the front loader's large teeth into the ground next to where Fredy was standing. Fredy stuck the marker in his back pocket, just in case, and went to work. As Dave swung the earth-filled bucket to the side and dropped it a few yards away, Fredy would play a game of chicken where he would track its movements and try to stand as close as he could to where Dave brought the bucket down before he'd smooth out the leftover dirt with his shovel. Old habits die hard.

On his fifth scoop into the newly widening hole, the guys heard a loud crack! Dave picked up what looked like a bunch of pine boards, their sharp corners sticking out from either side of the load of rocks and dirt. He dropped the big shovel again, this time making sure to get underneath the remaining part of the object and lifted it whole out of the ground. The sound of wood crunching under metal must have distracted him because Dave accidently dropped the load too early before he could lower the bucket. The force of its fall sent large pieces of splintered pine scattering over the dirt pile a few feet from where Fredy was standing. After days of digging around the large lot, the guys were used to finding all kinds of weird stuff: old building materials, small farm equipment, rusty tools, a child's stroller, even an Indian arrowhead. The broken pine boards turned out to be only the top of what was a larger wooden box that was still mostly intact. The box was now nestled atop the growing dirt pile they'd created.

Dave killed the backhoe's loud engine, jumped down from his cab and walked over to the pile. Fredy and Dave stared into the simple pine casket at the girl's lifeless body, now covered with fresh dirt and stones, partially decomposed but still apparent; her pale white skin, long dark hair and flower-patterned dress familiar yet made otherworldly by time and terrain.

The sight of the girl was almost unspeakable but the stench was worse—it hit the two of them like a foul wave in the Indian summer heat. Dave bent over his bulging middle and immediately tossed his Villa Combo, extra onions, he'd eagerly scarfed down only an hour before. Fredy, keeping a steady gaze on the face of the mangled figure in the pine box, felt a sudden swell of tenderness form within him for this singular girl who had played such a large part of his waking and dreaming life the past few months. He dropped down on one knee and, using his right shirtsleeve as protection from the fetid odor, leaned in close. In the softest, gentlest tone he could bring into being he whispered,

"Estrella, there you are."

~ ~ ~

Vale Maria

In the end it wasn't anything like falling.

More like life: unpredictable, unsparing. Unrelenting. The sea tossed her in every direction. And as she would almost every day of her life she tried fighting it. And when that didn't work, she tried moving away, escaping from it. If she could only keep moving, she told herself.

But each time she sensed relief—even the slightest chance of escape—another wave would come and overwhelm her. Toward or away, it didn't matter. There was only water.

And in the end, she submitted. As she descended, lower and lower into the boundless depths, crossing over into that other world, she could swear she heard a voice calling out to her. Her mother's god-awful Spanish, used only when she wanted something. Or when her mother felt the need to cast blame.

> *Bebé, y eras tan hermosa.* (I was beautiful, wasn't I, Mamá?)
>
> Or perhaps it was a lone gull, passing overhead and offering its final farewell:
>
> *Hail Mary, full of grace. The Lord is with thee.*
>
> *Pray for us sinners.*

And then the water swelled. Over, under and through her until it would leave her body swollen, later to be cast back onto the beach.

Chapter 38: September, the same day

"Hon, look what you've done to me? I've been a mess all day. My hormones are absolutely raging. You know that thing where you keep tasting it in the back of your throat but it never comes up? Echh. I can't even think about food at this point so don't expect me to make you dinner."

Butch had just walked through the door to their master bedroom to find Jeanine in her bathrobe, arms and legs splayed on the king-sized bed. The large wall-mounted TV was tuned to Bravo with the sound off.

"So you haven't heard," Butch said. He looked as pale Jeanine.

"What haven't I heard?"

"About the dead girl." This got her attention: Jeanine pulled herself upright against one of the dozen or so throw pillows lined up along the bed's expansive headboard. "Marty and his guys somehow dug up that dead girl's body over at our Sagaponack site today—you know, the girl that went missing from Wainscott this summer. On my fucking worksite."

"Why would she be—oh my God? That's horrible!" Jeanine began to cry, her voice breaking. She grabbed onto one of the pillows. "I'm sorry. Why would someone do that? What are the police saying?"

"Nobody knows how the hell she got there."

"Do they know who she is?"

"Now that they've got her I guess they'll find out. DNA and all that. I don't know." Butch's voice trailed off at the beginning of "I don't know."

"Oh my God, I just realized. Will this affect your presale of those properties? Has anyone purchased that lot yet? I mean, I might think twice about buying a house on the same spot where someone who was murdered got dragged and buried. That's a tough sell in any market."

Butch's eyes widened.

"Who said she was murdered!?" His usually tall shoulders sunk with the weight of it.

"I'm just saying. Did you talk to the police?"

"For like two hours. What can I tell them? I guess we just wait and see what happens."

Butch moved a pile of Jeanine's clothes from a chair to the floor and took a seat on its plush, new satin cover. Since the pregnancy Jeanine had removed any furniture in the room with hard backs or pointed edges and replaced them with soft, cushy pieces from Hildreth's. The cocooning had begun.

"Paul called me today but I let it go to voicemail. I was just too wrecked to talk to anybody. I guess this is what he wanted to talk about. Connor must know about it already too. Why didn't you call me earlier to tell me about this?"

"I didn't want to upset you. I mean, I thought it better to tell you in person. Whatever you do, don't talk to Paul about this, Jeanine. We need to keep things quiet, keep our name out of it. We don't want to have anything to do with this."

"Of course. Oh my God. I can't believe it." Jeanine reached out for Butch's hand. She seemed genuinely moved by his predicament. "It looks bad now, Honey, but once they find out who she is people probably won't even remember where they found her. Still, why would someone bury her there, on that property of all places?"

"I'd like to know that myself," Butch said. He sank back in the chair.

Jeanine's mobile buzzed and zigzagged on the dresser next to the bed, giving Butch a startle. She picked it up and looked at the caller ID.

"It's Paul. Butch, I have to take it. What if it's about Connor? He may be really upset about this thing."

Butch was too tired to object but everything about his stooped posture let Jeanine know he wasn't too happy about her taking the call.

"Paul, yeah, hi. What's up?"

"Jeanine, have you talked to Butch yet?"

"About the dead girl? Yeah, we were just talking about it. It's crazy, right? How is Connor doing?"

"Connor is fine. He is taking it extremely well, actually. He's in his room chilling out, chatting online with friends. More importantly, how is Butch doing?"

"Oh, thank God. I was worried about him. Hold on a sec."

Jeanine covered the phone with her hand and whispered to Butch: "He wants to talk to you."

"What? No."

She pushed the phone into his gut. "Take it!"

Butch held Jeanine's mobile away from his body like it was wrapped in a stinky diaper. Unable to fight Jeanine's insistent stare, he took the phone from her. He then walked the call into the carpeted hallway just outside their bedroom and closed the door. There were six bedrooms connecting the hallway on this level, only one of them currently occupied. Keeping its primary occupant happy was a priority for Butch, at least for the time being.

"Hey Paul, what can I do you for?"

"Butch, you seem rather chipper for a guy who just found out someone illegally buried a dead body on his property. Especially one that every detective from Maine to Florida has been looking for."

"Paul, unless you want to talk about something else maybe I should hand the phone back to your *ex*-wife."

"No, wait. I just want a statement. This kind of thing can't be good for business. Let me help you."

"Ha! Here is my statement: Go fuck yourself, Sandis!"

"Can you spell that for me? Not the name, just the first part."

"Very funny."

"How is Jeanine doing?"

"She's doing okay, considering. The pregnancy is making her nuts but otherwise she's fine." Butch leaned his girth against the doorframe and rested his forehead on the cornflower blue pattern of the hallway's custom wallpaper. Of course Jeanine had picked out the most expensive one among the options he showed her.

"That's good. Look Butch, I'm truly sorry. I'm sure there's a perfectly good explanation for all of this. If you find out *anything,* you be sure to let me know first, okay?"

"Oh yeah, I got you on speed dial. First position." Butch pretended to search the contact manager on his own phone. He held Jeanine's mobile away from his body and yelled into it: "Yep, let me see, here it is under 'A:' 'That *Asshole* Who Won't Stop Bothering Me.'"

"Wow, I didn't know your mobile could store that many characters. I'm honored," he heard Paul say through the little speaker.

"Goodbye, Paul. I'll get your paper an official statement tomorrow after I talk with our lawyers."

"Sure. Hey, give your lady a big hug for me, will ya?"

Chapter 39: September, a few days later

“So, tell me about your week.”

“I’m still having the dreams. The night terrors you called them.”

“I’m sorry to hear that.”

“Ever since they dug her up.”

“That was the trigger. But why do you think it’s still happening?”

“I dunno.”

“Things are going well in your life? I mean otherwise. Last time you seemed positive. About the future.”

“Yeah.”

“Before we can work on this you have to tell me about the accident. We’ve been talking for weeks now and you still haven’t touched on it. The details I mean. I think it’s time.”

“Why is it I can’t know anything about *you*?”

“It’s just how this works. I told you that.”

“Bullshit.”

“Why don’t you tell me why it’s so important that you know about *my* life?”

“Just is. Do I have to explain *everything*? Fuck this.”

“Alright then, ask me a question. If it means you’ll open up. But I can’t promise you anything.”

“Really? Okay, tell me: have you ever lost someone?”

“Of course I have. I know how painful that can be. My sister. When I was young. She was very beautiful. We were close.”

The patient brought his long legs up against his chest and let the air out of his lungs slowly. The chair felt too small for him. Lately, he had the feeling as if the whole world was shrinking while he stayed his same super-sized self.

"Have you ever killed someone?" he asked.

"Is that what you think you did?"

"*Know* I did."

"What do you 'know'? Take me through it. This is what we're here to do. You can feel safe here."

"You get off on this don't you?"

"Will, we're not going to make any progress if you don't trust me."

"Right. I'll tell you how *not* to kill somebody."

"Okay."

"It was her high school graduation. We planned to get together the day after. After all the stupid high school graduation parties out there. Then, around a week before, she texted me. Two words. Two fucking words: 'don't come.'"

"That must have been devastating for you."

"Yeah. I tried calling her but it kept going to voicemail. She wouldn't answer my texts. I just wanted to talk to her. Y'know when you don't hear back, that silence, you just fill it. I didn't know what to think. We weren't getting along the last few times we saw each other. She was acting all bitchy, bringing her friends along with us wherever we went. But to not talk to me at all? Maybe someone was manipulating her, trying to pull her away from me. Her parents or whatever. I had to talk to her."

"So you went out there anyway. To her house. Even though she told you not to come."

"Yeah."

Will shifted in his seat. He stared across the room at the books in the bookcase, the knick-knacks on the shelves all shrinks seemed to have. These were not your typical shrink artifacts: sharp shooting trophies, a "World Bestist Mom" coffee mug, old-timey cowboy and Indian statues, a Firestar Transformer toy.

"What else was going on before you went out there?"

"'Going on?'"

"The drugs."

"The drugs," Will repeated, mockingly. "Yeah, I drank a little too much that day. Did a couple of 80's from my regular stash. I smoked some weed on the way out there."

"80's?"

"Yeah. Oxycontin. 80 milligrams. I was 'self medicating'—isn't that what you guys call it?"

"Then what happened?"

"Okay, this is the funny part. I got to, like, Babylon or something and got pulled over for speeding by a county cop. One of the new Peconic guys. The cop leans his head in the car and he's like, 'you been drinking?' I hand him my license along with a PBA card my dad's friend gave me. Not the bullshit ones you get in the mail for a five-buck donation. The kind the cops give out only to their closest friends. So the county cop asks me to step out. I was a little wobbly. I'm sure he smelled it on me. But he just tells me to get back in the car while he calls in my registration. Comes back and gives me a warning. Not even a ticket. I'm thinking, damn, that was close."

"Why is that funny? Didn't you enjoy using whatever power you had to get free of a bad situation?"

"That's the thing. Sure, back then I remember thinking, 'Suckaaah!' I actually lit up a bowl after I got back on the road to celebrate. Now it's like, why didn't the guy pull me in for DUI? He knew I was fucked up. If I had brown skin, like Caridad's brother say, he would have taken me in like that. And if he did I would never have made it out there to her house. So that's the joke: he could have saved her life."

"And, how do you see your role in it?"

"My role? I fucking killed her. I told you that. But this guy should have stopped me. That's what cops are supposed to do."

"I'm confused. Didn't you also just tell me that cops give out little cards to make sure people like you can get away with stuff? Doesn't that make your father's friend culpable?"

"I dunno. Why does it matter? You're not getting this guy in trouble? He's one of my supervisors now."

"No. Tell me what happened when you got to her house."

"I pull up to her driveway–I came this close to turning around when I saw her mom was home–like it was more important that her mom not see me messed up. Anyway, I'm sitting there and I know she's home so I text her: 'I'm out front. Come out and talk to me.' So she comes out and gets in the front seat. 'I can only talk for a minute, Papi' she says right away. She looked so beautiful and smelled incredible. I love the way she smelled. It was hot that day and she was wearing this short little dress, her hair was wet. I remember that. Like she just got out of the shower. Her long dark hair matted against her back and neck, staining the top of the dress."

Will pulled on the rust-colored curls in the back of his head. He was starting to let his hair grow out again.

"I wanted to reach out and touch it. That's in the dream I told you about."

"You wanted to touch her hair then or only in the dream?"

"Both. I can't remember anymore."

"Go on."

"Then she started talking about the party she went to the night before, who drank too much, all this stuff I didn't care about. But nowhere in this conversation is anything about why she won't see me. Then she starts making a move to get out of the car but I can't let her go back inside. Not until she explains what's going on. I was pumped, nervous, like we were strangers now and I had to win her again. I wasn't thinking about how high I was, I just *was,* y'know? So I started the car and took off down the street. At first she seemed upset, 'Stop the car!' that kind of stuff, but then she's like, 'If you're going to kidnap me at least put on the air conditioning,' and she leans over and kisses me! So I roll up the windows and put on the AC. 'Did you get the earrings I sent you?' I ask her. 'Yeah,' she says. 'They're really pretty.' And as we're headed out to this park we used to go to, I'm thinking she's coming back to me but then she starts getting all these texts from her friends, her phone going off like every two seconds, not paying attention to me and texting back—probably some shit about me. I started driving too fast. I leaned over and tried to take the mobile away from her. Then...then we had the accident. That's it."

"Then what happened, after your car rolled?"

"Fuck you! You know what happened. You read the report."

"Will, I think you need—"

"—you don't know what I need. What I need is to not keep *living* it. To make it disappear. To not feel her on top of me, me fucking screaming my lungs out, tasting metal, tasting blood, tasting her wet hair against my face. She was right next to me all that time and I couldn't save her. The doors wouldn't open. I couldn't get at the fucking windows. Why did I close the windows? My legs... I kept kicking... the stupid fucking AC's still blowing and I couldn't get out. I needed to get out!"

"Will, listen to me. Even if you had somehow managed to get her out, she was already gone. You have to know that. There was nothing you could have done."

Will slowly lifted his head from his hands. Tears stained his face like war paint.

"You wanna know what's crazy? After all that time stuck in there, when I finally stop screaming and kicking at the windows, I push aside her hair and realize: she has no earrings on. She couldn't even bother to put on the pair of fucking earrings I got her. I still haven't forgiven her for that."

Chapter 40: November

"Butch! You've got to come and see this, quick," Jeanine yelled from the kitchen.

She was transferring gourmet takeout from plastic containers to plates to put in the microwave when the story's teaser appeared at the top of the local nightly news broadcast. Connor was supposed to be coming over for dinner but must have been running late.

She'd been experiencing that feeling again, that ache (it wasn't sadness—she had always managed to will herself away from feeling truly blue). It had been present ever since Connor moved out. Sneaking in around the corners of her day. Most intently in the early evening hours. Long, solitary stretches of time spent watching the waning autumn light through the majestic double-height windows of that big empty house.

There wasn't much else happening to distract her. Her own work was slow, dead really, even for this time of year. And now that Butch's new estate development project was in full swing she barely saw him. He would stop home for dinner, kiss her on the cheek and leave shortly after to work in his office for the next several hours, later stumbling home and flopping into bed beside her in time to catch the sports recap on the eleven o'clock news. Even on the weekends he seemed preoccupied, distant. Especially compared to the attention he had lavished on her earlier in the summer around the time of their wedding. A time when it felt as if he couldn't bear to let her out of his sight. They were on their honeymoon in Hawaii when he got word that the financing had come through for the big project. Since returning home he'd practically been a ghost.

At first she was against Connor leaving to go live with Paul but agreed to try it out as an experiment, hoping it would only be temporary. But whenever Connor came by the house to visit it was clear he was much happier with this new arrangement. And despite her apparent loneliness, maybe it wasn't such a bad idea.

In fact, she had been more conciliatory toward Paul since the pregnancy. Calling him up on occasion to talk, to catch up, even during those times Connor wasn't supposed to be at the house. Okay, part of it was to satisfy her curiosity about this new person he was dating. Some woman from the Res. Someone much younger who she'd mostly learned about through overheard whispers and overly polite descriptions from work friends who had seen the two of them around town.

And there was her coworker, Julia Manning it must have been, who had said,

"Good for him. The girlfriend won't be so free to walk around the house half naked. Believe me, there's nothing like having a teenager moping around your house to put a crimp in your sex life."

"No, no. Paul deserves this time with Connor before he goes off to college. It's his turn," Jeanine argued.

"That's what I'm saying. It was you who had to take care of the kid when you and Butch were starting out. Now it's his turn," Julia said.

On some of those long evenings she would phone Paul and he'd say he couldn't talk, he was busy with company. Then he'd finish the conversation with a mostly convincing, "*I'm sorry, Jeanine.*" After he hung up she'd continue holding the phone to her ear, listening to the silence on the other end, and not putting it down until the dial tone kicked in. Other nights he'd stay on the phone with her past the point at which either of them had anything left to say. She'd finally been able to set aside her anger regarding the circumstances around their breakup. And maybe it had been a mistake to end it so quickly, so definitively.

Perhaps making a new baby will do that. Get you to question things.

Jeanine was now eighteen weeks along and at her last appointment she'd asked the doctor to tell her the sex of the child. She'd always wanted a girl, even secretly prayed for one during those Ambien-free nights after the start of her pregnancy. She'd lay awake for hours in their big Swedish bed. Butch wheezing his snorer's chorus inches away. Jeanine staring up at the ceiling. Sometimes getting up and kneeling next to her side of the bed, hands clasped, eyes shut tight, her lips deliberately forming the words of her prayer. Once, when she was a little girl growing up on the Lanes, she caught a glimpse of her mother in this same position moving her lips in this way, lost in conversation with the Almighty. When she asked her mother why she did this, she said, "Didn't I tell you, sweetie? Your prayers don't count if God can't see your lips moving." Even then she thought it ridiculous but something made her do it just the same. Back then all she wanted from God was for her father to get well, to have him not leave her alone with her mother and little brother. How selfish could that have been? But God had other plans. "Maybe I didn't move my lips enough and God couldn't see them," she confessed to her mother in the backseat of the big black car on the way home from her father's funeral. "Maybe not, maybe we all coulda tried harder," her mother said. But this time

Jeanine's prayers had been answered, and against Butch's own stated desire for a baby boy.

And now there was a mother on the evening news with her own sort of prayer about a different girl, the girl they had found on Butch's property months after she had mysteriously washed up on the beach earlier that past summer. A summer that would soon seem in retrospect like a lifetime ago.

"Butch!"

"Okay, what is it? I was just getting a drink. Jeez." He walked into the kitchen and grabbed her playfully around the hips with his two meaty hands.

"Stop. Listen to this."

Jeanine used the remote to turn up the volume on the TV. The two of them stood side-by-side in the kitchen and watched.

A grieving couple roughly their age or perhaps slightly older was being interviewed by a reporter in front of a modest-looking suburban house. It was a scene Jeanine had witnessed on the news thousands of times. Another every-day occurrence in the ongoing spectacle. Only this time there was a banner superimposed at the bottom of the screen that brought the spectacle much closer to home:

Couple's missing daughter found dead in Hamptons' mystery

The mother was visibly distressed but showed no tears. Perhaps she had preferred to do her weeping privately and was already cried out. Her husband, the girl's father, stood in front of the camera without speaking, the look of a man who bore witness yet still couldn't fathom how life could have brought him to this particular moment. Still cameras clicked and whirred, their strobes casting unwelcome light on their faces. The mother held a piece of paper in her trembling hands. She kept her weary eyes fixed on the written notes, seeking comfort in the words she wanted to say. Her speech was halting and in a strong accent Jeanine didn't quite recognize.

"We lost our daughter Maria many years ago but always hoped to see her again. Yesterday we learned that we finally will be able to bring her home. As a mother I ask that anyone out there who saw our daughter or was with her when she died to please call the police and tell us what happened to our beautiful girl. Please help us bring whoever did this to justice..."

There was a catch in the woman's throat. She paused as the cameras continued to whir. Jeanine placed her arm around Butch to steady herself. The two of them stood transfixed at the TV screen as the woman raised her gaze from the paper and stared directly at those watching at home.

"...and know that whatever happened, whatever wrong you have caused, that we forgive you."

Jeanine lost it. She held onto Butch as tightly as she could, sobbing hysterically into his shoulder. This sad, small immigrant woman's words had cracked her wide open, bringing forth a flood of tears: for the memory of her warmhearted father, her mother's cool detachment and constant disapproval, her son's growing up and leaving her, the responsibility she felt but rarely admitted to in her failed marriage to Paul, and for rushing into a new one with someone she had otherwise rejected as unworthy of her love. When she was finally able to calm herself, she looked up and saw that Butch was crying too. She held his head in her hands and stroked his face, planting gentle kisses on his wet, ruddy cheeks.

"Honey, that is so sweet. You're crying. I love you so much," she said.

"Jeanine—"

"—oh, Hon, it's okay. You don't have to say anything. I think it's beautiful that you are so sensitive about this. I mean look at me, I break into tears watching the dumb commercials during the football game. But that woman, she really got to me."

"Jeanine?"

"What is it?"

She released her grip and took a step back to consider the man to whom she had entrusted her future happiness.

"Oh my God, Butch, you're shaking like crazy! What is it?"

"Jeanine, there is something I have to tell you."

Chapter 41: November, the following day

"Dad?"

"Connor, what's up? Where are you? I thought you were coming home last night. I didn't understand your text. Did you sleep over?"

"Yeah, still at Mom's. Dad, you gotta come over here." Paul could hear Connor panting through the line and a repeated *thud, thud, thud,* like he was racing up or down a set of stairs.

"What's wrong?"

A pause.

"Con—

"—just come over. I'll meet you downstairs."

"Look, I'm really busy here at the office. I'm supposed to cover—Buddy, are you crying?"

Connor's voice turned small and quiet. "Come over. Now."

"What is it? You're scaring me. Are you hurt?"

"Dad, it's too fucked. Just get over here."

* * *

The two of them were standing in Jeanine's bedroom amidst gaping chests of drawers, personal items scattered everywhere. The closets were rummaged and violated.

"C'mon. We're getting nowhere. Being here is making me uncomfortable enough," Paul said. He collapsed onto the bed and sprawled himself over the sea-green bedspread. "God, these guys own way too much stuff. I mean, how many fucking pillows does a person need?"

"Dad, get your shoes off the bed!"

Paul dug his heels in deeper into the bedcovers. “Where is Butch again?”

“He’s at his office. I think he’s avoiding Mom.”

“And when did you say your mom was coming back?”

“She’s at the haircut place. We got like another hour. Dad, I’m telling you. Let’s keep looking,” Connor said.

“Run through it again. What did you hear them say?”

“They were in the kitchen with the TV on. I was taking a dump in that bathroom off the pantry. The one the cleaning people use. Butch said, ‘Jeanine, I have to tell you something. That girl they found. I am responsible for her death.’ Mom screamed and ran up here into their bedroom. I tried listening from the other side of the door but I only heard like muffling sounds. Mom was crying.”

“And they didn’t hear you or see you?”

“No. I don’t think they even knew I was home. I snuck out and came back later.”

“And you’re sure you heard them talking about the girl?”

“Yes!”

“Nothing else? Was he cheating with this girl?”

“I don’t know. I told you I couldn’t find anything on his computer, at least the one he keeps here. Just the usual porn stuff. I can’t believe he pays for it! Anyway, I stayed up all night last night searching the rest of the house.”

“And he explicitly said, ‘responsible?’ He didn’t say ‘kill’ or ‘murder’?”

“Dad!”

“I’m sorry. I know this is a lot to take in,” Paul said. He pulled himself up to the edge of the bed next to Connor and put his arm around his son's shoulders. "Let's keep looking."

Paul stood up and felt the soft outlines of a woman's slipper against his heel. He used his foot to slide the slipper out from under the bed, and looked over at Connor. They both hit the floor like grunts going down for pushups.

As they were collecting up the shoes and slippers, Paul said, "When I was little my mom told me, when you put two pairs of bunny slippers under the bed, if you're lucky, you may find a third pair when you wake up. Guess it works for all kinds of shoes."

Connor didn't smile.

Paul stopped gathering shoes for a second, reached under the bed and grabbed Connor by the arm. "I don't think he's a murderer."

After forming two piles, they took turns shaking shoes and slippers, watching lint and dust balls fall to the carpet.

"Nice idea," Paul said, throwing down the last shoe, one of Butch's size twelve creamy leather slip-ons. He sat back on the bed and surveyed the mess they'd made when something caught his gaze: a framed picture hanging on the wall above the large chest of drawers disgorging Butch's overpriced polos and boxer shorts. It was the only piece of artwork in the room not chosen by Jeanine, Paul guessed. A photograph of Butch's boat.

"Hey Buddy?"

"Yeah, Dad?" Connor lifted his head from under the huge bed. He was still searching for clues there.

"You on Butch's boat much this past summer?"

"Nah. We were both too busy. I don't think he took it out much."

"He ever *say* anything about his boat? You know, talk about it."

"That's all he talks about."

"I mean specific."

"I dunno. He did say something earlier in the summer about having to fix something. He's always fixing stuff on it. Why?"

Paul walked up to the dresser. He lifted the picture off of the wall and turned it over to look at the back.

"Holy shit," Paul said.

"What is it!?"

"Nothing. Why didn't I think of it before? We need to go check out his boat."

After they put the bedroom back in order the best they could, Paul and Connor jumped into Paul's truck and raced over to Butch's yacht club out in Montauk. Connor made up some excuse to one of the maintenance guys to get him to open the gate, and the two of them clomped down "A" dock to Butch's boat.

First they searched the deck. When they came up empty they went below to check out the cabins. The space was unusually tidy.

"You know, I've never been on this thing," Paul said. He began ruffling through the shelves and storage compartments and accidently knocked over a framed 8x10 photograph. A picture of Jeanine and Butch, dressed in chic summer sailing attire surrounded by nothing but blue; water, sky. Placing the picture back on the shelf, he was thinking it could easily be one of those generic photos of insufferably happy couples they slip into cheap frames you see at Kmart. Though there was something slightly off about Jeanine's expression.

"You hate boats," Connor said.

"Yeah, remember when we went on that whale watching thing with your mom, out in Montauk?"

"You puked the whole trip. That was cool."

"I missed the whales. But I learned a powerful lesson. Stay off of boats. Hey, if you were a beautiful woman and brought your stuff on board some guy's boat, where would you put it?"

"Under the bunk?"

They searched the storage compartment under each of the sleeping areas using Connor's mobile as a flashlight, but couldn't find anything. Then they got to the deepest bunk, the one in the main cabin.

"It's really dark under there. Maybe if I had a better flashlight," Connor said.

He ran up to the deck, found a battery-operated spotlight in the cockpit and brought it down. The powerful flashlight beam lit up the whole lower cabin. Connor crawled back under the cabin bunk and shined the light.

"I—I think I see something!"

"What is it?"

"A reflection. From a broken piece of glass or something. It's wedged in there pretty good," Connor said.

"Can you get your hand in there? Careful."

Connor squeezed himself under the bunk and extended his arm out into the corner, but the object was just out of his reach.

Paul grabbed a cotton rag from the sink and handed it to him. "Hold on. Use this rag to grab it. I don't want you to cut yourself."

Connor reached in again, lengthening his arm as long as it would go.

"It's smooth. Wait a second, hold on, I think I got it!" Connor pulled out his hand and raised the thing up in the air, pushing it up from the cloth with his thumb like a magician demonstrating a magic trick.

"It's a bottle of nail polish."

"Let me see it," Paul said. "Don't touch it with your fingers. Keep it in the cloth." Connor handed it over to Paul, making sure not to put his fingers on the bottle. It wasn't broken after all.

Paul read the label:

Envy. An unforgettable green.

He used one end of the rag to grab the top and carefully screwed it off, exposing the applicator brush.

"What are you doing?" Connor said.

"You'll see."

Paul brushed a bit of the dark green lacquer onto his pinky fingernail. He then carefully replaced the top and set the bottle down inside the rag. He held out his hand, palm down, and blew on the nail to dry.

"Okay Dad, now you're creeping me out."

"Shhh. Just look."

Using his other hand, Paul removed the tattered color photocopy of Maria from his pocket, the one of her tattoo that also revealed parts of her hands and feet. He passed the photograph over to Connor.

"So?" Connor said.

"So watch."

Paul extended the tip of his newly painted fingernail so it

pointed to the girl's toes in the picture.

The color was an exact match.

"Damn," Connor said.

"Yep."

Chapter 42: Thanksgiving week

"I told you. She was dancing on the edge of the boat, lost her footing and fell overboard."

"You keep saying that but the facts don't add up. None of the people we've talked to knew her as a dancer," Detective Quinn said. "She had bruises on her legs—where'd they come from? There must have been a struggle. Maybe she got caught in the middle of one your drug deals? We've searched your property and found the remains of enough marijuana plants to put you away for a long time. Don't make it any worse."

"No. I told you already. I don't know how she got them. Or how those plants ended up at my house."

"Did the bruises happen before or after you tossed her overboard and dragged her to your property in Sagaponack?"

"Do I have to answer that?"

Butch was tired. They'd been questioning him in this little mirrored room for over eight hours. He deflected this last one to his lawyer sitting at his side in dolphin gray Hugo Boss. At five hundred bucks an hour, the headshake he just received cost him plenty.

Quinn was relentless, and not particularly bright, repeating the same questions over and over hoping for a different result—*isn't this the definition of insanity?* Still, Butch couldn't help respecting his interrogator. The detective was in good shape for a middle-aged guy. A large man like himself. Probably still worked out. Someone you might want working beside you on your crew, if he still had the ability to make those kinds of decisions. If this had been a week ago, he and Quinn could have easily been sitting down together and having a beer, talking football—or telling jokes about lawyers.

When the girl first showed up dead on his property he had to admit it was tough going. But after a week passed, then two, then three, it was clear he'd gotten away with it, could just wait it out. Even the properties where the girl was found were selling again. And later, when he broke down and told Jeanine what happened, she agreed with him that although a tragedy, it was better that "the incident" not destroy more lives. And especially not to go to the police. To keep it just between the two of them.

This was their agreement. At first. But two days later she changed her mind. A complete reversal. And she couldn't explain why. Must have been the damn hormones—and he was the one who wanted her pregnant! And that damn woman on the television. Her pleas reduced Jeanine to a puddle. Then that puddle turned into another thing he couldn't navigate his way out of. Jeanine, with her doe-eyed stare and reassuring caresses, her "everything will be fine because I'm here" rationalizations. She was just so goddamn convincing. Once she'd made up her mind he turn himself in, there was nothing he could do to change it. And somehow, through it all, she made him feel closer to her than ever.

"Honey, you are innocent. You need to tell the truth. Everyone will understand. I bet most of the guys out here would have done the same thing," she argued.

"But there is no *evidence*," Butch begged. Why do it now?

"Because it's the right thing to do. I'll stand by you, no matter what happens," she said.

That was Jeanine. A regular Tammy Wynette.

“I'm waiting for an answer,” Quinn said, leaning back in his chair. Butch stared at the blinking red camera light in the corner above Quinn's shiny head. If Butch squinted just so, the camera light became the red tower light on the tips of the jetties out in Montauk. The one he'd seen off in the distance while on that stupid early morning boat ride. A red light that should have told him to stop—or at the very least take the girl safely *below* deck before attempting what he did. Why the hell hadn't he thought this through? His male friends, jealous at the opportunity but forever mocking his ability as captain. Their wives thinking him a monster. His ex-wife Jill's shame and relief at having cut him loose. His daughters' love for him in retreat. And his beloved Pearl—towed to some evidence dock and picked over by government goons in surgical gloves.

Now this.

“That *fucker* Marty Cooper,” Butch mumbled under his breath.

“What's that? Was he the one selling the weed for you?”

“If only I went straight to that stupid meeting with Marty,” Butch said. He dropped his forehead onto the table and sighed.

Quinn wasn't showing pity. “We went over that already,” he said.

Butch lifted his head. “Look, if I wanted to hide this girl, why would I bring her to my own property? There's got to be a million places out here where you could hide a body.”

Butch's lawyer shot him a look that said, *ixne on the odybay*—but he shrug it off.

Fuck his five hundred bucks an hour.

“I don't know why she was there, OKAY ASSHOLE!? Like I've

been telling you. IT DOESN'T MAKE ANY FUCKING SENSE!" Butch screamed.

"Then make it make sense for me," Quinn said.

Chapter 43: December

The news spread quickly and devilishly.

Of course the TV people came. Camping out in front of Butch and Jeanine's manse at all hours, hoping for a glance, a word, any small gesture that might help their viewers better understand what might be going on in the heart of a killer. A reported drug kingpin. What kind of car(s) did he drive? How many rooms were there in that house? Was his real estate business legit? Where did he hide the illicit money? What was the true nature of his relationship with the girl? Were there other unfortunate souls he'd set sail with who may have never returned?

Jeanine, now five months pregnant, escaped to the quiet of her brother Tim's house across town.

And through the soft pretzel logic of the 24/7 story-hungry media, Connor became an unlikely celebrity. All of the drama without the responsibility or embarrassment of bloodlines. As a wannabee hip-hop star looking for street cred, having your stepfather charged with a felony—especially one allegedly involving sex with a beautiful younger woman—was almost as good as being charged yourself. Since he already had a large online presence through social media, it was easy for the alternative press to find its new darling. Some of the papers and online sites were even quoting his raps, sifting through his rhymes for any clues about his "abusive" and "violent" stepfather. There was even talk about a record deal.

Paul, meanwhile, kept his head down. He continued to crank out news stories based on his own understanding of events, ever conscious of his role as the engine that started the whole thing in motion. And with a new appreciation for the persuasive powers of his ex-wife.

A week later, around the time the public had tired of the story and was moving on—along with the esteemed members of the press camped out on Butch's front lawn—Paul got a visit at his office from the wiry surfer kid who knocked him down that June day when he was first trying to figure the whole thing out.

Fredy bounced in even more fidgety than the last time they met. In rapid-fire cadence, he apologized for clipping Paul on the ear, and sort-of-apologized for destroying Paul's yellow bicycle that day in front of his girlfriend's house.

"You get a new one yet cause that one looked pretty shitty even before I ran it over?" he asked.

"No. I'm taking a break," Paul said.

Fredy also thanked Paul for not pressing assault charges and for later writing a piece for the newspaper that tried to tell his side of the story (in a fit of compassion shortly after the girl was found, Paul wrote about how Fredy's arrest and subsequent interrogation was mishandled by Peconic County authorities, most of which Grace edited down to an inch of its life to downplay the negative stuff about a detective named Quinn who led the investigation).

Why had Fredy bothered to come in person to tell him? He could have easily used the phone.

Just as Paul was about to point this out, the kid made a sudden move, swinging his arm behind his back, like he was winding up for another strike. Paul immediately threw up his hands in front of his face. When he peaked through the space between his fingers, he saw that Fredy was only reaching around for something in his back pocket.

"Dude, why so jumpy?"

Fredy pulled out a piece of wood shaped like a cross and laid it on Paul's desk.

"What's this?"

"It's for you," he said, flashing a wide grin. "Think of it as my way of saying I'm sorry."

"Where'd you get this?"

"At work. That day we dug up the body. I totally forgot I had it on me and then later that night when I pulled it out of my pants pocket it I thought, 'I don't owe those guys shit'—you know, the cops—so I put it in a drawer and forgot about it. Then this builder guy—my fuckin' boss!—admits to being with the girl before she died and now I'm thinkin' this may be a clue or somethin'."

Paul held the object in his hand, the faded black letters still legible. He read them out loud for Fredy:

Dominus Vobiscum

"Did you say 'dominoes?'" Fredy asked.

"Close. *Dominus Vobiscum*. It means may the lord be with you." *Et cum spiritu tuo*, Paul mumbled.

"Huh?"

"You guys uncovered a grave that was probably marked by a Catholic. Whoever buried her cared enough to send her out with a message."

There was no way Butch would have done this. No one who is responsible for killing someone *and* hiding the body marks the grave with a Latin prayer for eternal peace, even if the death is an accident. But there was someone else who might.

"Hey, can I take a picture of this?" Paul asked

"Sure," Fredy said. "Do whatever you want with it. It's yours."

"Wait, what about the other guy? The guy operating the backhoe or whatever you call it? Didn't he see this?"

"Dave, yeah. He was so freaked that day I don't think he even remembers me picking it up. He didn't show up for work for like a whole week after that."

Paul proceeded to hug Fredy, jumped in his truck and drove straight to Southampton.

Once there, Paul rushed into Bert's office and dropped the marker on his desk.

"What the hell is this?" Bert said.

"That's what I said," Paul said. When he told him what it was, Bert did a dance around the office like the nerdy kid who finds out he's gotten into the school play. He immediately called Grace in to plan strategy.

"Will the kid be quoted that he found the grave marker that day?" Bert asked.

"Sure," Paul lied. At least he hadn't gotten his permission yet. He was too excited and forgot to ask if he could name him as the source. But Fredy ended up saying "Yes" after being told it would be sweet revenge and they couldn't charge him for withholding evidence if he didn't know it was evidence.

After Esra took pictures, Bert immediately handed the evidence over to the police. Quinn, the lead detective in the investigation, lobbied hard to block publication, with Grace making a passionate case for holding off until the police had time to react. Paul's article, along with the hi-res pictures of the homemade cross, was up on the website within hours.

The next day, and tens of thousands of hits on the story's web page later, Paul was back in the main office in Southampton working on his final edits for the print edition. He barely made it out of Bert's office when Grace pulled him aside and sat him down in her cubicle.

"You're meeting with Bert?"

She didn't look pleased.

"Yeah. He asked me to come over early this morning. It was a good meeting."

"Why didn't I know about it?"

"You'll have to ask Bert. I just follow the rules around here."

"Paul. I know what you're thinking. You're thinking you're a big shot now because you got a hot story. The *New York Times* calling you, *The Post*. Thousands and thousands of hits—wow, that's a lot of readers."

"Yeah, don't forget Yancy's profile of me in their paper. She's interviewing me later, after we get our version out."

"That's great, Paul. But allow me to let you in on a little secret: People may remember the story but they almost always forget the storyteller."

"Thanks, Grace." Paul wondered if his hero A.J. Liebling had to sit through this kind of torment with his editors. He'd have ride over to Green River Cemetery sometime and ask him.

"And I don't appreciate you going over my head on this," she said.

"Uh huh." Paul glanced up at the sailboat pictures behind her head. What the hell is it with these people and their boats?

"Paul, what are you looking at? I want to know what you two guys talked about."

"Is this about that Quinn guy?" he asked.

She pursed her lips but the words didn't come. Her face flushed. "None of your business," she said and then seemed to immediately regret it.

"It's okay, Grace. We didn't talk about him."

"I wasn't asking—"

Bert's head suddenly appeared, hovering like a cartoon dirigible. His chins took up the top six inches of Grace's beige-gray cubicle divider.

"Grace, Paul and I just had a good talk."

"Of course," she said. "Is there anything I can do?"

"Yes, in fact there is." Bert tried easing his mass into her cubicle. There was barely room for the three of them. Grace's posture quickly adjusted to the change in hierarchy.

"What is it Bert?" she asked.

"Paul and I went over his most recent draft earlier about this cross we found but there's something we're not getting. Before we go to press we got to get this right. I'd like you to make a phone call for me."

Grace looked confused. "Paul and I have already spoken to everybody, the town cops, the county guys. You know how they feel," she said. She glanced over at Paul.

"We got their statement, such as it is," Paul added, just a hint of a smile forming.

"I know. I'm not talking about the county," Bert said. "Paul gave me the idea—in our meeting just now. There's someone else I'd like you to call."

Bert tilted his big forehead up toward the water-stained ceiling tiles. With great drama, he gestured his chubby index finger skyward.

"*Jesus*, Bert, what is it?" Grace said.

"Not what but who, and you're close. I was thinking of aiming a little lower to start. How about the bishop?"

Chapter 44: December, a few days later

Tom Cole was just getting around to reading Paul's story about the little white marker in that week's *EET* when a familiar-looking priest snuck through his door dressed in his usual black garb, matching wool watch cap stuck to his head. His demeanor was much like the night of the fire some months before—overly anxious, excitable—which had the effect of lighting up his face like a monk in a Rembrandt painting. He untied the gray scarf from around his neck, removed his cap, and fell into the heavy oak chair across from Cole's desk.

"Father, so good to see you again and Merry Christmas. What do you think of our holiday decorations?"

"Nice, I guess." He turned his head to check out the paper cutout Santa smiling behind him.

"Well, we don't have a big budget but we try our best here."

Despite his cautious approach, Cole felt a certain kinship with the priest. After all, they both represented long established institutions, ones with fixed rules of conduct and honor and principles to uphold. And he could sense that like him, de la Rosa was someone who sometimes struggled to find his place in it. To hold onto what was good and true about the job, especially when the institution did its utmost to pull you down. Cole had wanted to follow up on his suspicions about Will Clifford and the fire from the beginning. He knew about the kid's past "indiscretions" and erratic behavior—the department was in possession of video of Clifford hitting the priest at an anti-immigrant rally for chrissakes—but Cole was told by higher ups not to pursue. There was nothing he could do about it.

He began the conversation with de la Rosa with his usual

speech about the "ongoing investigation" into the cause of the fire, commending the bravery of the Alvarez family and adding assurances that the police were doing everything they could to protect members of the Latino community. Investigators had concluded that turpentine-soaked rags in the garbage bins were the most likely cause. Although the owner couldn't recall placing anything there before leaving his house the day before, it didn't prove arson, Cole explained.

The priest had been nodding his head throughout Cole's speech when he cut him off abruptly.

"I suggested it. It was my suggestion," Father de la Rosa blurted out.

He had his handkerchief out and was wiping his brow repeatedly. His thick dark hair was plastered to the sides of his head.

"What was, Father? Oh, you mean your suggestion of arson? I know that—"

"—no, not arson," he shook his head.

"Good. Good. So you are no longer suggesting—"

"—the burial."

"What's that?"

"A parishioner came to me and asked me where they could bury the woman. They wanted her buried on sacred ground."

"What?"

"Maria. The girl from the jetty. I suggested it."

"You helped bury the dead girl!?"

"No. I *suggested* it. It was a suggestion. Given only after I failed to convince them to go to the authorities. I assure you."

"To bury the girl on Butch Weeks' building site?"

"No, no." He shook his head again, putting the handkerchief to his lips. "Church property. Someone must have mistaken the property line."

"Who did?"

"I am not at liberty to tell you. Our conversation was conducted in the sacrament of the confessional. The seal is inviolable."

"Inviolable. That's a big word, Father."

"It cannot be broken."

"I know what it means," Cole said, with a mixture of excitement and impatience. He leaned forward in his chair and looked into the priest's jumpy eyes. "From their mouths to God's ears, right?"

"Something like that."

"So it was more than one person?"

"I didn't say that."

"And what about your ears, Father? Why didn't you tell us this before?"

"I've spoken to my bishop. I am prepared to receive my punishment from him. And God, of course. I've asked for His forgiveness. I have no choice but to protect the silence of those who confess their sins through me. You see, when someone confesses their sin, it becomes my sin."

Cole couldn't believe what he was hearing or his good luck at having been chosen as the recipient but still, he couldn't help giving the Father a little dig, payback for the priest putting him on the spot the last time they spoke about the whereabouts of the dead girl.

"So, I take it this is *your* confession. After all these months?"

Cole asked.

"I guess you can look at it that way."

"Then let me ask you this, Father, now that you told me does the sin become *our* sin?"

A Sea That Has Cast Us

Chapter 45: Thursday, Beach Lane – The Understanding

Will Clifford raced his pickup toward the jetty, shading his eyes from the sun's intense glare. He struggled to maintain traction on the lumpy sand so maneuvered his truck to the smooth, flat rim of beach hugging the shoreline. The ocean's spray rose through his open windows and beat his face each time he veered too close to the incoming tide; he encouraged it—each rush of saltwater entering his cab making him feel more dangerous, important. It would take at least ten or fifteen minutes before the police showed up, even longer for the county cops. But he had to get back to the girl's body as fast as he could.

When he reached the jetty, he bounded out of his cab, this time making sure to leave Pico in the back of the truck. He climbed over rock and puddle until reaching the jetty's far end.

What the fuck—

The girl was gone.

He searched the horizon for any sign of her but there was nothing, only a calm blue sea. The ease with which the waves broke against the shoreline stood in stark contrast to the speed of his thoughts. Yet in that moment, he allowed himself a fantasy. There she was, still alive out there and in need of saving. He was jumping in, swimming out to a distance farther than he had ever swum before, cradling her in his powerful arms and carrying her back to safety. And then, with the little strength left in him, tendering to her the breath of life—breath from his own breath.

Climbing atop the tallest rock and looking due east, Will spotted something real—something far in the distance moving away from him in the direction of Main Beach. He hopped back in his truck and sped toward the other vehicle, following the same route along that flattened strip of shoreline. At first, the other vehicle remained at roughly the same distance from his as he moved toward it; he was almost sure to lose it if the driver chose to take the next beach exit. But now he could feel himself gaining, closing the distance between him and what now appeared to be another pickup truck. As he got closer, it became apparent that the truck, a blue Tacoma, had gotten stuck before reaching the next jetty at Georgica's ocean beach. The vehicle's heavy weight slouched to one side, its right rear wheel buried deep in the sand almost up to the doorframe. He parked his truck a few feet in front of the stalled vehicle and walked up to the driver's side where a man sat silently, elbow resting out his open window. A sign on the driver's side door read *Cardoza House Projects*.

"What's the problem here?" Will asked the driver. He was almost of out of breath, his heart about to leap from his chest. Will's eyes darted around the interior of the truck's passenger cabin and spied two other people: a petite middle aged woman sitting next to the man in front, and in the backseat a teenage girl, not much younger than him, with long dark hair and a pair of birder's field glasses strung around her neck. The girl looked at him hopefully, staring through thick eyeglasses, and then turned her head to face forward.

"I guess we got stuck in the sand," the man said nervously, his eyes fixed on some vague point in the distance.

"Where you headed?" Will asked, staring at the woman in the passenger seat who, unlike the others, had no problem staring right back.

"We were just going to Main Beach. To the parking lot," the man said. Will took note of the man's Spanish accent but there was something else. His response came across almost as a question, as if he wasn't exactly sure where his next destination might be.

"There's been a report of someone missing here on the beach. Do you mind if I check in the back of your truck?" Will asked.

The pickup had one of those generic-looking caps covering its rear bed, a dark blue color that didn't quite match the metallic shade of the rest of the vehicle. He walked around to the back but before he could lift the gate to look under the cap, the woman had already gotten out of the truck and appeared next to him. She stopped when she reached on the other side of the truck's rear bumper.

"You want to open it for me?" Will asked her. He inhaled deep and waited.

She stood there silent, completely still. Then she turned her head toward the infinite expanse of ocean. By now the morning's fog had cleared. The two of them watched as the sunlight sparkled like firecrackers off of the water's rippling surface. Will could feel the sun warming his cheek and neck, beads of perspiration trickling down his back under his T-shirt and plastic windbreaker. Taking her time, the woman turned her head back to face him. Her expression was grave yet revealed no clue as to what might happen next. Then she opened the gate and took a step back.

Inside were red plastic buckets, and rakes and nets used for clamming. And next to these fishing supplies was a brightly colored blanket rolled in the shape of a big burrito—rounded on its sides, the bottom quarter folded and tucked under itself.

"What is that?" Will asked the woman, pointing to the rolled-up blanket.

More silence.

Did she not understand him? In Spanish the question was—*que es, que es-something*—fuck, he couldn't remember the rest.

He reached in and tugged on the tasseled ends of the blanket closest to him, unfurling it slightly until the bottom came undone. Two delicate feet tumbled into view, blanched and still sticky from saltwater; the only color evident against the skin the chipped, blackened green of toenail polish. As his eyes adjusted to the darkness inside the covered truck he could now see the dead girl's wet hair clumped to one side of her head poking out of the opposite end. He pictured the slender shape of her body inside the blanket but refused to open it further.

He'd seen enough.

"Get out!" Will screamed at the man sitting in the driver's seat.

He was winging it. He carried no weapon. No badge. No handcuffs. Only a blue windbreaker spelling out words that spoke to his vague authority as an officer of the peace.

Pico, raising his haunches onto the side rail of Will's pickup, started barking in response to his master's command.

"Quiet!" Will yelled to the dog. Pico's head quickly disappeared behind the truck's tailgate.

"I saw you," the woman said. The man started to make a move to open the driver side door. The girl in the backseat began whimpering. Will tried his best to ignore her.

"What?"

“I saw you. At the beach before. What you did to that girl,” she said. “You beat her. You did something else I can’t repeat.”

Will was stunned. He could feel his throat closing, his tongue deadening.

It was starting.

“Who is this girl? Why is she in your truck?” he demanded.

“The girl is innocent,” the woman said. “You are her killer.”

“No, no, no. I don’t understand what you are saying.” Will held his hands up to his ears, as if this might block out the accusation. He was outside of himself now, looking down at the horrid scene.

Now the man was walking toward him with his arms out to his sides, pleading. Something he was carrying in his right hand caught a ray of sunlight and reflected it back for an instant.

Will spun and screamed: “You, back in the truck!” He turned his attention back toward the woman. “What is this? Where are you taking her?”

“You are the man who attacked Father de la Rosa,” the woman said, her face twisted into a look of disgust and reprobation. “We are protecting this girl—from you!” She reached into the truck bed and opened the blanket, exposing the girl’s face and the rest of her battered body. “Look at her. You did this.”

The man remained frozen in place outside the driver’s side door and stared at Will, still pleading silently. Will could see the object clearly now. In the man’s hand was a length of thick metal pipe.

Will glanced at the body of the girl in the truck and then over at the man holding the metal pipe. He collapsed onto the cool sand and began to weep. It took everything he had not to throw up on the spot.

"Why are you doing this? Do you know this girl?" he said between sobs. He looked down at his big, clumsy hands. They were shaking. He tried to fight what was coming next, his world closing in, the darkness tightening further around him.

The man walked cautiously toward Will and placed a hand on his shoulder.

"We only saw you and the girl. We don't know her. Please, my wife is only trying to help," he said.

Will looked up at the man, at his sun-marked skin, his graying hair sticking out of his laborers cap.

"Please let us go," the man said firmly now. "You can take the girl."

"Let me think," Will said. He brushed away the man's hand. He was speaking to himself as much as these three strangers, his voice barely rising above a whisper. "The police will be here soon. If I take the girl now how will I explain to them why I moved her? How she got in this condition? I don't know what you think I did but you have to believe me. I don't know her either." Will began to stand up, holding onto the truck's bumper for support. "She looks like someone I used to know but—"

"—you beat her. I saw it!" the woman cried out.

The girl in the backseat leaned her head out the window and screamed, "Mami! Stop!" She continued wailing, her cries competing with the sound of the surf lapping against the shore.

"No! Listen. She was already dead when I found her. I had to stop my dog from hurting her—I mean her body. Oh, God. Please believe me. That's what you saw."

The woman continued to stare at him, searching his eyes for the truth. Her expression slowly transformed from one of rage to pity.

"So what do we do now?" the man asked.

Will tried peering into the truck again. In the covered darkness the girl looked even more like Caridad than when he first discovered her—the long hair, dark eyes, even the dress. He'd messed up again and had to make things right.

"You take her," Will said.

His voice sounded unfamiliar, as if coming from someplace else. Someplace distant. He was speaking the words but somehow they didn't belong to him. Yet he was convinced this was the right choice: it was the only way he could ensure the woman's silence.

"But you see we are stuck here," the man said.

"I'll pull you out. That's something I know how to do."

Will walked around to the back of his pickup where Pico was lying. In that fractured second he imagined that they'd traded places. That it was he who was lying there instead of the dog. *Just tell me what to do, Pico. Tell me.*

He gave the dog a pat on the head. "Stay," he said.

Will removed a heavy metal chain from inside his toolbox and secured it to the front of the Tacoma's chassis. Then he attached the large hook on the other end of the chain to his rear hitch. He started up his truck, kicked it into first gear and spun wheels until he was able to pull the Tacoma out of the ditch and back into the parallel tracks in the sand.

He got out of his truck to collect his chain.

"Hey, what's your name?" he yelled out, looking up from the

sand-smeared front bumper as he unhooked their vehicle.

"Ixchel!" the woman answered.

"What?"

There was no further response. The woman simply stared at him from behind the windshield, expressionless, as if that one un-reproducible word were enough. Her husband sat at attention, hands nervously gripping the wheel, waiting for his chance to take flight.

"Go! Now! If I need to reach you I know how to find you," Will said. He took note of the Tacoma's license plate before getting back in his truck.

He turned his own vehicle around alongside them to allow their truck to pass, and watched as the woman got out of the truck one last time, carefully wrapped up the blanket and closed the rear gate. She returned to her place in the passenger seat, and the Tacoma jerked forward until its tires slipped into the deep grooves left by Will's pickup. As they were driving away, the girl with the binoculars leaned her head out of the back window one last time. She brushed aside her dark curtain of hair, smiled and sweetly waved goodbye.

CPSIA information can be obtained
at www.ICGtesting.com
Printed in the USA
LVOW10s1626270218
568056LV00005B/933/P